Alex Rutherford lives in London. *Raiders from the North,*
Brothers at War, Ruler of the World and *The Tainted Throne*
were the first four novels in the Empire of the Moghul
series; *The Serpent's Tooth* is the fifth.

By *Alex Rutherford and available from Headline Review*

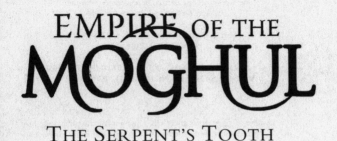

EMPIRE OF THE MOGHUL

THE SERPENT'S TOOTH

ALEX RUTHERFORD

headline
review

First published in Great Britain in 2013 by
HEADLINE REVIEW

First published in paperback in 2013 by HEADLINE REVIEW
An imprint of HEADLINE PUBLISHING GROUP

1

Cataloguing in Publication Data is available from the British Library

A format ISBN 978 1 4722 1707 3

Typeset in Bembo by Palimpsest Book Production Ltd, Falkirk, Stirlingshire

Printed and bound in India by Manipal Technologies Ltd, Manipal

Headline's policy is to use papers that are natural, renewable and recyclable products
and made from wood grown in sustainable forests. The logging and manufacturing
processes are expected to conform to the environmental regulations of the country
of origin.

HEADLINE PUBLISHING GROUP
An Hachette UK Company
338 Euston Road
London NW1 3BH

www.headline.co.uk
www.hachette.co.uk

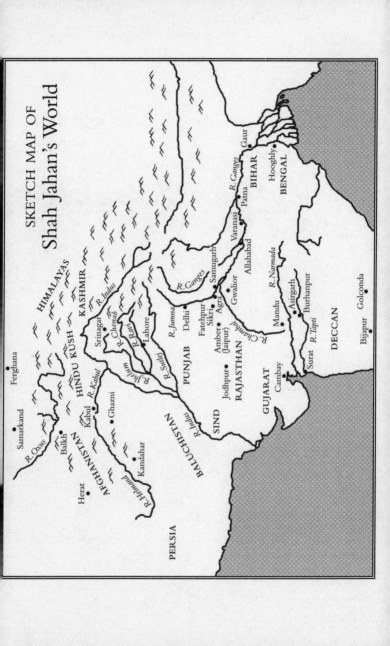

SKETCH MAP OF
Shah Jahan's World

Part I

'A thousand times good night!'
Romeo and Juliet, Act 2, Scene 2

Chapter 1

Agra Fort, northwestern India, 1628

The glint of the sunlight on the dagger's serrated blade caught Shah Jahan's eye at the last moment. As he flung up his right arm to protect his neck, he felt the blade slice into the muscle just below his elbow. Blood immediately began to drip down on to his silver throne. Launching himself with such force that the throne went crashing backwards, he seized the arm of his assailant before he could strike again. Using all his strength he threw the man, who was only slight, on to the marble dais on which his throne had stood. As his attacker hit the marble with a crash, the impact knocked his purple turban from his head and loosened his grip on his dagger. Twisting his assailant's hand back so hard that he heard the crunch as the wrist broke, Shah Jahan wrenched the weapon from his grasp and dropped with both knees and all his weight on to his would-be assassin's chest. Immediately his green-clad bodyguards were around him, but he knew that they would have been too late to save him.

As he got to his feet again the soles of Shah Jahan's sandals crunched on rubies and turquoises dislodged from the silver throne by its fall. He looked hard at his attacker, whom his guards had first dragged roughly to his feet and then, after pulling his arms out tight behind him, kicked to his knees. Shah Jahan half recognised his assailant who was dressed in court garb and appeared no more than a youth.

'Who are you? Why did you attack your emperor?'

At first the young man did not respond, then a black-bearded bodyguard kicked him hard in his kidneys, twice. 'Ismail Khan, nephew of Jani. She died because you killed her husband, your own half-brother Khusrau. She could not live without him. I owed vengeance to her. She took me into her family when my parents died.'

Yes, of course, Ismail Khan ... After his accession he had allowed him to remain at court at his own wife Mumtaz's pleading. Clearly he had been too generous, even naïve to believe that the divisions of the civil war in which he had come to the throne could be quickly or easily healed. Increasingly aware of the pain in his right arm, he looked down. The gashed gold cloth of his tunic was soaked in blood. It was trickling down his hand and fingers on to the white marble to form a small crimson pool. He must have the wound attended to quickly. He raised his arm to stem the blood flow as he had done when injured in battle. 'Have no doubt you will die, Ismail Khan, but first you will have a little time to fear death and to repent of your actions while I have the wound you caused your rightful emperor

4

dressed. The manner of your execution will depend on what you tell me of your accomplices.'

• ◆ •

'I confess, Majesty.' An hour later Ismail Khan was once more on his knees before Shah Jahan – this time in the parade ground outside the Agra fort.

'What else can you do? You were caught in the act,' retorted Shah Jahan. By an effort of will he had remained impassive while his *hakim* had used his needle to place ten stitches into the dagger slash in his forearm before smearing it with neem ointment and binding it tightly. The wound was still stinging but – as the continuing pure whiteness of the cotton bandages attested – no longer bleeding. It should soon heal. Unless . . . serrated weapons like Ismail Khan's lent themselves to poison. 'Did you poison your dagger blade?'

'No, Majesty,' Ismail Khan responded immediately, shock on his young face. 'No, I would not do so. It would be as dishonourable as your action in sending henchmen to kill Khusrau, already blinded by his father . . . I wanted to strike cleanly, in person, as a man.'

Even if he was scarcely the age to claim the status of manhood, Shah Jahan could not but admire the youth's courage, relieved as he was that he would live to fulfil those great ambitions he had had when crowned the fifth Moghul emperor only five months ago. Nevertheless, there could be no mercy, no pity, for any who dared attack the emperor. Ismail Khan must die. But first he must reveal his fellow conspirators.

'Who helped you? You couldn't have got through my bodyguards without some assistance.'

'I had no help. I acted from family honour.' There was defiance in Ismail Khan's young eyes now, and his beardless chin jutted forward. 'I take all responsibility. I knew that even if I succeeded, I would not escape alive. Your death would have been no crime, but just punishment for your sins. In killing you I would have been fulfilling God's wishes.'

Looking into Ismail Khan's face, Shah Jahan saw a martyr's self-righteous determination. He was almost certainly the sole instigator and inspiration for the attack. Although he must have had junior accomplices, not even torture would be likely to make him reveal them. Why delay then? 'Executioner, do your work.'

The executioner stepped forward from where he had been waiting just behind Shah Jahan. He was a burly man dressed in red with a red leather apron and had already unsheathed his sword, two feet long and curving slightly towards the tip. Quickly one of his assistants spread a jute mat on the ground. Two of the guards pushed Ismail Khan forward on to it. 'Extend your neck,' the executioner commanded. Moments later his sword flashed in the sunlight above Ismail Khan just as the youth's own dagger had done above Shah Jahan, but Ismail Khan's fate was set. His arms were pinioned and he could not raise them to protect himself. The sword swiftly sliced into the smooth skin and soft flesh of his young neck and then scrunched through the bone and sinew, severing head from torso. For a moment the head with its now sightless but still open eyes rolled towards Shah Jahan, but almost before blood had ceased to spurt from the crumpled body two of the executioner's assistants had gathered body and head into the jute mat and were carrying them away.

The crowd who had quickly assembled around the edge of the parade ground, and were being held back by the spear shafts of some of his men, cheered. Shah Jahan took little comfort from their enthusiasm. Life had taught him that the people's affections were fickle and that if fate went against him they would readily enough cheer his own execution. He must ensure it did not. Therefore, although he had granted Ismail Khan a dignified death, he could not spare his soulless body indignities. Raising both arms to command silence, he spoke. 'So will I reward all traitors whatever their status, however close to me in kinship or in favour. To remind my subjects great and humble of their fate, have Ismail Khan's body quartered and a portion placed at each corner of the marketplace until it rots. Have his head impaled for ever above the main gate of the fort.'

The crowd roared as he knew it would and at what he suspected was the instigation of some of his officers began to chant, 'Zinderbad Padishah Shah Jahan. Long live the Emperor Shah Jahan.'

Shah Jahan was still not finished. While his arm was being stitched he had asked Kamran Iqbal – his companion during both his long estrangement from his father and his subsequent fight for the throne against his half-brothers Khusrau and Shahriyar – to identify and arrest the guards through whom Ismail Khan had broken to attack him. He was sure at least one would prove to be an accomplice.

'Bring the prisoners,' he instructed. A few minutes later two men dressed in the Moghul green of his bodyguard,

7

but with their steel breastplates and helmets removed and their arms tied at the wrist, emerged from a low gateway in the fort walls and surrounded by an armed group of their comrades marched towards him. As they were halted a few yards in front of him, he recognised both. The first was Hari Singh, a member of a military family from Lahore whom he had taken into his service from that of Shahriyar on the pleas of the man's grandfather, a veteran of his own grandfather the Emperor Akbar's campaigns. The second, a grizzled Uzbek, Majid Beg, had been in Shah Jahan's armies for many years. Both looked composed.

'Kamran Iqbal said that Ismail Khan broke through the guard cordon between you two to attack me. Why did you fail in your duty? Why couldn't you stop him? He wasn't a powerful man, after all.' Neither man responded. 'Speak or I will have the torturers heat their irons.'

Suddenly Majid Beg blurted out, 'I felt Hari Singh move a little away from me just before Ismail Khan slipped between us despite my very best efforts to prevent him.'

So that was it, thought Shah Jahan, eyes turning to Hari Singh. He had retained a loyalty to Shahriyar, just as Ismail Khan had acted to avenge Jani and Khusrau. 'What have you to say for yourself?'

Hari Singh looked directly at Shah Jahan. 'Majesty, I did not shrink back, I swear. I tried to protect you . . . to prevent Ismail Khan getting through. I almost succeeded in knocking his heels together to bring him to the ground, as other comrades will bear witness.'

'And what about Majid Beg? Did he do his best as he claims?'

'I cannot say. Besides, he is my comrade.'

'It looks bad for you, Hari Singh. You must speak.'

Before Hari Singh could say anything more Shah Jahan saw the captain of his guard approach across the dry parade ground, from which the breeze was raising puffs of red dust. 'What is it?'

'As you ordered, we searched these men's military chests in their barracks and we found this in one of them.' As he spoke the captain up-ended a green velvet bag he held in one hand. Out into the dust tumbled several gold *mohurs*.

'Whose chest?' asked Shah Jahan.

'Majid Beg's.'

Taken aback that it wasn't Hari Singh's, Shah Jahan said nothing for a moment then demanded, 'What are they, Majid Beg? Your reward for treachery?'

'No, my savings.' Majid Beg remained impassive.

'That cannot be true, Majesty,' said the captain. 'One of the other guards told me Majid Beg is well known as a gambler and has been trying to borrow money for his daughter's dowry. He is guilty.'

'Come, Hari Singh, now you must speak,' urged Shah Jahan.

'I cannot condemn a colleague without being entirely sure, but he moved away from me, I'm almost certain.' Hari Singh spoke quietly, his eyes this time on the ground. As he did so, Majid Beg made a desperate lunge as if to run, but then as guards closed around him his whole body sagged.

'Majid Beg, it was you.'

'Yes, Majesty.'

'Who approached you?'

Majid Beg was close to breaking down. 'Ismail Khan himself. He said he had heard of my need for money from a guard who used to be one of his family retainers.'

'Were others involved?'

'No . . . Not to my knowledge, Majesty.'

'Like Ismail Khan you will die, Majid Beg, but unlike him, because you tried to divert blame on to an innocent comrade, you will die beneath the elephant's foot. Bring forward the execution elephant.'

Slowly a large elephant, the edges of its ears tattered with age, was urged forward from the shade of the fort walls by the equally elderly *mahout* sitting on its neck. At the same time bodyguards roughly spreadeagled Majid Beg on the granite execution stone and tied his wrists and ankles to the steel rings embedded in each corner. At first he did not resist, seemingly resigned to his fate. However, as the execution elephant reached the stone, casting its shadow over him, and began slowly to raise its right forefoot above his abdomen, he started to struggle, bucking and writhing. 'Remember my past service, Majesty! Pardon me!' he shouted hoarsely.

'I cannot,' said Shah Jahan. 'Proceed with the execution.'

At a tap on its head with the steel rod the *mahout* held in his hand, the elephant brought its foot down on to Majid Beg's abdomen. His screams rose to an animal pitch and there was a crunch as his pelvic bones broke, crushed against the hard granite. A pop of air followed as his stomach wall burst and the stench of human faeces rose as his intestines ruptured. After a few moments he ceased both his screams and struggles. At another command from its *mahout*, the elephant raised its foot, turned and slowly plodded back towards the fort, more orange dust adhering to its bloodied right forefoot with each step.

'So perishes another traitor,' Shah Jahan shouted as once again the crowd roared. Then he turned to Hari Singh. 'You are free, and for your refusal – even at peril to your own life – to implicate Majid Beg before you were certain of his guilt, take those gold *mohurs* spilled in the dust there. Let Majid Beg's pay for his treachery become your reward for loyalty.'

As guards cut Hari Singh's bonds and he bent to retrieve the coins, Shah Jahan turned towards the fort, brushing aside the good wishes of courtiers eager to congratulate him on his escape and to assure him of their loyalty. He must go to Mumtaz in the *haram*. While his injury was being treated he had given orders she was not to be told of the assassination attempt. It would alarm her less if she heard about it from him and saw with her own eyes that he was safe. But also, she might have tried to persuade him to pardon Ismail Khan. Jani's horrible end – she had swallowed a hot coal on learning of her husband's killing – had long preyed on her mind. But though he loved to make Mumtaz happy, for once he would not have been able to agree to her request.

• ◆ •

'No . . . no . . . Roshanara . . . !'

'Majesty, what is it?'

Mumtaz woke, body shaking and forehead damp with the perspiration that Satti al-Nisa, her strong-featured Persian lady-in-waiting, was already wiping away with a yellow silk handkerchief. 'I dreamed that the emperor and I were crossing the swollen Mahanadi river in a bullock cart when one of the animals slipped, tipping the wagon over . . . the torrent ripped Roshanara from my arms . . . I tried to swim after her but couldn't reach her . . . I knew she was drowning but the water was choking me . . . closing over my head, filling my nostrils . . . I couldn't breathe.'

'Hush. Nothing is amiss, madam. You've been having bad dreams again. Roshanara is with Jahanara. I saw your daughters together barely half an hour ago.' Satti al-Nisa's voice was as gentle and soothing as if she were speaking to a child rather than an empress aged almost forty. Lying back, Mumtaz willed her body to relax, but some minutes passed before her heart ceased its hectic thumping. She had fallen asleep just after the midday meal but the room was now in shadow. Surely she hadn't been asleep that long? Glancing around she realised that while she had dozed servants had covered the arched windows with *tattis* – screens filled with the roots of scented *kass* grass – to filter out the harsh summer sun. A dripping noise told her they had also begun trickling rosewater down the screens – a trick to create fragrant draughts of air. Perhaps the sound of the running water had prompted her sleeping mind to relive the moments when her younger daughter had nearly drowned.

Mumtaz turned on her side to watch the pricks of sunlight penetrating the screen create small, dancing pools of light on the rich Persian carpets around her couch. Shah Jahan had rescued Roshanara from the river that day – she would never forget his harrowed look as he had placed their daughter – sodden but still breathing – into her arms. Simply staying alive as they had been hunted across India by Shah Jahan's vengeful father, the Emperor Jahangir, was all that had mattered then. How strange that now she was empress, living in luxury and security, those bleak years should so often haunt her. Sometimes she wondered if Roshanara, young as she'd then been, retained some memory of the incident. More than any other of her children she seemed to need the reassurance of her mother's presence and love, hating to be alone for long.

'Satti al-Nisa, send word that I wish all my children to eat with us this evening.' Their company would revive her spirits, Mumtaz thought, impatient with herself for conjuring dark thoughts when she should be happy. Weren't her six fine children proof that, despite past trials, God had been good? And it was right that just now they should be together as much as possible. In two weeks' time Dara Shukoh would leave Agra with a Moghul embassy to the court of the Persian shah. Shah Jahan thought that at nearly fourteen and almost a man it was high time for Dara Shukoh to start gaining experience of imperial duties, and she had agreed.

Serenity regained, Mumtaz stretched. Soon she would prepare for the evening ahead. Her attendants would massage her body with scented oils, rim her eyes with kohl and dress her in the clothes her husband loved to see her wear – flowing pyjamas of muslins so gossamer-thin the court tailors gave them names like 'running water' and 'woven air' and an embroidered *choli*, a tight bodice. Suddenly she thought she heard the beat of the drum which announced that the emperor had entered the *haram*. Startled, she sat up – it couldn't be . . . Shah Jahan normally arrived just after sunset. Moments later attendants flung back the double doors and he entered.

One look at his face told her he was troubled. 'What is it? What's happened?'

He said nothing but pulled her to him and held her close. The warmth of her body, the familiar jasmine scent of her hair, made him give thanks yet again that Ismail Khan had failed in his attack. He didn't fear death but being parted from those he loved . . . At last he released her and stepping back slowly eased off his coat. Her eyes flew to his bandaged forearm. 'You have had an accident?'

'No. Not an accident. Someone tried to kill me . . . don't worry, there's no need. It's a flesh wound. The *hakim* has attended to it.'

'Who was it?' Mumtaz's voice was a horrified whisper.

'Ismail Khan. He burst through my guards and attempted to stab me.'

'Jani's nephew? But he's only a boy . . . Why? What possessed him? And what will you do to him?'

'He wanted to avenge Jani. He's already been punished. I was merciful – I granted him a quick death. I couldn't let him live . . . not after he'd attempted to murder me.'

'Perhaps not, but . . .' She stopped.

Shah Jahan took her face gently in his hands. 'Ever since we married everything I've done has been for us and for our children . . . to protect our lives and our future.'

'I've never doubted it, never . . . not in all these years. But it doesn't stop me feeling guilty – and also a little afraid. We have everything we ever wanted but there was a price and it was paid in blood.'

Shah Jahan's hands dropped to his sides. 'If I had not had them killed, my half-brothers would have killed me

... our sons as well. Their deaths are not something I'm proud of but they were necessary. It would be a lie to say I wished the deeds undone. Though the past troubles me sometimes – as I know it does you – there is nothing I'd change.'

'You did what you had to ... I understand that. But what if Ismail Khan was only the first? How many others will seek revenge because of your actions?'

'I am the Moghul emperor and rule over a hundred million souls. As such my life will always be at risk from many quarters. But I will protect myself and my family ... I will never relax my vigilance. I will keep us safe, I promise you.'

• ▬ •

Towards sunset Shah Jahan watched from his silver throne as a line of twelve imperial servants approached through the assembled ranks of his courtiers, every man bearing a gold candlestick in which a tall camphor-scented candle was burning. As each reached the dais he bowed before Shah Jahan, then carried his candle away to begin lighting the wicks in the giant brass *diyas* – large shallow saucers filled with mustard oil – set around the courtyards of the fort. The candle-bearers were followed first by the commander of the guard who assured him in formal tones 'The fort is secure for the night, Majesty', and then by his favourite court singer – a young Tajik with a fine, deep voice – who sang a verse in praise of the emperor before adding a prayer for the continuance of his auspicious reign. Shah Jahan enjoyed this nightly ritual which Akbar had instigated. Such links with his grandfather's long and successful reign were fitting, he

15

thought as he descended the dais and walked through the rows of his bowing courtiers towards Mumtaz's apartments in the *haram*. In his hand he held a scroll of paper tied with green velvet ribbons.

'I have a gift for you – a poem written in your praise by one of the court poets,' he said, bending to kiss her lips.

'What does it say?'

'It's a bit flowery but it says what I think.'

'Maybe that's because you told him what to write.'

'Well, perhaps. But should I read it to you?'

'Go on,' said Mumtaz, a gentle smile on her face as Shah Jahan loosened the ribbons and unrolled the paper.

> *'No dust from her behaviour ever settles*
> *On the mirror of the emperor's mind.*
> *She is always seeking to please the king;*
> *She knows full well the King of Kings' temperament.*
> *In her eyes she has the light of—'*

Before Shah Jahan could finish, Satti al-Nisa appeared through the thin muslin curtain embroidered with gold stars and moons covering the arched doorway.

'What is it?' demanded Shah Jahan. 'I gave orders not to be disturbed.'

'I'm sorry, Majesty, but Abdul Aziz has arrived from the south. I told him you and Her Majesty had retired for the night but he was insistent on seeing you.'

'I will come,' said Shah Jahan. What could have brought the son of his commander in the Deccan to Agra with such urgency that he was demanding to see him at this hour? One thing for sure, the news was unlikely to be good, he thought as he hurried from the room and across the *haram* courtyard, where two rows of fountains were bubbling in the silver moonlight. Reaching the gatehouse, by the light of the flaming torches kept burning there at night he recognised the slim figure of Abdul Aziz pacing to and fro beyond it. When he saw his emperor emerge into the main courtyard, the young man immediately prostrated himself.

'Rise,' said Shah Jahan. As Abdul Aziz did so, he saw that the man's face and garments were streaked with dust and sweat. He hadn't even paused to bathe and change before seeking the emperor's presence. 'What brings you to me so urgently?'

'My father sent me to report to you immediately about the reverses your armies in the Deccan have suffered. The rulers of Golconda and Bijapur have renounced their allegiance to you and invaded from the southwest. They overran our frontier defences and penetrated deep into our territory. My father assembled a large army well equipped with war elephants and modern cannon and confronted them about ninety miles south of the Tapti river. At first the invaders would not stand and fight but finally my father forced them to do so.'

'He is a good general.'

'Yes, Majesty, he was . . .' Abdul Aziz's face was etched with grief. 'The battle lasted a whole day with no quarter given on either side. Men collapsed and died simply from exhaustion from the heat and lack of water. Towards sunset the invaders began to give ground. My father mounted his grey stallion to lead a last charge to disperse them . . . I begged him to let me accompany him but he wouldn't.'

17

Tears were now running through the dust on Abdul Aziz's face. 'The weight of our horsemen's onslaught overwhelmed the invaders. Many fell. As my father attacked one of their cannon positions the artillerymen got off one last shot. By great misfortune the ball hit my father's right arm as he waved it above his head to urge our men on, severing the limb above the elbow. He wouldn't accept treatment until the position was taken and the enemy in retreat. Then he allowed the *hakims* to apply a tourniquet and dress and tidy the stump. Despite the pain and his loss of blood he slept well that night and I had great hopes for his speedy recovery . . .' Abdul Aziz paused.

'The next morning my father gave the order to pursue the enemy, whom our scouts reported fleeing south. Towards midday on the second day of the chase, intent on overhauling our foes we were marching through a valley with gently sloping hills on either side when a great number of Golcondan cavalry suddenly appeared over one of the ridges and immediately galloped down, smashing into our troops before we could form battle order. Their first impact cut our column in two. The attackers circled around the rear portion, where most of the cannon and baggage carts were, in a pincer movement, hacking and slashing as they went. Many of our men fell in the chaos. Some fled but most of the cowards did so in vain as the Golcondan horsemen cut at their backs as they ran.

'Others of the rearguard tried to form up and fight their way through their attackers to the front half of our column where my father now had musketmen in action. Their disciplined volleys were succeeding in holding the enemy back. Numbers of our cavalry did manage to join him but few of the infantry. I saw one party of orange-clad Rajputs all on foot defending themselves against the lances of the enemy cavalry. Several times horses struck by the Rajputs' swords reared up and threw their riders. But it was an unequal contest. The Rajputs could rarely get close enough to use their weapons effectively. There could be but one outcome. Only two of the Rajputs made it back to our lines, both bleeding heavily. Next the attackers fired arrows bound with pitch-soaked burning rags. These frightened our war elephants and some panicked, crashing into their comrades and overturning the gun limbers they were pulling, adding to the chaos.

'My father ordered all the remaining troops to fight their way towards a low hillock near the end of the valley around which we could regroup. We were doing so successfully despite the enemy's constant assaults when, just as we were approaching it, some mounted archers attacked, loosing off more of their flaming arrows as they stood in their stirrups holding their reins in their teeth. Three of their arrows penetrated the palanquin my father was being carried in because of his wound. Two set the palanquin alight, the third hit my father in the thigh, setting fire to his garments. His attendants bravely pulled him clear and smothered the flames on his clothes. He remained conscious but his wounds were such that he knew that this time not even the *hakims* could save him.

'Fighting against the pain, he handed the command of the column to his second-in-command, Zafir Abas, instructing him to conduct an orderly withdrawal as best he could. Then, summoning me to him, he clasped my hand and ordered me to carry the news of the defeat to you ... to tell you he was sorry for leading so many of your troops to their death and that many well-trained reinforcements were required immediately or all our territories in the south would be lost.' Abdul Aziz's whole body shuddered as he broke into a series of great heaving sobs. 'Majesty, the attendants had not been able to prevent the flames from setting fire to my father's beard. Burnt skin was peeling in strips from his face ... his blistered lips were bursting ... he could say no more. A few minutes later he died.'

'Your father was a great man. I honour his memory. You too have done your duty. Now you must sleep. We will speak further in the morning.'

As Abdul Aziz departed, his shoulders still shaking with grief at the memory of his father's death, Shah Jahan turned and walked slowly back through the gatehouse into the *haram*. His army in the Deccan had clearly suffered a great defeat. A new army and a new commander must be sent to restore order and take revenge. Who should the general be? If Mahabat Khan, his *khan-i-khanan*, commander-in-chief, had not been leading an army in the foothills of the Himalayas against incursions by the King of Nepal and his Gurkha warriors he would have been the obvious choice, but to recall him would take too long. As he walked past the still bubbling fountains, Shah Jahan went over the names of some other commanders. His loyal friend Kamran Iqbal, commander of the Agra garrison, was needed here. Besides, he had not yet fully recovered from the wounds he had suffered during the fighting against Shahriyar in Lahore and perhaps never would. His father-in-law Asaf Khan was ageing and might not be up to the rigours of campaigning. Others were either too impulsive or too cautious. Yet others were inclined to deal harshly with local populations, living off their lands without payment, and forcing them into unpaid labour. Such behaviour could only prove counterproductive among the proud, restless population of the Deccan. No. There was nothing for it. He must return south and lead his armies in person.

A few minutes later he was pushing back the gold-embroidered muslin curtains of Mumtaz's room once more. She was lying with her back against a lilac brocade bolster drinking a glass of watermelon juice. Looking up she asked, 'What did Abdul Aziz want?'

'We've suffered a major invasion and rebellion in the Deccan. I must assemble an army and lead it south immediately.'

'When do we leave?'

'I will go alone. You should stay here.'

'Why should this be any different from your previous campaigns in the Deccan? I accompanied you then and you were glad to have me with you.'

'Yes, and I would be happy for you to join me again if we hadn't just discovered you are pregnant once more. Your last pregnancies have been harder than the previous ones. You will have better *hakims* here.'

'And as I told you before you embarked on your first campaign, I refuse to be parted from you. The best *hakims* can come with us.'

'Perhaps.'

21

'No. There's no "perhaps". I and all our children and as many *hakims* as you wish will accompany you. Together we will march to victory.' Mumtaz's expression brooked no denial.

Chapter 2

Standing alone on the *jharoka* balcony of the Agra fort in the pale early morning light, Shah Jahan raised his sword and circled it three times above his head. At his signal, the artillerymen on the battlements fired their small cannons to set in motion the army that had been assembling in camps on the banks of the Jumna below in the fortnight since Abdul Aziz had brought the news from the Deccan. How magnificent it looked – not even the Persian shah could put a better equipped army in the field, Shah Jahan thought with a shiver of pride.

First of the twenty thousand men to move out were the vanguard of the cavalry, their green silken standards rippling. Elephants of state, gorgeous in velvet and cloth of gold and clanking with gold and silver chains and bells, followed, bearing his senior commanders. Next came the great bronze cannons pulled on wooden gun carriages by teams of milk-white bullocks, the tips of their horns striped green and

23

gold. Behind them Shah Jahan made out the advance columns of infantry marching twenty abreast. The enormous baggage train followed, its mass of pack elephants resembling a fleet of ships afloat in a sea of dust. In their wake came ranks of laden camels and mules and lines of ox carts.

Soon it would be time for him to mount his own elephant, descend the fort's broad winding ramp and proceed out through the gateway, while in the drumhouse above muscular bare-torsoed drummers beat their kettledrums to signal to the world that the Moghul emperor was riding to war. 'Don't understimate the power of spectacle and in particular the spectacle of power,' Akbar had once said to him with a smile. As a youth the aphorism had puzzled him but he was beginning to understand what his grandfather had meant. He was learning never to neglect the image of himself and his empire he presented to his people, whether on campaign or presiding over his court. That was why, while he was away, he had ordered his architects to modify the Agra fort by adding white marble pavilions to the existing sandstone edifice. The blood-red sandstone would convey his empire's martial power while the marble would show his wealth and opulence.

His jewellers would be busy too, creating a glorious *takht-i-taus*, a peacock throne, like that from which the great King Solomon once dispensed justice. He had allocated two thousand pounds of the purest gold and personally selected the finest gems in the Agra treasury, finding an almost sensuous pleasure in their glittering colours. He was determined his campaign would prosper. When it did he would return with fresh supplies of diamonds from the mines of Golconda, their sole source, and would have some inlaid into each of the three steps leading up to the throne's seat so that he would symbolically trample his enemies underfoot every time he mounted them.

Raising his sword once more in salute to his departing troops, Shah Jahan turned and left the balcony. He must go to Mumtaz. Entering the courtyard of the *haram*, he saw her gilded and curtained litter and the eight eunuchs who were to carry it waiting ready. A few moments later, Mumtaz herself appeared, followed by fifteen-year-old Jahanara and twelve-year-old Roshanara.

'I'm glad you've decided to use the litter – in your condition it's safer than riding on an elephant.'

'You advised it so often I could hardly disagree.'

'Something else. For the moment at least it's best that you and the *haram* party take a parallel route to avoid the thick dust the main column will raise. I've ordered eunuchs to walk beside your litter to cool you with peacock-feather fans and others to sprinkle the road ahead with rosewater. And you will be well protected. Five hundred of my best Rajput cavalrymen will escort you.'

'You fuss and worry too much about me.'

'Because I know a long and arduous journey lies ahead of us.'

'It's of my choosing. I'm stronger than you seem to think, as I've proved to you before. At least at the end of each day's journey I will be there to bid you "mubarak manzil", "welcome".'

• ➤ •

'I think we should increase our pace – the more days that pass, the more we allow our enemies to consolidate their

25

position.' Malik Ali's long face was earnest. 'In this terrain we could easily manage at least five ... even ten miles a day – more.'

'But why? According to despatches I received this morning, Zafir Abas has successfully withdrawn our forces back to Burhanpur with far fewer casualties than we anticipated. For some reason the forces of Bijapur and Golconda did little more than harry our rearguard.' Shah Jahan glanced around at the members of his war council, sitting in a semicircle around him in the canopied tent.

'Why haven't they followed up their advantage? I suspect a trick,' said his quartermaster Sadiq Beg, a grey-bearded veteran from the mountains of Baluchistan, taking an almond from the brass dish in front of him and crunching it with relish.

Shah Jahan shrugged his broad shoulders. 'It's difficult to think of what sort. More likely their early success surprised them as much as it did us and now they're arguing over their next move. Bijapur and Golconda have never made easy allies. Their jealousy and hatred of ourselves only exceeds a little that they have of each other. But there is some other news ... It seems that the invasion has encouraged one or two vassals within our southern borders to attempt to reassert their independence. My governor in Mandu reports that in the province of Mirapur the local raja hanged three Moghul tax collectors from a banyan tree and left their bodies swinging as meat for the vultures before leading his men to join our enemies.'

'Aren't such risings alone reason enough to push on as fast as we can?' Malik Ali persisted.

His master of horse was like a small dog refusing to let go of a rat, thought Shah Jahan. 'Some such risings were almost inevitable, and as long as they remain small in scale and few in number our existing forces should be able to suppress them and punish the foolish perpetrators for their insolence. The raja in Mirapur is a bit of a special case. He is nearly in his dotage and is said to be ruled by his new young wife – a member of the Bijapur royal family. She was always likely to push him to join the rebels. If we have real cause, we will of course hasten our march or detach an advance force to the Deccan. As it is, we're making better progress than I'd hoped. Rushing south would only exhaust our troops and pack animals so that they would need more time to recuperate before attacking the invader than if we proceed at a sensible pace. So, eager as I am to defeat our enemies quickly, we'd gain little advantage from increasing our speed.'

Sadiq Beg nodded. 'Yes. Let our enemies wait ... let them do the sweating. Give the rulers of Golconda and Bijapur time to contemplate their folly. Let them fall out with each other about who shall take precedence on the march and whose tent pride of place in the camp.'

• ◆ •

Shah Jahan turned in his howdah to glance back over his shoulder. Behind, as far as the horizon, hung a heavy curtain of dust but through it he caught the occasional glitter of the long, broad-headed lances of the mounted rearguard. The very earth seemed to shudder beneath so many feet, animal and human. From all along the line came the wail of long-stemmed trumpets and the steady beat of the mounted drummers whose job was to help the army

27

maintain its pace. His officials measured the length of each day's march with a piece of knotted rope and reported to him each evening. After six weeks they were approaching the town of Ujjain, over two-thirds of the way to Burhanpur. Tomorrow would be Mumtaz's birthday. In his mind he yet again went over the arrangements for the celebrations he was planning in the camp. Every detail must be perfect . . .

Suddenly Shah Jahan heard fast approaching hooves. A lone rider burst from a patch of scrub to his right and galloped towards him. At once his bodyguard closed ranks around his elephant, drawing their swords. But as the rider drew closer and reined in, Shah Jahan recognised the hawk-nosed features of one of his chief scouts – a young Rajput named Rai Singh – and gestured to his guards to let him approach. The scout slid from the saddle and touched his hand to his breast.

'What's happened? Speak!'

'A serious incident, Majesty. The wood and boat bridge we constructed over the Chambal river broke up as the first artillery and baggage wagons of the vanguard were crossing. Some of our men have drowned and we've lost two cannon and their bullock teams.'

'The bridge can't have been properly built. Who was the officer responsible?'

'Suleiman Khan. But, Majesty, he says there was nothing wrong with the bridge's construction. He believes someone deliberately cut through the bridge's rope bindings and ordered me to inform you at once.'

Sabotage? If so, this wouldn't be the first time it had happened, thought Shah Jahan. Two weeks ago someone had crept into one of the animal enclosures and hamstrung

28

some of the oxen. They had been discovered lowing piteously and close to death from loss of blood. There had been no alternative but to slaughter them for the pot. He had put that incident down to some local malcontent, but perhaps the invaders had despatched men north to harry his army's movement. 'Bring me my horse,' he ordered.

Ten minutes later Shah Jahan was galloping by Rai Singh's side towards the Chambal. As he breasted the dunes bordering the river's northern shore, a pair of herons took fright and soared, slender legs trailing, into the hot blue sky. Shah Jahan's attention though, as he reined in, was focused on the river below him. His soldiers were struggling in the fast-flowing green waters among a moving jumble of twisted wood and capsized boats to retrieve equipment and supplies and to prevent further damage to the bridge. Other boats had drifted a little downstream only to become enmeshed with floating debris in the thick clumps of reeds. As he watched, two men clambered up the slippery bank dragging a comrade whose face was contorted with pain and whose limp and bloodied arm had clearly been crushed. Two more men were carrying a rough wooden stretcher along the riverbank. On it lay a body, arms dangling. Further along the bank what seemed to be several corpses were piled up, feet protruding from beneath the rough cotton cover that had been thrown over them.

'Send Suleiman Khan to me at once,' Shah Jahan told Rai Singh, who kicked his horse down the steep, sandy slopes to the river. While he waited, Shah Jahan surveyed the destruction more closely. Over half of the boat bridge stretching from the middle of the river to the far side was still intact, but the rest had broken apart except for three or four tall wooden posts used to tether the boats. The long barrel of a cannon was sticking out of the water while nearby floated the body of a white bullock still entangled in the traces attaching it to the gun carriage. Two more lay lifeless at the water's edge. Was all this indeed the result of a deliberate attempt to slow his progress and endanger his men, or was it simply carelessness? He was not sure which he would find the more disturbing.

Anger and frustration were rising inside him as Suleiman Khan — a stout man — laboured up the dunes towards him, his tunic dark with sweat.

'Majesty.' He bowed his head.

'Tell me the truth. Have you been negligent in your duties?'

'Never, Majesty. This bridge was well and strongly constructed — I swear that on my life. We used good wood and the best rope. We completed it last night and I myself drove a heavy wagon across it to test its strength. The bridge broke up because someone tampered with it. Look, Majesty . . .' Suleiman Khan produced two lengths of rope from a jute bag slung across his chest. 'These were some of the smaller bridge ties we used close to the bank. See how the ends have been cut through — they're not frayed by wear. We found them caught in the reeds, together with others similarly cut. When we retrieve some of the bigger hawsers, I'm certain we will find the same thing.'

'Let me look.' Shah Jahan inspected the ropes then handed them back. 'You're right. This was deliberate. Did the guards see anything last night?'

'No, Majesty.'

'Quadruple the guard and repair the bridge as quickly as possible. I will send soldiers to the surrounding villages to offer a reward for information about the perpetrators.'

As he galloped back towards the main column, Shah Jahan pondered what had happened. The rebels and invaders did indeed seem prepared to adopt unconventional measures. As his army approached the south, the risks would grow. He must be vigilant and ensure his men were as well. He would increase the size of the screen of lightly armed but well-mounted horsemen who surrounded the column as it marched. But how vulnerable was his camp? The imperial quarters were secure, he reassured himself as his thoughts turned to Mumtaz. After each day's journey, she and their daughters were carried in their litters through the wooden gatehouse into an enclosure around which protective palisades had been set up. The walls were of thick, iron-studded oak panels draped with scarlet cloth and fastened together with leather straps.

What about the rest of the vast encampment? The tents of his senior commanders and courtiers were pitched around the royal enclosure. Beyond them radiated orderly lines of tents for their retinues and for Shah Jahan's soldiers and an infinity of roped enclosures for all the animals. But beyond that lay a world of chaos – the thousands of camp followers who always followed an army. Merchants and horse dealers, musicians and dancers, acrobats, magicians and prostitutes – all hoping to find employment. It would be hard to prevent enemies from penetrating that noisy mass, but he must try. He would treble the number of guards who patrolled the camp as well as post pickets around its boundaries to stop and search anyone who looked suspicious.

• ◆ •

Golden stars spattered the darkness as the first rockets soared skywards, leaving in their wake a shimmering veil like droplets of silver rain. His Chinese firework makers hadn't failed him, thought Shah Jahan. This was indeed a display worthy of an empress's birthday. Mumtaz, standing at his side by the *haram* tents, gasped as a great peacock spread its sapphire and emerald tail high above. Her pleasure lightened the dark mood that had descended on him since the incident at the crossing. So too did the knowledge that tomorrow the bridge repairs would be complete and he could recommence his advance after a thirty-six hour delay.

Savoury smells were rising from the campfires whose orange flames pricked the darkness. He had ordered thousands of sheep to be purchased and distributed to his men so they could feast. The imperial cooks had begun work even before the morning mists had lifted, plucking fowls, grinding spices, searching their sacks of provisions for the choicest dried apricots, cherries and plums, the best almonds and walnuts, to stir into the fragrant, delicate sauces of cream, ghee and saffron. His lame, elderly steward of the imperial household, Aslan Beg, had been hobbling about, checking the preparations, scolding the cooks and making sure that the correct gold and silver dishes had been unpacked and that the seals to be affixed in his presence to each dish before it was carried to the imperial table, to prevent any tampering with the contents, were ready.

He hoped Mumtaz would be able to do justice to the food. Though she denied it, he was convinced that her appetite – never large – had been diminishing. Her face sometimes looked pinched and the skin beneath her eyes bruised. But soon they would be ascending into the hills and perhaps she would revive in the cooler air.

As the last firework died in the heavens, he was aware of Mumtaz's scrutiny. 'What were you thinking about? You looked very serious.'

'Did I? It was nothing.'

'Are you sure? I know a messenger came to you earlier this evening. Did he bring some news about who damaged the bridge?'

'Only that a few days ago three riders were seen close to the Chambal river – southerners from their speech – asking detailed questions about our movements and where we were likely to build our bridge. I've sent horsemen to look for them but I expect they're long gone.'

'You think they were from Golconda or Bijapur?'

'I'm certain of it.'

'Don't worry too much. I know the delay is frustrating for you, but we'll soon reach Burhanpur. Then the waiting will be over and you can confront your enemies in the field as I know you're eager to do.'

'You're right. I want to conclude this campaign quickly. Rather than fighting to defend our present borders I want to expand our territories. Sometimes I think of reclaiming the homelands of my ancestor Babur . . . even of capturing golden Samarkand . . .'

'The time for such ambitions will come, but one step

at a time. Our enemies are strong. Take nothing for granted.'

• ◆ •

Shah Jahan's horse skittered sideways as a tangle of dried grass blew suddenly beneath its front hooves. The unusual movement jerked him from his reverie. Yesterday, the army had passed the dragon's teeth battlements of the fortress of Asirgarh, high on its red sandstone escarpment, where he and Mumtaz had spent so many anxious months of exile. Here he had learned that his father had declared him an outlaw, placed a price upon his head and sent an army to hunt him down. Though Aslan Beg had suggested that the imperial family should spend the night within Asirgarh's walls, he had chosen to sleep in the camp as usual – the fortress was not a place he wished to linger. And tonight they should at last reach Burhanpur. He could plan his campaign in earnest and Mumtaz would be able to rest.

At the thought of her, Shah Jahan wheeled his horse and galloped back to where the *haram* party was now travelling towards the rear of the main column for safety's sake since they were getting closer to enemy-occupied territory. Mumtaz was travelling alone in a covered litter being carried on the shoulders of eight eunuchs. Seeing Shah Jahan ride up through one of the gold mesh grilles inset into the curtains, she sat up and called a greeting.

'We've made good progress today – we'll definitely be in Burhanpur by sunset.' Shah Jahan reined his horse back to keep pace with the litter-bearers.

'Good. I've been noticing how parched everything looks.'

'Last year's rains were poor ... they tell me famine's breaking out. I'll learn more in Burhanpur.'

'Shah Jahan ...'

'What?'

'Does returning here seem strange to you? These past days I've felt it more and more. Everything – the smell of the dust, the way the red sun looks ready to explode just before it sinks, the stark beauty of these hills – rouses memories. The first time we came here we were young and life seemed very simple. It makes me sad to realise how swiftly time passes.'

'We are still young.'

'Are you sure?'

As he rode on, Shah Jahan pondered Mumtaz's words. The past – the good as well as the bad – was a dangerous place best left unvisited. Last night, with Mumtaz already asleep beside him, he had reread by candlelight some words of one of Akbar's chroniclers:

They told the great emperor that Burhanpur was a place of sinister reputation, ill-omened and dark, where no man could prosper but he laughed at their superstitions and captured it for the Moghuls, saying that he would make it a place of glory and victory ... and so he did.

He had always relished this reminder that from Akbar's time Burhanpur had indeed been a place of Moghul triumph. As a young prince he himself had ridden out from here to military victory – as he had every intention of doing again. Yet this time, instead of images of battle he had seen something else – purblind Khusrau, lying helpless

35

in his Burhanpur dungeon and starting as the door had creaked open. What had gone through his mind during those last moments of life? How would it feel to realise you were about to die and know that it was by your own brother's orders? He'd pushed the thoughts away, telling himself not to give in to weak sentimentality, especially when everything he had ever wanted was his. But now he felt a fresh unease. Had be been wrong to come to Burhanpur? He could easily have made his command centre somewhere else – Mandu perhaps . . .

A violet dusk was descending as Shah Jahan, again riding close by Mumtaz's litter, passed through Burhanpur's ancient gateway surmounted by two stone war elephants locked in combat, features blunted by the violence of sandstorms and monsoon rains. Reaching the inner courtyard of the *haram* where a fountain bubbled listlessly, Shah Jahan dismounted. Drawing back the curtains, he lifted the sleeping Mumtaz from her litter and slowly carried her inside.

Chapter 3

A musket ball whistled past Shah Jahan's head as, turning in the howdah of his war elephant, he shielded his eyes against the blazing sun, attempting to get a better view of the fighting suddenly erupting towards the rear of his force. Moments later another ball hit the *mahout* sitting behind the ears of his elephant in the throat. The man slipped slowly sideways, blood pumping from the wound, before falling to the stony ground. The elephant's pace faltered as it raised its trunk, trumpeting in alarm and swinging its head from side to side. As Shah Jahan grabbed the side of his swaying howdah for a moment to steady himself, the second *mahout*, who had been perched behind the first, quickly slid lower on to the beast's neck and leant forward to speak into its right ear. 'Calm, calm, Mover of Mountains,' he said, pressing his anka, the iron control rod, against the wrinkled grey hide of its shoulder. Reassured, the elephant lowered its red-painted trunk.

All around, the whole column was coming to a halt in disarray. Musketmen were jumping from their saddles and pushing powder and shot down the barrels of their weapons with steel ramrods, preparing to fire. A little way in front of Shah Jahan's elephant a junior officer – a squat man in a green tunic – was shouting orders to his small group of foot soldiers to form up. Shah Jahan heard another volley of shots and two of the infantrymen twisted and fell. One was immediately still. The other lay sprawled, heels twitching. One of his fellows, an elderly man with a thin grizzled beard, bent to help him but he too was hit. Dropping his spear he slumped over his comrade's body.

Everywhere was noise and confusion. Unless he acted quickly to master the situation panic could follow, thought Shah Jahan. And to do that he must dismount from his elephant and switch to horseback. Without waiting for the surviving *mahout* to bring the elephant to its knees, he climbed over the side of the jewel-encrusted howdah and dropped to the ground, bending his own knees to soften the impact. Landing lightly, he shouted to his *qorchi*, 'Bring me my horse!' But before the squire could do so a group of horsemen appeared through the dust and musket smoke, riding hard at the infantrymen in front of Shah Jahan. Encouraged by their green-clad officer, the foot soldiers stood their ground. At his command they crouched down in a rough V formation, their short spears ready to thrust at the horsemen. As the riders – a group of perhaps twenty – galloped closer, one, a slim figure with long black hair streaming behind his helmetless head, outdistanced the rest on his sweat-soaked grey charger.

Although the soldier at the head of the V formation bravely held his place his spear was shaking so much in his nervous hands as he thrust at the Bijapuran that he missed. His attacker's grey horse immediately rode him down, leaving him crumpled on the ground, his skull shattered by one of the horse's hooves. The soldier behind and to his left was made of sterner stuff. He waited until the last moment and after taking careful aim stabbed upwards from his kneeling position with his spear. As he intended, it caught the horse in the throat. Immediately it stumbled and fell, sending its rider somersaulting over its neck to crash headfirst to the ground where he lay still, blood and brains spilling into his hair.

Where was his own horse? Shah Jahan looked around to see his *qorchi* running towards him leading his chestnut stallion. Seizing the reins he leapt into the saddle and yelled to his bodyguard, 'Follow me.' Drawing his sword, he charged towards the enemy horsemen who were now surrounding the surviving foot soldiers. One of the attackers pulled so hard at his mount's reins to wheel it to face the new threat that his horse reared and threw him backwards. Another rider armed with a long lance turned his black horse successfully and kicked hard towards Shah Jahan. When they closed the man made a wild thrust at Shah Jahan which missed, but Shah Jahan's did not. As their horses passed he caught his enemy's arm with a slashing stroke of his sword. The rider dropped his lance and began to lose control of his horse which careered off, cutting across the path of another enemy rider who could not prevent the bolting animal from crashing into his own mount so hard that both horses fell, taking their riders with them.

A third horseman waving a long curved scimitar wildly above his head rode at Shah Jahan, who saw him only just in time to sway back in the saddle to avoid his flashing blade. However, recovering more quickly than his opponent, Shah Jahan thrust with his sword at the man's groin. At the last moment the Bijapuran parried the blow with his scimitar but the weapon snapped as he did so. Shah Jahan tried again. This time the thrust got through, penetrating his enemy's abdomen, and the man fell. Reining in, Shah Jahan saw that others of the attacking horsemen were now turning and beginning to gallop back in the direction from which they had so recently come.

Heart thumping with the excitement of battle, Shah Jahan's first instinct was to pursue and destroy this small band of enemy cavalry, but he quickly realised to do so would be foolish. As the army commander he should leave that to others. He must go to the rear of the column where the conflict had originally broken out to see how the fighting was progressing there. As he rode through the smoke and dust he noticed several of his men lying motionless on the ground and others being tended by their comrades. The body of a war elephant was slumped nearby, as well as those of several horses. Another horse, its left foreleg shattered, was standing neighing piteously. However, he saw little sign of fighting until he approached the rear where the baggage and powder carts had been travelling.

Through a gap in the increasingly thick smoke he made out a number of stationary six-wheeled ox carts. Two of the oxen pulling the leading vehicle were slumped in the shafts, wounded. Their drivers were struggling to cut them from the traces while those of the wagons behind were attempting to manoeuvre around them, shouting at their oxen and pulling at their yokes. Just then Shah Jahan saw six riders clad entirely in black galloping towards them. Each was carrying a double bow and was accompanied by another man holding in his gloved hand two arrows with flaming pitch-soaked cloths bound round them – the same tactics that had killed Abdul Aziz's father Ahmed Aziz, Shah Jahan just had time to think before the archers all took flaming arrows and fitted them to their bows. Rising in their stirrups they pulled back the drawstrings ready to fire at the wagons, where the drivers had now succeeded in cutting one of the wounded oxen from the shaft of the first cart. A musket ball hit a black-clad bowman before he could discharge his arrow and he pitched from his horse. As he did so his flaming arrow caught his clothing, setting it afire. Screaming in agony, he rolled over and over on the ground trying to extinguish it.

A great blast of hot air blew past Shah Jahan, deafening him and nearly unseating him. As he struggled to control his wildly bucking mount, he wondered what had happened. Then he realised the wagons must have been powder carts and that at least one of the archers' fire-arrows had penetrated an oiled cloth cover and ignited the powder bags inside. He succeeded in quietening his horse but felt a sharp pain in his left cheek. Removing his gauntlet and probing with his fingers he discovered a wood splinter protruding from it and plucked it out. Glancing down through eyes stinging with grit and dust, he saw several other splinters embedded in his horse's flank and his gilded saddle. Like him, both were splattered with patches of a red, sticky substance – the flesh of the oxen and their drivers. As the dust began to settle he saw that two of the wagons had exploded. The mutilated bodies of men with fragments of singed cloth still adhering to them were strewn across the ground, mixed with those of the oxen and pieces of the carts. The acrid smell of powder mingled with the sweeter one of burned flesh.

One of his officers rode up. Shah Jahan saw his lips move but could hear nothing. Soon, though, a little of his hearing returned and he made out what the man was repeating. 'They're fleeing, Majesty.' Although still groggy from the explosion, Shah Jahan knew that 'fleeing' was not the right word. He had not defeated his enemy. After inflicting casualties on his forces in a successful raid they were beating a hasty but tactical retreat. They – not the Moghuls – were the victors today.

This was not how it should be . . . not after the haughty Golcondans had predictably fallen out with the Bijapurans and retreated back to their own territories, leaving the latter to continue the war on their own. It was certainly not what he had anticipated when a month previously he'd led his column out from Burhanpur to sweep the rugged hinterland beyond the Tapti river where groups of the invaders had been raiding isolated fortresses and killing his *cossids*, his messengers, and his tax gatherers. In fact many things had surprised him. Like discovering that among those his men had captured were local people who had joined the invaders. Terrified for their lives, they had tried to excuse their treachery, some claiming they were desperate for plunder to help them buy food during what was becoming a serious drought, others pleading that their families were suffering because of the high taxes he had imposed to pay and feed his large army.

But he had had little choice. If he didn't raise the taxes, how could he recruit an army sufficient to deal with the invaders without depleting his treasuries? The expedition had scarcely been a success, even before this ambush. Nearly every time his army had encountered groups of enemy fighters they had fled before he could bring the full weight of his firepower to bear – but not before they had inflicted casualties as they had done just now.

An hour later, Shah Jahan's mood was grim as he addressed the senior officers clustered in a circle around him. 'How did the enemy succeed in taking us unawares?' He fixed his eye on his rearguard commander, Ashok Singh, one of the sons of the Raja of Amber and a promising young officer.

'They saw us approaching, Majesty. A prisoner told us how they hid in scrub some way from our column and our pickets until we had passed. They were all mounted – they even had spare horses to carry off booty and their own wounded – so they were able to circle to our rear. Then they galloped into the attack from directly behind our column, taking advantage of those great clouds of dust we were raising, which enabled them to be almost upon us before we were aware of them.'

'Didn't you post pickets to your rear?'

'No, Majesty. I am sorry.'

'You should be. But you are not the only one to blame. We must all learn from this. It's not just a question of designating more pickets but also of trying to see into our enemies' minds and understanding their tactics.' There was no response beyond some nods from his commanders, whose dejection was clear from their expressions, so Shah Jahan continued, 'Together we will succeed, I'm sure of that. But now we must consider what our immediate moves should be. How many of our men did we lose?'

'Not too many – fewer than a hundred, I think, but we also lost a lot of equipment in the attack on the baggage train. The massive explosion in the powder wagons knocked several cannon from their limbers and set some food supply wagons ablaze.'

'Well then, there is nothing for it but to return to Burhanpur, where we can rest and resupply,' Shah Jahan responded curtly. 'The council is dismissed.' As his officers turned away, Shah Jahan knew they were loyal and had felt the reverse as much as he had, but that was not the point. They should all – himself included – have learned better from Ahmed Aziz's initial defeat. It would be at their peril if they continued to underestimate their enemies' strength and cunning.

• ◆ •

'Look at those kites circling over there,' Mumtaz said to Shah Jahan as they stood with their arms around each other on one of the screened balconies of the Burhanpur fort, watching the sun set orange through the dust haze on the horizon. 'Some poor animal must be dying out there on the plain.' Shah Jahan nodded. It was becoming a common sight. The monsoon rains had still not come. The trees silhouetted against the sunset were stark and leafless. There was scarcely a blade of grass to be seen and all the crops had withered. The normally broad Tapti river was reduced to a muddy trickle. Man and beast struggled to get precious water from the stream and its few surrounding green slime-fringed puddles. Domestic beasts as well as wild ones were dying now, their carcasses dried husks of skin and bone on the dry earth.

According to reports from outlying villages people too were beginning to die, most from starvation, others killed by tigers driven by hunger from the mountains and jungles to gorge empty bellies on human prey. Some country people, hollow-eyed and skeletal, had made their way to Burhanpur, babies sucking at their mothers' shrivelled, and milkless breasts. He had ordered them to be given what food could be spared from the commissariat's limited supplies but his soldiers had to be his first priority with the rebellion still unquelled. Perhaps the latest sweep of the country on which he was embarking the next day with a division of his horsemen would succeed in bringing more of his enemies to battle on his terms than he had done previously. By changing his tactics and leaving his heavy weapons and infantry behind, he would enable his column to move faster and respond more flexibly to the feints and raids at which his enemies appeared so proficient. What's more, the very mobility of his new force might allow him to approach closer to the rebels before being detected.

As if divining the direction of his thoughts, Mumtaz broke into his introspection. Looking up into his face, she asked, 'Why must you lead the troops tomorrow? After all, most of the army will remain here and you have competent commanders enough. Why can't you trust them with the task?'

Shah Jahan smiled. It was a question he had debated with

45

himself, so he had a ready answer. 'I must go because my presence will hearten our men and I believe overawe many of the country people, some of whom may sympathise with the rebels, who are making them extravagant promises. I will wear my grandfather Akbar's gilded breastplate and helmet. He always told me that an emperor must project an image of power and authority beyond that of an ordinary man and that his people would love him for it. He proved the wisdom of his assertion time and time again.'

'But there is a risk in making yourself so conspicuous, isn't there? Don't forget you are as susceptible as anyone to weapons and wounds.'

'I know that I am as mortal as any man. To delude myself otherwise would be a first step to disaster and perhaps madness, but I must bear the increased risk for the sake of the empire and our dynasty.'

Looking down at Mumtaz in the gathering dusk he saw from her expression that she was not fully convinced so he added quickly, 'Besides, I will take care, and my equipment and bodyguard are the best there could be.' As he spoke the last rays of the sun dipped beneath the dusty western horizon. He bent and kissed Mumtaz. How much he had to lose.

• ◆ •

Rai Singh flung himself from his horse and hurried towards Shah Jahan. 'Majesty . . . we surprised a small group of Bijapuran horsemen as they rested after their midday meal. They were sheltering from the heat in the shade of a deserted herdsman's hut. Two got away – one who was guarding their horses and a second who had wandered off to relieve himself and somehow reached his mount – but we captured the rest. Look, they're coming now.'

Shading his eyes against the metallic glare of the late afternoon sun, Shah Jahan saw the scouts he had despatched under Rai Singh to sweep the arid country-side ahead of his main force galloping into the camp. Five were holding the reins of the horses on which, hands bound behind their backs, the prisoners were swaying. Four of the prisoners were men of about his own age but the fifth was much younger – a tall youth whose dirt-streaked red and gold tunic hung loosely on his slender frame. The guards were keeping him separate from the rest and the youth's eyes flicked nervously from side to side.

'Did you interrogate them, Rai Singh?' Shah Jahan asked.

'Yes, Majesty. Two of us took them individually into the herdsman's hut. We kept them blindfolded and my comrade interspersed promises of reward with my threats of torture. The four men were brave enough, refusing to reveal anything, but that youth began to piss himself with fear when I suggested that iron claws were being heated ready to rip his bowels from his belly. He was only too eager to accept my friend's subsequent softly voiced promises of his freedom and poured out all he knew. The other Bijapurans suspect he has betrayed them and have been yelling threats of what they'll do to him. That's why we've kept them apart.'

'Good work, Rai Singh. What did he tell you?'

• ◆ •

'Charge!' yelled Shah Jahan. He and his horsemen kicked their mounts into a gallop towards the Bijapuran camp one and a half miles away. The camp was a collection of

47

tents and makeshift shelters made from the dead branches of trees clustered around the sticky mud which was all that remained of a small lagoon. At the far side of the lagoon were the huts of what looked to have been a poor village even before the onset of the drought. After a brief consultation with his officers about the information provided by the captured youth on the whereabouts of his enemy's camp and their strength, Shah Jahan had decided on an attack just after dawn when his opponents should be preoccupied with their ablutions and their breakfast.

During the long moonlit ride towards the camp he had worried whether – since two Bijapurans had escaped – his enemy might be on high alert. However, he had convinced himself that even if his opponents attached any importance to the seizure of their scouts, from their past experience they would not expect his own forces to respond so quickly to any information they obtained. Neither would they expect them to cover the thirty miles between the point of capture and their camp so fast.

But his fears seemed to have been groundless, Shah Jahan had thought as, breasting some low hillocks, he and his men had looked down on the camp with its smoking cooking fires and lines of tethered horses and soldiers moving to and fro on their normal duties. His men had quickly overwhelmed the few sentries posted around the hillocks. Now as he and his troops galloped, green banners streaming in the wind and horses' hooves pounding the hard-baked ground, towards the Bijapuran camp his enemies were running towards the horse lines buckling on their swords, grabbing lances from their pyramid racks and preparing to face his onslaught. But they would not be in time, thought Shah Jahan, urging his horse into an even faster gallop.

Then above the battle cries of his men and the drumming hooves he heard a loud crash, and then another. The sounds were coming from his front and left. Turning his head in that direction he saw the branches of several of the Bijapuran shelters had been thrown aside to reveal cannon which were already being brought into action. Musketeers too were crouching behind the cannon, steadying their long-barrelled weapons on the limbers as they fired. Both cannon and musket balls were finding their mark.

Through the dust thrown up by his charging cavalry he saw the forelegs of one of the leading Moghul horses crumple. As it collapsed it propelled its rider – a standard-bearer – over its head to smash into the ground. Soon rider and banner were engulfed by the onrushing cavalry, but now other horsemen were falling. A wounded and riderless horse swerved across the path of a group of his Rajput cavalry, two of whom were unable to turn or rein in in time to avoid it so that all three crashed to the earth in a welter of flailing limbs and hooves. However, despite the casualties his men were, like him, pressing forward as hard as they could, urging on their mounts with hands and heels. They should soon be in the camp engaging their opponents at close quarters so that the Bijapuran gunners would be less effective, being unable to distinguish clearly friend from foe.

Noticing at the last minute a small thorn fence just ahead – probably originally constructed to house village cattle – Shah Jahan pulled on his horse's reins and leaning forward on its neck urged it to make the jump. As the animal landed safely he saw a group of enemy horsemen approaching him at the gallop. How had they been able to arm and mount so quickly? Or had the Bijapurans been expecting him, concealing battle-prepared riders as well as cannon in the tents and shelters? Too late to think about that now. He must concentrate on the battle ahead. The leading Bijapuran was mounted on a grey horse and carrying a long lance in his right hand and heading directly for him. Shah Jahan pulled hard on his reins so that his horse passed to the left of the onrushing rider, meaning he could not make a proper lance thrust at the emperor. As he went by Shah Jahan struck out with his sword, catching his enemy's horse in its rump causing it to rear up and throw its rider sprawling onto the ground. Another Bijapuran rebel slashed with his curved sword at Shah Jahan, who managed to parry the blow with his own weapon.

Wheeling their horses, the two men rode at each other again, kicking their heels into the heaving flanks of their mounts to urge them on. This time Shah Jahan got in the first blow but the Bijapuran ducked beneath his slashing blade and as he did so thrust his weapon towards Shah Jahan's breastplate. The armour proved its worth and the blow skidded off harmlessly. Again the two men wheeled and rode at each other. Again Shah Jahan was the quicker to strike – and this time decisively. His slashing blow caught his opponent under his unprotected chin, severing his windpipe and almost decapitating him. Without even a scream he fell backwards from the saddle.

Looking around him as he wiped the sweat from his face

with his cotton neckcloth and tried to regain his breath, Shah Jahan saw through the dust and smoke that his men were heavily engaged. More and more rebels were joining the fray, including some Shah Jahan could see galloping from the village beyond the lagoon. It was becoming clearer and clearer that the Bijapurans had indeed been anticipating his arrival, concealing forces wherever they could including in the village huts. He had underestimated his enemy once more and now they were gaining the upper hand. He must do something before it was too late.

Among the fast approaching riders his eye was caught by a small band of no more than a dozen led by two soldiers carrying long Bijapuran gold banners forked like serpents' tongues. At their centre was a horseman wearing a glistening breastplate almost the equal in splendour of his own, and a plumed helmet. This must be the Bijapuran general who, if reports were true, was one of the sultan's several sons. If he could kill him that would blunt his enemies' onslaught and give the Moghuls a much needed chance to regroup.

'Those of you who can, disengage and rally to me,' Shah Jahan shouted over the hubbub of battle to the men who were within earshot. As they began to do so, he charged towards the Bijapuran general and his entourage who were now less than six hundred yards away. His horse was blowing hard and there was a thick scum of white sweat on its neck but it was willing and began to outdistance the rest of his men.

In less than a minute he was among the Bijapuran group. His first blow bit deep into the unprotected left leg of one of the standard-bearers, catching him just above the knee and slicing through sinew and flesh to judder against the bone, almost jolting the weapon from Shah Jahan's grasp. However, he held on to the hilt as the banner-bearer fell, dropping his golden standard into the dust. Another rider struck at Shah Jahan but the sword slid off his breastplate. Nevertheless, the force of the impact knocked the emperor back in his saddle. Within moments though, he had recovered his balance to see that he was in striking distance of the general. Putting all his weight into the stroke, he caught the man just beneath his glistening breastplate. Although he retained his seat on his horse, the general dropped his sword and doubled up clutching his belly. Quickly Shah Jahan aimed another thrust designed to finish him off, but as he did so he felt a crashing blow on his own head and his helmet falling. He put up a gauntleted hand in an attempt to steady it but his ears were buzzing, his thoughts scrambling and white stars and flashes appearing before his eyes and hampering his vision. He must get away from the conflict for a little to recover his senses.

Instinctively he kicked his mount forward, urging it on with his hands and heels. The willing animal gathered speed but then the flaring lights and the ringing in his head intensified. Overcome, he fell forward on his horse's neck . . .

• ◆ •

What was that plucking and pulling at him? He and Mumtaz were cocooned in the stars but something or someone was snatching at him, dragging him away from her. Mumtaz's pale face held a look of horror and pleading. Then she seemed to recede into the velvet darkness. He couldn't understand. Was she being pulled away from him and not him from her? It couldn't be . . . he mustn't let it happen. He tried to stretch out a hand, feeling a more distinct tug at his clothing. Someone was indeed clawing and probing at his body, pulling at his limbs, drawing him away from Mumtaz. 'No, no,' he muttered, jerking his head as he spoke. 'Mumtaz, I will stay with you.' Then he felt what could only be sharp-nailed fingers grasping at his throat.

Eyes opening but still dazed, he saw a blurred but gaunt face with hollow cheeks and bright eyes only inches from his own. Its lips seemed half open in surprise, open enough to reveal the blackened stumps of teeth. Strands of long grey hair were falling from the plait in which it was tied back. Thumbs were digging into his throat, seeking his Adam's apple. The apparition was definitely trying to strangle him. Instinctively Shah Jahan brought up his hands and knocked the bony fingers from his throat. Then he grasped at the devil's face. It felt surprisingly warm as it fought back, foul and sour breath polluting his nostrils. He wrenched the head back, twisting it as he did so. There was a crack and the apparition ceased to struggle and slumped forward on to Shah Jahan, warm saliva dripping from its slack mouth on to his face. Although light, the figure had some weight.

The pressure of it, together with the sensation of the spittle running down his cheek, cut into Shah Jahan's brain, reviving him towards full consciousness. He pushed the body off him, his mind clearing and his eyes focusing. He sat up and looked about him. The sun was blazing from its midday zenith with dazzling ferocity. Except for the body he was alone in a coppice of leafless trees. Slowly, to his horror, Shah Jahan realised that the figure with its head twisted at an unnatural angle, tongue lolling and eyes staring, was a woman, an old woman what's more. The edges of her tattered red sari were blowing in the breeze, exposing her bony ribcage and beneath it the slack skin crater where her stomach should have been. She must have been starving. He had killed her. Why? And why was he alone?

Slowly, splintered memories – weapon clashes, battle cries both of encouragement and of pain – coalesced in his mind. He remembered his headlong charge towards the Bijapuran camp, the drumming of his horse's hooves and after a while his attack on the enemy general, but what had happened next? Finally came a recollection of a blow to his head, a memory of falling forward ... His horse must have carried him several miles from the battle. He could neither see nor hear signs of conflict, nor, he realised with dismay, of his horse. Scrutinising the surrounding sandy ground he did make out some hoof prints. After he had fallen his horse must have wandered off. But how did the old woman fit in? Looking more closely at her corpse he saw on the ground beside it one of his rings – a large carved emerald – and yes, there was one of the silver clasps that had held on his light cloak, now carefully folded beside her. That must be it – she had been looting his body and when she had felt him stir attempted to kill him.

Clearly, the instinct to survive had overwhelmed any more feminine feelings of care and protection. That same instinct must account for her being alone. Had she left her village in search of food after the death of her family?

Were they lying somewhere too weak to move? Or had they in fact abandoned her? Survival was truly paramount in the human mind. That was why she had tried to kill him . . . why he had killed her . . . why indeed, he reflected, he had had his half-brothers killed. Now he himself must strive to survive once more.

Picking up his cloak from beside the woman's body he wound it roughly round his bare head to protect it, aching as it was from the fierce sun. The glint from his breastplate might betray him to searching enemies as well as burdening him as he walked. He quickly unbuckled it and, after scraping out a small depression in the sand, buried it. Then he looked at what he had assumed were his horse's hoof prints. His mount seemed to have come from the northwest before he fell from the saddle, after which it had headed off to the south. Should he follow it and try to recapture it or should he retrace his steps in the direction of the battle? He should go after the horse, he reasoned. It would probably have stopped quite soon. Besides, the outcome of the fighting had been highly uncertain. He might be returning to the scene of his column's defeat and face capture or death.

Slowly he began to pick his way southwards through the leafless trees, following the horse's tracks, which became less and less distinct as the ground grew more flinty towards the edge of the coppice. How he wished he had spent more time with his scouts learning the secrets of tracking. Lifting his eyes from the faint hoof prints, he scanned the horizon in the hope of catching sight of his mount. Instead, he saw some riders perhaps a mile away, approaching from the north in a cloud of dust. He couldn't tell whether they were friend or enemy and took cover behind the trunk of one of the larger trees, straining his eyes to pick out any identifying signs. He could not, and remained still behind the trunk as the squadron came closer. Then it divided. Half the men headed around one side of the coppice, the remainder around the other, both halves clearly bent on a thorough search. As they came even nearer, Shah Jahan shrank back against the tree trunk, trying to make himself as small and inconspicuous as he could. Suddenly to his intense relief he recognised the leading officer – a tall Rajput mounted on a black horse and wearing saffron robes beneath his steel breastplate. It was Ashok Singh. The troops were his own. He emerged from the shelter of the tree trunk and ran to the edge of the coppice.

'Majesty, is that you? Are you wounded?' Ashok Singh shouted, dropping from his saddle.

'Yes – and no, at least not seriously. Praise God you have found me. I was knocked out and my horse carried me here, I think, before I collapsed from it.'

'We found it wandering not too far away.'

'Were we victorious in the battle?'

'Yes, Majesty. We gained the upper hand in the fighting during which we lost sight of you and drove the Bijapurans from their camp, inflicting many casualties on them as they retreated.'

'Is the pursuit still continuing?'

'No. Our losses were also high. In your absence your generals thought it better to regroup and tend our wounded rather than maintain the chase. They feared another ambush of the type that overtook Ahmed Aziz and of course we needed to discover what had happened to you.'

So the victory was by no means complete, thought Shah Jahan, but better a partial success than the setbacks he had suffered previously.

Two hours later, once more wearing his breastplate, which one of his soldiers had retrieved from its hiding place, Shah Jahan mounted his horse. Nearby the pyre hastily constructed by his Rajputs from the coppice's dead trees crackled and burned. By her dress the old woman had clearly been a Hindu and it had seemed only proper to accord her the rites of her faith. But with the flames licking around the cotton-wrapped corpse there was no need to linger. Let the old woman crumble to ash alone in the desert. The important thing now was to re-join the main body of his troops before demoralising rumours spread that the emperor had been injured, even killed. Casting a last look at the spiralling black smoke of the pyre, he urged his tired horse to a canter.

For the first few miles not a living thing crossed their path in the arid and featureless terrain, but then Shah Jahan noticed what looked like a small village – no more than six or seven shacks – away to their right. Perhaps there was a well not yet dry where they could water their horses. Signalling to his men, he turned his mount in the direction of the low mud-brick houses. As they approached, an old man staggered up from his charpoy beneath a withered banyan tree which had retained just a few of its leaves and stumbled forward on stick-thin legs that looked too weak to bear even his frail weight.

'Food, gentlemen, food, I beg you …' he cried out through cracked lips.

Shah Jahan reined in his horse. The old man's eyes

stared unnaturally bright in sunken eye sockets above prominent cheekbones. 'Are your stores exhausted? When did you last eat?'

'Our grain was gone six weeks ago. A few days later our animals began to die. We ate their carcasses – skin and entrails too. We even ground their bones to make a kind of flour. We were lucky our well still had a little water. But other than that we've eaten nothing but dried leaves and two geckos we caught a few days ago.'

'Where are the other villagers?'

'They left three days since to seek food elsewhere but my wife was too weak and I've remained with her.'

'Give him what food we have and any spare water bottles,' Shah Jahan told Ashok Singh. 'I hadn't realised the extent of the famine.'

'It is bad, Majesty. Around the walls of Burhanpur I have seen proud men fight over undigested grain one had extracted from animal dung. But it seems far worse in these outlying regions. Parents are said to be selling their children into servitude for a few coins in the hope that both they and the children may thereby live. There are even rumours of cannibalism among some of the hill people whose flocks of sheep and goats have perished.'

As his Rajputs handed the man food and water Shah Jahan could not get the thought of people grinding bones for flour and even descending to cannibalism from his mind. Perhaps he shouldn't be surprised. After all, it was only a few hours since he himself had killed the old woman. However, as he rode on another thought struck him. The man must have truly loved his wife to stay with her rather than desert her to seek his chances away from the village, just as he himself would have stayed with Mumtaz. If survival was a basic and selfish instinct shared with animals, man also had other more noble ones . . . like love.

Chapter 4

Supported by Satti al-Nisa and wearing a shift of sapphire silk, Mumtaz stepped carefully down the three white marble steps into the pool of rose oil-scented water. Despite her bulk – in a few weeks she would give birth – her every move was graceful, thought Shah Jahan, watching from the doorway into the *hammam*. The apricot glow of the candles accentuated the curves of her body. For a moment he allowed himself the luxury of just watching her as she lay back in the pool, resting her head against its side as attendants poured more water down two marble shoots carved in a fish-scale pattern to make the droplets ripple and dance. At least here within the encircling walls of Burhanpur he had created a haven for Mumtaz. Red lilies and sweet-scented *champa* flowers bloomed in the courtyards and the ancient fountains had been coaxed to new life.

Yet beyond the walls lay an unforgiving landscape

where men and beasts struggled beneath a pitiless sun that was daily sucking them and their land dry. In their temples his Hindu subjects were beseeching their gods to relieve their suffering – even making blood sacrifice to the many-armed Kali. Some were blaming the Moghul emperor for failing to aid his people. Last week two *saddhus*, bony ash-daubed bodies pale as ghosts, had walked up to the gates of Burhanpur, shaking their sticks and denouncing him. He had given orders they should not be molested and they had remained in the blistering heat for an hour. Before departing they had placed what looked like the body of a young child on the ground. When his soldiers investigated they found it was only a bundle of sticks wrapped in dirty cloth with a dried gourd for a head but the message was clear. Children were dying and he, the emperor, was to blame. He hadn't told Mumtaz.

As he stepped towards the pool, she heard his footsteps and turned her head, smiling. 'I felt so tired tonight – I thought a bath would revive me.'

He waited until the tall figure of Satti al-Nisa and the other women had withdrawn, then sat on the pool's marble ledge. 'The famine's getting even worse. Every day I receive reports of whole villages emptying as people take their surviving livestock west to seek water. I've ordered the imperial granaries in the affected areas to be opened but there's just not enough grain to go round – only enough to feed the people for a few weeks, not their flocks. Yet without their animals their future is bleak. In some places the Bijapuran rebels are raiding the grain stores.'

'You are doing what you can.'

'But I feel helpless. Despite my wealth and power what is needed is water, not gold. If the rains don't come quickly many more will die.'

'Not even you can defeat nature.'

'I should be able to do better for my people and I can't while this war distracts me . . . I must end it quickly.'

'You're being impatient again. I'd rather stay here a year, two years even, than see you hazard yourself for the sake of a short campaign.'

In the candlelight Shah Jahan saw the earnestness in Mumtaz's eyes. Leaning forward he stroked her cheek. 'You're right. I am impatient. I always have been. It's not only that I want to deal decisively with my enemies and be free to turn my ambition elsewhere – I want to be able to take you back to the comfort and security of Agra. Long ago, when we first married, I vowed to protect you from dangers of all kinds and to give you the life of peace and luxury you deserved. But when my father turned against us I couldn't keep that promise. Since we've been here in Burhanpur I've worried that I've failed you again and exposed you to unnecessary hazards. This is no place for you.'

'It was my choice. I refused be parted from you, as I've always done . . .' Mumtaz sat up, then, gripping the marble ledge, pulled herself upright. 'Help me out.' Standing before him she took his face between her hands and kissed his forehead. 'The present is as it is. Again I made my choice, and again it was to be with you. As for the past, we survived it together. It is over, as I've told you so many times. Why keep tormenting yourself with unrectifiable regrets?'

'You're right. I must look ahead, but some things are hard to forget. By defeating my enemies quickly I can do what is best for those I love and win my subjects' respect for me as their new emperor.'

'You already have it. Your father himself gave you the title "Shah Jahan", "Lord of the World", and time and time again you proved your worthiness of it.'

'That was a long time ago. Much has happened since then and my people don't yet know me.'

'You are as stubborn as our son Aurangzeb. Go if you must. But promise me one thing, at least – that before charging headlong into battle you will think what may be in your enemy's mind ... Others can be as clever and cunning as you. Each time I bid you farewell I need to believe you will come back to me.'

'I promise to take care.' He saw that Mumtaz was shivering despite the warm air. 'You should put on dry clothes – I will summon your attendants.'

He was about to ring the silver bell hanging from a green silk cord when Jahanara appeared through the cusped doorway, breathing hard as if she'd run quickly. 'It's Dara ... a rider has just brought the news ... He'll be here tomorrow.'

'You're sure? He wasn't due to reach Burhanpur for another two weeks,' Shah Jahan said.

'The messenger says Dara has been insisting on riding all day and much of the night.'

Shah Jahan glanced at Mumtaz, whose face was glowing at the thought of seeing their son after so many months. 'I'll send troops at once to meet the party.'

'Let Aurangzeb go with them so he can share in the

glory of his brother's return,' Mumtaz said. 'Young as he is, I know how much he envied Dara the opportunity of going to the Persian court.'

Shah Jahan considered for a moment. 'If we were at peace I'd agree, but the Bijapurans are impudent enough for anything. I'm not sending an escort for show but to ensure Dara and the rest of embassy reach Burhanpur safely. I think it best that Aurangzeb remains here.'

• ◆ •

Seated on his throne on the sandstone platform in the middle of the courtyard of the Burhanpur fort, Shah Jahan waited, hiding his impatience. There were few times when he wished himself an ordinary family man, free to behave as he pleased, but this was one of them. The neighing of horses and the clatter of hooves on flagstones from beyond the arched gateway had told him that Tuhin Roy, his envoy, and his party had arrived. He found it hard not to rush to greet his son but protocol demanded a formal ceremony. That was why his courtiers and commanders were standing in rows before him, while on a low dais to his right his three younger sons waited, dressed in brocade coats of Moghul green with ropes of pearls round their necks.

Thirteen-year-old Shah Shuja was looking around grinning but the stockier, square-jawed Aurangzeb, two years his junior, was solemn-faced. Soon he must find suitable tasks for them both, just as he had for Dara. An imperial prince's training couldn't begin too early. Shah Shuja needed to learn that life was about more than hunting and hawking and Aurangzeb to appreciate that the exercise of power might not be as easy as he sometimes seemed to think from his reading about his ancestors. At least it would be some years before he need worry about the six-year-old Murad, who was trying without success to attract Shah Shuja's attention by tugging on his sash.

The trumpets sounded and, as precedence required, Tuhin Roy as the head of the embassy appeared first through the gateway. Elderly but still upright, his beard dyed black, he approached with slow, stately steps and bowed low before the throne.

'Welcome back, Tuhin Roy. Did your embassy to the shah prosper?' Shah Jahan knew perfectly well that it had – the envoy had sent regular despatches – but it was important to announce the success of his mission in public.

'The shah sends you his greetings and calls you brother. I carry a letter from him. May I read it aloud, Majesty?'

'Proceed, Tuhin Roy.'

The envoy opened an ivory case and took out a paper. Unfolding it he began to read, starting with a flowery passage extolling the greatness of the Moghul empire at which Shah Jahan suppressed a smile – the Persian shah and the Moghul emperor had long been rivals rather than allies. But then the envoy came to the meat: '*I, Shah Abbas, am graciously pleased to accept the trading rights you offer in Herat in return for which I pledge myself not to levy taxes on the merchants of the Moghul empire passing through my city of Isfahan.*'

'You have negotiated well, Tuhin Roy, and you will be well rewarded. But first you must rest, as you have had a tiring journey. For that I know I must blame my son and his eagerness to return to his family. Forgive me, but I am equally eager to be reunited with him.'

Tuhin Roy looked a little hurt to be dismissed so quickly, but bowed and withdrew. At Shah Jahan's signal a trumpet sounded and Dara Shukoh appeared through the gateway, the ranks of courtiers bowing like stalks of wheat in the breeze as he passed between them to acknowledge the return of the emperor's eldest son. Dara was smiling as Shah Jahan descended his dais and enfolded him in his arms. Then taking Dara by the right hand he turned to his assembled courtiers. 'To celebrate the safe return of my beloved son, I hereby present him with a yaks-tail banner – since the days of my ancestor Babur one of the highest honours an emperor can bestow.'

That night, as darkness fell and a new moon cast its pale reflection across the fortress of Burhanpur, the *haram* was a place transformed. Burning wicks flickered in glass balls of red, green and blue suspended on chains from trees in the main courtyard, their light softening the austerity of the sandstone masonry. Shah Jahan sat cross-legged in the centre of a dais spread with rich Persian carpets – gifts from the shah. His three eldest sons were still eating. Mumtaz was lying back against a yellow brocade bolster, Jahanara and Roshanara beside her, heads close as they laughed together. Little Murad was on his back sleeping the deep sleep that comes only to the very young.

Shah Jahan's first thought on learning of Dara's return had been to order a celebratory feast, but Mumtaz had taken him on one side. 'Should we do such a thing during a famine?' she had asked. 'Won't it seem uncaring if we feast lavishly? The smells from our cooking fires will waft over the walls of Burhanpur to those who may not know when they will eat again.' He had realised at once that – more sensitive than he to what others might be feeling – she was right. She usually was. Instead of the great celebration he had planned, at Mumtaz's suggestion he had ordered an extra issue of grain to the surrounding villages in Dara's honour and instructed his cooks to prepare a plain meal for his family to share alone here in the *haram*.

Shah Shuja was quizzing Dara Shukoh about the Persian court. It was good to see them so easy in each other's company, Shah Jahan thought. How different from his own boyhood – even in his early years he and his half-brothers had never been close, and later ambition for the throne had severed any bonds there might have been. If he had had a full brother – as his sons were to one another – things might have been different . . .

Something Dara was saying – Shah Jahan had been too caught in his own reflections to pay attention – was making Shah Shuja shake his head in disbelief.

'What is it, Shah Shuja?'

'Dara was telling us what the shah told him – that many years ago the Persians helped our great-great-great grandfather Babur in his struggle against the Uzbek leader Shaibani Khan . . . that the Persians rescued Babur's sister from the Uzbeks and sent him a drinking cup made from Shaibani Khan's skull. It can't be true . . . When were the Moghuls ever in such thrall to the Persians, Father?'

But it was Aurangzeb, sitting a little behind the other two, who answered. 'The story's true, as you'd know, Shah Shuja, if you ever bothered to read the chronicles – especially

Babur's own account. You'd also know that one of the reasons Humayun finally won back Hindustan was because the Persians loaned him an army.'

'I am impressed, Aurangzeb. Your tutors told me you were studious but I didn't realise how much. Perhaps one day you'll be a great scholar,' said Shah Jahan.

'A scholar? No – I'll be a warrior like you!'

'Perhaps.'

'I mean it, Father.' Aurangzeb's serious young face was flushed. 'What I read tells me the Moghuls won Hindustan by the sword – not by the pen. That's how we'll keep it.'

Shah Jahan suppressed a smile. Aurangzeb's sense of humour was not strong and his feelings were easily bruised – something his brothers, who often teased him, understood only too well. 'I'm sure you will be whatever you wish to be.'

As Shah Jahan looked at his family, reunited once more, his eyes met Mumtaz's and she gave a tiny, almost imperceptible nod – her signal to broach the subject that they had talked of deep into the night.

'Dara Shukoh, Tuhin Roy praised your tact and discretion in Persia. You acquitted yourself as a man, not a boy, and your mother has a suggestion for how we might declare this to all the world.'

'What do you mean, Father?' Dara Shukoh's clear hazel eyes looked from Shah Jahan to Mumtaz.

'It is time for you to marry. Your mother has suggested your cousin Nadira as your bride. She has noticed how much you like her . . .'

Dara Shukoh's somewhat abashed but delighted expression showed that Mumtaz hadn't been wrong. So did the knowing grins on the faces of Shah Shuja and Aurangzeb. Even though he hadn't been aware of the attachment till now, Shah Jahan was pleased. If one day Dara had to take other wives for dynastic reasons it was good that his first marriage should be to a woman for whom he cared. He hadn't been much older himself when he'd been betrothed to Mumtaz. And it was a good alliance for the dynasty. Nadira was the daughter of his half-brother Parvez, whose passion for drink and opium had killed him at the age of only thirty-eight at a time when conflict had divided the dynasty. A union between Nadira and Dara Shukoh would heal at least some of the wounds of the past and bind the wider imperial family closer. She was also beautiful – short but voluptuous – and with a ready wit that she had already showed was a match for Dara's agile mind at the family gatherings where Mumtaz had observed their mutual attraction.

'Well, Dara, what do you say?'

'It would make me very happy to marry Nadira,' Dara replied, his voice betraying a mixture of pleasure and embarrassment – the latter doubtless fuelled by his brothers' smirking scrutiny.

'I'm glad you approve. I'll start planning your wedding. It will be a welcome distraction during these final weeks of waiting for your new brother or sister to join us,' said Mumtaz, looking down on her swollen belly.

Shah Jahan lay back against the cushions, already visualising the splendour of the marriage procession. The ceremony would take place as soon as possible after their victorious return to Agra. It would mark not only the nuptials of a beloved son and an imperial prince but also the true start of his own reign when, with the rebels of the south subdued, he could begin to take the Moghul empire forward to new splendours and new conquests.

• ◆ •

'Majesty, Rai Singh has located a large Bijapuran force some thirty miles to the west.' The messenger's sweat-stained clothing showed the speed with which he had ridden to Burhanpur.

Shah Jahan felt a shiver of excitement. At last this might be the opportunity to deal his elusive enemy a decisive blow. For a moment his mind raced, but then it was made up. 'Take a fresh horse and return to Rai Singh. Tell him I'm bringing a force of horsemen and cannon-equipped elephants to join him. You said the Bijapurans were thirty miles away? If I ride hard with the vanguard of the cavalry, I can be with Rai Singh in under three hours.'

As he hurried towards the *haram* after giving the necessary orders, Shah Jahan was smiling. He was tired of being played with by a disciplined enemy who appeared now here, now there, in hit and run raids only to melt away again before he could engage them fully.

Mumtaz was sitting on a stool while Satti al-Nisa combed out her long hair. Jahanara was sitting close by reading aloud from a volume of poems by the Persian Firduz that Mumtaz loved. Jahanara was as much of a scholar as Dara or Aurangzeb, thought Shah Jahan.

'What is it? You look excited?' Mumtaz asked, stretching out her hand to him.

'Good news at last – at least I hope so. My men have encountered a large group of Bijapurans. If I am quick we may finally have the battle I've been hoping for.'

Mumtaz's smile faded. 'You again mean to go yourself, don't you?'

'I must. This is too great a chance to turn the campaign decisively in our favour to neglect.'

'I hope it is indeed the turning point . . . and I'm sure it will be. Take care.'

'I will.' He bent to kiss her warm lips, then, at her urging, placed his hand for a moment on her belly to feel the kicking of the new life within her. The child wasn't due for another month. He would be back long before then and perhaps with his campaign over. As he half ran from Mumtaz's room, his mind was already focused on the fighting ahead.

Three hours later Shah Jahan, who had just ridden up with the main body of his troops, followed the pointing arm of Rai Singh. 'The rebels have occupied the old fort on that rock-strewn hill over there, Majesty.' On the crown of the low hill about half a mile away he could see the crenellations of a dilapidated mud-brick fort. Some stretches of the wall appeared to have collapsed completely. The small fort would provide only limited protection for the enemy horsemen and foot soldiers he could make out moving about on the slope, but the hilltop position was a clear advantage. Some of the rebels were stationing themselves behind the stronger, more intact-looking portions of the walls. Others were dragging brushwood into the gaps in the defences or trying desperately to pile up fallen bricks and other rubble into makeshift barricades.

'How long have they been up there?' Shah Jahan asked.

'We clashed with some of their scouts at first light.

Once alerted to our presence the enemy quickly began to move up to the hilltop.'

'I'm surprised they did not simply retreat, disappearing into the countryside as they have before.'

'They have more infantry with them than I have known previously, and those men would not have got far on foot.'

'About how many of them are there?'

'No more than two thousand or so.'

'We outnumber them then, but that's no bad thing . . . As we attack up the slope we will be much more exposed than they will be behind the walls.' Shah Jahan turned to Ashok Singh. 'Have our horsemen surround the hill. Then once the war elephants with the small cannon arrive we will advance. There is no point in delaying.'

The elephants took longer than he had anticipated to appear, during which time he could see the rebels continuing to work feverishly with their hands as well as picks and shovels to strengthen their makeshift fortifications. Shah Jahan could not relax. He ordered small parties of his musketmen to scramble up the hillside, water bottles and spare ammunition slung across their backs together with their muskets, to take up positions behind rocky outcrops just outside the range of enemy fire so that they could join the action quickly when it began.

Once the elephants had arrived and the gunners had loaded the cannon in their howdahs with powder and ball, sweating in the afternoon heat as they rammed the shot down the barrels, Shah Jahan gave the command for them to advance. They began to do so steadily and slowly, with groups of musketeers, archers and foot soldiers running along behind them, taking advantage of the protection afforded by their bulk. His scouts had told Shah Jahan that they did not believe the rebels had even small cannon. Nevertheless, he waited apprehensively for a crash and burst of white smoke from the hillside to show that they had been mistaken and he had once more underestimated his enemies' strength and cunning. None came.

By now, his leading elephants were more than halfway up the slope and the gunners in their howdahs were bringing their small cannon into action. Shah Jahan saw a long portion of the fortress's brick wall collapse after being hit by some of the cannon balls. Some enemy horsemen who had been sheltering behind it rode out through the dust but Shah Jahan was sure others had been trapped by the falling debris. Still there was no answering cannon fire from the Bijapurans. His scouts must have been right – they had no cannon, he thought with relief. The assault was going well and now was the time for him to join it with his main body of horsemen. Waving his sword as the signal to attack, he began to gallop forward. As they saw him and his bodyguard advance, other horsemen surrounding the hill took up the charge until, green banners billowing, they were riding at the fortress from all sides.

Kicking his horse onward while taking care to avoid the scattered rocks, Shah Jahan soon came up with the war elephants. Suddenly one – a massive beast with three gunners as well as a small cannon in its open howdah – raised its red-painted trunk and began to trumpet in pain.

A lucky musket shot had hit it not where the overlapping steel plates of its armoured surcoat gave some protection but in the right eye socket. With blood pouring down its cheek and running on to its curved tusk, it turned from the advance and slowly crashed to the ground, dislodging both the gunners and the bronze cannon. The weapon fell into the path of the mounted bodyguard immediately on Shah Jahan's right, bringing his horse to the ground and trapping its rider by his leg between its flank and a large jagged rock.

The bodyguard's scream of agony reached Shah Jahan's ears above the other sounds of battle. As it did so, he himself felt a sharp pain in his left ankle and his mount skittered sideways, half rearing. The fallen horse, thrashing its legs, had kicked both of them. Hot pain searing his ankle, Shah Jahan reined in his horse and tried to bring it under control, but for some moments it crossed the line of his advancing cavalry, slowing their charge up the hill, which was particularly steep at this point. Just as he regained mastery of his mount, Shah Jahan became aware of a party of at least thirty enemy horsemen galloping from the fortifications now no more than three hundred yards away, intent on exploiting the temporary chaos in this section of his advance.

Musketeers firing from the elephant howdahs knocked two enemy riders from their saddles before the rest, benefitting from the impetus provided by the slope, crashed into Shah Jahan's troops. One bearded rider, yelling wildly, thrust his lance deep into the cheek of a war elephant, which veered sharply away from the attack and crashed back down the hill, trampling some of the foot soldiers who had been following in its wake. Another rebel horseman caught the grey mount of one of Shah Jahan's bodyguards full in the chest with his long lance, killing the animal almost instantly. A third spitted from his saddle one of Shah Jahan's young *qorchis*, whose first battle and now almost certainly his last it was.

Shah Jahan kicked his own horse towards the attacker, who was trying to extract his lance from the squire's chest as the young man lay squirming and screaming on the ground. The rebel could not turn to face Shah Jahan in time and the emperor's sword struck him hard above the knee before knocking his lance from his hand to land beside the dying *qorchi*. Leaving others to finish the rebel off, Shah Jahan attacked another man who was so intent on scything the head from an imperial musketeer that he did not notice the emperor's approach until he felt the blow which split his own skull. Twisting in his saddle, Shah Jahan saw that the rebel attack had been blunted and his own men and horses were advancing up the hill again. Despite the pain in his rapidly swelling ankle, he urged his mount forward once more.

As his horse leapt one of the makeshift brushwood barricades, Shah Jahan felt another sharp impact, this time on the point of his left shoulder blade. A spent ball had caught the edge of his breastplate before thudding into his shoulder. A second ball hissed through the air close to his head. Then he was upon the musketeers, who were desperately trying to reload in the shelter of some rocks. One, reversing his musket, whirled it by its long barrel over his head in an attempt to knock Shah Jahan from his horse, only to be felled by Shah Jahan's sword cut which laid open his cheek, leaving his teeth exposed.

Within minutes Shah Jahan and his men were inside the mud-brick walls of the fort, hacking and slashing at their increasingly desperate enemy as the Bijapurans tried to retreat from one position to the next. Soon some rebels were throwing down their swords and falling to the ground to beg for mercy. Others, mainly horsemen, were trying to flee but in most cases were ridden down by the emperor's cavalry or shot from their saddles by his musketeers. One rider – a large man in billowing white robes – fell from his horse only for his foot to be caught in his stirrup so that he was dragged behind his mount as it careered downhill, his head smashing to bloody pulp as it ricocheted from rock to rock. Another man who from the look of his garments was an officer was brought to the ground, arms flailing, by a shot fired by a musketeer at Shah Jahan's side which must have travelled nearly two hundred yards. Shah Jahan was turning to congratulate the man and promise him a reward for his skill when from his hilltop vantage point his eye was caught by a small group of riders approaching fast from the direction of Burhanpur.

Shah Jahan hesitated a moment. The battle was won and he was curious to know who the riders were. Calling to his bodyguard to follow, he kicked his horse forward and galloped down the hill towards a clump of trees where the riders had reined in. As he got closer he saw there were six of them – five soldiers and a white-haired man in dark green robes. As the man turned his head, Shah Jahan recognised Aslan Beg. What could have brought his elderly steward from Burhanpur to the field of battle?

Kicking his tired horse so hard it snorted in protest and

flattened its ears, he outstripped his escort and thundered towards the little knot of men. 'What is it? What's happened?' he called out as soon as he was in earshot.

'Majesty, the empress has gone into labour before her time. The lady Jahanara asked me to send word . . . I felt it was my duty to come myself . . .' The old man was swaying with fatigue; the exertion of the hard ride had clearly drained his strength.

Shah Jahan felt a sudden coldness in the pit of his stomach. What had prompted Jahanara's message? If all was well, wouldn't they have left the good news of the birth to await his return? 'How is the empress?'

'I don't know. The *hakims* were with her when I left . . . I did not wait to ask them. Your daughter was insistent no time be lost.'

Shah Jahan hesitated. His every instinct was to ride at once for Burhanpur but he mustn't throw away a longed-for victory gained at such cost. He thought quickly, then turned to his captain of bodyguard. 'Tell Ashok Singh he is to assume command here. My orders to him are to pursue the Bijapurans as far as seems prudent but to take no risks, to garrison this fort and then to bring the rest of the troops back to Burhanpur. And quickly bring me a fresh horse.'

As he rode, urging his new mount on, Shah Jahan's eyes were fixed on the hazy horizon, willing the battlements of Burhanpur to come into view though he knew many miles separated him from his goal. His injured left ankle was throbbing painfully and glancing down he saw that his garments were spattered with blood – whether his own or his enemies' he couldn't be sure – but memories of the conflict were already fading. All he could think of was Mumtaz and how soon he could be with her. At least it would ease her mind to know he had come safely through the fighting.

At last, through the fast fading light, he saw the Tapti river before him and overlooking its northern bank the square tower in which were Mumtaz's apartments. Urging his blowing horse down the bank, he splashed through the shallow, sluggish waters and rode on up to the gateway through which each evening his elephants were led down from their stables, the *hati mahal*, to the river to bathe and drink. This wasn't the way he usually entered his fortress but it was the quickest. He saw the guards' surprise as he cantered into the small courtyard outside the *hati mahal*, jumped from his saddle, pain shooting through his ankle, and half running, half limping, made for the stairs leading into the heart of the fortress and the *haram*. He mounted the steps as fast as he could, unbuckling his breastplate which he thrust into the hands of an attendant as he reached the entrance to the *haram*. Normally he would have washed away the blood and sweat of battle but he rushed towards Mumtaz's apartments just as he was.

His appearance was so sudden that there was no time for the usual cry of 'the emperor approaches' to precede him. Jahanara was standing by the half-open door to her mother's room. Hearing his steps on the stone floor she raised her head and he saw tears running down her face.

'Jahanara, what is it? What's happened?'

'The baby will not come. She has been in such torment these past hours. Nothing seems to help. I tried to calm her but all she will say is that she must see you . . .' Before Jahanara could finish, there came a long agonised scream more animal than human. Fear such as he had never felt on the battlefield took hold of Shah Jahan. Stepping forward, he pushed the door fully open and looked inside.

Mumtaz was lying on a low divan, knees drawn up, back arched, her hands clenching the sides of the bed. Her white shift was soaked in sweat and her long hair was plastered to her contorted face as raising her chin she screamed again. Satti al-Nisa, who was kneeling by the divan, attempted to take her in her arms and hold her still but Mumtaz was threshing so wildly that she couldn't. Two *hakims*, one elderly, the other a youth, were standing in a corner of the room by a small brazier of burning charcoals over which some bitter-smelling potion was bubbling in a copper pot. 'Leave her be, madam. The opium is almost ready and will ease her pain,' one of them said.

Looking up, Satti al-Nisa saw Shah Jahan in the doorway. Her face wore the same helpless expression as his daughter's as she rose and stepped aside. Slowly Shah Jahan approached the bed. Somehow Mumtaz sensed he was there and turned her head towards him as another spasm racked her body. She gasped but this time did not cry out, and as he knelt beside her she managed a smile. 'You came,' she whispered.

'Of course. All will be well.'

'No. The baby won't come . . . I've tried and tried . . . I don't want it to die inside me.'

'It will come when it is ready . . . try to relax.'

'That is what the *hakims* say but I can't. My body feels about to split with pressure and pain but nothing happens.'

'Majesty.' The older of the *hakims* was by his side, a cup in his hand. 'This medicine will relieve her suffering.'

'Give it to me.' Kneeling by the side of the divan, Shah Jahan held the cup to Mumtaz's lips. 'Drink . . .' At first the amber liquid trickled down her chin but at last she swallowed some.

'That will soothe her, Majesty, relax some of the tensions building within her. This is the sixteenth hour of her labour and she is exhausted. In a few minutes she will grow drowsy,' said the *hakim*. But as if to contradict his words, Mumtaz began to cry out again. As she struggled she knocked the cup from Shah Jahan's hand and it rolled across the floor. 'It's coming,' she gasped. 'Thank the heavens, it's coming at last . . .' Her nails dug into the flesh of his right forearm as she clung to him.

'Transfer her pain to me. Let me be the one who suffers,' Shah Jahan found himself praying.

Suddenly Mumtaz let go of him and dragged herself into a sitting position, knees doubled up beneath her shift. Then she flung back her head but this time her cry was one of triumph rather than despair. The next moment Shah Jahan heard the sound of a baby crying.

'Majesties, look. A beautiful girl.' Satti-al Nisa was holding out a tiny bundle already wrapped in a piece of green linen – fit clothing for this newest addition to the Moghul line.

Feeling dazed, he got to his feet and looked briefly at the child, but all his thoughts were for Mumtaz. 'I knew all would be well . . .' he began. But as he looked at her again he saw not joy but terror on her face and realised that her shift, in fact the entire divan, was crimsoning with her blood. He didn't need the *hakims'* cries of consternation to tell him that this was not the ordinary blood-letting of childbirth.

He moved aside to allow them room to work while Satti al-Nisa, who had handed the child to an attendant, rushed to fetch the cotton pads for which the doctors were calling to staunch the blood. Mumtaz was lying back, eyes closed and her body very still. As the minutes passed, it seemed to Shah Jahan that the *hakims* were doing nothing except mopping up the bright red flow which continued to stream from Mumtaz. Water from the copper basins in which they were rinsing out their cloths slopped crimson on the floor.

'Surely you can do something,' he heard himself say but there was no reply, only a shaking of heads and a muffled conversation between the two doctors.

'Leave us!' Mumtaz's voice suddenly rang out sharp and clear. 'I wish to be alone with my husband. Go ... go now!' Never in twenty years of marriage had he heard her sound more commanding.

The *hakims* and Satti al-Nisa looked at Shah Jahan. 'Do as the empress says but remain within earshot,' he ordered.

'Mumtaz ...' he began as soon as they were alone.

'No, let me speak. My life is flowing from me with my blood. I'm dying ... I know it. There is nothing anyone can do. I must have these final precious moments with you. Put your strong arms around me ... let me feel the beat of your heart.'

Kneeling down again he cradled her in his arms. 'You have given birth to a fine child and you will recover ... the *hakims* will stop the bleeding ...'

'No, my heart tells me that it isn't so. Listen to me . . . our remaining time together is short. I have things to ask of you while my mind is still clear . . .'

'Anything.'

'Please don't marry again . . . if you have more children by another woman they will be a threat to our own sons. That mustn't happen . . . rivalries between half-brothers bring nothing but sorrow. We both know that.'

'I could never marry another. You are everything to me . . . everything.'

'That gives me such comfort – knowing that I can endure anything, even the pain of parting from you. But I have something else to beg of you. In my dreams I've seen a white marble tomb, luminous as a great pearl . . . build me such a resting place where you and our children can come to remember me.'

'Don't speak of tombs. We will have many more years together.' He held her even tighter, as if by doing so he could make the life force pulsing within him flow into her and give her strength.

'Please . . . you must promise me . . . you must. Then I can go in peace to whatever awaits me.'

'When the time comes I will create you a paradise on earth. I will spare nothing, no cost, no effort. It will be the marvel of the world not only for its flawless beauty but because people will know it represents a flawless love.'

He heard Mumtaz give a deep sigh as if what he said had satisfied her. For a few minutes they clung to one other in silence, then Mumtaz whispered, 'You mustn't spend your life in regret, not you or Dara, Jahanara or any of our children . . . Love them as I did . . . They have so much before them, as I once did, the night I first saw you at the Meena Bazaar. Do you remember that night? All the lanterns hanging on the trees and how you came to my stall. You didn't bargain very well … Shah Jahan, in the years to come remember how much I loved you – more than I ever thought it possible to love another …'

'And I love you … that is why you mustn't leave me …'

'My fate is written. I don't have a choice. Stand up and let me look at you one last time …'

As if in a dream Shah Jahan released her and rose. Her pale face held such an expression of yearning that tears came pouring down his face as all sensation drained from his body and he struggled to find words. 'Mumtaz …' was all he could manage. He knelt and cradled her once more.

A veil was already falling over her beautiful eyes. So many times on the battlefield he'd seen that look on the face of friend or foe at the very moment the soul was about to flee the body. 'Don't forget me …' she whispered as her head fell back. As he looked down on her small, blood-soaked form it seemed to him that her last words to him on this earth still lingered, though the woman he loved was gone for ever.

Chapter 5

The face reflected in the mirror of burnished silver was a stranger's. Shah Jahan studied the gaunt features, the bags beneath the swollen eyes and the locks of hair straggling from beneath his cap that looked silvery white when they should have been dark. The mirror must be faulty. He flung it against a stone pillar and watched the tiny seed pearls dislodged from the frame roll over the carpet. What did it matter what he looked like anyway – whether he ate or drank ... whether he saw another sunrise or not? Without Mumtaz his life was over.

From beyond the double doors of his room he caught the murmur of voices and frowned. He had ordered that no one was to disturb him ... not even his sons and daughters. For the past five days nobody had dared intrude on his grief though now and then he had heard footfalls and subdued voices, doubtless debating how long the emperor intended to seclude himself. He hardly knew himself. Perhaps for ever ... resuming court life was unthinkable. How could he listen to petitions from fawning courtiers concealing selfish ambitions beneath honeyed words or decide between plaintiffs arguing about trivial matters when his whole being was empty and drained of emotion?

For the first hours after Mumtaz's death he had moved in a kind of numb trance, distant from the horror and the shock. He had watched Satti al-Nisa gently cleanse Mumtaz's body with camphor water, untangle her long hair with an ivory comb and dress her in a plain shift as tears ran down her own cheeks. When she had completed her work and the imams had recited verses for the dead from the Koran, everyone had left the death chamber so that he could take his final leave. As he had kissed those already chill lips goodbye, for a moment his hand had strayed to the dagger in his sash, so strong had been the temptation to end his own existence and join her in Paradise.

And now Mumtaz, wrapped in the traditional woman's shroud of five pieces of white cotton, was lying in her temporary resting place across the Tapti river within the walls of an old Moghul pleasure ground – the Zainabad Gardens – her head to the north and her face turned towards Mecca. He had followed her bier dressed in the plainest of clothes, wearing not a single jewel and barely conscious of the procession of elephants bearing his children and his courtiers following behind, their solemn pace set by the slow beat of a single drum.

Walking over to the casement Shah Jahan looked across the Tapti, imagining that through the pearly early morning light he could see the glow of the thousand candles he had ordered to be kept burning around Mumtaz's grave. Suddenly his head began to spin and he gripped the edge of a marble table to stop himself falling. With shaking hand he reached for a pitcher of water and emptied its contents down his throat. As the liquid hit the pit of his stomach he thought he was about to be sick. Slumping to the ground, he leant back against the wall and closed his eyes.

'Father . . . Father . . . wake up!'

A gentle voice was intruding into his troubled sleep and a hand was shaking his shoulder. Shah Jahan opened heavy eyes to see Jahanara kneeling by him. 'Why are you here? I said I wanted to be alone . . .' he muttered. The sun was slanting through the casement but he had no idea how long he'd been sleeping.

'I've been so worried about you, we all have . . . We couldn't obey your order not to be disturbed any longer.'

Shah Jahan pulled the cap he had been wearing from his head. As he ran a hand through his hair he heard Jahanara gasp.

'My appearance shocks you, but I've no more use for fine clothes or rich gems . . . I followed your mother's bier in these coarse garments and I'll wear them until they fall from my body.'

'It's your hair, Father . . .'

'What d'you mean?' He tugged a lock forward and examined it. When he had ridden from the battlefield to Mumtaz's side it had been dark as night. Now it was mostly white. The mirror hadn't lied. 'God has truly cursed me. He has punished me for my sins and cast me out. This is one of his signs.'

'Father ... Father, please ... Shock and grief are the cause ...'

'No, it's a message. God is reminding me that despite my power, my wealth, I'm only human – born to suffer just like the peasants who are dying because of the drought.' He gave a mirthless laugh, then stopped as a yet darker thought came to him. What if Mumtaz's death was God's retribution for the deaths of his half-brothers? As he stared down at the carpet, the swirls of crimson red and indigo blue danced before him and he felt himself growing dizzy again. Leaning forward he put his head in his hands and began rocking gently to and fro.

'Father, you are making yourself ill. You must eat something,' Jahanara was saying. 'Let me order your attendants to prepare you some food.'

'The very thought turns my stomach.'

'You must try, for the sake of our family. We need you. And you forget you have a new daughter. Satti al-Nisa is caring for her as tenderly as our own mother would have done, but we need to know your orders for her care ...'

Shah Jahan held up a hand. He had no wish to think about the child whose birth had cost Mumtaz her life. 'Tell Satti al-Nisa I am grateful to her but that such matters must wait.'

'You can't just stay here avoiding the world.'

'I don't intend to. It is exactly a week since your mother died. Tonight I will go again to her grave.'

'Let me come with you, Father ... Dara too. As your eldest children it would be fitting – and we want to.'

His first impulse was to tell her he would make the

journey alone, but his children had the right to mourn Mumtaz as well. 'Very well.'

That evening, three palanquins decked in purple so dark it was almost black bore Shah Jahan, Jahanara and Dara Shukoh out of the same gateway through which Mumtaz's bier had been carried head first from Burhanpur and which hadn't yet been bricked up. The country people, who dreaded ghosts, believed that a corpse must be carried that way and the route of its final journey blocked to confuse the spirit and prevent it from finding its way back to the place where body and soul had parted. Shah Jahan had always thought it a foolish superstition but now he wished that it was true – to have Mumtaz return to him even in spirit would be some balm. Her ghost could never frighten him.

The bearers crossed the river at a ford where the river was little more than a foot deep and continued up the bank towards the Zainabad Gardens, whose semi-ruined arched gateway emerged out of the darkness. 'Set me down here,' Shah Jahan ordered. Stepping from the palanquin, he waited for Jahanara and Dara Shukoh. Then, with them following, he approached the gateway, acknowledging the salute of the Rajput guards with a brief nod. Through the arch the white marble pavilion beneath which he had ordered Mumtaz's grave to be dug glimmered palely as a crescent moon appeared through the scudding clouds. Beneath the canopy over the simple white marble slab bearing Mumtaz's name flickered the mass of small candles.

Shah Jahan's eyes blurred with tears so that everything seemed suddenly magnified and multiplied as he walked towards the grave. Reaching it, he dropped to his knees weeping helplessly, his tears splashing on the marble. Bending lower, he kissed the cold stone. Mumtaz had been his lover, his friend, his guide through life's complexities. To face each new day without her would be a torment. But it was his burden to bear. For the sake of Jahanara and Dara Shukoh, whose hands he could feel resting on his shoulders, and his other children he would devote himself to strengthening the empire and securing the future of their dynasty. Though Mumtaz had passed into another life, he would take the empire to even greater glory in her memory . . . But even as he made that pledge it echoed hollowly round his mind, bringing him little comfort. What did any of it matter without her beside him? There was greater consolation in the promise he had made to her in the last moments of her life. Raising his head he whispered, 'I will build you a tomb like Paradise on earth in Agra. You won't lie long in this famine-struck land.' As he knelt by the grave Shah Jahan lost all sense of time.

'Father . . . are you all right?' Dara Shukoh's tone was hesitant.

This was the first time his son had ever asked him such a question. Until now it had been his role as a father to nurture and protect his children. How often had he spoken those very words to one of his sons after a fall from a horse or a tumble during a wrestling contest? Life was strange. A week ago, hair still dark as ebony, he had been riding to war against his enemies, never realising how close – or in what way – he was to tragedy. Now he was an object of the compassion, pity even, of a son barely out of his boyhood. 'I am an emperor and as such I must and will weather this as I have weathered setbacks in battle and plots against my life. But as a man, no, I'm not all right. This wound will never heal. The pain may lessen but it will never go away and I wouldn't wish it to, because the absence of hurt would mean I had forgotten your mother.'

'Nothing will be the same for any of us,' Dara said. At her brother's words, Jahanara took him in her arms and held him for a moment, just as she had when they were children and he needed comfort, even though she was barely a year older.

His children were so young, so vulnerable, thought Shah Jahan as slowly they made their way from the garden. Though tragedy had overtaken his family he must protect them from its consequences. For the first time since Mumtaz's death, his mind returned to the war he was fighting. Though he had suffered a mortal wound he must conceal it from his enemies, who would already be scheming how to exploit his misfortune. They might even expect him to leave the Deccan and return in mourning to Agra.

Shah Jahan frowned. The Bijapurans' treachery had forced him south. If they hadn't risen up, he would still be in Agra. Mumtaz would have stayed in the comfort and security of the *haram* to give birth instead of enduring an exhausting journey to this desolate part of his empire. She might have lived . . . His enemies would die repenting their foolhardiness.

• ◆ •

Shah Jahan looked up reluctantly from the drawings spread out before him. His master builder had followed his guidance but the result looked wrong. The tomb itself seemed dwarfed by its position in the middle of a large square garden. Yet he'd intended the garden as merely the setting for the flawless jewel that would be Mumtaz's mausoleum. 'I know the effect I want but I can't see how to create it . . . This looks too ordinary. What do you think, Jahanara?'

'I'm not sure . . . it's not easy to tell.'

He looked broodingly at the drawings once more. 'I asked not to be disturbed. Why are you here, Jahanara?'

'Because I must speak to you. It's six weeks since my mother died yet I and my brothers and sisters still hardly see you. Neither do your courtiers or your counsellors. I mean no disrespect but I know that my mother would say the same thing if she were still alive. You must not neglect your duties because of your grief for her.'

'How am I neglecting my duties? My commanders have their orders and are in the field against the rebels. We are driving them back. What more do you expect of me?' He saw Jahanara flinch and softened his tone as he added, 'Please understand. I can find no rest until I have decided the plans for the mausoleum.'

'I know how much that means to you, but you still haven't seen your new daughter. You haven't even given her a name. And now I hear that you intend to send her to Agra to be brought up in the imperial *haram*.'

'You don't understand. I wish the child to be well cared for, but the thought of her is painful to me.'

'She's not "the child". She's your daughter. At least look at her once before you send her away.' Without waiting for his answer Jahanara clapped her hands. At the signal Satti al-Nisa entered the room. Cocooned in a soft woollen blanket in her arms was the baby. 'Majesty.' She bowed her head, then held the bundle out to him.

Shah Jahan hesitated. He was on the point of ordering Satti al-Nisa to withdraw, but something stopped him. Slowly he stepped closer and with a hand not quite steady drew back the blanket. The baby was sleeping, one curled fist pressed against her mouth. How could he feel animosity towards such a tiny, innocent creature . . . Yet he felt no fatherly tenderness. It was as if he had lost the power to feel anything much at all.

'Majesty, the empress often talked about the names you and she might give the child if it were a daughter. There was one name in particular she was fond of,' Satti al-Nisa said.

'What was it? I don't recall . . .'

'Gauharara.'

'Then let it be so.'

Gauharara suddenly woke and began to thresh about in Satti al-Nisa's arms, then to wail.

'Take her back to the *haram*.' Shah Jahan turned away as Satti al-Nisa carried his daughter swiftly from the room.

'Don't send Gauharara from us, Father. Satti al-Nisa wishes to care for her.' For a moment Jahanara rested her hennaed fingertips on the coarse-woven cotton of his tunic. Since Mumtaz's death he had decreed that all the court should wear only the plainest garments.

'Very well.' At the relief on Jahanara's young face he felt regret for causing her anxiety, yet he couldn't help himself. Since Mumtaz's death it was as if a barrier had sprung up between himself and the rest of the world, including his family, whom he knew he loved. Even now he was wishing Jahanara would go away and leave him to his thoughts, but it seemed she had more to say.

'Father, there's something you should know. A few days ago Aurangzeb came to me in great distress. A mullah had told him that God had taken our mother away because you are a bad Muslim who flouts Islamic law by employing Hindus and other non-Muslims at your court. I told Aurangzeb that the mullah was talking nonsense – that you rule as our great-grandfather Akbar did by showing tolerance to all – but he would not be convinced.'

'Perhaps he was right not to be. Maybe the mullah is speaking no more than the truth. These past weeks I've asked myself over and over how I could have offended God so badly to be punished in this way. Perhaps I have been too lax, too indulgent towards those of other faiths, like the arrogant Portuguese Jesuits who travel the length and breadth of my empire proclaiming that they alone have God's ear. They are corrupt, and venal as well. Remember how they expelled us from their settlement on the Hooghly river when we were fugitives, even though your mother was so weak? They acted without the care and compassion they boast is at the heart of their religion because they wanted to gain favour with my father and Mehrunissa. I've often thought of them over the years but now I've acted. Two weeks ago I despatched soldiers to expel the priests from their settlement and to burn their buildings down so that they cannot return. I am also thinking of forbidding the construction of further Hindu temples in my cities.'

'What?' Jahanara looked stunned, and it was a moment

or two before she could gather her words. 'Father, expel the foreign priests if you must – they have done something to deserve it – but don't turn on your loyal subjects just because they are of a different religion. Your own mother, your grandmother, were Rajput princesses. Hindu blood flows in your veins and mine. What's more, your Hindu subjects have done nothing to offend you and they share in our grief . . . Think of the messages of condolence we have received. The courts of Amber and Mewar and Marwar mourned with us, observing the forty days as strictly as we did ourselves. Don't repay them by restricting their religious freedoms . . . It isn't just.'

Shah Jahan stared at his daughter as if seeing her properly for the first time. Her strained expression, the passion in her voice, told him she was speaking from the heart. And there was so much of Mumtaz in her – she had her mother's courage and her gentle persistence. Even her tone was so like Mumtaz's that for a moment, if he closed his eyes, he could imagine that his wife was still with him. The thought brought pain but also consolation of a kind.

'Perhaps you are right. I will think further before I act. But in return I've something to ask. I've decided to send your mother's body back to Agra for temporary burial until the tomb I will build there is ready to receive her. The golden casket I ordered will arrive in two or three days' time and there's no reason to delay any longer. My mind will be easier knowing she has returned to rest in the place she loved. I can't leave the Deccan myself until I have beaten my enemies, so I'd like you and Dara to accompany the funeral cortège. As you reminded me once before, as my eldest son and daughter it is fitting.'

• ◆ •

Shah Jahan charged at the head of his men towards a large squadron of Bijapuran horsemen. He had encountered them as they crossed in front of his own forces on one of his sweeps of the countryside. At the urging of his officers he had reluctantly re-joined his forces for the first time a few days after the departure of Mumtaz's cortège for Agra, but now he found that the excitement and risks of the search and ensuing pursuit were almost the only things that dulled his grief for Mumtaz, forcing him to concentrate his mind on present dangers rather than the past. He had been glad to embark on this, the third such sortie.

'Majesty, you are outdistancing us. Rein in a little or we cannot protect you,' he heard the captain of his bodyguard yell above the thunder of the charging horses' hooves. He paid no attention. If his fate was to die so be it. He would join Mumtaz in the gardens of Paradise. Within moments he clashed with the foremost Bijapuran, a squat man on a white horse whose opening stroke with his curved scimitar whistled through the air above Shah Jahan's plumed helmet as he ducked. Shah Jahan's horse was galloping so fast that it carried him beyond the man before he could get in a stroke of his own. Another Bijapuran horseman thrust at him with his long lance but he turned it aside with his sword before giving a backhand slash with his own weapon which thudded into the rump of the rebel's chestnut horse, causing it to rear and unseat its rider before bolting.

Shah Jahan struck at a third Bijapuran but his blow

glanced off the rebel's breastplate. Moments later, he found himself alone on the far side of the Bijapuran ranks. Several enemy riders were wheeling to attack him. Realising the danger his impetuous and foolhardy charge had brought him into, he immediately headed, heart thumping, towards the nearest man, still battling to turn his horse, and before the rider could react thrust his sword deep into his abdomen below his steel breastplate. As Shah Jahan wrenched his weapon free his adversary collapsed on to his horse's neck, dropping his short lance.

A second Bijapuran had been quicker to turn and at once attacked the Emperor. His sword struck the pommel of Shah Jahan's saddle as the emperor swayed back out of the way, simultaneously striking out with his own bloodstained blade and knocking the Bijapuran's domed helmet from his head. Undaunted, the horseman rode again at Shah Jahan, this time joined by two of his comrades. Shah Jahan pulled back hard on his reins purposely causing his horse to rear up, front legs flailing. One of its hooves caught the foremost Bijapuran, who fell backwards. Immediately Shah Jahan, gripping his reins with his left hand to turn, slashed at the next rider catching him in the muscle of his upper right arm and forcing him also to drop his weapon. Struggling desperately to turn his horse to face the third attacker, the helmetless man, Shah Jahan realised that he was not going to be able to do so before the Bijapuran got in his blow. Instinctively he tried to make himself the smallest target possible. Then the Bijapuran's head split before his eyes into a mess of blood and brains. The captain of his bodyguard had forced his way through the column and cleft the man's unprotected skull in two. Others of his bodyguard were appearing and straight away charging into their enemies' disintegrating ranks. The Bijapurans who could disengage themselves from the fight – by no means all of them – were beginning to kick their horses into a gallop to escape, leaving their fellows to die or be taken prisoner.

Forty-eight hours later – a period during which he had scarcely left the saddle, never mind slept – Shah Jahan was standing with Ashok Singh on a flat outcrop of rock looking down on the small walled town of Krishnapur sited in the ox-bow bend of a dried-up river. From his interrogation of some of the Bijapurans captured during the earlier skirmish Shah Jahan had discovered that the town had become a base for their activities. Sparing neither himself nor his men, two hours earlier he had reached Krishnapur to find its gates firmly closed against him. His men now encircled the town.

'No, Ashok Singh! I will not bargain with them. They must surrender unconditionally. They've ignored the proclamation in which to honour the memory of my wife I offered clemency. Now that they are surrounded why should they expect me to renew my mercy?'

'I will tell their emissary.' Ashok Singh hesitated for a moment as he was about to leave. 'Forgive me, Majesty. If deprived of any hope of mercy might they not fight the harder?'

Perhaps Ashok Singh was right, Shah Jahan reflected. 'Very well. Tell the envoy that any who leave the town within one hour of his return will live. I make no promises as to whether as free people or slaves, but they will live.'

Fifty minutes later Shah Jahan was sitting on his horse

in front of the main gate of Krishnapur just out of arrow and musket shot. The gatehouse was a substantial sandstone building with an intricately carved hissing serpent relief above the double gates themselves. Shah Jahan had ridden down from the outcrop to see if anyone would accept his offer of life and to make his preparations in case they did not. He was determined that as soon as the hour was up he would order his forces to make an all-out assault on Krishnapur. The best route of attack would be across the dried-up riverbed since the town walls were lower and looked weaker at that side, doubtless because in normal times the river formed a first line of defence.

'Majesty . . .' Ashok Singh was again at his side. 'If the invaders choose to fight, I and the captain of your bodyguard have a request. Please don't expose yourself recklessly in the battle as you did the day before yesterday.' The young Rajput prince paused before continuing, 'All the court knows the grief you feel at the empress's death . . . that you say your life has become empty. I too lost my beloved wife, not in childbirth but from the spotted fever – she died before I could be told and rush back from a tour of inspection of some of my father's outlying posts. I too was devastated and held my own life cheap, risking it recklessly in battle and on the hunting field until my father took me aside and lectured me sternly. He made me understand that it was for the gods and not for a man to decide when he dies. It was the more so for me as a prince with responsibilities to my destiny and to him and the dynasty. Even though you are not a Hindu I believe your religion too teaches that a man should submit to God's will. What's more, your responsibilities are much greater than mine. You are not a younger son but head of a dynasty that controls a vast empire many times larger than the state of Amber. What would become of it and your family if you got yourself needlessly killed?'

Shah Jahan was silent for a moment before replying. 'You're right, I know. My sons are not yet of an age or experience when they could easily succeed me. I know too that Mumtaz herself would have said the same to me, and my daughter Jahanara has already done so. But from your own experience you must know it is easier to give such good advice than receive it and put it into practice.'

'But you will heed my words, Majesty?' Ashok Singh persisted gently.

'Yes. Should the Bijapurans sally out of Krishnapur I will stay back in a position where I can command the whole action rather than rush forward to lead the charge.'

Moments later, almost as if in response to his words, the main gates of Krishnapur swung open. Was it to be a sortie or surrender, Shah Jahan asked himself. Capitulation, it seemed, as a column of women emerged through the gates, many gripping the hands of small children, others holding their palms outstretched in supplication. Nearly all were thin to the point of emaciation. The drought had not spared Krishnapur any more than anywhere else. Shah Jahan was just turning to give Ashok Singh the order for his men to go forward to receive their captives when suddenly armed horsemen burst through the gateway. Scattering women and children alike before them, they swerved their mounts round Krishnapur's walls, hell-bent on their own escape. More followed. None slowed to avoid the prone bodies of those whom the first riders had knocked over but simply trampled them beneath their hooves.

'Fire on those riders! Don't let any get away!' Shah Jahan shouted to Ashok Singh. His outrage at the Bijapurans' treatment of the townswomen immediately overwhelming his promise to hold himself back from the action, he kicked his horse forward. Before he could get far, however, he heard a disciplined volley from the band of musketeers he had ordered to be stationed near the walls in anticipation of just such a Bijapuran sortie. Their firing emptied several saddles. It was a reduced enemy squadron which closed up as best it could and kicked on, heads bent low over their horses' necks in the hope of safety, leaving their fallen comrades like the trampled women and children to care for themselves.

Shah Jahan had reined in briefly to see the effect of the musket shots. Now as he pushed on again his bodyguard and Ashok Singh's Rajputs were around him. Together they were gaining fast on the Bijapurans when about a dozen of the hindmost wheeled their horses to turn back and attack their pursuers – clearly prepared to sacrifice themselves to save their comrades. Sacrifice themselves they certainly would, but no one else would escape either, thought Shah Jahan grimly as, drawing his sword, he prepared to meet the rebels, now only yards away.

The first of them – no more than a youth – crashed into the front rank of Shah Jahan's bodyguard. He got in only one stroke of his sword, cutting into the muscular arm of a bearded Rajput, before being swallowed up by the charge of Shah Jahan's men and knocked from his horse to die crushed beneath their onrushing hooves. His fellows fared little better. Only one succeeded in unhorsing a member of the bodyguard before he was himself spitted by a Rajput lance and carried out of his saddle. Soon Shah Jahan's riders were beyond the melee and gathering speed once more, leaving crumpled bodies and riderless horses in their wake. Within five minutes they were up again with the remainder of the Bijapuran horsemen who were galloping along the rutted riverbed. Suddenly, as if as one and clearly in response to a shouted order, the whole Bijapuran column, still over fifty strong, reined in and threw down their weapons.

'Take care. Don't approach them too closely in case it's another trick,' shouted Shah Jahan.

A tall Bijapuran horseman wearing a cloak of gold cloth rode through their ranks, dismounted and prostrated himself. 'We surrender, Majesty. We accept your offer to let us live.'

'What?' shouted Shah Jahan. 'You expect my offer to stand after you have ridden down women and children and caused the death of some of my own men? You had the chance to live but you forfeited it by your brutal behaviour. You and your officers will die. Your men will be sold into slavery.'

'Majesty, I implore you . . .'

'There is no point in pleading. Accept your fate with dignity. Death comes to us all sooner or late. Yours will not be pointless but will serve as a deterrent to anyone else contemplating invasion or rebellion.'

An hour later Shah Jahan watched as his men laid the first stones of the tower he had ordered to be built to display the severed heads of those he had had executed, already piled nearby in a bloody heap around which hordes of blue-bodied flies were buzzing. His warrior ancestors had built such towers in their homelands on the Asian steppes and Akbar too had followed the practice early in his reign when he had faced stubborn enemies. Looking skyward, he saw vultures already circling, eager to feast on eyes and the soft flesh of cheeks and lips as soon as they felt it safe to do so. This bloodstained, reeking monument would signal to the Bijapurans as nothing else could the futility of their continued resistance to his authority and the unflinching harshness of their punishment should they persist.

As he rode back through the gateway into Burhanpur a few days later, Shah Jahan saw Aslan Beg waiting for him in the sunlit courtyard, a letter in his hand. 'Majesty, a rider brought this yesterday. It is from the Lady Jahanara. I thought you would wish to see it immediately.'

Shah Jahan broke the seal at once.

Father, I wanted you to know as soon as possible that we have reached Agra safely after ten weeks of travel and that my mother's body has been laid in a temporary grave on the banks of the Jumna exactly as you wished. As we approached the city, wailing crowds lined the highway, covering their heads with dust and weeping. So has it been throughout the journey, as if the indigo of grief had descended on our land. I will write later at greater length.

As he read, Shah Jahan felt a familiar dark desolation steal over him, dissipating his pleasure at his military success. When he and Mumtaz had left Agra he had never imagined that their life together was almost over. With her by his side he had looked to the future and the fulfilment of his ambitions to expand his empire with confidence, but now, whatever triumphs he achieved as an emperor, what could they mean to him as a man when so much joy and warmth had been taken from him? What consolation could he find in building a cold tomb? He had promised Mumtaz he would not give way to despair, but was that a promise he could keep?

Chapter 6

'Welcome to Burhanpur, Ustad Ahmad.'

'I am honoured you sent for me, Majesty. I came as quickly as I could.'

Shah Jahan scrutinised the tall, slenderly built man bowing low before him, hoping that at last he had found an architect who could help give expression to the vision of Mumtaz's tomb that had begun crystallizing in his mind but was still incomplete. 'My father-in-law Asaf Khan wrote to me that you have designed buildings of great beauty for Shah Abbas. The task I have for you is greater than any the Persian shah can have set – to design a mausoleum for my wife of such unique beauty that later generations will still hail it as a wonder of our age. The thought doesn't intimidate you?'

'No. It's a challenge no true artist could resist.'

Clearly Ustad Ahmad was not a modest man, but that was a good thing, Shah Jahan thought. Others he'd consulted – like his master builder – had been over-eager to please, praising everything he himself had suggested and contributing few ideas themselves. He waved the architect to sit at the long low table. 'What thoughts do you have for me?'

'I think you are familiar with the way the Persians design their gardens?'

'I've seen paintings and drawings. I know they call them *pairidaeza*.'

'Exactly, Majesty, "gardens of Paradise", with two bisecting watercourses running north to south and east to west to represent the sacred rivers of Paradise. Such should be the setting for the tomb of her late Majesty.'

'But I have already written to you saying that I wished the tomb to be built in the centre of a garden. Do you have nothing new to suggest?' Shah Jahan couldn't keep irritation from his voice but Ustad Ahmad didn't seem abashed.

'I do, Majesty. I believe the tomb should not sit in the centre of the garden – instead it should overlook it, dominating the eye. The land you have purchased on the banks of the Jumna is perfect for what I have in mind.'

Shah Jahan looked at Ustad Ahmad, trying to picture what he meant. Ashok Singh had suggested he acquire the site which was immediately downstream of an almost right-angled bend in the Jumna river, from his father, the Raja of Amber, because it was so close to the fort – barely a mile and a half away – that the tomb would not only be visible from the battlements but could be visited by boat. The architect continued. 'I propose building the tomb on a raised platform on the riverbank with the gardens laid out below.'

'But can the bank take the weight? My builders say the soil is sandy and light and the force of the river may cause erosion.'

'The bend in the Jumna reduces the thrust of the current at that point. Besides, there are ways of reinforcing the bank to support the buildings.'

'Buildings? You're suggesting more than one?'

'Yes. Let me show you, Majesty.' Ustad Ahmad took a large folded paper from his battered green leather satchel, opened it and spread it on the table. 'I have drawn everything on a grid so you can see clearly the layout I'm proposing. The mausoleum would stand on two platforms – a large one surmounted by a smaller plinth for the tomb itself.'

'What are these structures you've marked on either side of the tomb?'

'To the west a three-domed mosque and to the east a similar structure to be a resthouse for pilgrims but also the *jabab* – the echo – of the mosque, enhancing the symmetry which is so important to my design. And look, Majesty, to complete the effect, at the far end of the north–south waterway, directly opposite the tomb, I propose a southern gatehouse. As they enter, visitors will see the mausoleum rise before them as if floating against the limitless backdrop of the sky.'

Shah Jahan scanned Ustad Ahmad's drawing – he had indeed created an image of perfect balance. Yet everything would depend on the design of the tomb itself, which was marked only by a circle. 'What about the mausoleum?'

The architect produced a silk-wrapped bundle from his bag. 'Before I show you this let me explain my thoughts. I recently visited the Emperor Humayun's tomb in Delhi. What if, I wondered, the late empress's mausoleum was, like Humayun's, built to an octagonal plan but fuller of light, better befitting the memory of a woman? I experimented over and again with the proportions and concluded that the base should be a cube with its vertical corners chamfered to produce the octagon. The sarcophagus itself would lie in the middle of a central octagonal chamber surrounded by eight interconnecting chambers on each of two levels. The exterior façades would consist of two storeys of arched recesses. But enough words, Majesty. Allow me to show you what I mean.'

Ustad Ahmad opened his parcel and took out some wooden blocks which he began carefully arranging into an octagonal structure. 'Look, Majesty – on each of the four main sides would be *iwans*, entrance arches, whose top border would rise above the rest of the façade. The height from the ground to the top of the dome would be two hundred and forty feet.'

'And the dome itself?'

'I suggest a double one. Again, allow me to demonstrate.' From his pocket this time, Ustad Ahmad took out two pieces of polished alabaster. 'In the Emperor Humayun's tomb inner and outer domes rest on a low drum. What I propose here is an inner dome rising eighty feet from the ground and a swelling outer dome shaped somewhat like a guava, topped by a golden finial.' As he was talking Ustad Ahmad balanced the inner dome on the model's octagonal walls then carefully slid the elongated outer dome over it. 'Finally I suggest placing four *chattris*, domed kiosks, used in so many of the palaces of your Hindu allies, around the main dome, like pearls surrounding the central gem in a ring.'

Shah Jahan stared at the model in front of him. It was perfect. How had this man understood his wishes so well when he had been unable to articulate them properly even to himself? Ustad Ahmad was looking hard at him, perhaps uncertain how to interpret his silence.

'I'm appointing you my architect to oversee the creation of the empress's mausoleum. Return to Agra immediately. Whatever you require – money, materials, labour – you shall have it.'

'Majesty, I have one further question. What material should we build in? Sandstone?'

'For the subsidiary buildings perhaps, but the mausoleum itself is to be of the purest white marble – I have already told the Raja of Amber that I will purchase the entire output of his quarries at Makrana and asked him to arrange the safe transport of the marble the two hundred miles to Agra.'

For the first time Ustad Ahmad looked startled. 'No one has ever built anything on this scale in marble . . . the cost will be . . .'

'Do not concern yourself with the cost. You promised me a heaven on earth and that should be your sole concern.'

That night Shah Jahan fell into a deeper sleep than for many months, anxiety over how best to fulfil Mumtaz's dying wish quietened by Ustad Ahmad's sublime design.

In his dreams he stood beneath the great southern gateway, gazing at the shimmering mausoleum. As the hours passed he remained there transfixed, watching the white marble flush pink in the dawn light, glitter diamond bright beneath the hot midday sun and soften to violet as dusk descended and shadows shrouded the pearl-like dome. Then, through the velvet darkness, a lantern glowed and a woman appeared in the moonlit doorway. He couldn't see her face but he knew it was Mumtaz . . .

Slowly he walked through the gardens, breathing the heavy scent of white-petalled *champa* flowers and following the marble channel through which water rippled silver towards the tomb. As he passed, each of a row of marble fountains burst into life, sending jewel-bright droplets into the air. All the time his eyes were fixed on Mumtaz waiting in the entrance. He tried desperately to walk more quickly but his legs wouldn't obey him, even when she raised her arms in silent entreaty. Her face was still in shadow but jewels glittered around her neck, waist and wrists. Just a few more steps and he would be with her, but suddenly the figure shimmered and dissolved before him.

In anguish he climbed the stairs to the pale tomb and touched the milk-smooth marble, expecting it to feel cold. Instead the translucent stone was silken and warm as human flesh – Mumtaz's flesh. An erotic longing possessed him and he pressed his lips to the stone. The mausoleum was Mumtaz herself. He would adorn it with the gems she loved in life. Emeralds and rubies, amethysts and corals, would shine against the white marble as they had glowed on her body. He stretched out his arms to embrace the tomb but suddenly there was nothing but the gloom of his bedchamber.

Shah Jahan sat up and looked around him, dazed. Rising, he walked to the casement and peered into the darkness at the dim outline of the Tapti winding on its sluggish way, reminding him how far he was from Agra and Mumtaz, lying in her temporary grave. How weary he was of these empty barren lands that had robbed him of so much. Before Mumtaz's death they had often talked about the visit they would make to the Vale of Kashmir when the fighting was over. They would never go there now – never wander its purple crocus fields or feel the cool wind blowing off its snow-dusted mountains or glide in a barge across its lily-strewn lakes. But as he gazed into the night he made Mumtaz – and himself – a vow. He would end this war quickly and return to Agra to oversee the construction of her tomb himself.

• ◆ •

From the protection of the awning of his scarlet command tent pitched on a small hill Shah Jahan surveyed the surrounding low-lying countryside. Heavy raindrops were splashing from a leaden monsoon sky into the already deep puddles around the tent. The drought had broken three weeks earlier and since then the much delayed rains had been almost incessant. Everywhere the ground had been baked so hard that at first it had been unable to absorb so much water so fast. In places flash floods had swept away humans and animals who only days earlier had been longing for water. Now green leaves had begun to sprout on the trees and shrubs. Small orange-pink jungle flowers were appearing and many more birds were singing, all part of the natural renewal of life and at odds with Shah Jahan's sombre mood and continuing sense of final and irreplaceable loss.

Eager to speed his departure from Burhanpur, despite the atrocious weather he had led a division of his army out into the water-logged and scarcely populated plains on receiving reliable reports that the last sizeable detachment of Bijapuran invaders had taken refuge in a forested area barely two days' ride away. Now after much thought during another of the many sleepless nights he had suffered since Mumtaz died he had devised a plan of attack.

'Send my officers to me,' he shouted to an attendant. Soon they came splashing through the puddles to sit around him on low stools placed under the awning by his servants. Despite the rain Ashok Singh was colourfully and immaculately dressed as ever in a gold-trimmed maroon tunic and surcoat, his extravagant dark moustache brushed and perfumed, but several of the other commanders were mud-spattered. Standing slightly to one side was Aurangzeb. At his persistent urging Shah Jahan had allowed him to join the expedition instead of Shah Shuja, whom he had intended to bring had the boy not dislocated his shoulder playing polo while riding a half-broken pony against his groom's advice.

When all had arrived, Shah Jahan began. 'I've decided how we will put an end to these invaders once and for all. They descended on our lands like ravening animals and we will deal with them as such. Just as my ancestors on the steppes hunted game by driving them into a confined

111

space, so we will encircle and trap our enemies leaving them no chance to flee. According to our scouts they've withdrawn into an area of thick jungle about five miles away to the south. Ashok Singh, I want you to select five thousand of our best horsemen and order each to take a musketman up behind him. They are to surround the jungle – our scouts tell me it is around six miles in circumference. Then, keeping no more than four yards apart from one another, they are to advance.'

'You intend to take the Bijapurans unawares?'

'At first yes, but as our noose tightens I want our enemies to know we're coming. At a signal from me, as our men move through the trees and the length of our perimeter shortens, I want them to start shouting, even to blow trumpets and strike gongs. With noise on every side and realising they're surrounded, the enemy won't know which way to run and we will herd them together as we do wild animals in the hunt before we fall on them and slaughter them. Just in case any succeed in breaking through our cordon I want further horsemen backed up by musketmen and archers stationed round the jungle edge. Are my orders clear?'

'Do we take prisoners, Majesty?' Ashok Singh asked.

'No, no prisoners.' Seeing Ashok Singh's look of surprise, Shah Jahan said, 'You Rajputs expect no mercy in battle and fight to the death. But the Rajputs are honourable warriors. If they were ever my foes instead of my allies – as I hope will never be – I would spare any who asked for mercy. But these Bijapurans have brought nothing but havoc and bloodshed to my lands and cost my wife her life. They have spurned every opportunity to surrender and thus have forfeited any right to mercy – even if they beg for it.'

Ashok Singh said nothing, and it was Aurangzeb who spoke next. 'Father, can I accompany you to the attack?'

Shah Jahan hesitated. He himself had fought his first battle when he'd been only a little older. 'Very well. But you're to take no part in the actual fighting.'

'Father . . .'

'No! I won't change my mind. You'll remain at a safe distance or not come at all.'

'It wasn't that. I just wanted you to know I think you're right not to give the Bijapurans quarter. They don't deserve it and should be made to pay the ultimate price for their treachery.'

'Good.' Shah Jahan nodded. Despite his youth Aurangzeb was not backward in advancing his forthright and usually stern opinions. He had a dogmatic sense of what he believed just or unjust and in disputes with his brothers was usually the most determined in maintaining he was in the right, using his fists if he had to.

An hour later, the column had already covered three miles. If all went well – and even allowing for the rain falling in a constant veil around them there was no reason why it shouldn't – they should reach the thick jungle and be ready to attack by midday. Glancing over his shoulder, Shah Jahan saw Aurangzeb riding not far behind him. He was wearing a chain mail tunic and silver breastplate and had an expression of deep concentration. Turning his attention to guiding his own horse across the increasingly soggy ground, Shah Jahan soon found mud flying up all around him, spattering his horse's steel head armour and speckling his face beneath his jewelled helmet. Soon though the rain began to ease and Shah Jahan could make out the thick jungle ahead of him to the south. A quarter of an hour later a small group of riders appeared from that direction led by Rai Singh.

'All is well, Majesty,' called the scout, long hair hanging in wet tendrils. 'The Bijapurans are still in the jungle and as far as we can tell have no idea of our presence. Now that the rain is stopping they've begun lighting their cooking fires – look.'

Sure enough thin trails of smoke were spiralling from several points within the jungle. The Bijapurans' bivouacs seemed to be scattered rather than concentrated in one large encampment. 'If they want to eat they'd better be quick – it'll be the last food they'll taste. Continue to keep watch. If you see anything suspicious send word at once. Otherwise we will advance into the jungle as soon as we have surrounded it.'

Quickly Shah Jahan issued his final orders to his commanders. 'Deploy your men around the forest. I will join those entering from its northern edge and will send my orders along the line from there. Aurangzeb – you stay here. Vikram Das – I am making you responsible for my son's safety.' The officer nodded, then glanced a little nervously at Aurangzeb as if doubting his ability to control the young prince. Shah Jahan saw the look. 'Aurangzeb – do I have your word of honour that you will remain here and not attempt to join the fight?' His son hesitated a moment, then nodded.

Shah Jahan kicked his horse onward, his bodyguard around him, as he joined the horsemen fanning out to surround the forest. The musketmen mounted behind the riders had their long-barrelled weapons and ram rods strapped to their backs while their powder horns were slung from their shoulders. So much moisture dripped from the trees as Shah Jahan and his men pushed through the branches that it seemed still to be raining. Water was trickling down their necks and running beneath their breastplates and the forest floor was sodden. The horses were soon sinking up to their hocks in places as they struggled to pick their way through and around the deep puddles and soft oozing mud. All the time the vegetation was growing denser.

Shah Jahan listened hard, but above the squelching of the horses' hooves and their occasional blowing and snorting could hear nothing. The Bijapurans must still be too far off to be aware of his advancing forces, but not for much longer. Shah Jahan raised his sword. At the sign, Ashok Singh flung back his head and yelled the ancient war cry of the Rajputs, 'Onward, children of fire, sun and moon, to glory or to death.' All around men began shouting, clashing weapons, sounding trumpets and banging drums. As the cacophony rolled around the jungle, samba deer barked their alarm call and doves and pigeons whirred in panic from the shelter of the trees. Soon it would be time for the musketmen to drop to the ground and set up their weapons ready to shoot down any Bijapurans who tried to break out of the circle into which the horsemen were driving them. Heart pounding, Shah Jahan scanned the dripping foliage, right hand fingering his sword hilt.

Within moments shouts of alarm rose ahead. Suddenly

over an area of lower bushes slightly to his left, Shah Jahan made out a clearing with a number of tents and some horses tethered nearby. 'Musketeers, dismount and take up your positions. Pass the order along,' he yelled. 'Horsemen, keep the line as you advance – let no one through.' To his right and left, Ashok Singh's riders, their lances at the ready, pushed their mounts on through the thinning undergrowth, picking up speed despite the cloying mud.

As he burst with them into the clearing Shah Jahan felt something graze his cheek. A black-flighted arrow embedded itself in the mud close by him. Glancing around he spotted the archer – a long-haired youth – standing in the doorway of a tent not thirty yards away and fumbling with nervous fingers to fit a second arrow to his bow. In a single movement, Shah Jahan pulled one of his two steel-bladed daggers from its scabbard and sent it spinning through the air with all the force he could muster. The dagger tip hit the youth in the throat and he dropped to his knees, blood spurting through his fingers as he clawed at his neck.

Around Shah Jahan, his horsemen were making swift work of the Bijapurans, of whom there appeared to be no more than thirty. As he watched, Ashok Singh, bending low from his saddle, scythed another bowman's head from his shoulders with a single sweep of his weapon, sending the head rolling away to rest, mud-covered, among the roots of a tree. The torso remained upright for a few moments before toppling sideways with a splash into a puddle. Other Bijapurans were attempting to flee deeper into the jungle while the smell of powder and the crackle of muskets behind him told Shah Jahan that a few had

116

been foolish enough to attempt to break through the cordon of his musketmen. 'Set fire to their tents and turn their horses free,' he shouted, but at almost the same moment he heard a cry of 'Bijapurans, over here, to me!'

Wrenching his horse round, Shah Jahan saw a group of thirty or forty well-armed riders led by a tall man in a gilded helmet crash through the scrub on the far side of the clearing. They'd obviously had more time to prepare than their comrades here in the encampment, where red blood now stained the muddy ground. 'Regroup,' shouted Shah Jahan to his men. 'Re-form your line.' There might be more Bijapurans concealed in the trees beyond and he didn't want his soldiers rushing into a trap.

From Shah Jahan's right and left, out of his range of vision, came the sounds of battle as his men clashed with other pockets of Bijapurans. He could not tell precisely what was happening but he trusted his men to maintain discipline and remember their orders. The important thing was to keep the encircling cordon tight and intact and continue the advance, driving his enemies into a tightly packed, disordered mass where they would be easier to destroy.

The Bijapuran riders, seeing they were outnumbered, knew better than to stand and fight in the clearing. Instead, pulling two or three survivors from the conflict up behind them, they were already turning their horses and disappearing deeper into the jungle.

Urging his own mount after them, Shah Jahan realised that the vegetation ahead was growing less dense – nearly all scrubby bushes rather than trees – and that the ground, now lit here and there by shafts of sunlight, was growing even more sodden. At first the tracks of the retreating Bijapurans were easy enough to follow. With luck they would lead to the main encampment. As the sun began to shine more strongly, reflecting mirror-like from the puddles, the air grew humid and sweat ran freely down between Shah Jahan's shoulder blades. With mosquitoes whining in his ears, he glanced around, on the lookout for any Bijapurans lying in ambush amid the brush and fallen branches. He could see none.

Suddenly Shah Jahan's mount slithered and plunged forward, nearly throwing him. He struggled to keep the animal upright and succeeded, but as the horse tried to walk on it stumbled again. Raising an arm to halt the advance on either side of him, he quickly dismounted and ran his hand over the horse's front fetlocks. As he touched the left one the beast whinnied in pain. 'My horse has lamed itself,' he called to Ashok Singh. As he waited for a spare mount to be brought, a lone rider appeared on a low hillock about fifty yards away. His gilded conical helmet gleamed in the sunshine. It was the officer who had come to the aid of the Bijapurans in their camp. In his hand was a banner of golden yellow silk – the colour of Bijapur – obviously intended as a flag of truce. The officer shouted with all the power of his lungs, 'I bring a message from our commander. Majesty, we know that your forces have encircled us. To spare further bloodshed on both sides we wish to surrender.'

'You have a short memory, Bijapuran,' replied Shah Jahan. 'Once before you offered to surrender, then broke your word and innocents died. Today there'll be no bargaining. Traitors have no right to the protection of a flag of truce, so be gone before I seize you.' As the man rode quickly away, Shah Jahan glanced up into the sky. From the position of the sun it was still only early afternoon. By sunset, God willing, he would be victorious.

A ragged volley of enemy musket fire forty minutes later was the first sign that he had located the main body of Bijapurans. One ball hit a young Rajput a few yards to his left in the thigh and, blood pouring from his wound, the youth toppled sideways from his horse. Another rider cried out, then slumped forward in his saddle, dropping his lance. The mount of a third, hit twice in the throat, slowly collapsed, allowing its rider time to jump clear. For a moment the animal's body twitched convulsively, its blood pumping into a puddle, before becoming still.

'Keep low,' Shah Jahan yelled, kicking his horse forward. Through the spindly bushes he could see a large encampment on to which most of the Bijapurans seemed to have fallen back. They had overturned their few baggage carts to use as barricades, but surrounded as they were, they didn't seem to know how best to position them or on which side to take refuge. From all around came the cries of the advancing Moghul troops. The cordon had held and his men had advanced together just as he had planned, Shah Jahan thought as, determined to finish the campaign, fresh energy surged through him.

Yanking on his left rein, he swerved round a tent to slash at a Bijapuran musketeer struggling to reload. His blade caught the man's right arm and dropping both his musket and his ram rod he screamed and turned to run. Shah Jahan struck again, cleaving the musketman's back open to the bone. Looking round, he spotted a huge man

119

in a yellow turban standing with his back to an overturned cart, a spear in his right hand. At that moment a Moghul cavalryman swept past and the man thrust his weapon hard into the horse's stomach. It fell, trapping the Moghul rider beneath it by his thigh. As he struggled to free himself, the yellow-turbaned Bijapuran leapt on him and holding his already dripping spear in both hands raised it above his head. So intent was he on despatching his victim that he didn't notice Shah Jahan until it was too late. Leaning low from his saddle, Shah Jahan cut with his sword into the nape of the man's neck, half severing the head so that it flopped forward in a froth of blood as he fell.

But suddenly the world was spinning around Shah Jahan as he found himself flying through the air to land with a thud on the squelchy ground. Dazed and winded, he looked about to see his horse on its knees in the mud. It had clearly stumbled over the shaft of the overturned cart. His sword was lying a few feet away. Dragging himself to his knees he reached for his weapon but at that moment a boot caught him in the small of his back and sent him sprawling forward into a deep puddle. His mouth and nose filled with muddy water and he spluttered for breath. He tried to get up but felt a hand pull off his helmet, grab hold of his hair and force him face down into the water again. He was starting to choke and his lungs felt as if they were on fire. Gathering his remaining strength he tried to dislodge his attacker but the man was too strong, while every attempt to breathe just brought another mouth and noseful of muddy viscous liquid. With a last desperate effort he felt in his sash for his second dagger and managed to grip its hilt. Pulling it from its scabbard he lunged blindly upwards. The weapon cut through empty air. Blood pounding in his ears as if the drums were about to rupture, he tried again. This time the blade penetrated muscle. A startled, high-pitched scream followed and the hold on his hair relaxed.

Pushing his opponent from him and rolling sideways, he gulped in air. His enemy – tall and heavily built – was writhing doubled up on the ground, clutching at a wound in his left side. Taking a few more deep breaths Shah Jahan got up and staggered across to him, pulled him over onto his stomach and thrust his head into the same puddle where just a moment ago he had been struggling for his own life. Straddling the man, he pushed his head down as hard as he could into the liquid mud. The Bijapuran threshed and bucked, trying to dislodge him, but he held on. For some moments the man's feet kicked furiously but then his body grew limp. Standing, Shah Jahan retrieved his sword. Then he stood for a moment, back against the overturned cart, trying to gauge the progress of the battle.

'Majesty, are you all right? I lost sight of you in the fighting.' It was Ashok Singh, leaning from his saddle.

'That new horse of mine tripped and fell.'

'Give me your hand, Majesty. Pull yourself up behind me. Even if the fighting's nearly over it's still safer on horseback than on the ground.' Ashok Singh was right, Shah Jahan thought, though most of the bodies sprawled on the earth were Bijapuran and resistance seemed to be over. As he watched, four yellow-clad soldiers emerged from a tent and threw down their weapons while a few yards away a Moghul cavalryman pinioned a Bijapuran whose sword was still drawn to the side of a baggage cart with the tip of his lance.

'Majesty. We have taken a number of prisoners. Are your orders still the same?'

'Yes. Execute them. But do it quickly and cleanly.'

Their death agony would be short, Shah Jahan thought, gazing at the carnage around him, unlike the death of Mumtaz and the long agony of his own grief. He felt no joy in the death of his foes, just an overwhelming weariness and gratitude that the fighting was over and he was victorious. At last he could return to Agra to raise his monument to love – his love of Mumtaz.

Chapter 7

As he topped the crest of the low ridge, Shah Jahan signalled the column to halt and, shading his eyes, looked north towards Agra. The familiar sandstone walls of the fort glowed red in the noonday heat. In the centre of the plain extending from the bottom of the ridge to the outskirts of the city he could make out a long line of troops – some on horseback, others on elephants – coming to escort the Moghul emperor and his victorious army on the final mile of their journey home.

He would re-enter his fortress with fitting ceremony – drums would beat in the gatehouse and green banners flutter on the battlements – but he had ordered that there should be no throwing of flowers or showering of silver and gold coin, no processions of dancers and musicians, as there would have been if Mumtaz had still been at his side. Ever since Dara and Jahanara had accompanied her coffin back to Agra he had longed for the moment when he could follow. Now, the thought of riding alone up the fort's familiar winding ramp to the imperial apartments, refurbished during his absence for an empress who would never see them, was inexpressibly painful.

Yet he must, it was his duty. His astrologers had named today as the most auspicious for his return for many weeks to come. Such things mattered to the people if not to him. Though he had lost his empress he must make it appear that an aura of good fortune still surrounded him and his dynasty. To reinforce the message he would ride slowly through the streets of the city to the fort accompanied by his sons. Dara Shukoh would arrive with the escort while Shah Shuja, Aurangzeb and Murad, dressed in the white of mourning as he still was and riding matched white horses with green trappings, were waiting just a few yards behind him, ready to take their place in the procession.

As soon as the ceremonials were over he would go by barge along the Jumna to inspect the progress on Mumtaz's tomb. Ustad Ahmad's reports had been buoyant. Narrowing his eyes, Shah Jahan looked beyond the fort and across the bend of the river, trying to identify the site, but it was masked by the dull apricot shimmer on the horizon.

'Father, look, there's Dara . . .' Shah Shuja broke into his thoughts.

Peering down towards the bottom of the ridge, Shah Jahan saw a figure urging his horse up the path. The sight cheered him. God had taken Mumtaz but with four fine sons his dynasty would live on. He had much he should be grateful for.

• ◆ •

The next morning Shah Jahan glanced up into the pale, almost colourless sky. According to the scientific instrument an Italian trader had brought to his court, today was the hottest of the year so far. The curious-looking device consisted of a glass bulb filled with water attached to a long tube, also of glass, on which a series of lines had been etched. According to the Italian, a man named Galileo had invented it and it was in common use in Europe. The trader had shown Aslan Beg how to use it. The complicated process fascinated Dara Shukoh, though he himself doubted the instrument's utility. Wasn't nearly every day on the plains of Hindustan hot?

Approaching the place where the brick core of the sandstone platform was taking shape and Ustad Ahmad was waiting for him, Shah Jahan coughed as the coarse dust hanging in the air caught at his throat. 'Majesty, if you accompany me to that mound over there you will see better and the air will be clearer.' Shah Jahan followed Ustad Ahmad across the hard-baked ground to a small hillock. His architect was right – the view was better from here. He could clearly distinguish the perimeter of the vast platform – 970 feet long and 364 feet wide according to Ustad Ahmad – on which the mausoleum would stand.

'It still seems to me incredible that ground so close to the river can support the weight.'

Ustad Ahmad smiled. 'Majesty, I've checked my calculations again and again and I am entirely certain, provided we strengthen the bank in the right way, that it will. I've already ordered the workers to dig shafts close to the riverbank, varying their depths to compensate for the slope, and then line them with bricks and a cement made of lime and sand and fill them with rubble and more cement. I've also ordered them to position piers on top of the shafts to support the platform.'

'But aren't labourers digging down on the riverbank too?'

'Yes, Majesty. They're excavating large holes in which they're burying cement-filled ebony boxes to provide added reinforcement against the rise and fall of the Jumna.'

Shah Jahan nodded. Ustad Ahmad had thought of everything.

'We now have twenty thousand workers. Those are their living quarters.' The architect pointed to the south of the building site. 'As well as their huts there are four caravanserais for the merchants whose camel and mule trains arrive daily and for the boatmen bringing materials by barge along the Jumna. They have named their city Mumtazabad in honour of the late empress. I hope that doesn't offend you, Majesty.'

'No, it's fitting. But tell me, have you everything you need? Is enough sandstone arriving?'

'Yes, we already have a good supply. While you were still in the south, I obtained Prince Dara's permission to construct a road of packed earth ten miles long so that the teams of oxen can haul their carts laden with stone from the local quarries here more easily. Would you like to see the masons at work, Majesty? A group are over there beneath that cotton awning.'

A middle-aged man in a white dhoti with a red Hindu tilak mark on his forehead was bending over a large, square block of sandstone, watched by two youths who by their looks were clearly his sons. As Shah Jahan drew closer he saw that the mason was hammering a straight row of small nail-like wedges into the block. Suddenly aware of the emperor and his architect, the man jerked upright.

'We didn't mean to disturb you. Please continue,' said Shah Jahan.

With a nervous look at his visitors the mason resumed his work, sweat beading on his muscular arms as he drove the line of wedges deeper into the stone. After several minutes he passed the hammer to one of his sons, who continued hitting the wedges until suddenly the sandstone split cleanly. Using a large length of wood, the younger man levered one of the pieces aside. The mason ran his fingers over the newly cut surface with a grunt of satisfaction, then took a fine chisel and began almost tenderly to smooth the edges.

'The masons work the stone with their chisels and polish it with grit until the surface becomes as smooth as alabaster,' explained Ustad Ahmad. 'When each block is ready they will lift it into place and secure it with cement, iron dowels and clamps. You'll not detect a crack between them.'

But Shah Jahan's attention was on the mason, who was incising a triangle into the stone. 'What are you doing?'

'Making my mark. This is the greatest project of my life and I want to leave some sign that it was my work.'

'Other masons have been doing the same, Majesty. I saw no reason to forbid it.'

'And I don't either. I'm pleased the craftsmen have such pride in their work. Here, take this.' Shah Jahan handed some coins to the mason. 'Thank you for your dedication and your skill.' Then he turned away. 'Ustad Ahmad, you've created a design of great beauty, but something is still lacking.'

'Majesty?' Ustad Ahmad looked more surprised than disturbed.

Ever since his dream of a bejewelled Mumtaz standing in the doorway of her tomb, Shah Jahan had been thinking how best to put his vision into effect. 'I want more ornament for the tomb. I want gems inlaid into the marble. Few people know more about jewels than myself. I will select the best from my treasure houses. If there isn't enough of any stone – green jade, perhaps, or dark blue lapis lazuli – I'll import it from beyond my borders. When I have chosen the materials I will have some of my Hindu subjects who are, I know, skilled in the art they call *panchi kura* – the inlaying of stone – do the work. I may also employ European craftsmen – I remember two Italians who visited my father's court when I was a boy. They brought pictures of the city of their birth – Florence, they called it – which looked like paintings but in fact were composed of tiny pieces of semi-precious stones.'

'What patterns do you want inlaid into the marble, Majesty? Geometric designs, perhaps?'

'No. Flowers, green leaves and curling tendrils that look as real as if they were truly growing over the mausoleum, so that my wife's tomb becomes a living thing. I want some further decoration too. I wish other craftsmen to breathe life into the cold marble walls with relief carvings of tall irises and slender-stemmed tulips bending in the breeze as they do in Kashmir. I know it can be done.'

• ◆ •

But O thou soul at peace,
Return thou unto thy Lord, well pleased, and well pleasing
unto Him,
Enter thou among My servants,
And enter thou My Paradise.

'What do you think, Father? Have Dara and I chosen well from the Koran? It wasn't easy.' Jahanara spoke softly.

Shah Jahan nodded. Soon after returning to Agra he'd asked his two eldest children to suggest some wording. The verse was exactly right to inlay around the frame of the gateway, reminding visitors that they were entering both a spiritual place and an earthly heaven. 'I'll order Amanat Khan to lay out the words for the stonecutters to chisel out.'

'He is a true artist. His calligraphy is so fluid.'

'That's why I summoned him from Shiraz.' Shah Jahan looked down at the table on which stood a wooden model of the entire complex. The four white minarets – one at each corner of the marble plinth – were an inspired touch. In his excitement to convince him they would enhance the design, Ustad Ahmad had called them 'ladders to heaven'. Just to look at the model gave Shah Jahan pleasure, but then his smile faded. 'It will be many years, of course, before the tomb is ready to receive your mother's body. Meanwhile I can do little except inspect progress and authorise the payment of the bills my treasurer keeps presenting.'

'Would you like me to see to the bills? As First Lady of the Empire I should have some responsibilities.'

'I gave you that title because it was your mother's, not to make a drudge of you.'

'It wouldn't be any more onerous than dealing with the correspondence and petitions your steward sent me on your behalf while you were still in the Deccan. Anyway, it would provide me with an occupation. You've been giving Dara more tasks – why shouldn't I do more too?'

It was true. He had begun entrusting Dara with increasing responsibility, like a review of the army's equipment. Jahanara's role must of necessity be more prosaic – things a woman could do from the *haram*, as Mumtaz had done before her – but she was intelligent enough to know that. 'Very well. I will have the bills sent to you and I'll find you other duties if you want. I'll also give you your mother's ivory seal to authorise imperial *firmans* on my behalf.'

Shah Jahan saw Jahanara's delight. If he was honest, he'd be as glad of her help as he was of Dara's. With their open natures and quick minds the two of them were so similar. Small wonder they were close. But what would his eldest daughter's future be? Akbar had established the rule that an emperor's daughters should not marry, to reduce the potential for the bloody disputes between rival family claimants to the throne that had tainted the Moghuls' early years in Hindustan. Yet why should royal daughters be denied the happiness their brothers enjoyed?

Mumtaz would have known instinctively what was both prudent and fair . . . but maybe fairness didn't come into it. What mattered most was ensuring the dynasty's survival, as Akbar – wise and humane though he was – had understood. Shah Jahan glanced at Jahanara, absorbed in the model. He would find other ways of making his daughters happy.

'Jahanara, what you've said reminds me that you're a grown woman. If you'd like an independent household I will give you your own mansion. There's that handsome one that used to belong to your great-grandfather Ghiyas Beg. Would you like that?'

She considered but only for a moment. 'Yes, thank you, Father. But I forgot ... I've some news. Satti al-Nisa tells me Nicholas Ballantyne has returned to Agra. He's living in the bazaar.'

'Nicholas?' The last time Shah Jahan had seen the young Englishman had been soon after he'd come to the throne. Hadn't he departed on some trading venture ... to Kabul or perhaps Herat? Nicholas had remained faithful to him during his family's dangerous years as outcasts and exiles. He had even been his emissary to his father Jahangir, helping them to make their peace. 'I would like to see him again. He was our friend when we had few.'

Next day, as Nicholas Ballantyne bowed before him, Shah Jahan thought he had broadened over the years since he had last seen him. His shoulders strained against his tight-fitting leather tunic and his calves beneath the outlandish slashed pantaloons these foreigners wore were knotted with muscle. But when he raised his head Nicholas's eyes were the same piercing blue beneath his unruly butter-coloured hair, streaked almost white by the hot Indian sun.

'Welcome back to my court. I hear you're lodging in the bazaar. My steward can find lodgings for you within the fort if you wish.'

'Thank you, Majesty.'

'What's brought you to Agra?'

'To be honest, I hope to find employment at your court.'

'Didn't you decide to try your hand as a trader?'

'Yes, but I didn't prosper. With the money I'd earned in your service I went to Kabul and bought Persian carpets and Chinese silks in the great bazaar to ship back to Europe. However, Ghilzais ambushed the return caravan I joined as we descended the narrow Khoord-Kabul pass just before dusk. They killed many merchants in their initial attack. The few of us who survived only did so by scrambling up the hillside and taking refuge behind the rocks in the half-light. Once the Ghilzais had seized our mules with their cargos they lost interest in us.' He smiled a little ruefully.

Shah Jahan, though, was frowning. Nicholas's words had reminded him that for some time his governor in Kabul had reported growing lawlessness among the tribes inhabiting the passes – Afridis and Kafirs as well as Ghilzais. 'What did you do after you were robbed?'

'I made my way south to Kandahar and eventually across the Helmand river into Persia, where I joined the shah's army for a time.'

'Did you never think of returning to your own country?'

Nicholas shook his head. 'No. There's little for me there. My parents are dead – my elder brother has inherited my father's estate. Besides ... I love this land – I have ever since I came ashore with Sir Thomas. That's why I returned here from Persia. I'm not ready to go home – at least not yet.'

Sir Thomas Roe ... Shah Jahan had almost forgotten

the spindly-shanked English ambassador whose *qorchi* Nicholas had been.

'Nicholas, you were always loyal to me. To show my gratitude, I'll appoint you a captain in my army headquarters – you'll find some familiar faces there. Your knowledge of the shah's army – especially his weaponry – will be useful. I suspect – indeed I know – he has ambitions to seize territory on the fringes of my empire. I've asked my eldest son to review my army's preparedness. You can help him.'

'I'd be glad to, Majesty. I remember Prince Dara well.' Then Nicholas added more hesitantly, 'I learned of the empress's death while I was in Persia. I was truly sorry.'

Shah Jahan nodded but said nothing, then rose, signalling the interview was over.

Twenty-four hours later Shah Jahan looked round the familiar faces before him in his marble audience hall. This was the first time he'd summoned his full council since returning to Agra. Raising his hand to quell the hubbub of expectant conversation, he began to speak.

'The tribes in the north think they can act with impunity, plundering our merchants in the passes leading to and from Kabul. I have heard first-hand accounts of their crimes and studied reports from my governor in the city. Perhaps these criminals believe I've been too preoccupied with the Deccan to notice their misdeeds . . . if so, they'll soon discover their error. I'll not tolerate their defiance. Unless our roads are secure, trade can't prosper.'

All around, his counsellors were murmuring agreement. 'Ashok Singh,' Shah Jahan continued. 'You proved your courage and ingenuity in the Deccan. I have chosen you to rid me of this menace. I've decided to place you in command of ten thousand troops – horsemen and musketeers. You will advance up through the passes and punish these bandits as they deserve. Execute the ringleaders, pull down their forts and villages and drive off their flocks. Make them understand that death and destruction are the only alternatives to accepting Moghul authority.'

'I suspect the Persian shah has been offering the tribes money to stir up unrest. A show of force may make him think again,' Asaf Khan said quietly.

'I'm sure that's right.' Mumtaz's father was growing more frail in body but his brain remained as acute as ever.

'I'll assemble my forces quickly so that we can complete our mission before the next cold season puts an end to campaigning. I have only one question: should I take cannon? We'll move more speedily without them,' Ashok Singh said.

'What do you think, Kamran Iqbal?' Shah Jahan asked.

'I agree. They will only hold him up. If he needs cannon the governor can supply them from Kabul.'

It was good advice, even though his old comrade's face looked drawn with pain. The stump of the arm he had lost at Lahore had never healed properly. 'So be it, then. I'll have the necessary instructions drawn up.'

Later, when the details of the campaign had been debated and agreed and his counsellors and commanders had departed, Shah Jahan sat for a while. He was glad he'd acted decisively. He mustn't let his preoccupation with Mumtaz's tomb make him neglect his empire's security ... Yet though he knew he'd sounded firm and authoritative, he'd felt curiously detached during the meeting. He'd been reminded of watching some puppets a group of travelling players from the east had once brought to his court. Cut from pieces of leather to resemble the outlines of men and women and mounted on sticks, the puppets themselves had been concealed by a silk screen behind which a row of oil lamps had been lit. Only their shadows had been visible as they went through their act. That was how he had felt – a shadow emperor, moving mechanically to create an illusion for his audience.

Was that how it would always be from now on? Trying to do what he must but always acting a part? He had once had such a desire for greatness. By discipline and effort he must force it to return.

Chapter 8

Seated beneath a scarlet awning on a specially constructed dais in the courtyard of the Agra fort, his commanders and courtiers before him, Shah Jahan listened to the clashing of cymbals and the beating of drums. For the first time since Mumtaz's death two years ago he had permitted music at court. It was also the first occasion when he had laid aside his simple white mourning garb for rich clothing and jewels. His gleaming green brocade robes, the stiff jewelled belt round his lean waist and the ropes of gems round his neck and wrists felt unfamiliar and he had no pleasure in their splendour. But this was Dara Shukoh's wedding day and, as Asaf Khan had reminded him, Mumtaz would have wished him to dress with imperial magnificence to honour the marriage of their eldest son, his grandson.

The cheering of the crowds outside the fort as well as the music told him that the groom and his brothers were approaching. An hour ago Shah Shuja, Aurangzeb and Murad had ridden to the mansion along the banks of the Jumna that he had given to Dara as a wedding present. Now all four brothers would be returning, Dara mounted on a splendid black stallion, and preceded by a hundred gold-sashed attendants carrying round trays laden with gems, gold and silver as well as mounds of vividly coloured spices – orange saffron and yellow turmeric – and scarlet pomegranates, purple figs and green guavas to symbolise the prosperous and fertile future that awaited the groom and his bride.

Sure enough, three trumpet flourishes announced Dara's arrival and he entered, followed by his brothers. As Dara reached the dais, he glanced briefly at the carved screen high in the wall beside the throne through which his two elder sisters would be watching. Jahanara had been eager to be allowed to make the wedding arrangements and Shah Jahan had agreed. As she'd gone about the task, planning everything from the *pulaos* studded with dried fruits and nuts wrapped in gold leaf for the wedding feast to the whirling Rajasthani dancers in their bright spangled clothes, and the fireworks that at midnight would transform dark night into dazzling day, he'd been surprised how rapidly his daughter was growing in confidence and authority.

It was time for him to place the groom's pearl marriage crown on Dara's head. As Aslan Beg, limping more heavily than ever, stepped forward with the velvet cushion on which sat the crown, Shah Jahan rose. Taking the crown with both hands, he raised it high so all could see it, then placed it on his son's head. 'I ask everyone here to witness that I give my blessing to the marriage of my beloved eldest son to his cousin Nadira, the daughter of my half-brother Parvez. May God look kindly on their union and bless it with many healthy children and many years of great happiness.' Then, taking Dara by the shoulder, he turned him to face the assembled courtiers. 'I have something else to announce. I hereby appoint my son to the rank of commander of twelve thousand horse – the same rank my own father awarded me at his age.'

Shah Jahan saw the pleasure in Dara's hazel eyes. Soon Shah Shuja too would wed and he would award him honours as well, but perhaps not with quite the same satisfaction. Dara was everything a son – and a Moghul prince – should be. He was a good swordsman and an accomplished wrestler who could outwit far heavier men. Yet he was also a scholar with the same fascination with science and the natural world as his grandfather Jahangir. By contrast, Shah Shuja's chief interest was the pursuit of pleasure – natural enough in a young man, but too many of their Moghul forebears had died not at enemy hands but from their own weaknesses, Nadira's father among them. Parvez had died young, a hopeless drunk.

Dara seemed free of such vices. If he continued to prove himself, perhaps he should soon declare him his heir. It was what Mumtaz would have wanted and surely only what Dara's younger brothers would be expecting. It would bring the stability and certainty lacking in earlier generations, the absence of which had caused so much fraternal bloodshed and hazarded the empire. If he could achieve that it would be something he could be proud of and one of his most important legacies to future generations. Yet, he thought, his family was different from his forebears' – his sons were full brothers, not half-brothers, and the bonds between them consequently deeper and stronger. Dara was only nineteen and his own rule still young. Perhaps after all he had no need to hurry to name a successor.

• ◆ •

'Majesty, the elephants are ready to begin their fight.'

Reining in his horse, Shah Jahan wiped the sweat from his forehead. He was pleased he could still compete with his sons in the sport of racing on horseback to be the first to spear a melon placed on the ground three hundred yards away on the banks of the Jumna. To the roars of the spectators clustered on the battlements of the Agra fort on this the fourth day of the celebration of Dara Shukoh's wedding, he had challenged and beaten both Shah Shuja and Aurangzeb, albeit by the closest of margins in the case of Aurangzeb who, although two years younger, had outdistanced his brother and to Shah Jahan's amusement had looked disgusted that he had not succeeded in beating his father, throwing his gauntlets into the dust.

Turning his sweat-scummed horse, Shah Jahan could already hear the trumpeting of the elephants in the enclosure built specially for their fight a little further along the riverbank. As he rode up, accompanied by Ashok Singh, he signalled the *mahouts* to remove the green silk scarves tied over their elephants' eyes and for the fight to begin. His mount whinnied nervously as the two elephants, facing each other across the great wall of earth that divided the enclosure and separated them, raised their trunks and bellowed defiance at one another. Shah Jahan whispered reassuring words to his horse and tautened his reins, gripping harder with his knees. As he did so he saw that Aurangzeb and Shah Shuja had already arrived and were seated on their horses a little in front of him, just by the enclosure wall. The lances they had used in their previous contest with him were slung from their saddles. Dara was watching from the opposite side of the enclosure with Asaf Khan.

At first Damudar – a huge beast with sharpened tusks and a scarred trunk, named after one of Akbar's most famous fighting elephants – seemed to be having the best of it. Goaded by his *mahout* he mounted the internal dividing wall, dislodging some of the earth, to strike at his opponent Jhalpa, inflicting a long jagged slash in his tough grey shoulder. Ashok Singh's father, the Raja of Amber, had sent both animals to Dara as a wedding gift. Rising up on his hind legs, Damudar inflicted a second gash, but then, as he hurled himself forward yet again, he slipped on the crumbling earth of the wall and crashed sideways to the ground, sending his *mahout* flying through the air like a child's doll to hit the hard ground with a crash, where he lay crumpled and seemingly unconscious as a pool of crimson blood grew around his head. Seeing his chance and urged on by his own *mahout* perched on his neck, Jhalpa pushed forward despite his wounds. Red-painted trunk coiled, he trampled through what remained of the earth barrier before, lowering his head, he tore into the recumbent Damudar's right ear with his tusk, half severing it.

Blood dripping down the side of his head, Damudar staggered up and stood swaying and trumpeting defiance, but Jhalpa was again quicker to react, swinging his great domed head at Damudar and this time catching his opponent in his left flank. Suddenly, Damudar seemed to have had enough. Turning, he lumbered towards the wall of the enclosure close to where Shah Shuja and Aurangzeb were watching. Twisting slightly, he hurled his right shoulder against it. Though the wall was five feet high and almost as thick, as Damudar struck it for a second and then a third time the red earth crumbled under the pressure. The *mahout*-less elephant blundered out of the enclosure and on to the riverbank and began to lurch towards a group of spectators who were on foot.

Frightened once more by the elephant's appearance, Shah Jahan's horse began to rear. As he fought to control it, Shah Jahan saw Aurangzeb kick his own mount forward, endeavouring to put it between the enraged animal and the onlookers, several of whom had children on their shoulders, and most of whom appeared rooted to the spot by fear. Something about Aurangzeb – perhaps the flash of the diamonds in his turban or the metallic clinking of his mount's jewelled bridle – caught Damudar's attention and he turned his bloodstained head towards him. Then, curling up his trunk, he gave a deep roar and charged.

'Aurangzeb, get back,' yelled Shah Jahan as Damudar lumbered towards his son, who was surely about to be knocked from his horse and trampled or gored.

Yet the fifteen-year-old Aurangzeb looked far from frightened. Controlling his horse with one hand, with the other he reached down to the side of his saddle where his lance was tied and tried to pull it free. But before he could do so, Damudar was on him, catching his horse a glancing blow in the shoulder with the tip of his right tusk, causing it to rear and throw Aurangzeb backwards from the saddle. Somehow he managed to get to his feet and draw his sword while attendants began hurling firecrackers at Damudar in an attempt to drive him off. As acrid smoke filled the air, Damudar appeared to hesitate as if confused by the explosions.

'Shah Shuja, no!' shouted Shah Jahan, still struggling to prevent his bucking horse from bolting, as his second son rode into the drifting smoke brandishing his own lance, followed immediately by Ashok Singh. As Shah Shuja flung his weapon – which bounced harmlessly off Damudar's thick hide – his skittering horse tripped over some obstacle hidden by the smoke and fell, sending Shah Shuja too tumbling to the ground. Ashok Singh wheeled his mount and succeeded in interposing himself between the two unhorsed princes and Damudar. But then came a thundering so great that the earth seemed to shake. Jhalpa, having dislodged his own *mahout* who up till then had been struggling to control him, pushed through the gap in the enclosure wall made by Damudar, seemingly determined to get at his enemy. Turning, Damudar for a moment stood his ground, head down, but then his courage failed him again and with a desperate trumpeting roar he rushed down the riverbank and into the Jumna, pursued by Jhalpa, as spectators scattered before them.

Shah Jahan flung himself from his quietening horse and ran towards his sons. Both were now on their feet, covered in dust and breathing hard but looking unharmed. For a moment Shah Jahan closed his eyes in silent gratitude and then he embraced them. 'You both showed great courage.

You were true *bahadurs*, heroes. You too, Ashok Singh.'

'It was no more than my duty to intervene, Majesty. Damudar was a gift from my father.'

Shah Jahan turned back to his sons. 'Aurangzeb – you were too rash. You shouldn't have tried to fight the elephant alone but waited for some of the bodyguards to join you.'

Aurangzeb shrugged. 'There wasn't time and I wasn't rash. Yes, I knew there was a risk but I wanted to protect the spectators. If I'd died there would have been no dishonour. Death comes to us all. What matters is how we meet it. The shame would have been in doing nothing.' As he spoke he glanced towards Dara, on the other side of the enclosure, jaw set in that way he had when he wanted to make a point. What was Aurangzeb implying? That his eldest brother was a coward for not having tried to intervene? If so it was unfair. Dara had been too far away. But surely it was nothing – just the conceit of an adolescent boy embracing the glory of the moment and unable to resist a snipe at an elder brother. He mustn't let memories of past family rivalries make him see anything more sinister in it.

Chapter 9

Shah Jahan's eyes were closed as he thrust harder and harder, throwing back his head at the exquisite moment of release. Then, panting, he collapsed on to the Baluchi woman's soft-fleshed body which like his was beaded with sweat. She was voluptuously beautiful, he thought, with her full breasts and lushly rounded hips. Her shinning hennaed hair spilled over the brocade cushions and her kohl-rimmed eyes looked confidently into his. She thought she had pleased him.

The *khawajasara*, the superintendent of the imperial *haram*, had chosen well. 'What are your tastes, Majesty?' she had asked. 'Slender or curvaceous? Tall or short? Dark or fair?' Shah Jahan had stared at her. In all his years of marriage to Mumtaz he had never asked for a woman from the *haram*. Other rulers – eager for the Moghul emperor's favour – had sent him women but until recently he had never given them a thought. 'You choose for me,' he had replied. 'I don't care.'

For a long time after Mumtaz's death he'd never even thought of having a woman, but latterly he'd felt the stirrings of physical desire which had grown stronger until he had decided he must satisfy it.

'Majesty, you are a stallion among men,' the woman was saying, stretching her body invitingly before him. 'I have never known such vigour . . .'

Shah Jahan rolled from her and standing up looked at her with a feeling bordering on disgust – but with himself, not her.

'What is the matter? You look displeased, Majesty.' She too rose from the bed and moving towards him pressed her naked body against his own so that he could feel the tautness of her henna-painted nipples. 'Have I offended you?'

Despite himself, Shah Jahan felt a fresh surging in his loins and her soft laugh told him she had detected it as well. 'Perhaps I haven't displeased you after all.' Her hands were caressing him and suddenly he was pushing her back on to the bed, burying his face in the tangled masses of her scented hair as once again he entered her. This time the climax took a little longer and as he pulled away from her to lie face down, head in his arms; his body was still shaking, but no longer with the dying moments of sexual fulfilment. Tears pricked his eyelids. What had he done? How could he have betrayed his unique and sacred love for Mumtaz?

'Go now,' he said, not raising his head as self-loathing welled within him again.

'Majesty?'

'I said go. I've no further use for you.'

•◆•

'He barely eats and his *qorchis* say that despite his proclamations of abstinence he sometimes calls for wine and has ordered fresh supplies to be sent from the province of Ghazni. Occasionally he dissolves pellets of opium in it ... Four mornings ago his attendants found him almost impossible to rouse for his daily appearance to the people on the *jharoka* balcony. They had to half carry him on to the balcony and a *qorchi* supported him on each side as he gave the blessing. Sometimes he can go weeks without touching either wine or poppy but even then Aslan Beg can't get him to deal with court business. Instead he sits for hours staring into the middle distance without saying anything and rebuking anyone who dares approach him. I've seen it with my own eyes. I do what I can. I've talked to him but though he is never sharp with me he takes little notice.' Jahanara shook her head.

'I could tell from your letters you were worried, but I hadn't realised how serious it's become.'

'You've been away some time. I visit Father nearly every day. I'd hoped he was finally overcoming his grief – after all it's nearly five years since our mother died – and for a while it seemed like it. But either I was wrong, perhaps only seeing what I wanted to see, or he's relapsed ... He's becoming more melancholic and isolating himself from the world again.'

'Does he at least still take an interest in the building of our mother's tomb?'

'Yes. He inspects progress most days, giving detailed instructions, especially about the inlaying of the gems into the marble. But he doesn't stay long and as soon as he returns he relapses into brooding introspection. If he isn't careful it will either erode his sanity or lead to internal rebellions, but he doesn't realise the danger either to himself or to the empire . . .'

'Danger? You really think things have become that bad again?'

'I'm not sure, but quite possibly . . . I can only tell you what I've observed recently. Father is once more finding it difficult to concentrate. The deaths of Kamran Iqbal and our grandfather Asaf Khan following each other in such quick succession have unsettled him, severing further links with his past. What's more, both of them felt able to speak to him frankly about problems they saw arising and advise him how to deal with them before they grew. Without their prompting he's become ever more reluctant to turn his mind to issues like official appointments or taxation.'

'But these things matter.'

'Yes. They're what bind our empire together. It's essential for the empire's well-being that he retains not just the outward loyalty of his commanders and officials but their genuine support and enthusiasm, but he won't take time to listen to their petitions and complaints, nor will he read the reports from the provinces. However, I read them and I see what's beginning to happen . . .'

'What do you mean?'

'We're growing lax. We're alienating our nobles by disregarding their ambitions at the same time as relaxing our scrutiny of their activities. Though they remain outwardly faithful and deferential much of it is mere show – they feel free to flout obligations like maintaining troops for imperial use in return for the gold we pay them. While you were away, the commander of the Agra garrison wrote to the Governor of Ajmer asking for five thousand men to escort the imperial court when we journey to Lahore in three months' time. However, the governor replied that the local landowners couldn't raise that number of men so quickly.'

'But they're supposed to keep them ready for action in case of sudden war. Aren't we still sending inspectors to their estates to check that they're maintaining the correct numbers of troops and collecting the taxes efficiently?'

'Yes, but the landowners must be bribing them. I asked Aslan Beg for the records of the Ajmer inspections, and discovered that our officials were there three months ago but reported nothing amiss.'

'They must be punished, and severely, to make an example, and the Governor of Ajmer as well. At the least he was weak in allowing such corruption. At worst he was involved. I will attend to it even if Father won't. As you say, it mustn't be thought even in the most remote outposts that the emperor's eye is elsewhere or his authority weakening or we will face more rebellions like that of the Raja of Orchha . . . What do Shah Shuja and Aurangzeb think about all this?'

'I don't know. I've written to them, of course, but Aurangzeb has been so preoccupied he hasn't been in Agra for a couple of years. His campaign to quell the Orchha rebellion was harder and took longer than either Father or anyone else could have anticipated. Now that he's viceroy in the Deccan the region's still so unsettled that he's busy dealing with several local risings as well as incursions from beyond our borders. Shah Shuja must have his hands full in Bengal too. The Arakanese are a constant threat to our traders in the Ganges delta.'

'I heard that Father's just given Shah Shuja Orissa to govern as well?'

'Yes. Shah Shuja asked and Father agreed before I knew anything. Otherwise I would have advised against it. Although he enjoys the power and status such appointments bring, I don't think Shah Shuja yet has the capacity for such wide responsibilities or such hard work and may never do, but perhaps I misjudge him.' Jahanara took Dara's hands and smiled. 'I'm glad you're back in Agra. I've missed you. There are few people I can talk to about such things ... Satti al-Nisa sometimes and Roshanara who I'm sure thinks I exaggerate because she doesn't spend as much time with Father as I do. In fact she's delighted with him at the moment – she asked him to reinstate the Royal Meena Bazaar and he's agreed. But enough of such matters. I want to hear about you. Was your journey to Surat successful?'

'Yes. It was a good idea of yours to take Nicholas Ballantyne. He was useful as an interpreter and helped me negotiate good terms. The English East India Company have agreed to supply ships to protect our trading vessels and our pilgrim fleets on their voyages across the Arabian Sea to Mecca. There are no better soldiers than the Moghuls but we don't understand how to fight at sea as the English do. They'll deal with the pirates for us.'

'The Surat merchants must have been honoured that a Moghul prince came to negotiate in person.'

Dara grinned. 'Surprised too, I think. I put on a mighty

149

show – one hundred elephants caparisoned in gold and a thousand mounted retainers in green turbans and tunics. These foreigners are easy to impress – their jaws dropped to their knees as they gawped at the opulence.'

'Father will be pleased with the outcome. The pirate raids on our ships have angered him . . .' Jahanara paused. 'But there's something else you should know about him . . . Nearly every night he sends for women from the *haram*, sometimes two, even three. He's even built a mirrored hall inlaid with gold and pearls so that he can observe his love-making.'

Dara stared. 'How do you know all this?'

Jahanara smiled a little sadly. 'It's common gossip around the *haram*. I asked Satti al-Nisa to speak to the *khawajasara* who confirmed it all. Apparently he never sends for the same woman twice and scarcely utters a word to them while they are with him. She also said that he is taking dangerous quantities of aphrodisiacs – he's especially fond of some concoction called "the Making of the Horse" . . . Of course, I was shocked at first. I couldn't understand how he could act like this when he loved our mother so much . . . but then I felt pity. He has never recovered fully from her death and now he is seeking whatever solace he can. It's as if he's begun testing his potency as a man when he should be more concerned about demonstrating it as an emperor.'

Brother and sister looked at one another in silence. Then Jahanara said, 'I've never told anyone this, but in Burhanpur, while our mother was lying in agony waiting for our father to come to her, she made me promise that if she died I would watch over him and keep him from harm. I wasn't sure what she meant or what I could do. But I believe she understood his character – that without her guidance and support, and in particular her insight into human nature, for all his strength and courage, all his wealth and power, he would be rudderless – a vessel adrift from its moorings. We must rescue him from himself and anchor him back in the world, Dara . . . for his sake and for the empire's. The question is how.'

• ◆ •

Thousands of coloured lanterns hanging in the trees lit the main courtyard of the Agra fort. In the centre stood the vast tent of maroon velvet that workmen had laboured for a week to erect for the eighteen-day Nauruz – the New Year festival introduced by Akbar. Inside, every surface was covered with thick, soft silk carpets and brocade hangings embroidered with gold, pearls and precious stones. Each night since the festival's start Shah Jahan had either held court in the tent, receiving the gifts and good wishes of his nobles, or visited their own resplendent pavilions pitched nearby. This evening, though, would be different. It was the night of the Royal Meena Bazaar, when the wives and daughters of the nobility spread stalls with trinkets and lengths of brilliant silks and played at being traders. It was one of the few occasions when the women of the court dropped their silken veils and men could gaze openly on their faces.

He had first seen Mumtaz at a Royal Meena Bazaar on a warm night just like this . . . Standing beneath the gold awning of the imperial tent he began to regret allowing Roshanara to persuade him to allow the bazaar to take place once more, arguing that it was the most important event of the year for the women of the royal household. The Meena Bazaar recalled too many bitter-sweet memories perhaps best forgotten ... how the fourteen-year-old Mumtaz had looked standing behind her stall, pearls and diamonds shining in her hair ... the sweet smell of the white jasmine growing on the wall behind her ... the bright golden *mohurs* he had tipped into her hand in payment for a small vase.

But he must do his duty. The emperor's tour of inspection was the official start of the Royal Meena Bazaar. He climbed into the gilded palanquin waiting for him and it rose shudderingly into the air as eight muscular female Tartar *haram* attendants raised it to their shoulders. Then, preceded by the *khawajasara* bearing her carved ivory staff of office, and escorted by smooth-faced eunuchs, he began his tour, smelling the attar of roses made by Jahanara to a recipe invented by her Persian great-grandmother and tasting sweetmeats of sugar and butter prepared by elderly royal matrons.

As he reached the less prominent parts of the courtyard where the wives and daughters of his courtiers and officials had their stalls and went through the motions of praising the wares and pretending to bargain, it was the women not their goods who increasingly caught his attention. He recognised some but others he'd never seen, like a tall woman in a purple silk robe whose plaited hair was interwoven with marigolds. She was broad-shouldered for a woman but had a slender waist. Her black eyes looked boldly into his as, play-acting the role of stallholder, she beckoned to him, urging the claims of her wares over the other women's.

'Who is that?' he asked the *khawajasara*.

'Kalima Begum, wife of your governor in Lahore. He married her while you were in the Deccan but she is not his favourite. He has another wife he wed five years earlier whom he has taken with him to Lahore, leaving Kalima behind. Do you wish to inspect her stall, Majesty?'

'No. But I want you to send her to me tonight.'

'She is a married woman, Majesty . . .'

'That isn't your concern. So long as she herself is willing, do as I have ordered.'

Why had he done it, Shah Jahan asked himself an hour or two later. It was one thing ordering the *khawajasara* to select him suitable women from among the occupants of a *haram* he'd taken no interest in for over twenty years, quite another to ask her to procure him the wife of one of his governors. What could have possessed him? The hope of assuaging his grief by a coupling as meaningless and crude as a dog mounting a bitch in the street? . . . No . . . He would tell the *khawajasara* that he had changed his mind.

He reached for the enamelled bell to summon an attendant, then paused. No one could ever replace Mumtaz in his heart . . . every time he bedded a woman it only left him feeling more bereft. Yet the feel of a woman's body beneath his brought a fleeting comfort. Also, making love to other women demonstrated their imperfections in mind as well as body compared with Mumtaz, proving yet again the perfection and uniqueness of their love.

What would be in Kalima's mind now as the *khawajasara* prepared her for his bed, he wondered. That assumed, of course, that she was willing, but recalling the look in her eyes he didn't doubt it. Would she be nervous or perhaps already planning how to turn the situation to her advantage? And what about himself? He was intending to use his power to take another man's wife, just as David had stolen Bathsheba. Was that the act of an honourable man? Probably not, though if Kalima were willing to make love with him it would prove she didn't deserve whatever love her husband had for her. He would be robbing neither husband nor wife of anything that mattered, like the love that Mumtaz's death had robbed him of.

Shortly before midnight he heard a gentle tapping at the door and the *khawajasara* entered, the taller figure of Kalima close behind enveloped in a cream robe, its deep hood concealing her face. 'I have brought Kalima Begum, Majesty,' said the *khawajasara*. 'Should I return to the *haram* until you send for me again?'

'No, wait outside.' Now that the woman was before him, Shah Jahan's doubts had returned and he wondered afresh why he was doing this. As soon as he was alone with her, he stepped towards her and gently pushed back her hood. This time, instead of being tightly plaited, her hair was loose about her shoulders, shining and luxuriant. She smiled at him as confidently as she had at the Meena Bazaar. Her right hand went to her throat and she started to undo the silver clasp securing her cloak.

'No, not yet.'

'Majesty?' Her hand dropped.

'Why do you think I sent for you tonight?'

'Because I please you. I saw you watching me at the bazaar.'

'What about your own feelings? Will you willingly give yourself to me?'

'Of course, Majesty.'

'But you're married. What about your husband?'

'I haven't seen him for many months. Anyway, I mean as little to him as he does to me. He married me for my dowry – my father's lands adjoin his in the Punjab – and he has another wife whom he prefers to me.'

'Isn't it your duty to be faithful to him?'

'Isn't it also my duty to obey my emperor when he calls for me?'

Smooth words came easily to her, thought Shah Jahan. She was no better than the courtesans of the imperial *haram* who had instructed him in the arts of love when he had been a young prince, ignorant of women and fumblingly eager to learn.

'Take off your robe.' Shah Jahan watched her undo the clasp and let the cream robe slide to the floor. She was naked, her skin shining with scented oil, save for a gold chain hung with tiny golden leaves about her waist. 'Turn around for me.' She revolved slowly, the golden leaves shivering as she moved. Her square shoulders were more like a boy's than a woman's; so were her tapering back, high, rounded buttocks and long, muscular legs. She was striking enough but far from beautiful – at least not to him. As she turned to face him once more, he was about to order her to pick up her robe and cover herself. Then, unbidden, she raised her hands and throwing back her head ran them through her glorious hair. The gesture was achingly familiar. How often had he watched Mumtaz do the same? An urgent, unexpected desire possessed him.

155

'Lie down over there.' As she walked across to the low brocade-covered divan he undid the coral buttons of his own robe. Lowering his body on to hers, he sought her nipples with his lips. Moments later, as with his right hand he parted her lean thighs – so different from Mumtaz's soft, yielding flesh – and began to caress her, Kalima began to whimper with pleasure – simulated or real, he couldn't tell – and then to cry out, sharp-nailed hands clinging to his back. Yet it wasn't her voice he heard but Mumtaz's gentler one, urging him on and whispering her eternal love for him.

Two hours later, Shah Jahan sat up, body soaked with sweat. He put his head in his hands, grateful for the comforting darkness, though through the casement the paling sky told him dawn wasn't so far off. He had dismissed Kalima as soon as he had slaked his desire but her scent still clung to the bedding. He reached for a silver ewer on the marble table beside him and poured a cup of water, emptying it with a single gulp. His body was still shaking with the horror of the dream from which he had just awoken, and which had nothing to do with Kalima. He had seen Mumtaz's tomb rising up ghost-like on the banks of the Jumna, perfect in its marble purity. He'd stood at the gateway marvelling at the beauty of his creation but then the sharp, rigid outline of the white dome had begun to soften and tremble – no longer a piece of cold inanimate stone but the warm mound of a woman's breast, Mumtaz's breast. Suddenly, before his horrified eyes, bright red blood had begun spurting from the tip of the dome, running down in scarlet rivulets . . .

The tomb had faded to be replaced by other visions –

Mumtaz in the agonies of labour, soaked in blood and sweat, screaming for the baby to come and for relief from her pain . . . then more blood, this time dripping from the executioner's blade as the head of his half-brother Shahriyar rolled across the floor . . . then a different scene: Jani, stricken with grief at her husband Khusrau's death, approaching a brazier of burning coals with tongs . . . gazing into its red-gold glowing heart . . . carefully selecting a small, single coal . . . lifting it out . . . feeling its scorching heat on her face as she brought the tongs closer . . . closing her eyes and opening her mouth to receive it . . . her screams as she swallowed it. Then, certain he could smell Jani's singeing flesh, he had woken, shaking and confused.

There had been so much death and destruction within his family. What had the Moghuls done to deserve it? God had allowed them unbounded power and wealth but denied them the peace and harmony that even the humblest family had a right to expect. His name meant 'Ruler of the World', yet as he sat there, alone in the darkness, the words seemed to mock him.

• ◆ •

Shah Jahan shifted his position a little to get more comfortable. The Turkish concubine, with her wiry dark hair and startling amber eyes, had departed at dusk back to the *haram*. She had exhausted his body but his mind was restless. He had not slept for several nights. He must tonight. Standing, he went over to a locked chest on a low table and turning the key took out a small bottle of wine, into which he dropped a pellet of opium. He knew Mehrunissa had damaged his father with such potions but he must sleep. Soon he was drifting into a world of sensual, soft-scented dreams. He and Mumtaz were lying beneath a jasmine-covered arbour in the garden of their first mansion in Agra, bodies close. He touched Mumtaz's cheek and, seeing her answering smile, pulled her gently to him. Slowly he began unfastening the emerald buttons of her *choli*, marvelling at the velvet swell of her breasts beneath the tightly fitting silk.

'Please, wake up ... the cloth has been spread for the evening meal and we've been waiting for you ... had you forgotten?'

A voice – a woman's voice – was intruding into his idyll. Opening his eyes he tried to focus but the pink-clad figure in front of his divan was only a blur. Even when she came closer and knelt beside him, he still couldn't distinguish the features, half hidden as they were by a sweep of dark hair. Slowly he sat up, confused. Was it Mumtaz? Yet how could it be if she was lying beside him? But as the figure leaned yet closer he caught the scent of orange blossom – one of Mumtaz's favourite perfumes which she distilled herself. It was her after all. Reaching out, his fingers touched the yielding smoothness of her breast and began to caress it.

'Stop it! What are you doing? ... Please don't ...'

As she tried to pull away, he gripped the breast harder and with his other hand felt for the mound between her thighs. Through the soft fabric of her clothes her flesh felt firm and warm and welcoming, contradicting her words, which she couldn't mean ... Mumtaz had never denied him anything. This was just a teasing game to heighten his desire ...

As she continued to struggle, Shah Jahan relinquished

her breast and putting his arm round her neck pulled her down beside him, breathing in the fragrant scent of her body. 'You know what you mean to me ...' he whispered, feeling her heart beating against him. She had always responded to him. From their very first night she had known how to give and to receive pleasure and so it would always be between them. But as he moved closer, she suddenly twisted away and scrambled off the divan, hair tumbling about her face. 'Where are you going? Don't go ...' Shah Jahan leapt up but as he reached for her she grabbed a brass bowl and flung it at him, catching him on his right temple. Blood streamed down his face and he felt dizzy. Gasping with pain he gripped a pillar for support and for a moment shut his eyes.

'Father!'

Opening his eyes again, he saw Jahanara, the front of her *choli* ripped open, revealing her breasts. What was happening? He shook his head as if that motion could drive away the clouds in his mind. As he stared at his daughter ... saw the shock and revulsion on her tear-stained, kohl-smudged face ... he began to grasp what he had tried to do. 'Jahanara ... I didn't mean ...' He took a step towards her but she backed away, the breeze blowing in from the terrace behind her ruffling her pink muslin skirt.

'No ... don't come any closer!' Her voice sounded strange – hoarse and high-pitched – and he saw her glance towards the doors leading from his apartments, but he was blocking her path. He let go of the pillar and was about to move aside when he stopped. How could he let her go like this? He must make her listen to him ... 'Let me explain ...'

'No!' She stared at him, then without warning turned and darted out on to the terrace.

'Jahanara . . .' Shah Jahan staggered outside. At first his eyes couldn't focus as he peered into the soft light of the oil lamps and wicks burning in their saucers of oil, but then a noise told him where she was – near a stairway at the far end of the terrace that led directly down to the *haram*. 'Wait . . .'

For a moment she looked back at him, then gathering her muslin skirt she turned and ran towards the stairs. Suddenly she lost her footing and tumbled forward, putting out her hands to try to save herself. As she came crashing down, the hem of her skirt brushed a naked flame. Shah Jahan watched in horror as a tongue of orange fire spread into the fabric and his daughter began to scream.

Shah Jahan half ran, half lurched forward, but before he could reach Jahanara female *haram* attendants who must have heard her cries ran up the stairs. Seeing what was happening, two dropped to their knees beside Jahanara, one trying to beat out the flames with her bare hands, the other trying to remove the burning skirt. They had some success until one leaned right over Jahanara and her long hair caught light and she too began screaming and clawing at her head. Almost simultaneously the second attendant's clothes caught fire and as she rose and ran towards a fountain a breeze fanned the flames, turning her into a human torch.

By now other servants were pouring ewers of water over Jahanara, dousing the flames before turning to help the other two women. But Shah Jahan had eyes only for his daughter. Kneeling low over her, he began peeling away the shreds of burnt clothing, fearful of what he was about to see. She was lying on her face, parts of her back and left leg horribly burned and much of her once lovely hair frazzled. As the smell of scorched flesh caught his nostrils, he began to heave.

'Your *hakims* are coming, Majesty,' he heard someone say. With the fumes of intoxication dissipating under the shock and tears coursing down his face, he tried to stand as strong arms reached out to help him. Minutes later, he watched as two *hakims* bent over Jahanara. 'She's breathing, but the burns are bad,' one said at last.

'Where should we take her, Majesty? Back to her own mansion?' asked the other.

'No ... Prepare apartments for her in the imperial *haram* here in the fort. Also give every attention to her attendants – they risked their lives to help her.' Shah Jahan watched as, following the *hakims'* instructions, attendants covered Jahanara and her two waiting women with cotton sheets soaked in water and lifted them carefully on to litters. As they carried them from the terrace Shah Jahan followed slowly. Glancing for a moment towards the Jumna river he made out the pale shape of Mumtaz's half-built tomb. 'Don't let my daughter die like her mother,' he found himself praying. 'Punish me, instead. I deserve it.'

Chapter 10

Shah Jahan leant closer as Jahanara muttered something. Briefly her eyelids flickered but then she lay quiet and still again in the half-light of the sick chamber. Though she was getting no worse the *hakims* were worried. Her periods of full consciousness were brief and her burns, pink and suppurating beneath their dressings, terrible to look at. So it had been for the past ten days. He was spending all the time he could by her bedside, making only the briefest of appearances in his audience chamber. As he sat head bowed, his mind returned again and again to that night. In his opium-laced longing and confusion he had mistaken Jahanara for Mumtaz and tried to make love to her, his own daughter, a sin before God and man. He could not forgive himself and therefore how could he ever expect Jahanara to do so?

Dara and Murad often joined him in the sickroom. Soon Aurangzeb would arrive from Burhanpur and Shah

Shuja from Bengal. His family would be reunited again, but in what terrible circumstances. How could he admit to them what had really happened? Where was that aura of good fortune he had striven to preserve on his return to Agra after Mumtaz's death? . . . Yet it wasn't that fate had turned against him. He had cast her off through his own weakness, and even if she survived Jahanara's scars would remind him for ever how he had betrayed his daughter's trust. He was so lost in his thoughts that at first he didn't hear one of the *hakims* enter the room and he started when the man came close and whispered, 'Majesty?'

'What is it?'

'The foreigner says he knows of a European doctor who might be able to help Her Highness. I'm doubtful but I promised to pass his message to you.'

'What foreigner? . . . Do you mean Nicholas Ballantyne?'

'Yes, the Englishman.'

'Send him to me at once. If he knows anyone or anything that might help I want to hear about it.'

Half an hour later Nicholas stood before him on his terrace, just a few feet from where Jahanara's skirt had caught alight.

'Well? I understand you know a doctor who you think can help the princess?'

Nicholas nodded. 'He's a French physician now settled here in Agra. I met him many years ago – he helped cure my master Sir Thomas when he was racked by stomach fluxes – and I know he is highly skilled. I told him about the Lady Jahanara's burns and he described a remedy that he invented to help soldiers burned by flaming arrows or exploding cannon during battle. It combines medicines from Arabia, from his own country and from Hindustan and he swears that it reduces the pain. He also says that if applied soon enough it encourages the burnt skin to renew itself. He's outside. I brought him with me in case you wished to speak to him – I could interpret. He speaks little Persian.'

'Bring him in.'

The physician was a short, squat man and his dark belted robe was stretched tight across a rounded belly.

'What treatment d'you propose?'

Nicholas translated, then listened carefully to the physician's response before turning back to Shah Jahan. 'Before he can decide what to recommend, he says he must examine the patient. He asks whether it's true that her shoulders, back and legs have been severely burned?' Shah Jahan nodded. The doctor reflected a moment then spoke again. 'He says he's treated similar cases here in Agra where thatched roofs are so dry that a few sparks can ignite them. Last month just such a fire swept through a row of houses in the north of the city. Several women died because they feared to break purdah by leaving their homes but he was able to save a few ... As well as the salve I told you about he has invented other treatments, all of which can ease the patient's suffering.'

'He talks of easing pain. Can he restore the sufferer to health? My daughter's two attendants have died of their burns.'

'I know the answer to that, Majesty – I asked him myself. He says he will try but he can make no promises – at least not until he has seen the princess.'

'And the disfigurement? If my daughter does survive, can he lessen that?'

164

Nicholas consulted the physician. 'No, Majesty. He cannot obliterate the scarring that inevitably results from burns.'

'That is a lesser matter. Tell him that if he saves my daughter's life I'll give him anything he wants.'

After a further whispered exchange Nicholas replied, 'He asks how soon he can see her?'

'She is being cared for here in the imperial *haram*. Only in the most extreme circumstances are my own *hakims* allowed to enter. No foreign man has ever been admitted. Though such rules are foolish in desperate times like these, I must show some regard to them. I will allow the two of you to visit the *haram*, but my eunuchs will lead you with your heads covered until you reach my daughter's room.'

The Frenchman was saying something else and Nicholas lowered his head to catch the words. 'Majesty, he asks for complete control over everything the princess eats or drinks.'

'Tell him my daughter is barely conscious and that all that has passed her lips since the accident has been a concoction of water and opium to deaden her pain, especially when the dressings are changed.'

'The doctor insists she must eat as soon as she is able – mashed fruits, especially bananas – but in particular she must also be made to drink as much water as possible. Her body needs fluids.'

Half an hour later Nicholas put his hand on the shoulder of the French doctor, standing directly in front of him, as the *khawajasara* instructed. Then a eunuch – smooth-faced and willowy – arranged a piece of green brocade over both the foreigners' heads, twitching it into place until satisfied that neither would be able to see anything when they entered the *haram*. The brocade tickled the back of Nicholas's neck as at the *khawajasara's* command he and the doctor stepped slowly forward, the doctor's hand resting on the eunuch's shoulder.

'I was in a *haram* some years ago,' the Frenchman whispered, 'in the household of the Moghul Governor of Gujarat. One of his wives thought she had been poisoned. In truth, she had simply over-eaten and I recommended a purge. But I've never forgotten how difficult it was to take the woman's pulse. She had so many ropes of pearls wound round her arms that at first I couldn't find it.'

As the doctor chuckled, Nicholas heard doors thrown open and warnings shouted ahead that two foreigners were approaching and the *haram* inmates should keep out of sight. As he and the doctor shuffled forward, he felt soft carpets beneath his booted feet and smelled the spicy sweetness of frankincense. A few twists and turns and then he caught a rasping of hinges as more doors were opened. This wasn't how he had imagined entering the exotic, erotic world of the *haram*. Lurid stories of these sexual pleasure grounds had fascinated him ever since he'd arrived in India. Now, though, his thoughts returned to the injured, possibly dying, princess. Of all Shah Jahan's children, Jahanara and her brother Dara Shukoh were the ones he remembered most clearly from their childhood. Jahanara had especially enjoyed questioning him about customs in his own country – how women lived and how one had become its sole ruler.

Suddenly, Nicholas was blinking in soft candlelight as

the cloth was pulled from his head. He and the doctor were in a large room smelling of herbs and camphor. He looked around for Jahanara. All he could see were three serving women holding up a length of silk to screen something. It must be her sickbed.

'The doctor may approach Her Highness to examine her wounds,' announced the *khawajasara*, 'but the interpreter must remain on this side of the screen.' Nicholas watched as the doctor pulled his leather satchel from his shoulder and took out a pair of thick-lensed spectacles which he stuck on the end of his nose. Then, as one attendant raised the silk a little, he ducked beneath it. Nicholas paced up and down anxiously. After what seemed an age, but was probably no more than fifteen or twenty minutes, the doctor re-emerged.

'Well? Can you help her?' Nicholas asked.

'Her burns are serious and weeping – I have applied the salve and will leave two jars of it here for her attendants to use – but the injuries are not quite as bad as I feared. My guess is that she will live. Her pulse is regular and her breathing good, but her recovery will still take time and much dedicated care.'

'The emperor has promised you everything you need, any reward you desire.'

'I know. These great men think their wealth can buy them anything or anyone, but in this case the princess's youth and strength will be her greatest help, not me.'

• ➤ •

Jahanara re-read the verse before laying the ivory-bound book down on the coverlet. She had been curious to read poems written by Dara himself. How wonderful to open her eyes one day and find her brother by her bedside. When she had smiled, tears had pricked his eyes – whether tears of happiness that she was alive or of sorrow for her disfigurement she wasn't sure. Reaching for the small mirror she kept by her bed, she examined her face. The skin of her left cheek was scarred by a smooth, shiny red mark that broadened as it spread down her neck. What her back and left leg looked like she'd no idea – she was still too weak and stiff to twist to see – but she could guess.

At least the pain was gradually growing less and her mind was clearing, though that brought problems of its own. The memory of Shah Jahan's behaviour on the night of the fire was as fresh and sharp as if it had only been three days ago instead of six weeks ... her horror and revulsion as her father had grabbed her breast ... the strength of his grip ... the passionate look in his eyes. Her only thought had been of flight ... she recalled lashing out with some object and running from him but after that all was shadow and searing pain. As she had returned to longer periods of full consciousness, she had vague recollections of her father sitting by her bed and of hearing him and the *hakims* discussing her progress. At first, weak as she was, she hadn't realised what had happened to her, but from their conversation she had gradually pieced together that she had been badly burned because her muslin skirt had caught alight.

Once her recovery was beyond doubt, she had noticed that her father had ceased coming to her room alone. Someone – usually Dara, Murad or Roshanara – accompanied him. When sleep evaded her and she lay in the darkness, her mind returned again and again to that terrible night, seeking an explanation that she could reconcile with the love that, despite everything, she still felt for her father. How could he have been so lost to everything as to treat her, his daughter, like that?

Of course she'd spoken to no one about what had happened – not Satti al-Nisa, old and trusted confidante though she was, not her brothers, not Roshanara . . . Even her sister might not believe her, and, if she did, might not understand.

'How are you today, Jahanara? You look better!'

She hadn't heard Aurangzeb enter. He was carrying something concealed beneath a yellow cloth. She suppressed a smile – probably yet another gift. Her brothers seemed to be competing to keep her amused as if they thought her a sick child needing to be distracted by baubles. Yesterday, Shah Shuja had presented her with a necklace of coral and pearls from Bengal.

'Every day I feel an improvement.'

'Good. Look what I have for you.' Aurangzeb lifted the cloth to reveal a gold birdcage. Sitting on a perch of carved ivory was a dove with feathers of palest mauve and a collar set with amethysts.

'It's beautiful. Thank you.'

'What's this?' Aurangzeb picked up the book she'd been reading and flicking it open began to scan its pages.

'Some poems Dara's written. On his way to Surat he met a Sufi mystic whose teachings inspired him to write these verses. He's invited the Sufi to Agra so that they can talk further.'

'Why's Dara so interested? And just look what he's

written here: '*I rejoice that it is for every man to find God in his own way.*'

Aurangzeb's contemptuous tone surprised her. 'Isn't Dara right? Surely each of us has a duty to strive for spiritual knowledge ... spiritual peace ... in whatever way we can.'

'What about the holy mullahs and their writings? They are our conduits to God. Ignoring them and their judgements to pursue our own path is not only presumptuous and misguided – it's heretical.'

'Is it? Dara thinks some mullahs are obstacles on the road to enlightenment – they insist on interposing themselves between the people and God merely to preserve their own power. I agree with him.'

'That's dangerous nonsense.' Aurangzeb snapped the ivory covers of the book shut and tossed it back on to her bed. 'When your body and your mind are stronger you'll realise that.'

'Perhaps. Or maybe because I've been nearer to death than you, you'll accept that I may be nearer to understanding the true nature of existence. Don't be angry with Dara and me just because our beliefs aren't your own ...'

'I could never be angry with you. But since I've been back at court I've seen how arrogant Dara's become and how he disregards the views of others. He was bad enough as a child, always thinking he knew best and telling the rest of us what to do. He doesn't realise the bad example he's setting. Since I've been in the south, I've had time to observe the Muslim kingdoms like Golconda, Bijapur and Ahmednagar. To suppress and bind them into our

170

empire we must show our power – not only our military strength but our religious strength as followers and promoters of the true faith. One of the excuses for their rebellions against our father is that he is three-quarters Hindu and married a Shia Muslim . . .'

'Our father is the emperor. It's not for them to question his birth. As for our mother, Sunni or Shia, she was a devout Muslim, kind and good to all . . .' Jahanara's voice shook with anger. 'If we allow ourselves to be influenced by such narrow, bigoted talk not only do we defile her memory but we'll alienate the majority of our subjects.'

'I'm sorry. I didn't mean to agitate you . . . let's talk about something else.' Aurangzeb knelt by her bed. 'You told me when I first returned that a foreign doctor aided your recovery with a "miracle" ointment. Who was he?'

'A friend of Nicholas Ballantyne – he recommended him. He has remarkable powers – for an infidel,' she couldn't resist adding. A flash in Aurangzeb's dark eyes showed her little barb had found its mark. Good. Aurangzeb meant well but even if he was right that Dara could sometimes seem patronising he himself was growing narrow-minded and intolerant.

Two hours after Aurangzeb had left her, when her attendants were lighting the oil lamps in the niches around her room, Jahanara heard cries of 'The emperor approaches' and a few moments later Shah Jahan entered. He was alone. 'Leave us,' he told the elderly *hakim* sitting in the corner to keep watch over Jahanara. As the double doors closed behind the doctor, she felt suddenly nervous as the memory of what her father had tried to do returned in all its vividness. She wished someone else was in the room with them.

Instead of coming to her bedside Shah Jahan walked to an open casement and for a while stared out into the dusk. The only sound was the mournful shriek of a peacock roosting in a neem tree in the courtyard outside. Then, slowly, he turned to face her, but it was still some moments before finally he spoke and when he did his voice sounded hoarse. 'So many times I've been on the point of coming to beg your forgiveness or at least to ask for your understanding . . . I never realised I was a coward until I found I lacked the courage to do so. Now that I have come, it's so hard . . . my feelings overwhelm me and the words won't come . . .'

'No, please . . .' The bleak look on his face banished her fear of him. 'Let's not speak of that night . . . we must both try to forget it.' Jahanara sat up, wincing with a pain that was more mental than the physical result of the stretching of the not yet fully healed scars from her burns.

'You are too generous. You nearly died because of me . . . because I violated all the natural bonds between father and daughter. That is why I must speak . . . I can't bear to think you might ever look at me again the way you looked at me that night. I make no excuses, but I was confused by the opium I had taken to help me sleep. I was in another world . . . in my semi-conscious state I thought you were Mumtaz and had returned to me . . . I thought I was reaching out to her. I never meant to violate my own daughter . . . I didn't know it was you until it was too late and you were fleeing from me.'

'You thought I was my mother?'

'Yes. I'd been dreaming of her and confused my longings with reality. It will never happen again, I promise you. Not a drop of wine or grain of opium has passed my lips since your accident.'

'That at least makes me very happy.'

'But can you forgive me . . . not only for what I did but for the terrible consequences?' Shah Jahan bowed his head. 'I torment myself that just as your mother's death was my punishment for ordering the killing of my half-brothers, your injuries were my punishment for my actions towards you – an eternal reproach.'

Jahanara was silent for some time. She could see now how the incident had happened. It was not some vicious act by her father but the result of a grief he could neither control nor come to terms with. If she did not say she forgave him – and make herself mean it – the events of that night would corrode both of their souls, eating away at their relationship. Before the fire her greatest anxiety had been her father's withdrawal from the world. If she rejected him now he would isolate himself even more.

She composed her face into a smile and said simply, 'Yes, I forgive you.' Moments later she felt Shah Jahan tentatively take her hand. Using all her self-control she did not withdraw it, and not wishing to explore either of their emotions further said briskly, 'Don't let's ever talk of the night of the fire again – it can only bring pain to us both. Instead we should look to the future. Won't you send me some of your petitions for me to deal with, just as I used to?'

'I would be grateful for your help again.'

Seeing relief flood her father's countenance Jahanara added, 'As soon as I can walk properly again – the doctors tell me it won't be long – will you take me by barge down the river to visit my mother's tomb? I would like to see what progress there's been. You were not the only one to love her, Father. We all did.'

Her willingness to include him in her family once more brought a tear to Shah Jahan's eye as he responded, 'We will all go. It's been a long time – far too long – since our family was together.'

Part II

'Sharper than a serpent's tooth . . .'
King Lear, Act 1, Scene 4

Chapter 11

As Shah Jahan approached through the scented gardens, the white marble mausoleum beneath its teardrop dome seemed to float against the backdrop of the pinkening sky. Its sheer perfection still made him catch his breath. Earlier, one of his court poets had presented him with verses to commemorate today, the sixteenth *urs*, the anniversary, of Mumtaz's death.

> *The back of the earth-supporting bull sways to its belly,*
> *Reduced to a footprint from carrying such a burden.*
> *The eye can mistake it for a cloud.*
> *Light sparkles from within its pure stones*
> *Like wine within a crystal*
> *When reflections from the stars fall on its marble,*
> *The entire edifice resembles a festival of lamps.*

The poet had caught both the awesome size and the spectral radiance of Mumtaz's final resting place. Four years ago, on the twelfth anniversary of her death, her body had been taken from her temporary grave, carried into the crypt and laid in a white marble sarcophagus inlaid with jewelled flowers, their curving fronds suggesting vitality and renewal as if they were truly growing over the marble. A simple epitaph inlaid in plain black marble told the onlooker that here was THE ILLUMINED TOMB OF ARJUMAND BANU BEGAM, ENTITLED MUMTAZ MAHAL. He had spent an hour alone in the crypt before mounting the stone steps to join his family and courtiers in public mourning for his dead empress, just as he was about to do now.

If he had believed those who had consoled him that the passing of time would blunt his pain, he would have been disappointed. Although the pressures of ruling might preoccupy him for a time, immediately afterwards his mind returned to his loss. His emotions were as raw as on the first *urs* to be held in the mausoleum. Yet not to feel loss would mean he was forgetting Mumtaz, something he could never do ... He could at least find comfort in what he had created. His love and loss could not have found more perfect expression.

Even now the tomb was not quite finished. Craftsmen were still putting the final touches to the pavilions of finely carved red sandstone set into the boundary walls where musicians would play, and he had ordered further embellishments to the mosque and guesthouse. Only last month, his comptroller of revenues had reported that the costs of building the tomb had reached fifty *lakhs* of rupees. He had hinted that such great expense might soon become a drain on the imperial treasury, but Shah Jahan had cut him short – the Moghul empire was wealthy and powerful enough for any project he wished to pursue including the bejewelled Taj Mahal, as people had begun to call the tomb from a shortening of 'Mumtaz Mahal'.

What a legacy he, Shah Jahan, would bequeath to future generations ... what majesty his buildings would convey, whether the Taj Mahal, his monument to his personal loss, or his new city of Shahjahanabad in Delhi, a symbol of his imperial power. History would not easily forget his reign. He had extended the Moghul empire's boundaries farther south than ever before and who knew what further expansion he and his descendants might achieve to the north?

That thought made him glance over his shoulder at his four sons – all dressed like him in mourning white and matching their pace to the sombre beat of a single kettledrum from the gatehouse as they followed him, walking beside the central north–south water channel with its softly bubbling marble fountains. As he neared the mausoleum, he heard the voices of his dark-robed mullahs as they prayed for the repose of Mumtaz's soul in the gardens of Paradise. Reaching the sandstone platform, he led the way up the steps on to the smaller marble plinth and into the tomb's central octagonal chamber. Silk wall hangings gleamed in the light of golden chandeliers and smouldering frankincense crystals spiced the air.

Shah Jahan took his place before the latticed screen of polished jasper. Carved from a single block of stone to resemble filigree and inlaid with gems, it veiled the white marble cenotaph that was an exact copy of the sarcophagus in which Mumtaz lay in the crypt below and over which was spread a sheet of perfectly matched Arabian pearls.

The ritual of commemoration enveloped him, but when the formal prayers were over and he was left once more to his memories and the sharp pangs of grief they evoked, he felt an intense and urgent need to be alone. Leaving the tomb, he walked swiftly back towards the southern gateway whose white marble *chattris* stood out pale in the moonlight. He did not pause as the guards stood to attention but continued down to the riverbank where his barge was moored. The crew, who had not been expecting the emperor so soon, ran to lower the gilded gangplank. 'Take me to the gardens opposite,' he commanded.

While Mumtaz's tomb had still been only half built, he had had his gardeners create him a *mahtab bagh*, a moonlight garden, planted with heavily scented night-flowering shrubs, on land directly across the Jumna from the Taj Mahal where his great-great-grandfather Babur had once laid out a pleasure ground. Now it was his private retreat where he could walk and think as he contemplated the mausoleum.

Although the barge swayed a little in the Jumna's swirling current, Shah Jahan remained standing. As soon as the boatman nosed the prow on to the bank, he stepped ashore without waiting for the gangplank and made his way into the garden to a small marble pavilion overlooking the river. Sitting down, he leaned his back against one of the pillars and closed his eyes. The only sound was the gentle lapping of the water.

For a while his only thoughts were of Mumtaz. He would never forget the look on her face that night as she realised she was dying – or her courage in those final moments they had shared together ... It sometimes seemed to him that only then, at the moment of parting, had he truly and fully understood the woman he had loved so intensely. In all their years of marriage he had taken her unconditional love for granted – drawing strength from it in the darkest of times. Her beauty and sweet temperament had sustained him like meat and drink, but had he really appreciated her selflessness and fortitude? Her final thoughts had been for him and their children. And there, perhaps, he was failing her. She had been the beating heart of their family ... the one to whom their children revealed their thoughts and feelings. Empathy had come naturally to her. Why couldn't he be the same? Sometimes he felt his children were strangers to him. Was it because his relations with his own father had become so strained? Or was the reason simply that as emperor he must necessarily become distant and preoccupied with the affairs of the empire, a father and a figurehead to his people with less time for his own offspring?

Times of crisis had united the family, of course. During the long, anxious months of Jahanara's recovery from the fire, he had drawn comfort from the presence of his children. Yet over the years since then they had seldom all been together – not even at the annual *urs* for Mumtaz. As a result, how well did he really know some of them, especially his sons? Thirty-two-year-old Dara was his frequent companion, seldom absent from court, but what about Shah Shuja, a mere fifteen months younger? He had come to Agra for the *urs* but was clearly eager to return to his governorship of Bengal. If his behaviour in Agra these past weeks was anything to go by, it was probably because he enjoyed the freedom of being far from court – and his father – rather than because he relished responsibility or nurtured ambitions for the betterment of his province. To Shah Jahan's critical paternal eye he remained indolent and pleasure-seeking. Yet weren't those the usual vices that afflicted wealthy high-born young men, although they had not been his own?

Shah Jahan frowned. His third son was a greater puzzle, even if no one could accuse him of frivolity. Aurangzeb, now nearly thirty, had returned from the Deccan even more intense and self-contained, seldom sharing his thoughts although Shah Jahan suspected he had plenty. He spent hours reading or discussing religious points with members of the *ulama*, and praying. He ate and drank sparingly, never touching alcohol, and spending his energies honing his military skills. Such an austere, disciplined life, though hard to criticise, seemed almost unnatural in a young man. It was a pity Aurangzeb didn't have more of Dara's engaging manner. Both were interested in religion and philosophy but while Dara was open and curious – ever ready to debate ideas with those who disagreed with him and even to change his opinions – Aurangzeb seemed to prefer the company of those whose stern view of the world mirrored his own.

His son's detachment – coldness even – was disconcerting. Though he found it easy to talk to Dara he never knew quite what to say to the taciturn, serious-minded Aurangzeb. Perhaps it was because he saw less of him; Aurangzeb was as eager as Shah Shuja – though probably for very different reasons – to leave Agra as soon as possible. Shah Jahan had agreed he could go. Yet on reflection it might be better for him to remain at court a while longer and learn the art of pleasing others that seemed to come more naturally to his eldest brother.

Suddenly Shah Jahan heard approaching footsteps and opened his eyes. 'Who's there?'

'Only me, Father.' He heard Jahanara's voice, then saw her pale figure emerge from the darkness and further behind her, some soldiers. 'I saw you leave the tomb through the women's screen. I was worried about you.'

'Did you come alone?'

'Roshanara offered to accompany me but I told her there was no need. I crossed with some of my attendants and some of your guards.'

'Ask them to withdraw to a distance. Please ...' he added, suspecting she was about to remonstrate with him.

'But you will let me stay with you, won't you?'

Shah Jahan hesitated, then nodded. Jahanara hurried back down the path to speak to her escort, then returned and sat down.

'I was just thinking about you and your brothers and sisters ... How things have changed since your mother died.'

'We were so young then – Dara and I barely grown up, the rest just children.'

'And now you are men and women and I'm getting older. When I was young time seemed to stretch out for ever – a summer was a lifetime. Now the seasons are always on the turn. Even the fruits on these trees I had planted here seem to form, ripen and fall in the blink of an eye.'

Jahanara said nothing, but drew her shawl a little closer around her as a cool breeze blew from the river.

'Perhaps it's time I decided where I should be buried,' Shah Jahan continued.

'Father, please . . .'

'Why not talk about it? Death claims us all. I've often thought of building a tomb identical to your mother's here in this moonlight garden but of black marble, not white. I've even sometimes contemplated a silver bridge to connect the two across the Jumna so that at night my soul could rise up and cross the bridge to be with her . . . But perhaps that would be too fantastical even for a Moghul emperor.'

Jahanara looked at him, wondering whether he was serious. It was sometimes hard to tell these days. At times he was still the pragmatic, decisive, dominating figure she remembered from her childhood, at others a whimsical melancholy seemed to cloud his mind. She had long ago found it in her heart truly to forgive – if not entirely forget – the incident in which she had been burned and over the years they had grown closer again. Now as she watched him, visibly ageing as well as mentally troubled, her eyes filled with tears. If only he could become his true self again.

• ◆ •

'I need your opinion, Father. I think my builders have done a good job but there is still time to make changes.'

'I'll come this afternoon. You should too, Aurangzeb.

It'll be your last chance to see Dara's new mansion before you return to the Deccan.'

'I'd prefer to remain here in the fort. Buildings don't interest me. Anyway, I promised to visit Roshanara today.'

'You can do that later. I wish you to accompany myself and Dara.' Shah Jahan's tone was sharper than he'd intended, but as so often these days Aurangzeb was exasperating him. 'Now leave me, both of you. I have matters to attend to.'

Two hours later, Shah Jahan rode along the banks of the Jumna, Dara and Aurangzeb on either side of him and a small escort behind. Though still dusty and raw-looking, Dara's new sandstone mansion glowed handsome in the warm March sunshine. As they dismounted in the courtyard, Dara's yellow and gold liveried attendants ran forward to take their reins. Shah Jahan looked around with interest as Dara led them through the network of airy rooms and terraces on the ground floor and then up to the flat roof in the centre of which stood a domed *chattri*. 'So Nadira and her women can catch the evening breezes,' Dara explained.

Shah Jahan nodded. 'Your builders have done well.' As they reached the ground floor again he turned to Aurangzeb. 'What do you think?'

'It's very fine, but I imagine cost wasn't an issue.'

Dara looked surprised. 'As I told you, Father gave me the land and the money to build this new palace some while ago to mark the birth of my second son Sipihr.'

'If our tour is complete, with your leave I would like to return to the fort,' Aurangzeb addressed his father. A report arrived this morning about tax gathering problems south of Burhanpur that I haven't finished reading.'

It was Dara who answered. 'The tour's not quite over. You haven't seen my underground chamber. I've had it lined with giant mirrors imported from Aleppo and my architect has designed a series of wind tunnels – such as they have in Persia – to keep it cool in summer. Father, I'd rather show it to you when it's nearer completion – the decoration's not finished yet and it's still dusty and dirty – but I'd like Aurangzeb to see it before he leaves Agra.'

Shah Jahan nodded and was already turning away when he heard Aurangzeb reply in a strange tone, 'No, I'd rather not.'

'Aurangzeb.' Shah Jahan looked back towards his sons. 'Surely your business from the Deccan can wait a few moments.'

Aurangzeb was silent for a little, then replied, 'No. As I said, I don't want to see the underground room and must ask to be excused.'

Shah Jahan stared, unable to believe his ears. Aurangzeb's expression was set and determined. What on earth was the matter with him? Was it pique that he had given Dara such a generous present? If so, it was unfair. He was open-handed to all his sons. He wasn't in the mood for childishness. 'I wish you to visit the chamber as your brother requests.'

'Father, please think before you order me or I will have to disobey you.'

Shah Jahan's temper was rising. 'I don't understand your behaviour. You are being discourteous to your brother and insolent to me. I am no longer asking you to do as Dara asks as your father, I am ordering you as your emperor.'

186

'Then, as your subject, I refuse!'

Shah Jahan strode over and grabbed his son by his thickly muscled shoulders. 'What's the matter with you? Do as I say or I'll have you punished!'

'Perhaps, but at least I'll keep my life. I've heard about this room — that only one door leads in and out. I don't understand its purpose — unless it is a trap.'

Dara gasped. 'What are you suggesting? That I plan to murder you?'

'How can I be sure that you don't?'

Shah Jahan pushed Aurangzeb away from him. 'If you are accusing your brother of wanting to kill you, you're insane. I won't force you to go down to the chamber but I want you out of my sight immediately.' Walking out into the courtyard where their horses were tethered, he shouted to the captain of his escort, 'Take half your guards and escort Prince Aurangzeb back to the fort at once. The rest of you wait here.' As the enormity of his son's behaviour hit him, Shah Jahan struggled to keep his voice low as he re-entered the house. He had no wish to be overheard by the soldiers outside. 'Aurangzeb, you will return to your quarters in the Agra fort immediately.'

'Father, I . . .'

'Silence. I've no interest in your excuses. Just go!' Shah Jahan turned his back as his son walked quickly out into the sunlit courtyard. Soon came the sound of hoof beats. Shah Jahan realised he was shaking with anger. Some troublemaker must have seeded in Aurangzeb's mind the idea that Dara wanted him dead — his obstinate expression, the utter determination in his voice had seemed the result of genuine conviction. Otherwise why make allegations that he must have known would bring trouble upon him? Shah Jahan stood a while longer, caught between bafflement and rage. Glancing at Dara, he saw that his son's handsome face was averted as if not wishing to meet his eye.

• ◆ •

'Aurangzeb, I have a right to an explanation.' Shah Jahan's anger hadn't abated during the hour it had taken to return to the Agra fort and then make his way to his son's apartments. It would have been better to wait until he was in a cooler frame of mind, but he couldn't rest until he knew the reason for his third son's extraordinary behaviour.

'I've no more to say than I said at the time.' Aurangzeb's expression was unflinching.

'You made it clear that you suspected Dara's motives in inviting you to his subterranean room.'

Aurangzeb nodded but said nothing.

'Why?' Shah Jahan shouted. 'Answer me!'

'Even if I tell you, you won't believe me. Dara has poisoned your mind against me.'

'Aurangzeb – do not play games with me.'

His son hesitated, then shrugged. 'Very well, since you insist . . . Ever since my return to Agra I've noticed how Dara has changed. He was never modest but now he struts around the court like a peacock. While Shah Shuja and I have been trying to serve you in distant parts of the empire, he has remained here, pampered and preening . . .'

'So that's what all this is about – you're simply jealous!'

For the first time Aurangzeb smiled. 'Jealous? No. I despise Dara. He is all show and no substance. I'd suspected it for years. All he cares about is the image he presents. He acts as if he was already your acknowledged heir and we his brothers are of no account. He should take care how far he tries our loyalty.'

'Be very careful what you say, Aurangzeb . . .'

'You demanded to know my true thoughts and feelings. It's not my fault if you don't like what you hear. As I said, Dara is arrogant and ambitious . . .'

'But if, as you claim, he thinks his brothers unimportant, why should he contemplate killing you?'

'He maintains to the outside world that he is your acknowledged favourite, basking in your approval with no fears for his position. Secretly, though, he is weak enough on the inside to fear that one day one of us may challenge him. Hasn't that always been our way, "throne or coffin" as they called it in the old days? You too had to fight for the throne and in so doing you disposed of two of your half-brothers. I respect you the more for it.'

Shah Jahan was silent, anger and guilt contending within him. Eventually, keeping his voice level with an effort, he said, 'That was different. I had no choice. I only did what I did because otherwise my half-brothers would have killed me – and indeed you – to rid themselves of potential rivals. But such times are long gone. I'll not tolerate such barbaric notions within my family. All my sons are full brothers, brought up by a caring father and mother to love one another – not the offspring of rival wives and concubines scheming against each other.'

'You think because we are full brothers that will unite us? Ask Dara if that's what he believes! Have you forgotten Cain and Abel? Fraternal rivalries are a part of fallen man.'

'You've still given me no evidence that Dara wants to hurt you – that your fears are anything but fantasy . . .'

'No, far from it. As I was saying, Dara suspects that when the time comes one of his brothers may challenge him for the throne. Shah Shuja is idle at heart even if he enjoys power and has his own ambitions. Murad is young and unproven. The one Dara should most fear at present is me and I'm sure he does. He knows I'm as able as he – perhaps more so. I could tell he didn't welcome my return to court from the Deccan. It suits his purpose better that I – and if it comes to it Shah Shuja – should be far away from the centre of influence and from you. And it would suit him best of all if I were permanently out of the way. He knows that I disapprove of his ideas – his passion for Sufi mysticism, his denigration of our religious traditions. Only a week ago one of our mullahs warned me that Dara had said that the empire had no need of bigots like me . . .'

Shah Jahan held up his hand, his head so full of Aurangzeb's assertions and accusations that he hardly knew where to begin. 'You're wrong. It's natural that you and Dara should have your differences, even your rivalries. You are young men close together in age. But I cannot tolerate your unfounded suspicions, your wild accusations. Who is this mullah who has tried to set you against your brother?'

'I cannot tell you. He spoke to me in confidence and I will never reveal his name.'

'I have had enough of your arrogance and your disobedience . . . of your assertions of what you will or will not do, as if you – not I – were emperor. You disobeyed my order to visit Dara's underground chamber and now you tell me you will not give me a name I ask for.' Shah Jahan began striding up and down the room. 'You accuse Dara of high-handedness and ambition but you're the one who's consumed by them – and by jealousy of your brother, even if you try to deny it.'

'Perhaps I am jealous, though not for the reasons you think. Even when Dara and I were children given up by you as hostages to Mehrunissa, I knew you loved him more. I can still remember what happened when you came to rescue us from the dungeons of the Lahore palace . . . how you called out Dara's name first, not mine – how saving him was your main concern.'

'That's madness. I loved both of you – still love you. You are my son just as much as Dara.' Shah Jahan stared nonplussed at his son.

'You say that, but it isn't true. If it were, you'd have sent Dara away to govern a province just as you did Shah Shuja and me. Instead you keep him here by your side at court like a mother hen with a favourite chick. What has he ever done? Has he fought as I have, risking his life for the empire? No! Because in your eyes his life is too precious to be hazarded. Instead he lives a soft life in his palace on the Jumna, as spoiled and pampered and indulged as any woman in his *haram*.'

'Silence! I can listen to no more of this. Everything you accuse me – or Dara – of is fantasy. But it is dangerous fantasy. What would happen if it leaked out to the court that two of the emperor's sons were locked in rivalry – that one was even planning to murder the other? Just think what capital our enemies within and beyond our borders could make of it . . . how much mischief they could stir. I tell you, Aurangzeb, this one-sided feud with your brother must cease here. So must your accusations against me.' Shah Jahan stopped pacing and turned to look at his son.

Aurangzeb, though, said nothing, his face was set in that expression Shah Jahan knew only too well. Exasperation with his son's crazy views mingled with concern that he should think himself so unloved, so unappreciated, yet for the sake of his family and his empire he must show strength, not weakness, and put a stop to this behaviour now, or where might it not lead? 'I have made my decision. Until I can be certain that you have returned to a more rational way of thinking, I cannot allow you to continue as my viceroy in the Deccan.'

For the first time since their meeting had begun, Shah Jahan saw that his words had struck home. Aurangzeb seemed visibly to recoil. 'Father . . .'

'No. I haven't finished. You will remain in the Agra fort indefinitely. I can't risk having you far from my sight in your present frame of mind. I hope that in the months to come you will reflect on your foolish behaviour and your unjust accusations. You have shocked and disappointed me more than you realise.'

Back in his own apartments, Shah Jahan sat for a while, still deep in thought. The incident had helped him reach a decision. It was time that he signalled to his family and the wider world which of his sons he wished to succeed him and end all doubt – or misplaced hope – that any of his younger sons might have. They could reconcile themselves to their disappointment while he still lived and could restrain them from any conflict.

Two days later, as he took his place in the Hall of Public Audience upon his glittering peacock throne, he felt proud. What other ruler could have created such magnificence? His courtiers and commanders, arranged before him in order of precedence, were dressed in their finest clothes and jewels, just as he had instructed. Ashok Singh was resplendent in orange silk robes and a diamond-hilted dagger in his sash. So it should be for one of the most significant proclamations of his reign. Glancing to where Dara was standing, flanked by Shah Shuja and Murad, he raised his hands to command attention, though the silence in the many-pillared hall was already absolute.

'I have summoned you here today to honour my beloved eldest son, Dara Shukoh, before my court. I hereby award him the estates of Hissar Firoza and the right to pitch the scarlet tent.' Even before he had finished speaking he saw the quickly exchanged glances. Everyone knew what he meant – he had as good as declared Dara heir to the Moghul throne. It wouldn't take Aurangzeb, still confined in his apartments, long to hear the news and understand its implications. Perhaps, at last, Aurangzeb would see the world as it really was and understand that the throne would never be his. He should have acted faster to dispel false hopes and prevent the souring of fraternal love but, God willing, he was in time. Aurangzeb would reflect on his folly and come to accept that he would never have been his father's choice while Dara lived. He would also realise that Dara would have had no need to dispose of him – that he had never been a rival – though that would be hard for a proud man like Aurangzeb to stomach.

Chapter 12

'Father, I must ask you something ...'

'What is it, Jahanara? There's nothing wrong, is there? Your health ...?'

Ever since receiving her message Shah Jahan had been wondering what had prompted her request that he visit her in her mansion when nearly every day she travelled by palanquin to the fort.

'I'm fine, Father. It's not about me, it's about Aurangzeb.'

'So he's asked you to intercede for him, has he?'

'No. He has no idea that I'm doing so. But when I see something so amiss in our family I can't ignore it. Forgive me, Father, but perhaps I notice things you don't.'

The rebuke, gentle though it was, hurt. 'I see clearly enough. Aurangzeb only has himself to blame. I thought he was a man, but he didn't behave like one.'

'I agree ... and I think Aurangzeb himself understands that now. I've spent a lot of time with him, listening to his outpourings and trying to make him see reason. He accepts that his accusations were foolish and wants only to regain your favour. He begs you to allow him to return to the Deccan . . .'

'I've found an excellent replacement and have no need of him.'

'Father – when I was ill and you were keeping watch by my bedside I sometimes heard you promise God that you'd do anything so long as I survived. God indeed returned me to life, and it's I – not He – who now asks this favour of you.'

'Jahanara . . .'

'Please! Aurangzeb is unhappy. Forgive him, as you once asked me to forgive you. Release him from his confinement.'

'What then?'

'Find him some new appointment. If not in the Deccan, then somewhere else where he can use his talents and his energy instead of wasting them and growing bitter. He won't disappoint you, Father, and that's not just my opinion. I've talked to Dara. Although at first he was angry with Aurangzeb – and offended by his preposterous claims – he says the dispute was not of his making and he is prepared to overlook what happened and see Aurangzeb reinstated if he is contrite.'

'Why does Aurangzeb dislike Dara so much? Is it simple jealousy?'

'Perhaps – but it's not all Aurangzeb's fault. As long ago as when I was recovering from my burns I saw tensions building between them. Now Dara is so confident in his own abilities and in your favour that even to me he can seem patronising – though unintentionally, I'm sure. Aurangzeb is devoid of humour where he himself is concerned and swift to detect a slight – intended or not – particularly from Dara. Rivalry is a part of it, of course.'

'Some rivalry is natural, I know, but Aurangzeb spoke as if he hated Dara. What has his brother done to offend him so deeply?'

Jahanara hesitated, then said, 'There's the religious divide between them, of course.'

'Religious? I know that Dara is interested in Sufi teachings and Aurangzeb spends much time with the mullahs but I've never imagined religion to be a serious source of conflict between them.'

'You're wrong. You know what Dara's like – tolerant and so curious about everything . . . Aurangzeb is drawn to the certainties of our Sunni scholars and mullahs and believes that deviating from their orthodoxy is heresy. He believes Dara's philosophising is heretical and a danger to our rule. I've often heard him say that the problems of the Moghul empire are because we have fallen away from the true and strict Muslim path of righteousness. He blames the Hindus and the Shias in your employ for the corruption that he believes is tainting our administration. He told me that while he was in the Deccan he found numerous instances of usury and injustice perpetrated by our Hindu subjects – whole villages exploited as slaves by landowners who keep them in poverty and debt.'

'It is not religion but character that counts in such matters. If he knew of crimes, it was his duty as my viceroy to put things right.'

'Of course, and he says that is what he tried to do. But

he argues that the rottenness goes to the very heart of government. Encouraged by the more extreme mullahs, he would like every Hindu – "infidels" as he calls them – thrown from high office.'

'Then he is a fool. My grandfather understood that the way to bind our empire together and make it prosper was to be fair to all its subjects – Hindus such as Ashok Singh as well as Muslims. As you yourself once reminded me, Hindus are among my most trusted and loyal courtiers and generals, and royal Rajput blood runs in our veins.'

'That's what Dara says, and that's why they argue. The last time, only a day or two before the visit to Dara's mansion, they nearly came to blows when Aurangzeb said we should prohibit the building of more Hindu temples.'

'Perhaps they both forget that I am still emperor and that it's for me to decide who holds high office in my empire and who doesn't and what religious buildings we permit.'

'I didn't mean to make you angry. I just wanted to explain one of the things that has gone wrong between my brothers.'

'Nothing you've said explains why Aurangzeb should suspect Dara of seeking to murder him.'

'Aurangzeb knows now that he was being absurd. But look at things from his point of view. Dara isn't always tactful. Indeed since they were children he's enjoyed baiting Aurangzeb. Now that they are men he knows just where to direct his barbs so that Aurangzeb has begun to think Dara his enemy and to harbour exaggerated suspicions, seeing malice in Dara's every action . . . But he says that is over now and that he was wrong about the underground room and wants to regain your good opinion. I believe him.'

Shah Jahan was silent. Was she right? Since the incident in Dara's mansion, Aurangzeb had been living quietly in the fort. Although he'd had a discreet watch kept there'd been nothing suspicious. Not a hint of sedition or even resentment at Dara's elevation to emperor-in-waiting in all but name. Aurangzeb was either a good dissimulator or else genuinely contrite.

'Please, Father. Show him you forgive him and allow him the chance to prove his worth. At least allow him to attend your council meetings like Dara and Murad. By excluding Aurangzeb you slight him in the eyes of the court. He is, as we both know, a proud man and, although he would never show it to you, it hurts him.'

'It wasn't my intention to humiliate him but to teach him a lesson about the strife behaviour such as his could cause. If, as you suggest, he has learned it, I will allow him to come to the council. It all depends on him. If he behaves himself I may even find a fresh position for him. If not, he will not find me so lenient again . . .'

• ◆ •

Four months later, as servants lit the evening candles in the Hall of Private Audience, Shah Jahan prepared to address his counsellors, Dara, Aurangzeb and Murad among them. In recent weeks Aurangzeb had listened gravely to the discussions but had said little himself except on several occasions to agree almost fulsomely with points made by Dara as the counsellors debated taxes or the suppression of rebellious minor vassals or improvements to the great trunk road that bound the empire together, north to south. Perhaps the animosity between the brothers really was over. Shah Jahan hoped so. The opportunity that had suddenly presented itself to his dynasty might never occur again – at least not in his lifetime – and he couldn't let foolish arguments between his sons distract him or his senior commanders, nor would he allow them to do so.

Raising his head, he began. 'This is no ordinary meeting of my council but a council of war. As my governors in Kabul and Badakhshan have been reporting these past weeks, the Uzbek tribes beyond the Oxus river are at each other's throats and anarchy rules their lands. Their chaos is our opportunity.'

'What do you mean, Majesty?' asked Ashok Singh, immaculate as ever in a gold brocade tunic.

'I mean that the Uzbeks are in no position to defend themselves. If we act quickly, we can advance north and seize Balkh. The city is a valuable trading post and control of it would greatly benefit our merchants in Kabul. But Balkh would only be a stepping stone. Once in Balkh, we can cross the Oxus and take Samarkand just a hundred and seventy miles beyond the river. The golden city can be ours if we grasp the opportunity that fate offers . . .'

Shah Jahan paused and looked at the faces around him, some expressing enthusiasm, some doubt, but most simply stunned. He'd told no one of his decision, not even Dara. It was the fulfilment of a long-nurtured ambition. Often when unable to sleep, he'd lain in the darkness listening to an attendant reading from his great-great-grandfather's diaries. He had loved the *Baburnama* ever since he was a boy – Babur's frank depiction of his years as a young raider prince in quest of a throne, never losing faith however desperate his circumstances, however great the danger, had inspired him. But one thing above all had resonated – Babur's determination to rule Samarkand, a city he seized not once but three times during his turbulent life. When the reports of the Uzbek disturbances had arrived he had determined to act.

'You look surprised,' he went on. 'You forget that before the Moghuls came into Hindustan we ruled beyond the Oxus. My ancestor Timur made Samarkand his capital and my great-great-grandfather Babur also captured it. The Moghuls have inalienable ancestral rights to those lands.'

'But Babur couldn't hold Samarkand, however hard he tried. Ultimately the Uzbeks defeated him,' said Dara.

'That was because he was outnumbered. He didn't have the resources of a great empire behind him, as I have. Also he faced an enemy united under a great Uzbek warlord, Shaibani Khan. At the moment the Uzbeks have no such leader.'

'I understand what you're saying, Father,' put in Aurangzeb. 'It's our destiny to reclaim our birthright across the Oxus. And if we succeed, we'll rule from Samarkand to beyond the Deccan – something not even Timur managed.'

Shah Jahan nodded. Aurangzeb was the only man in the room who looked as if he truly understood what he was proposing and was excited by it, and that disappointed him. Perhaps the rest were still adjusting to the idea.

'You're sure the reports are correct, Father?' Dara was frowning a little. 'Can we be certain the Uzbeks are fighting each other to the extent we've been told? And even if they are, won't they put their differences aside and unite to resist a foreign invader?'

'I trust the reports of my officials. One describes a massacre by one Uzbek clan of another when at least five thousand people were killed, women and children as well as men. Uzbek blood feuds run deep. They should be too intent on avenging themselves on one another to pay much attention to us until it's too late. But of course the situation might change. That's why we must act now.'

'You mentioned resources, Majesty. How many troops would you send north?' asked Ashok Singh. 'We would need a large and well-supplied army. Conditions in the mountains are tough, and the weather is extreme.'

'We'll debate the details later but I suggest at least fifty thousand horsemen and ten thousand musketeers with cannon and infantry to match to take Balkh, then more if necessary to cross the Oxus and move on Samarkand. It depends on the strength of the Uzbek resistance.'

'But such a vast army will take time to raise. Remember how many of our governors are saying they need longer to assemble troops than in the past . . . that our nobles grow ever laxer in maintaining standing armies for imperial use,' Dara persisted.

Dara shouldn't be so cautious or so questioning, Shah Jahan thought. 'I know, but any noble who is slow to send troops will be punished. Also, I've decided to employ foreign mercenaries. I have already put the Englishman Nicholas Ballantyne in charge of recruiting three thousand of them.'

'Who will lead the army?' asked Ashok Singh, posing the question that had most troubled Shah Jahan.

Towards the back of the room, Shah Jahan saw Aurangzeb stand and look towards him. He had proved a capable and decisive commander in the Deccan and was the obvious choice, as he himself must know. Dara had had little direct experience of fighting, Shah Shuja was away in Bengal and would take too long to recall, while Murad was young and untried. He had sat up deep into the night pondering whether he should indeed give Aurangzeb the command. He had very nearly decided to – in most ways it would be the logical decision – but he had not been able entirely to dismiss memories of his son's irrational and unpredictable behaviour from his mind. The more he had thought about it the more worried he had become. Could he take the risk of Aurangzeb's suddenly deviating from his orders because of some obsession, or indeed of his either imagining or provoking dissent among his senior officers? As dawn had seeped into his room he had decided that Aurangzeb must wait a little longer for fresh responsibilities.

'I have decided to give the command of my armies to Prince Murad.' There were gasps of surprise and a look of pure amazement flashed across Murad's face. 'I know this is your first major campaign, Murad, but it's time you learned the art of warfare and I know you won't disappoint me. To advise you and to take day-to-day management of the troops I am appointing you, Ashok Singh, who have proved your courage – and your military skill – time and again since we fought together in the Deccan all those years ago. My son can have no better mentor.'

'But Father . . .' Aurangzeb took a step forward. 'You should send me. Haven't I just shown I alone understand your ambition? Haven't I demonstrated to you what I'm capable of as a leader of armies ever since my first campaign against the Raja of Orchha? Did I yield a single patch of scrubby land in the Deccan? Haven't I made the rulers of Bijapur and Golconda fear me on the battlefield and grovel in their eagerness to secure a treaty with the Moghuls? Let me go to Balkh and you'll see how quickly its walls tumble beneath the onslaught of our cannon . . .'

'No, Aurangzeb. I've made my decision.'

'It's the wrong one and you'll regret it.'

Shah Jahan heard sharp intakes of breath all around the hall. This was the very insubordination he had feared. He had been right in deciding not to send Aurangzeb and immediately took a further decision – unpremeditated but one his son had just brought upon himself. 'I repeat that my mind is made up. In any case, I've decided on another appointment for you. I'd not intended to announce it today but I'm sending you to Gujarat. My governor there is elderly and ill and you will replace him. One of your tasks will be to see how well the English are keeping their promise to protect our merchant vessels and pilgrim fleets from pirates.'

'Gujarat?' For a moment Aurangzeb said nothing more but stared straight ahead. Like most of the other counsellors, Dara was looking at the carpet, as if wishing to avoid anyone's eyes, while Murad was glancing between his father and Aurangzeb and back again. 'If you insist, Father, I will of course go to Gujarat,' Aurangzeb said at last, the fire in his eyes belying the meekness of his words.

'Good. You will depart within the next few days. Now let us turn our attention back to details of the Balkh campaign – I am determined to send my army well equipped and provisioned and we have little time to lose.'

Chapter 13

'You are the only person I can turn to now. You've been loyal to us in dangerous times as well as more prosperous ones.' Jahanara could still scarcely believe that she had asked Nicholas Ballantyne to visit her in the courtyard of her palace on the banks of the Jumna, but many hours of careful thought had convinced her she must. 'Forgive me. You must be thirsty.' Turning to an attendant, she said, 'Fetch some iced sherbet, please,' before gesturing to Nicholas to sit opposite her on cushions piled beneath a canopy to protect against the afternoon sun.

'How can I help, Highness?'

'In a few days' time my father's armies depart for the north and you will go with them.'

'Yes. To lead the foreign mercenaries.' Nicholas's expression betrayed his puzzlement.

'Can I be frank? I am worried about Murad. This is my brother's first important campaign. He's had no experience of command or real training for it. I believe my father has made a grave error in appointing him, though I cannot say so.'

'Ashok Singh has experience of the north. He quelled the tribes in the hills around Kabul some years ago. He will guide the prince.'

'He will try, but you don't know Murad. He was only an infant when my father became emperor and still very young when our mother died. He's grown up in the *haram*, spoiled and indulged for his good looks and high spirits. He is no fool but he's used to having his own way and can be impulsive ... headstrong even if the mood takes him. My father doesn't see that side of him. Murad is in awe of him – ever respectful and obedient in his presence – but I know his real nature. Once Murad is far from court, power may go to his head. Equally, it may overwhelm him. Though my father doesn't agree, I think Ashok Singh – good and loyal general though he is – will find it hard to understand and control Murad's reactions if my brother is confronted by the unfamiliar or unexpected.'

'Forgive me, Highness, but wouldn't you do better to discuss this with your other brothers?'

'Dara Shukoh doesn't share my concerns. He thinks it will do Murad good to shoulder some responsibility.' Jahanara frowned, recalling her brief conversation with Dara, currently so absorbed in the philosophising of the Sufi he had invited to court that he had had little time for what he casually dismissed as her female fluttering and fussing. 'Shah Shuja is far away in Bengal and Aurangzeb is on his way to Gujarat. In any case ...' She hesitated and cast Nicholas a searching look. Yet if she didn't trust him, why had she invited him here? She forced herself to continue. 'Aurangzeb couldn't be expected to have very much sympathy with my concerns. He thought my father should have given him the command of the army and he was right. Aurangzeb is a resolute campaigner and experienced fighter and was the obvious choice.'

'Then why didn't the emperor appoint him?'

'As you and all the court know, some while ago he and Aurangzeb had a ... disagreement. That was why my father terminated Aurangzeb's appointment in the Deccan so suddenly. I believe he gave Murad command of the Uzbek campaign partly to teach Aurangzeb a lesson – put him in his place, you might say. To be truthful, I'm worried about Aurangzeb too – that his relationship with Dara and my father is broken beyond any but the most superficial repair.'

Jahanara paused, tears forming in her eyes as she watched Nicholas sip the rose-flavoured sherbet from the jade cup, his unruly fair hair flopping over his sunburnt face. Why couldn't life be as it had been in the past when her mother lived and their family was united against the world by their difficulties? Suddenly she was a child again, peeping through the curtains of her litter and seeing Nicholas, a reassuring presence, riding close when she and her family were in flight from Jahangir in the swamps of Bengal. With those recollections came lighter ones – Nicholas playing with her and Dara in the Portuguese compound at Hooghly, distracting them from the worry of their mother lying ill, of his teaching Aurangzeb swordplay and carving a toy soldier for Murad.

Straightening her back, Jahanara began again. 'You were always kind to me and my brothers and sister when we were children. That is why I'm appealing to you now to help me allay at least one of my worries by keeping watch over Murad and advising and restraining him if you can. As a foreigner and commander of his elite mercenaries as well as someone he has known since childhood you can be more blunt with him than the other commanders, who will feel they must treat him with the deference due to an imperial prince, however foolish or unconsidered his actions.'

'I am not one of his most senior commanders, and though you think being a foreigner may give me an advantage it may equally exclude me from his inner circle.'

'Even so – and strange as my request may sound – please do your best. And write to me by the imperial post riders when you can.' Jahanara glanced at her three waiting women, standing impassive. If only she could be alone with Nicholas . . . but such a thing was unthinkable. It wasn't that she didn't trust her attendants, but the temptation to gossip could be irresistible to even the loyallest.

Rising, Jahanara went to Nicholas and bending for a moment laid her small henna-painted hand on his sleeve. 'Please, Nicholas . . . You know enough of our customs to realise I wouldn't have invited you here if I wasn't really concerned about the future of my family. You move in the world of men, whereas I . . .'

· ◆ ·

'Majesty, a further despatch has come for you.'

As he took the folded paper from his steward, Shah Jahan saw from the seal that it was from Ashok Singh and opened it with impatient fingers. It was nearly a month since he had last had news of Murad's campaign and that had been merely a brief report that the army was making progress towards Balkh.

Majesty, as we advanced towards Balkh the local rulers harassed us hard, making darting raids to plunder our baggage and killing any who straggled. However, we were not dismayed. When ten days ago Uzbeks under a prince descended from your ancestor Babur's great enemy Shaibani Khan attacked us at dusk as we made camp, we fought them off, maintaining our discipline as we fired from behind our wagons. The next morning with your son's permission I led our horsemen in pursuit of the retreating enemy. We caught up with their main body and scattered it to the winds, killing many and suffering few losses ourselves. The Uzbek prince sold himself dear when surrounded with his bodyguard but I am proud to report a Rajput lance put an end to his life and to his men's resistance. Our victory cleared the way to Balkh which we reached three days later.

At first the city's commander rejected our offer of terms with bellicose and abusive defiance. However, after a day's cannonade from our largest weapons had damaged his walls he changed his mind and in most abject and humble terms craved our pardon and promised to surrender if only we would renew our offer. To save time — one of the most precious commodities in regions such as this which have only a limited campaigning season — as well as to spare human life, your son on my advice agreed. We entered Balkh in triumph, green banners high and trumpets sounding to the heavens.

Since then we have despatched an advance force to the Oxus to locate a suitable crossing place – the river is broad and its currents treacherous – and then to assemble vessels from which they can construct a bridge of boats and to find sufficient wood – not plentiful in this area – to make enough rafts to float our cannon and heavy baggage across. God willing, in a few days' time we will be over the river and advancing on glorious and golden Samarkand. The Uzbeks know we are coming and the news of our success and our strength may unite their warring factions, but nevertheless if we move quickly – as I am advising most strongly – they will still be no match for us and we will ride in triumph into Samarkand as we did into Balkh.

Your son asks me to send you his deepest respects, to tell you he rejoices in the conquests he has made on your behalf and to assure you he will spare no effort not only to take Timur's great capital but to achieve an absolute and lasting victory and the permanent expansion of your dominions.

Forgetful of those around him, as he finished reading Shah Jahan let out a great shout of joy and raised his clenched fist in a victory salute. Samarkand with its great palaces and *madrasas*, its orchards and gold-bearing river, would be his – the fulfilment of his long-nurtured ambition. Not even his grandfather the great Akbar had thought of such an audacious plan. After one and a half centuries the Moghuls were reclaiming their ancestral lands. That would be something for his chroniclers to write about and for his descendants to glory in when they sat on his peacock throne. What's more, Murad was proving his worth. Neither Aurangzeb nor even Dara could have done better.

Soon he would summon his council, but first he wanted to share the good news with his family. A few minutes later eunuchs flung open the great gilded wooden doors of the *haram* and his Rajput guards bowed low as Shah Jahan entered. Dara, he knew, was out hunting but he hoped to find Jahanara there – she often visited her younger sisters. But as he came into Roshanara's apartments, to his disappointment he saw she was alone. She looked up and smiled.

'I've received great news from Murad's army. They have taken Balkh and will shortly be across the Oxus and in a few more days in Samarkand.'

'That's wonderful! Our empire will know no rivals! Will you give a feast to celebrate?'

'No ... not yet. Let's wait for news of Samarkand and then I will give the greatest celebrations Hindustan and the Moghuls have ever seen.'

'Aurangzeb will be glad to hear of the success of our armies. Should I write to him in Gujarat – and also to Shah Shuja in Bengal – so they can both share in our happiness?'

'No. Let me have that pleasure. But where is Jahanara? I must tell her.'

'In her own house. Satti al-Nisa has taken Gauharara there today.'

'After I've told my council the news, I will ride there.'

He was already turning to leave when he heard Roshanara say, 'Father, I'm not sure if this is a good time, but there's something you should perhaps know.'

There was an edge to Roshanara's voice that did not bode well and Shah Jahan turned back. 'What's that?'

'Some months ago I recommended a young Gujarati noblewoman called Nasreen to Jahanara as an attendant. I had always found her diligent and thought she would serve my sister well. Nasreen has an aunt here in the *haram* and when she visits her she also sometimes comes to see me. A few weeks ago she told me something I haven't been able to dismiss from my thoughts – that not long before Murad and the army left Agra, Nicholas Ballantyne visited my sister in her mansion. He was with her for nearly an hour, and though Nasreen couldn't overhear what they were saying she said they spoke very earnestly.'

Shah Jahan blinked in surprise. What could Nicholas Ballantyne and Jahanara have to discuss? And how could his daughter be so blind to propriety as to entertain a man in her palace?

'You look angry, Father. I shouldn't have mentioned it.'

'Did Jahanara herself say anything to you about Nicholas's visit?'

'No, and that in itself seemed strange.'

'Why didn't you ask her?' The directness of his question seemed to surprise Roshanara. For a moment she looked down, then shrugged. 'I was too embarrassed – it might have looked as if I were prying. Besides, it's hardly my place to question her. She is the honoured First Lady of the Empire while I'm only her younger sister.'

Recognising the sense of grievance implicit in her remark, Shah Jahan felt more of his earlier elation at the news from Balkh seep away. 'What made you decide to tell me? And why did you wait so long?'

'I wasn't sure what to do at first but then I began to worry about my sister's reputation – especially as she doesn't live here in the *haram* but has her own establishment. It's all too easy for wild stories to circulate at court. I insisted Nasreen promise to tell no one else and also to swear the other attendants present that day to secrecy. I decided I should tell you, not only because you are our father but so that you could talk to Jahanara . . . make her understand that such behaviour could damage her position . . .'

'You were right to do so. As you yourself said, malicious gossip spreads fast and redounds to no one's credit. Now, though, put the matter from your mind.'

After Shah Jahan had left her apartments Roshanara stood for a moment. When her father was buoyed by a great triumph had definitely not been the time, she now realised, to raise Jahanara's behaviour. But even so, his reaction hadn't been the one she'd anticipated. Shah Jahan had seemed as suspicious of her motives as of Jahanara's – but why was she so surprised? Jahanara was perfect in his eyes. Yet she herself had done nothing wrong . . . Everything she'd told her father had been pure truth, and if Jahanara – for all her status – was foolish enough to be indiscreet then she deserved any consequences. Nasreen had already told her that Nicholas was writing regularly to Jahanara though she had never managed to read any of the letters – Jahanara always locked them in her jewel chest. She would continue to watch and listen. Perhaps one day Nasreen would provide enough evidence to prove to her father that he should have paid more attention to her and to teach Jahanara a deserved lesson. Her father was blind to his two elder children's faults and both of them too confident of the place they held in his heart. As a consequence both did as they pleased and acted as if their younger brothers and sisters didn't matter. But let them wait . . .

• ◆ •

'I summoned you at this late hour because the news is too grave to keep until tomorrow.' Shah Jahan looked round at his counsellors, whose sleepy faces and hastily pulled on apparel showed that many had not long left their beds. He could still scarcely believe what he had read in the two despatches that had just arrived within half an hour of each other despite having been written over a week apart. For many days he had been waiting for the news that his army was safely across the Oxus and advancing on Samarkand, but it hadn't come. Instead every despatch had related a series of excuses – the river was too high to cross and they were waiting for the level to fall . . . the supplies of fodder for the baggage animals were running low and they were waiting for more . . . fever had broken out among the foreign mercenaries, who were unused to the food and the climate . . . Uzbeks had been seen on the opposite bank of the Oxus preparing to oppose their crossing so they might need to feint to cross elsewhere.

He had tried to be patient, telling himself that the reasons for the delay were understandable and that there was still enough good campaigning weather for Samarkand to be taken. However, as time went by he had begun to suspect he was being played along. Ashok Singh himself would never do such a thing but, as the Rajput general made increasingly explicit, he was only writing what Murad instructed him ... More and more he had begun to detect in Ashok Singh's words a hesitancy, embarrassment even, and so it had now proved. Holding the first of the new despatches in a hand still trembling with anger, he began to read its contents out loud: '*Majesty, your son commands me to inform you that the Moghul armies have had no choice but to retreat southwards. It is still too hazardous to ford the Oxus while all the time our enemies are gathering, their recent differences forgotten, with a single aim – to annihilate us at the first opportunity. Only a week ago an Uzbek raiding party crossed the river several miles upstream of our camp and massacred some of our pickets. We found them the next morning, their heads sliced from their shoulders and their severed genitals protruding from their mouths. Our men are becoming disheartened and complaining that they are unsuited to fight in these lands which are unknown to them. Also, the season is now against us – the first snow has fallen and our men are ill equipped to withstand the rigours of a harsh winter. We are therefore on your son's instructions falling back on Balkh where we will await your further orders. Ashok Singh.*'

As Shah Jahan stopped speaking a heavy silence fell. Not a single man was willing to meet his eye. He knew only too well what they were thinking – that Murad had little stomach for a fight. And they were right, especially given this second and latest despatch, written this time by Murad himself.

'That is not the worst of it. There is more, this time from my son in a despatch which almost overtook Ashok Singh's. *Father, by the time you read this I and your forces will have withdrawn from Balkh and will be on the road back towards Hindustan. It was impossible to hold the city. Learning that*

215

thousands of Uzbeks were pouring over the Oxus intending to besiege us, I decided to fall back to Kabul rather than risk the massive losses that would have followed. I did not want the blood of so many of our men on my conscience and trust that you will understand and agree with my decision. Your dutiful son Murad. Dutiful son!' Shah Jahan could no longer contain himself. 'He has disobeyed me. He knows his orders were to move immediately on Samarkand. Instead he invented excuses until the time when decisive action would have resulted in certain victory had passed. Now he has forfeited what gains he made without a fight. I have decided to strip him of his command. But the immediate question is what orders to send north to Ashok Singh who, until I appoint a new commander, will take charge of my armies. What do you advise?' He waited, but again no one spoke. 'Well, doesn't anyone have anything to suggest?'

But as he looked around his counsellors, Shah Jahan knew in his heart that this was as much his fault as it was Murad's. Wanting to teach Aurangzeb a lesson, he had sent an inexperienced youth into the field in pursuit of his long-held goal of Samarkand. But he could never have anticipated that Murad would fail him so badly.

'Majesty.' A veteran counsellor at last broke the silence. 'The present year's campaign cannot now succeed – too much time has been lost and snow will soon block the northern passes leaving your armies cut off from Hindustan. Why not order your forces to overwinter in Kabul? Then, when the thaw comes, they can advance north again – perhaps taking a different route through the Hindu Kush to surprise our enemies.'

Shah Jahan reflected for some moments then nodded.

'Of course you are right. Just because one attempt has failed is no reason to give up, especially after the expense of raising and equipping a large army. I still believe we have a realistic chance of succeeding. Also, to give up so easily would demean us in the eyes of our enemies, whether Uzbek or Persian, and encourage them to think the Moghul armies have lost their teeth.' All around him his counsellors, now thoroughly awake, were murmuring their approval. 'Good. In that case I will send immediate orders to Ashok Singh that the army is to winter in Kabul and send instructions to the governor there to make arrangements to accommodate and feed them.'

'And the new commander, Majesty? A decision is needed,' the veteran counsellor prompted.

'I intend to recall Prince Aurangzeb from Gujarat. He was anxious for the command. Let him now prove he is worthy of it – and of my trust.'

Chapter 14

Nicholas swerved to avoid the spear hurtling towards him. It missed by inches, thudding harmlessly into the sandy ground, but his enemy – crouching a few feet away behind his dead horse for cover – wasn't finished with him. As Nicholas wheeled his own mount, intending to ride him down or slash at him with his outstretched sword, the man drew a long curved knife from his sash. When Nicholas was almost on him, he flung it. Nicholas jerked his head back but not quite in time and felt the sharp blade cut into his cheek, sending red blood running down his stubbled face and into his mouth. Ignoring the pain, he leant forward and thrust at the man, but he had misjudged. As the tribesman ducked down again behind the horse's carcass, Nicholas's sword swished through empty air. He wrenched his horse's head round to attack the man once more but as he did so the beast stumbled, lost its balance and crashed to the ground. Nicholas felt himself catapulted over its head to hit the ground with a thump.

Dazed by the fall, he spat the metallic-tasting blood from his mouth and struggled to his feet, but in a moment the tribesman was on him. Nicholas smelled the stench of sweat as his opponent, a squat burly man, knocked him back to the ground and straddled him, pushing his grinning face with its sour garlic breath close as his strong fingers fastened on Nicholas's windpipe and squeezed, intent on throttling the life out of him. Bucking and kicking, Nicholas tried to dislodge him but the man was heavy and his own strength began to fade as he fought for breath. His lungs felt as if they were filling with hot sand and his eyes seemed ready to burst from their sockets when suddenly a spray of blood blinded him for a moment and the man's grip relaxed. Wiping his eyes with the back of his hand, Nicholas saw that someone had severed his assailant's head. His saviour – whoever it was – had already disappeared but Nicholas gave him silent thanks as he pushed the dead torso aside and, still gasping for air, got to his knees and looked around him.

The attack on the Moghul vanguard had come out of nowhere as they had advanced through a defile on one of the final stages of their long march north from Kabul through the jagged mountains of the Hindu Kush, still snow-capped even in summer. The defile had been so narrow in places that no more than three men could ride comfortably abreast. The overhanging cliffs, rising two hundred feet, had meant travelling in almost perpetual shadow. Perhaps that was why the scouts hadn't spotted the tribesmen perched in the jumble of rocks above, who had suddenly begun firing down on them with deadly accuracy. Unable to see their assailants and with men falling from their saddles all along the column, they had had no option but to kick on their horses and ride as hard as they could through the defile, zigzagging wherever there was room to put off their enemy's aim. More riders had fallen but eventually the remainder had emerged, men and horses alike breathing hard, out on to these stony plains, as barren as the defile but at least with enough space for the Moghul troops to deploy.

At last they had been able to see their enemy – a mass of mounted warriors in the striped green and red robes, sheepskin jerkins and shaggy black woollen hats of the Turkomans – who, seated on their wiry ponies, had been waiting, correctly anticipating that their musketeers would flush the leading Moghul troops out of the defile and into their path. Five hundred of Nicholas's foreign mercenaries with about a thousand of Ashok Singh's Rajputs whose turn it had been to form the vanguard of Aurangzeb's army that day had tried frantically to form a line as the Turkomans galloped towards them, waving their weapons and yelling their wild war cries. In the chaos Nicholas had heard Rajput officers shouting commands as they tried to rally their men but all too quickly the Turkomans had smashed into them, slashing with their broad scimitars and rising in their stirrups to fire balls from their long-barrelled muskets – *jezails* they called them – or arrows from their double-curved bows.

Sword still gripped in his right hand, Nicholas backed against the dead horse and again looked around. His own mount had disappeared after throwing him. As far as he could tell, the fight was in the balance but if anything the Moghuls were getting the worst of it. To his left, orange-clad Rajputs, steel-tipped lances in their hands, were galloping towards a cluster of Turkoman musketeers and archers firing from behind some large boulders. Above the clamour, he heard a Rajput scream as an arrow tore into the exposed flesh of his neck; then a second and a third Rajput simultaneously tumbled from their saddles, both hit by musket balls. Directly ahead, he made out a group of his own men – Frenchmen and Danes – fighting desperately but determinedly as, outnumbered, they tried to break through a ring of Turkoman horsemen who had surrounded them. Suddenly one man, blond hair streaming from beneath a domed helmet, broke through the Turkomans' cordon only to be hit by a musket ball and slip from the saddle. For a moment his foot caught in his stirrup but then the stirrup leather broke and after rolling over on the ground a couple of times he lay still. Nicholas recognised him as one of the Danish pirates who had joined the mercenaries after his ship had been wrecked off Bengal. He must find himself a horse and go to his men's aid if he could . . .

Suddenly, he heard a drumming of hooves and turning saw fresh Moghul troops galloping out of the defile and debouching across the open ground towards the fight. A cluster of fluttering orange banners emblazoned with a flaring yellow sun at their head told him that Ashok Singh himself was leading them, and sure enough he glimpsed the Rajput's straight-backed figure in his glittering steel breastplate riding a tall white horse and closely surrounded by his bodyguard. Their drawn swords glinted before them, bright as fire in the slanting evening sunlight. But Nicholas had no further time for reflection. A huge Turkoman with a curly black beard on a bay horse had spotted him and was galloping towards him, intent on riding him down. Looking round, Nicholas saw a spear lying close by. Discarding his sword, he bent and grabbed it just in time. Leaping to one side, out of the rider's path, he swung the shaft horizontally and succeeded in inserting it between the animal's hooves, bringing it crashing down on to its flank and trapping its rider's left leg beneath it. As the Turkoman struggled vainly to free himself, Nicholas, taking care to avoid the horse's flailing hooves, leapt on him and drawing his dagger cut though the man's jugular in a single, swift movement.

Breathing heavily Nicholas clambered to his feet, bloodied dagger in hand, looking around for the next threat and expecting any moment to feel a musket ball or sword blade cut into his flesh. Seeing the dead man's bay horse standing nearby, Nicholas lunged for the rope reins. Though shaking with shock, the animal seemed unharmed beyond a gash on its right front fetlock where the spearshaft had caught it. Patting its neck, Nicholas hauled himself into the saddle, and urging it cautiously forward headed for a piece of higher ground to get a better view of what was happening. Now that Ashok Singh and his men had appeared, they could surely put the Turkomens to flight . . .

Bending over the horse's neck to whisper words of encouragement, he guided it carefully around dead and dying bodies and gained the hillock safely. Looking down, he saw Ashok Singh about a quarter of a mile away fighting like a man possessed. Nicholas watched him decapitate one Turkoman with a swing of his double-headed battle axe, then hack into the right arm of a second who dropped his spear and turned away, his arm hanging limp at his side. All around, Turkomans suddenly seemed to be riding or scrambling across the stony ground out of the battle. His own French and Danish troops had fought their way clear of their encircling opponents and were joining up with Ashok Singh's men. Not for the first time in the campaign the Rajput prince and his warriors indeed seemed to be turning the battle in the Moghuls' favour.

Exhilaration surging through him, Nicholas kicked his horse and galloped towards Ashok Singh, who acknowledged his arrival with a smile and a wave of his gauntleted right hand. 'They've had enough – they're running away,' Nicholas gasped. It was true. Surveying the action he could see that in some places the fighting was nearly over. Elsewhere knots of Turkomans were determinedly holding their ground but only because their path of escape was cut off. To Nicholas's right about thirty of them had formed a defensive ring but were steadily being cut down by Rajput swords and lances. Nearby a smaller group had taken refuge behind an overturned wagon, but some of Nicholas's mercenaries were now driving them out from behind it into the open and despatching them one by one.

Two hundred yards away to his right he noticed a group of dark-robed riders. They were still fighting fiercely, sweeping and lunging with their broad-bladed scimitars as they attempted to force a way through some

Moghul horsemen. Better mounted and better equipped than most of the Turkomans, they were led by a bushy-bearded man on a black horse. Perhaps he was a local khan and they his bodyguard.

'We're teaching these savages a lesson.' Ashok Singh grinned. 'Perhaps they'll think twice about attacking Moghul troops again.'

Before Nicholas could reply he heard the beat of hooves on stony ground behind them. Turning, he recognised one of Aurangzeb's young *qorchis* with an escort of six soldiers. Reining in, the youth addressed Ashok Singh. 'Highness, I have a message from Prince Aurangzeb.'

'You can tell the prince that when he leads the main troops out of the defile he'll have nothing to fear – we've routed the men waiting to ambush us,' said the Rajput.

The youth looked from Ashok Singh to Nicholas as if uncertain what to say and his face, speckled with pale dust, was anxious. 'I'm sure my master will be glad to hear that, but I bring an order from him. You are to retreat immediately.'

'What? Did I hear you right?' Ashok Singh leant forward in his saddle.

'Prince Aurangzeb wishes you to fall back and re-join him in the defile.'

'Why? If we fall back now the enemy will reoccupy the ground we've fought so hard to capture. We'll have to fight them all over again to secure our troops a safe passage as they exit the defile.'

'My master didn't give his reasons.'

Glancing at Ashok Singh Nicholas saw a vein pulsing at

his temple. Ashok Singh and Aurangzeb had lately often been at odds, the latter seeming to resent the Rajput's advice, something which the proud and occasionally quick-tempered Ashok Singh was finding increasingly difficult to accept. As for himself, he could scarcely believe what the *qorchi* had said. To give up and turn back when they had almost succeeded in coming through the mountains and an easier road awaited ahead seemed insane.

'What's happening in the defile? Are those musketeers in the rocks above still firing down on the main army just as they fired on the vanguard? Is the prince recalling us because he needs our help?' Ashok Singh demanded, failing to keep anger as well as disbelief from his voice.

The *qorchi* shook his head. 'When I left we had secured much of the higher ground.'

'Why then must I retreat? It makes no sense militarily. To withdraw now without good cause would be an affront to my honour and to the memory of my men who have died securing this position.'

'I can only repeat that these are the prince's orders and he was insistent that you should obey them immediately.'

While Ashok Singh sat in grim-faced silence Nicholas and the *qorchi* eyed one another uneasily. Not for the first time Nicholas reflected how glad he was not to be a senior commander bearing all that weight of responsibility upon his shoulders. A few moments ago he and Ashok Singh had been brothers in arms, equals, sharing a moment of victory. Now he was only a subordinate, waiting for orders.

'If the prince has ordered my return, I must, of course,

obey,' Ashok Singh said slowly before, voice rising, he added, 'but he previously ordered me to clear the exit from the defile and that task is not yet quite accomplished. Since I received that order first I will complete it first.'

Before Nicholas realised what Ashok Singh was intending to do, the Rajput drew his sword and throwing back his head yelled the hoarse battle cry of his people. Then, driving his heels hard into the sides of his white stallion, he shot forward towards the battling khan and his dark-robed warriors without even waiting for his bodyguard who, as soon as they saw what was happening, urged their own mounts in pursuit. Nicholas didn't hesitate either. Galloping across the stony ground, one hand on his reins, one on his sword hilt he tried to see ahead but his view was obscured by the riders in front of him. Suddenly a gap appeared as two Rajputs swerved to avoid a rock. Nicholas caught the flash of Ashok Singh's white horse and saw that the Rajput prince, still far in advance of his bodyguard, had almost reached the fighting. Then he saw something else: a single spear arcing through the air towards the prince. Instinctively Nicholas shouted a warning, but the noise of battle muffled his cries. Ashok Singh flung up his arms, grasping at the spear transfixing his neck, before sliding slowly from his horse to fall beneath the hooves of his bodyguard behind.

Nicholas hurled himself into the fighting, cutting and slashing with grim determination. Barging two of his opponents aside he aimed for the bearded warrior. The khan thrust at him with his scimitar but Nicholas turned the weapon aside with his sword, before jabbing his own blade into his opponent's groin. The man screamed and fell. Reining in, Nicholas saw that most of his followers lay sprawled on the ground, dead or dying. Like that of the whole battle, the outcome of this hard-fought skirmish had never been in doubt, but Ashok Singh had chosen to sacrifice himself to save his honour. Nicholas pondered the waste and pity of it as four muscled Rajput warriors, honed by countless battles but openly weeping, retrieved their prince's battered and bloodied body and hoisting it on their shoulders carried it away as the sun, a blood-red ball, began to sink beneath the mountains. Soon, using whatever wood they could scavenge among these grey desolate hills, they would build a great funeral pyre whose flames would light the night sky as they reduced Ashok Singh's mortal remains to ash.

Wearily, Nicholas sheathed his sword and turning his horse called to one of his mercenary captains, a scarred French veteran from Navarre. 'Gather our men. The prince has ordered us to retreat. The reason why defeats me, but do so we must.'

• ◆ •

Alone on the terrace of his apartments Shah Jahan stared ahead, blind to the grace of a flock of geese flying in arrow formation across the Jumna. Once more, just as when the *cossids* had first brought news of the disaster in the north three months previously, all he could see were thousands of his men lying dead or crippled through hunger and frostbite in the chill passes of the Hindu Kush as they had tried to fall back once more on Kabul. So many casualties as well as twenty million rupees lost to the imperial treasuries and not a single inch of territory gained. These campaigns were proving the first serious and lasting military reverses of his entire reign . . . Once more he asked himself how Aurangzeb could have failed him so badly, even worse than had Murad the previous year. This time the Moghul army hadn't even reached the Oxus . . . hadn't exchanged a single sword stroke with the Uzbeks. Instead they had allowed motley bands of hit and run Turkoman and Afghan raiders to hold them up so long that winter – the most relentless and implacable foe of all – had overtaken them as they had tried to retreat back to Kabul.

And now this latest news. The Persian shah had taken advantage of his stalled Samarkand campaign to send an army against Kandahar, and after a siege of only fifty-seven days the spineless Moghul garrison had opened their gates to the triumphant Persians. The more he'd thought about it, the more his resentment had grown against Aurangzeb, now waiting for an audience following his return last night to Agra in response to his father's urgent summons. Aurangzeb's failures were harder to forgive than Murad's because he was more experienced. Everything Dara had said was right . . . Aurangzeb had a conceited view of his abilities and now his shortcomings had been exposed, as Shah Jahan was about to tell him.

'Send Prince Aurangzeb to me,' he ordered a *qorchi*.

Five minutes later his son stood before him, dressed in his usual plain garments. One look at his posture, straight shoulders, head held high, told Shah Jahan that he was in a combative rather than either a humble or penitent mood and that made him even angrier.

'Well, what do you have to say for yourself?' Shah Jahan demanded as soon as they were alone.

'The narrow mountain passes defeated us. Though we

managed to drag some of our heavy cannon through several of them the wheels of many of our gun carriages were damaged and some shattered on the rocky ground.'

'So you abandoned the cannon rather than halting to repair the carriages!'

'Yes. I saw no alternative. Repairs would have taken time and the damage would have reoccurred. Besides, the guns were slowing our progress and were useless.'

'They wouldn't have been useless once you were out of the mountains and on to the flat steppe. How could simple tribesmen have withstood artillery? You should have tried harder. With cannon to support you, you could have been over the Oxus by now!'

'In my judgement it was impossible to get them to the Oxus, Father.'

'Did you ever consider advancing without them? No! You retreated in defiance of my orders and brought shame on both me and the Moghul army. No wonder Ashok Singh – a good friend as well as one of my best and most honourable generals – preferred to die.'

'You call his behaviour honourable? I call it stupid to sacrifice yourself needlessly rather than live to fight again. Whatever he might have thought, my actions were correct. Struggling with the guns delayed us too long. The enemy knew we were coming and with every day that passed were massing to oppose us. What they lacked in modern weaponry they made up for in numbers. I couldn't take the guns forward. I couldn't risk the lives of my men by continuing without them.'

'You could scarcely have lost more men if you had. How many was it?'

'Almost twenty thousand – five thousand in battle and fifteen thousand dead from disease and cold. The snow and ice came earlier than for many years ... Father, for once have some trust in me. I did all that I could. Everything was against me, and the men were restive. They lacked commitment – particularly those from the plains – and there were many deserters. Without my efforts our losses would have been even worse.'

'Nothing's ever your fault, but someone else's! Isn't that always your excuse? You've shown no respect for me either as your father or as your emperor, and far too much belief in your own opinions and abilities. You have disappointed me more than I thought possible. What's more, you have cost me the lives of too many – including Ashok Singh.'

'Why harp on Ashok Singh? These Rajputs aren't like us – their beliefs are warped and their pride insufferable. He would have served the empire better had he simply obeyed my orders and helped me manage the retreat instead of indulging in grandiose gestures.'

'How dare you deride Rajput pride! The Rajputs' bravery and loyalty are beyond question and they have been responsible for many of the Moghuls' greatest conquests. Hold your tongue and listen to me. I summoned you to me in private because what I have to say would reflect no credit on our family if I said it in public. Weakness was something I never thought to have to accuse you of, but you and no one else have brought disgrace on our dynasty by making us appear weak. Because of you, laughing Persians are pissing down on us from the walls of Kandahar ...'

'I see your mind is made up. There is strength, not weakness, in knowing when to suspend your ambitions and how and when to pursue them, so I bow to your will. What do you intend to do with me?'

'Were it not for the watching eyes of the world, I would banish you to the remotest part of my empire, or perhaps send you on the *haj* to Mecca since you seem so fond of praying. But I won't give our enemies the satisfaction of knowing the extent of my anger. You will return to your former post in the Deccan but I will be keeping a close eye on how you conduct yourself. At least all seems peaceful there, so you are unlikely to face any military challenges beyond your capabilities. You will depart within the week. Now leave me.'

• ➤ •

'He understands neither me nor my ambitions and never has because he doesn't want to.' Aurangzeb shook his head.

'But at least he's sending you back as his viceroy in the Deccan.' Roshanara moved a little closer and placed a comforting arm round her brother's shoulder as they stood on a terrace of the Agra fort.

'He's only done it to save face – his face, not mine. He wasn't interested in why the campaign failed – only in what people will say. I'm sure Dara has been stirring him up against me. Both of them should take care not to push me too far.'

'You may well be right in suspecting Dara has influenced Father against you. While you were away, they spent a great deal of time together. I felt quite left out, Jahanara was so often with them.'

At the mention of his oldest sister Aurangzeb's face softened. He had always been fond of Jahanara, Roshanara reflected. But it was time he realised that his eldest sister's first loyalty was to Dara, not him, and that if he wanted a sisterly ally she, Roshanara, was willing and waiting. Perhaps he should know that the First Lady of the Empire might not be as perfect as he seemed to think.

'Nicholas Ballantyne returned to Agra with you, didn't he?'

'Yes. He was wounded in the leg in the final stages of the retreat but has recovered. Why do you ask?'

'Because of something that happened just before Murad left on campaign. Nicholas Ballantyne visited Jahanara in her mansion. Since then they have been exchanging letters, even while he was away fighting for you . . .'

'That can't be . . . Who told you that? How do you know?' Aurangzeb looked stunned.

'One of my former waiting women is in her employ and tells me what is going on. I tried to talk to Father about it, but you know what he's like where Jahanara's concerned, especially since the fire. But who knows the real purpose of their letters? I'm not saying there is anything truly improper, just that Nicholas doesn't understand our ways and perhaps has been giving Jahanara information about your conduct of the campaign, and she's been using that to help Dara turn Father against you.'

'Jahanara wouldn't do such a thing.'

'Are you sure? Father is growing older. Perhaps she's already looking ahead to a time when she might have to choose between her brothers. If she wants Dara to become the next emperor, she'll do her best to help him. That doesn't make her your enemy – I know how fond you are of her, as indeed I am – but love of position and of influence changes people and I believe it has changed her. After all, she's not content to live in the *haram* as I and Gauharara do, but has her own palace and household, gives her own parties and entertainments. And her relationship with the Englishman is another symptom of her arrogance. She thinks she can ignore the conventions that bind the rest of us.'

'Not just conventions but the tenets of her religion that condemn such immodesty,' Aurangzeb said quietly.

'Don't be so angry with her. She loves you as a brother, I'm certain. It's just that she perhaps favours Dara for the throne.' Roshanara smiled, but won no answering smile from her brother. Instead he was staring at the ground. That he might hold second place to Dara in Jahanara's heart was painful. If he'd ever thought about it at all, he'd assumed she loved them equally. Yet the more he pondered, the clearer it became that Roshanara was right. Didn't Jahanara always take Dara's part in their disagreements? Didn't she sympathise with his philosophic musings? When it came down to it, mightn't she prefer the weak rule of Dara with his lax and flexible views to the stricter and sterner regime he would impose?

Roshanara's soft voice intruded into thoughts growing ever more bitter and suspicious. 'If I gain further information about Jahanara's relationship with the Englishman, what should I do?'

'Speak to our father again and this time in such terms

as to make sure he listens. And tell me . . . I need to know everything so that I'm prepared. Can I count on you for that? I'll not stand for anyone – not even Jahanara – conspiring against me.'

Chapter 15

Jahanara re-read Nicholas Ballantyne's letter more slowly. If she'd hoped a second reading would bring any more comfort than the first she was disappointed. How could things have gone so wrong? She simply didn't understand, however hard she tried. Shah Jahan's dismissal of Aurangzeb back to the Deccan had been so peremptory that she'd had no opportunity even to see her brother, let alone talk to him and hear his side of the northern campaign. When she'd tried to raise the subject of Aurangzeb with her father he had refused to discuss him with a tight-lipped obstinacy that had both surprised and wounded her.

Dara thought she was wrong to worry about Aurangzeb. 'He has a hot head but a cold heart. Firm treatment is the only thing he understands. I've told our father so.' Dara had looked unusually stern as he'd spoken those words, but perhaps he'd never truly forgiven Aurangzeb's accusations during their inspection of his mansion.

At least she had Nicholas Ballantyne to turn to. Just as he had honoured his promise to write to her about Murad he was again at her urging proving a candid and reliable informant, this time about Aurangzeb and the debacles in the Hindu Kush. He had replied quickly to the message she had sent to his lodgings within the Agra fort asking about Aurangzeb and the reason for the failure of his campaign. If only she could have found something in his letter to help her understand her brother better ... Glancing down, her eyes fell again on the passage that had disturbed her most − Nicholas's account of a skirmish early in the campaign.

Though this particular ambush − only one among many − was unexpected and made in greater strength than usual, our greater discipline and better weapons made our victory certain − at least I thought so. Your brother was in the heart of the fighting − he's certainly no coward − and was about to charge with his bodyguard against a group of Kafir tribesmen firing down on us from a crest some two hundred yards away. He had ordered me to lead some of my French mercenaries to circle round to support him. We were ready to move, weapons unsheathed, hearts thumping and our horses pawing the ground. We expected him to give the signal at any moment but instead he did something that made us gasp with astonishment.

After gazing up into the sky for a few moments, Aurangzeb suddenly dismounted and pulled something from his saddle. As he lifted it clear, I saw it was a prayer mat. With his bodyguards forming a cordon around him, Aurangzeb laid the mat on the ground and kneeling down began to pray, leaning forward to touch his forehead to the mat, then sitting back on his heels again and again. Glancing up at the sky myself, I realised by the position of the sun that it was the hour of evening prayer.

By now musket balls and arrows were flying all around us. The captain of his guard was one of several killed or wounded as we continued to wait, but their screams had no effect on your brother. He went on praying calmly and without hurry. When he had finished, he rolled up his mat, replaced it on his saddle, remounted and gave the order to charge as if nothing had intervened. We still put the enemy to flight. That evening his mullahs, travelling as always with the army, their tents pitched close to his, commended his piety and his bravery, telling him that both would bring him victory. However, others – myself included if I am honest and Ashok Singh too – were disturbed. A commander who breaks off in the thick of the battle to pray is reckless as well as pious and courageous. However keen he is to ensure his own place in Paradise he has no right to be so careless of the earthly lives of his men.

From that time we suffered a number of desertions, particularly among troops not of your religion. I suspect your brother knew that he was losing the confidence of some of his men. In consequence he almost ceased asking his officers' advice. His orders became ever more autocratic – even sometimes irrational – as he sought to impose his will and enforce his men's loyalty. Ashok Singh did what he could to maintain the army's morale but after his death – a matter of great personal sorrow to me; I cannot help worrying whether I could have done anything to save him – I think your brother doubted his ability to hold his army

*together through a long and dangerous campaign and that
I believe was why he aborted the mission. He is unlike
other commanders I have served, being austere and cold. It's
hard to tell what is in his mind and I suspect he would
have it thus.*

Jahanara touched her scarred cheek. In those terrible
weeks after the fire Aurangzeb had hurried back from the
Deccan to be at her bedside. Could that tender affectionate
brother have become the remote, self-contained man
conjured by Nicholas? Yet now that she thought back she
realised how little Aurangzeb had ever revealed of himself,
his feelings and ambitions, even during the hours they'd
spent together at that time. If he was indeed a man such
as Nicholas described, what had made him become so?
Did some seam of bitterness run through him like a vein
of marble or of granite, cold and unyielding, hidden until
you dug deep enough? As the eldest of her parents'
children – and as a sister who loved him – it was her duty
to try to find out . . . She owed it to her mother who, had
she lived, would surely have penetrated her son's reserve.

Sitting down cross-legged at her desk she took her pen
and began to write again to Nicholas.

*Thank you for your letter, even if it has caused me great
heartache. How can a woman living such a protected life as
I understand fully what is in men's hearts – their thoughts
and feelings, their true desires. What you have said raises so
many questions that I cannot rest until I know more.
Please, I must see you. Come to me here in my palace
tomorrow evening, as you did before.*

Heating a stick of wax over a candle she let the red tallow trickle in a little pool on to the bottom of the letter. Then, taking her mother's ivory seal, she pressed it firmly into the wax. She would have given the letter to her steward but his daughter had just given birth to his first grandson in the town and he had gone to visit her. This time she would have to entrust the errand to someone else.

'Nasreen!' she called to her attendant. 'Come quickly. I have a task for you.'

• ◆ •

As he often did, her father had ordered that he was not to be disturbed that evening, but the piece of smooth ivory-coloured paper in her hand gave Roshanara the confidence she needed.

'I have information for my father that cannot wait,' she told the captain of the Turkish female guards who protected the main entrance to the emperor's apartments from the imperial *haram*. The Turk – broad-shouldered and muscular as a man in her tightly belted leather jerkin – hesitated a moment then bowed her close-cropped head. At her signal the guards flung open the silver-clad doors to admit Roshanara into a long torchlit corridor at the far end of which was a second set of doors, also flanked by Turkish *haram* guards.

Accompanied by the captain of the guard, Roshanara took her time as she made her way towards them, the hem of her turquoise silk robe rustling as it brushed the ground. After all, she'd already waited long enough ... indeed she'd even begun to think that Nasreen would never obtain any useful information, but finally her patience had been rewarded. She had something to dislodge Jahanara from her patronising pedestal and prove to her father that he should not have treated her so roughly when she had first voiced her suspicions. She paused while the captain of the guard tapped on the second set of doors and informed the *haram* eunuch who appeared that the Princess Roshanara had urgent business with her father.

A few moments later she was in his familiar apartments overlooking the Jumna. Shah Jahan was on the terrace where he often stood at night, gazing across the river at Mumtaz's mausoleum by the light of an almost full moon.

'What is it, Roshanara?' He looked tired, but there was no reproach in his voice for disturbing him so late.

'I thought you should see this, Father.' She held out the piece of paper.

'What is it?'

'A letter from Jahanara to Nicholas Ballantyne. Yesterday Jahanara asked her attendant Nasreen – the one I spoke about to you before – to take it secretly to Nicholas's lodgings. However, anxious that her mistress seemed to be conducting a clandestine correspondence with this man and afraid that she might be blamed for helping, she brought it to me unopened. At first I wasn't sure what to do. Then I remembered that when I told you Nicholas had visited my sister in her mansion you said I'd been right to tell you … I opened the letter, hoping and believing I would find it was nothing, but I confess the contents shocked me. I knew it was my duty to bring the letter to you at once.'

'What does Jahanara say?'

'You should read it yourself, Father. Here.'

Shah Jahan took the letter and moved closer to a torch burning in a sconce. The flickering orange light danced across the page as he read. At first he couldn't believe what he was reading, the words jumping before his eyes, jumbled up and making no sense. He took a deep breath to steady himself and looked again. This time his daughter's elegant script – written in the pale blue ink she always used – stood out only too clearly, though the hand in which he was holding the letter was beginning to tremble. *How can a woman living such a protected life as I understand fully what is in men's hearts – their thoughts and feelings, their true desires . . . Please, I must see you . . .'*

Shah Jahan shook his head. Could this be anything but a letter from a woman to her lover? How could Jahanara bring shame on herself and her dynasty like this? He closed his eyes but all he saw was his daughter's face as it had been before the fire, smiling at him just as Mumtaz had used to smile. He had lost the dearest thing to him on earth – his wife – and now by her own thoughtless and disgraceful acts he was losing Jahanara . . . For a moment he pressed his knuckles to his eyes as if by so doing he could drive away the images in his mind.

'Father, are you all right?'

Shah Jahan struggled to speak but his emotions choked the words. Shock and doubt whirled in his head but as the letter's contents sank in he felt something else – a scalding anger such as he'd not felt for many years, perhaps not since the time when Mehrunissa had demanded two of his sons as hostages. In those days he had been forced to submit to what could not be helped but no longer – he

241

was an emperor whose word was life or death to a hundred million people. No one – not even a much-loved daughter – could escape his anger when they had transgressed.

He opened his eyes again to see Roshanara standing before him with a half-smile on her face. This was nothing to smile at. He took her none too gently by the shoulders and pulled her towards him so that her face was only inches from his. 'Does anyone else know the contents of this letter?'

She shook her head, her smile banished. 'No. Only I read it and I told no one.'

'Good. So it must remain. I'll not have your sister's reputation dragged through the mire of court gossip any more than I can help. Return to your apartments and act as if nothing had happened. Do you understand?'

'I understand.' Roshanara was trembling in his grasp. She had expected her father to storm and rage but his voice was so quiet it was almost a whisper and there was a coldness in his eyes. For the first time she realised how merciless he must have looked on the battlefield, or as he was about to pronounce death on a traitor in the court of justice. She almost regretted what she'd done. She'd wanted to see Jahanara humbled in their father's eyes and to pay her back for her disparagement of Aurangzeb. Now she wondered what she might have unleashed on her sister.

• ◆ •

'Highness, please, you must wake up.'

Jahanara opened startled eyes to see Satti al-Nisa bending over her, lined face anxious. 'What is it? Has something happened to my father?'

242

'No, it's not that. It concerns you. Someone has betrayed you. As soon as it's light the emperor intends to summon you to the fort to account for yourself.'

'What do you mean? You speak as if my father suspects me of some crime.' Jahanara sat up and pushed her long hair back from her face as she struggled to make sense of Satti al-Nisa's words.

'He does, Highness. If what I heard tonight in the *haram* is true he has come by a letter written by you to the Englishman.'

'My letter to Nicholas Ballantyne? How did my father get it?'

'One of my oldest friends told me your attendant Nasreen claims you gave her a letter to take to him but that instead she made sure it found its way to the emperor. She is saying that he is your lover and boasting she's to receive a rich reward.'

'My lover . . .' Jahanara gasped and gripped Satti al-Nisa's arm. 'But it's not true. How could anyone think such a thing . . . there was nothing in that letter. All I said was that I wanted to talk to him about Aurangzeb . . . to understand more about the northern campaign and what caused my brother to act as he did.' Still dazed, Jahanara got up. Though the night was warm, shock and dismay chilled her as for the first time she considered how others might interpret her words. How could she have been so careless? But she had never expected one of her servants to be so deceitful. Anyway, she tried to comfort herself, when her father understood that only anxiety about her brother had made her write in that way surely he would forgive her . . . After all, what was there to forgive?

'I must go to my father at once and explain.'

'No! Be careful, Highness. Though I have admired your father for many years – even before he became emperor – I can't be blind to his faults. His bitterness against the world since your mother's death still eats away at him. He has turned in on himself and does not always react rationally. Of all his children he loves you and Dara the most – that is common knowledge – but if he feels that one of you, his special ones, has let him down, his rage will be all the greater. Remember you have further to fall than either of your sisters.' Satti al-Nisa took Jahanara in her arms. 'After Mumtaz's death, while you were trying to be a mother to your brothers and sisters, I tried to be a mother to you. And it is in that role that I came here tonight – to counsel as well as to warn you. Do not rush to the fort. Allow your father's anger time to cool and give yourself time to think what you will say.'

Satti al-Nisa was right, Jahanara thought, as the older woman comfortingly stroked her hair in the way she had done when Jahanara was a child. But suddenly she jerked away as a new and terrible thought struck her. 'If my father is angry with me, how will he feel towards Nicholas Ballantyne? He'll have him killed . . . I must warn him.'

'Yes, but no more letters, Highness. Let me be your messenger. Now that I have told you all I can I will return to the fort and go to his apartments. He knows me of old and will listen to what I say.'

'Tell him to leave Agra immediately and to do so in disguise – to get as far away as he can, perhaps even to take ship for his homeland from the English settlement at Surat.' For a moment she saw Nicholas's frank open face beneath that unruly golden hair as he spoke his reluctance to communicate with her before he left for the north. He had become a familiar and trusted part of all their lives, yet by her thoughtlessness she had put his life at risk. 'And tell him I am sorry . . . none of this is his fault. Go, Satti al-Nisa. Go now! I pray it's not already too late.'

• ➤ •

'Approach no further!' Shah Jahan was seated on a silver chair in his Hall of Private Audience beneath the green silk, pearl-sewn canopy. His stiff embroidered robes, the strands of emeralds and rubies round his neck, the jewels glittering on his fingers, told Jahanara how carefully he had prepared for this interview. She knew him well enough to realise that at his most distressed or vulnerable he retreated behind the magnificence of his imperial image. Though they were entirely alone with all the doors tight shut she felt as if the eyes of all the court as well as her father's were watching her in judgement.

'Father, you don't understand . . .'

'Silence! You will not speak until I give you permission.' Jahanara was close enough to see the taut skin around his unblinking eyes and pursed mouth, the rapid rise and fall of the jewels on his chest and the tightness with which his hands gripped the lion's head arms of his chair. Taken aback by the vehemence of his words and expression, she looked down at the floor.

'Well may you bow your head in shame before me. I've known for some time that you once invited Nicholas Ballantyne to your mansion. Because I trusted you I assumed it was for innocent reasons. I refused to think badly of you and pushed the incident from my mind.

Now I discover I was wrong. For two years at least letters have been passing between you and the Englishman and they were not innocent!'

Reaching inside his robe, Shah Jahan pulled out her latest letter and flung it to the ground. 'You, an imperial Moghul princess, the First Lady of the Empire, write to a man of feelings and desires ... In our ancestors' days on the steppes you would have been killed at once for shaming our house. Jahanara ...' his voice cracked a little, 'I trusted you, gave you everything you could desire ... even your own mansion ... and this wantonness is how you repay me.'

Jahanara wanted to shout out 'It is only you who ever behaved wantonly, not I' but knew she must not. In the effort to keep silent, she dug the nails of her manicured right hand into the palm of her left.

'All night I sat up in my apartments wondering what punishment would fit the crime – and a heinous crime I consider it. One thing and one thing only has made me stay my hand from harsh measures – the knowledge that the physical scars you bear are my fault. My actions robbed you of some of your beauty and that loss has perhaps caused you to forget yourself and seek the touch of a man, however dishonourable and improper. At least that is what I have tried to tell myself as I struggled – still struggle – to find excuses for your immorality. Until I have considered further you will be confined in the imperial *haram* within this fort. As for Nicholas Ballantyne, this morning at dawn I ordered his arrest, but when my guards went to his lodgings he had fled ... hardly the act of an innocent man. But I promise you this – he will be found and brought back to Agra where I will have him castrated before wild horses rip him apart.' Shah Jahan rose from his chair and descending the shallow dais took a few steps towards her, his face an expressionless mask. 'Now I have said what I wished to say, you may speak.'

Jahanara opened her mouth, but the will to defend herself and Nicholas was draining from her. What was the point? That her father could treat her like this hurt with a pain more deep-seated than that of her burns had ever been. He was judging her as arbitrarily and distantly as if she and Nicholas were strangers dragged before him, and what was more using the standards of his own moral weakness to do so. She'd done nothing to be ashamed of; just the reverse. Rather than indulging in selfish desires she had been trying to hold his family together. She would not stand abject before him. Neither, having done her best to secure Nicholas's escape, would she plead with him. If he had so little trust in her, let him do with her what he would. Whatever happened she would keep her pride and her honour and one day her father would once more beg her forgiveness. She straightened her back. 'I have done nothing to dishonour you or our family or – most important – myself. I swear so before God, my immortal judge. Do with me as you will.' Jahanara's eyes flashed defiance. 'But before you do there is one thing I must know. Who was it who brought my letter to you?'

'Someone with more regard for our family's honour than you. Their identity is no concern of yours. Now go.'

As father and daughter turned stiffly away from each other both had tears in their eyes – in each case tears of righteous anger, betrayal and loss.

Chapter 16

Shah Jahan leant against one of the columns of the pavilion in his *mahtab bagh*, his moonlight garden across the Jumna from Mumtaz's tomb. Here, among the waxy white *champa* flowers and orange trees, was one of the few places he could find peace. On nights like this he could almost imagine Mumtaz herself was beside him. What would she have said about the state of his relationship with their children? But that was a foolish question – if she'd lived their children would never have drifted so far away from him or apart from each other, and they themselves might have turned out differently.

As so often in recent days his thoughts returned to Jahanara. His initial anger had blunted a little over the week since he had confined her to the imperial *haram*, but he couldn't forgive her behaviour with Nicholas Ballantyne. Of all his children she was the one he'd thought he'd understood the best, believing they had recreated the bonds that had existed before the incident leading to the fire. Clearly he had been deluding himself, seeing what he wanted to see rather than the reality. Wasn't that what men often did as old age claimed them? Her duplicity had hurt him far more than if it had been Roshanara or Gauharara. Though his younger daughters were affectionate enough they'd never meant the same to him. He missed Jahanara ... her daily visits, her companionship and wisdom.

At least Dara would soon return from his inspection of the new fortifications on the great trunk road near Gwalior. What would he make of the scandal that had enveloped his sister? As for his other sons, he'd not seen any of the three for many months. Aurangzeb was still in the Deccan. Despite his stubborn pride and confidence in his rigid view of the world, he was at least showing himself a diligent and effective administrator even if his reports were short and uninformative. Taxes from the wealthy south were flowing smoothly into the Moghul treasuries and for the moment the empire's southern borders seemed quiescent. He was glad that his third son appeared to have at last put the humiliation of the northern campaign behind him. He must find some important honour to confer on him and summon him to court to receive it. Aurangzeb's claim that he had never loved him still lingered ... it wasn't true and he would prove it to his prickly son ...

He might also recall Shah Shuja to court to reward him for his management of Bengal which too seemed prosperous and peaceful, although his despatches were as terse as Aurangzeb's and even less frequent. Shah Shuja's hard-working officials probably deserved the real credit but it would be good to see his son again. As for Murad, he must certainly soon summon him to Agra. Unlike his brothers, he was not performing well as a governor. Only last week a private report from Gujarat's loyal and honest revenue minister, Ali Naqi, had informed him – respectfully but unambiguously – that even though Shah Jahan had personally ordered Murad to levy higher dues on the rich English traders of Surat, the foreigners had easily bought off the prince with rich gifts which he was squandering without a thought for remedying his province's dilapidated finances. Would Murad take his strictures to heart? All the evidence suggested that he remained shallow and vain and – if his letter attempting to excuse his behaviour over the Surat merchants was anything to go by – full of bluster when challenged about his inadequacies just as after the failure of his northern campaign.

Shah Jahan closed his eyes, feeling weary as he now quite often did. A few hours hunting or hawking exhausted him. The days when he'd galloped hundreds of miles yet still had energy to wield his ancestors' sword Alamgir in battle were long gone. Perhaps that was to be expected now he was in his mid-sixties. Soon he would hand the sword to Dara – it was fitting that his eldest son should have it, especially since he himself was now the father of promising sons. Suleiman was a fine horseman and marksman but also a thinker and scholar like his father. Young Sipihr closely resembled their Moghul mother Nadira, sharing her charm and intelligence. The dynasty's blood ran strong and vigorous through their veins.

Shah Shuja, Aurangzeb and Murad also had sons though he scarcely saw them. If they arrived at court tomorrow he would barely recognise them. That was a pity. He would like to know them better so that they could learn from him, just as he had from his own grandfather, Akbar. That thought made him especially pleased that Dara, who had always seemed to him to resemble Akbar in so many ways, would not be away too much longer.

Hearing the hooting of an owl, Shah Jahan opened his eyes to see the bird's dim shape soaring into the sky. How bright the star-dusted heavens, so loved by his great-grandfather Humayun, looked. He took a few steps away from the pavilion the better to appreciate their beauty. But as he did so, the world began spinning around him. The stars were whirling at his feet while the sky sprouted flowers and fountains. Was it an earthquake? He reached out for something to hold on to but his hand seemed to extend into nothingness and he felt himself falling forward . . . He could hear voices, but faint and far away. Dark mists enveloped him.

• ◆ •

'What do the *hakims* say? Tell me everything, please, Roshanara . . .' Jahanara's heart thumped as she scrutinised her sister's face.

'They're not yet sure what the problem is but they say he's exhausted, both in mind and in body. Of course they blame his onerous responsibilities, the time he must spend in the Hall of Public Audience administering justice . . . the long hours he has to spend privately with his counsellors and commanders. But of course recently he's had other worries . . .'

251

Jahanara flushed but said nothing. This was the first time Roshanara had visited her since she'd been confined to the fort's *haram*. At first she'd wondered whether Shah Jahan had forbidden her sisters to see her but Satti al-Nisa had assured her it wasn't so. Doubtless her sisters didn't wish to associate themselves with her disgrace. Now that Roshanara had finally come, she didn't want to say anything that would send her away, at least not until she had learned everything she could about their father's health. 'How serious is it? How long do they think it will take him to recover? He will recover, won't he?'

'The doctors believe so but say it may take some time. One of them – old Ali Karim – has suggested that when our father is strong enough he should go north to Lahore where the cooler air will do him good. I will accompany him if he goes – Dara too. He has been informed of our father's illness and is hastening his return to Agra.' Roshanara smoothed the heavily embroidered border of her sleeve.

'And our other brothers? Have you written to them?'

'No, not yet. I didn't want to alarm them. I considered it better to wait a few days when Father's condition will be clearer and there may well be good news to report.' That wasn't quite true, Roshanara thought as she continued to play with her sleeve. She had written at once to Aurangzeb. He had been so grateful for the other information she had sent him about what was happening at court – what she heard in the *haram* through wives of their husbands' rivalries and alliances, their secret ambitions and weaknesses. She liked to feel important to someone – not something she'd experienced often in her life.

Unlike Dara and even her father, Aurangzeb at least knew how to value her.

For a little time the sisters were silent, each immersed in her own thoughts. Then Jahanara said awkwardly, 'I'm glad to see you, Roshanara. How have you been ... and Gauharara? Satti al-Nisa told me you gave a party together last week, here in the *haram*.'

'We're both very well. Gauharara has a pet mongoose, sent to her by Dara's wife Nadira. When it hears the notes of a flute it stands on its hind legs and revolves for as long as the music lasts.' Roshanara glanced towards the door, clearly thinking of leaving.

Suddenly Jahanara could contain herself no longer. 'Sister, why are we discussing such trivialities? Why don't you ask me straight out about what happened between myself and Nicholas Ballantyne ... don't you want to know the truth? Though my father will not listen to me, it would grieve me that you, Gauharara and my brothers should think ill of me. I promise on our mother's memory that you have no cause to do so. I'm guiltless. Make them understand my innocence too. Be my ambassador.'

'Why should I be the bearer of your lies?'

'Roshanara!' Jahanara stared at her sister, shocked by her tone and the hardness in her eyes. 'I would never lie to you or to our father. As I told him, I've done nothing to be ashamed of. My relationship with Nicholas Ballantyne was innocent.'

'How can you say that? I saw your shameless words to him and I ...' Roshanara fell silent, but it was too late.

Jahanara moved closer to her sister and looked into her face. She saw the flicker of dismay and suddenly she understood . . . 'Was it you who betrayed me? Did Nasreen bring my letter to you, instead of to Nicholas?'

Roshanara said nothing and Jahanara felt a sudden urge to slap her smooth, round face, angry with herself as well as with her sister. She'd assumed that a curious Nasreen had not been able to resist opening the letter and, reading the contents, had seen an opportunity for reward. She wouldn't have been the first attendant venal enough to seek to profit from her intimate position in an imperial household. But it had never crossed her mind that Nasreen had simply been doing another's bidding . . . and not just anyone's but that of her own sister! 'You planned it all, didn't you? That was why you urged me to take Nasreen into my household . . . to be your spy. How could you do such a thing? And even if she did bring you my letter why didn't you come to me first instead of taking it to our father? You never gave me a chance to explain.'

'No, I didn't plan it. It was natural Nasreen and I should talk when she visited the fort and when I saw your letter it required no explanation. I knew at once that it was my duty to take it to our father.' Roshanara turned but Jahanara moved quickly to stand between her and the door. She would not permit her sister to leave until she had answered all her questions.

'I'm not a fool. Nasreen has been in my household for two years at least. All that time you must have been hoping she'd bring you some evidence to use against me. What I don't understand is why. You're my sister. I've always done my best for you!'

'Have you? For years you've either patronised or ignored me as if I were nothing beside you, the great First

Lady of the Empire. You've always been by our father's side, behaving as if you were the new empress and the rest of us just your acolytes. That night at our mother's *urs* when our father left the mausoleum to cross the river to the moonlight garden you told me only you need follow, as if I were of no account and only you had the right to go and only you could bring him comfort.'

'It wasn't meant to be like that . . . I'm truly sorry if it seemed so.' Seeing sudden tears in Roshanara's eyes, Jahanara tried to take her in her arms but Roshanara jerked away, dashing the back of her right hand across her eyes and smudging the kohl rimming them.

'Don't!'

Jahanara's arms fell back to her sides. 'Ever since our mother died I've tried hard to look after you all . . . to do what was in your interests . . .'

'If you think that, it's only because you've never troubled to see things from our point of view. You were so certain you knew best that you never asked us what we thought or wanted. Now you've got what you deserve for playing the great lady while all the time conducting a squalid liaison with a foreigner . . . Now you will know what it feels like being excluded from everything that matters.'

'There is – there was – no liaison. Not ever! I wrote to Nicholas Ballantyne asking him to visit me because I was worried about Aurangzeb. I knew he'd quarrelled badly with our father over the failure of the northern campaign. Nicholas was on that campaign. I hoped he could explain what had happened and help me put matters right between Aurangzeb and Father.'

'I don't believe you. That's just a story you've invented to save yourself.'

'You don't understand . . . Nicholas Ballantyne had my confidence because he'd helped me before. When Father appointed Murad commander of the northern army, I summoned Nicholas and asked him to try to advise Murad and keep me informed of the campaign. He didn't fail me and I knew I could trust him over Aurangzeb.'

'If that's true, why did the infidel flee Agra?'

'Because our father would have had him executed if he'd stayed because he didn't believe my story any more than you do now.' Jahanara's voice was rising and it was only with the greatest of efforts that she was remaining as calm as she was. 'You deride Nicholas as an infidel – you call him a guilty man. That's all too easy, labelling him rather than trying to understand. Don't you remember how good he was to us as children . . . his loyalty and courage when we were all hunted fugitives? Our family has given him very shabby thanks and that makes me ashamed, as you should be.' Tears ran down Jahanara's cheeks. Sometimes the weight of everything that had happened was too heavy to bear. At least Nicholas was safe. Satti al-Nisa had brought her a letter he'd written from Gujarat where he was thinking of taking ship from Surat for England.

'It's not only that Nicholas Ballantyne ran away.' Roshanara's tone was more confident now that her sister's anger had turned to tears. 'I've seen how you've looked at him, heard your voice soften when you talk about him, as it did just now. Earlier you told me not to take you for a fool. Well, I could say the same thing!'

'You're wrong if you think I have feelings – feelings like that for him . . .' But Jahanara blushed nevertheless.

'Am I? Anyway, if you would please move out of my way it's time I returned to my place at our father's bedside.'

◆ ▶ ◆

Startled by a sudden urgent rapping at the outer doors to her apartments, Jahanara put down her book of reflections by her favourite preacher, the twelfth-century mystic Abdul Qadir-al-Jilani. A visitor at this late hour – it must be nearly midnight? Surely her father hadn't relapsed? It was more than two months since he had first fallen ill and he had been recovering, if only slowly. She had only just got to her feet, pulses racing with anxiety, and taken a few steps forward towards the doors when they were flung wide to admit a tall cloaked figure. As he pushed back his hood her heart soared.

'Dara!' She rushed into his embrace. 'I'm so glad you've returned. How I've waited for this moment!'

'I came straight to you,' Dara said, releasing her. 'Our father doesn't know I'm here yet. How is he? It's some days since I received any report on his health.'

'The news is good. Satti al-Nisa tells me he has been keeping up his improvement. Recently he's been strong enough to get up for three or four hours a day – and he's eating better, not just the mint and manna soup which was all he would take at first. He is still frail, though, and the *hakims* are insisting that he is not troubled by any affairs of state.'

'Then he doesn't know . . .'

'Know what?'

257

'As soon as it's light I must go to him. I've news that he must hear and soon, however frail he is.'

'What is it, Dara? What's happened?'

Dara hesitated and in the flickering candlelight she saw the strain in his face. 'I know you've had your own troubles, but there is no way of breaking this to you gently. Aurangzeb, Shah Shuja and Murad have risen in revolt, claiming our father is too sick to rule. They are preparing to march on Agra with their armies.'

'But that can't be true . . .' Jahanara stared at Dara, aghast. 'Are you sure?'

'Yes. I found it hard to credit myself when the initial reports reached me. Many roads meet near Gwalior. The first news I received was that Aurangzeb was returning to Agra. I thought he must wish to be at our father's side – as he did to be at yours after your accident – and, being further from Agra than I, had not heard the reassuring news about his recent improvement. So I thought little of it. The next day, a *cossid* bringing a birthday message to the ruler of Gwalior from his eldest son, our governor at Allahabad, told one of my *qorchis* of rumours that Shah Shuja was also heading for Agra but with an army. Alarmed, I immediately sent relays of messengers down towards Allahabad to investigate. Thirty-six hours later the true position became clear. My vizier's son rode into my camp demanding to see me. He had been serving at Aurangzeb's headquarters in the Deccan and knowing that I was at Gwalior had ridden night and day to alert me. He told me that Aurangzeb was claiming to his senior officers that our father was dying or more probably already dead and that I was concealing the fact to strengthen my grip on the succession. Therefore he was marching on Agra to save the empire from me. He claimed that he was acting in concert not only with Shah Shuja but with Murad too.'

Jahanara felt so numb with shock she could scarcely think, let alone speak. This wasn't how she'd imagined her reunion with Dara would be. Many times she'd dreamed of telling him of her innocence, knowing he'd believe her, of how he would go to their father and explain, how Shah Jahan would return with him to her apartments to beg her forgiveness. Now, with her father still sick, three of her brothers in arms against him and the empire perhaps about to dissolve into civil war, her own problems suddenly diminished. 'I've heard nothing,' she finally whispered. 'Even though I'm confined to these rooms Satti al-Nisa visits me every day. She'd have told me at once if such rumours had reached the court.'

'I gave orders that all imperial *cossids* were to be diverted to me as I made my way back to Agra. I didn't want Father alarmed if I could avoid it until I was back at his side. In the week it has taken me to return I've received more messages. In particular those I sent east confirm that Shah Shuja indeed has an army on the move. It can't be long until this news becomes common knowledge.'

'We must prevent it from doing so for as long as we can, at least until we've sent messengers to our brothers telling them our father is recovering . . . that in any case their behaviour is treason.'

Dara smiled a little sadly. 'They probably know both those things – certainly the latter. They've also known for a long time that he intends me to be his heir. They've seized on his illness as an excuse to act before he makes

259

any formal announcement. It gives their claims greater legitimacy.'

'But what do they intend to do? Fight you and our father's armies for the throne?'

'I don't know, but this is clearly a conspiracy planned some time ago for just such a contingency. They must have agreed that if anything happened to our father they would act together. Perhaps they've agreed some sort of plan to divide the empire between them. Whatever the case, I'm certain Aurangzeb is their leader.'

'Why do you say that?'

'He hates me,' Dara said simply. 'I've seen it in his eyes many times, however conciliatory his words. Behind my back he derides my beliefs and interest in other religions and calls me a heretic to anyone who will listen, and many I suspect do through self-interest if nothing more. I thought that in the Deccan he was too far away to do much harm but I was wrong. I've been too confident in Father's favour and in my position here at court. I should have paid more attention to what was happening elsewhere. I have let down my own sons. If I fail now, Suleiman and Sipihr as well as I will surely pay the price.'

'All this can still be stopped. Before he was taken ill our father was in command of his empire and he can be so again. The most important thing is to quash the rumours that he's too ill to rule or dying or dead ... As soon as possible – tomorrow at dawn if he is in any way strong enough – he must resume his daily appearance on the *jharoka* balcony to prove to his people that their emperor still lives. And he must be told at once what has happened. God willing he's not too ill to take command of the situation himself. Surely our brothers won't dare to defy his authority if they know he is himself again.'

'Your words are wise as always . . . I won't wait until the morning. I'll go to him now . . .' Dara hurried to the door but then stopped to look back at her over his shoulder. 'Do you want to come with me?'

'I can't. He still refuses to see me. Even when I asked to be allowed to visit his sickbed he would not permit it. I fear the sight of me will only disturb him and distract him from more pressing matters.'

'I'll tell him how wrong he has been to suspect you. Satti al-Nisa wrote to me informing me exactly what had happened. I'll make him listen. All will yet be well – I promise you.'

But would all be well, Jahanara wondered, listening to Dara's fast receding footsteps. She wasn't so sure. Her father's accusations and ready belief in her guilt . . . the knowledge that her own sister had had a hand in her downfall . . . had rocked her faith in her family, her belief that they were united and not each out for their own interests. And now this dreadful news about her brothers had confirmed her fears exceeding anything she could have imagined in her worst nightmares. Who would ever have believed it could come to this? *Taktya takhta* – throne or coffin – the brutal code her Moghul ancestors had brought with them from the Asian steppes. Strip away the fine clothes and jewels, the formal etiquette that governed their lives as imperial princes, and what were her brothers? Not civilised scions of a great and enlightened empire but wild animals, snarling at each over a carcass that wasn't yet even dead meat . . . snarling like the flat-eared tiger on her father's worn, heavy, gold ring that had once graced Timur's hand.

• ◆ •

Shah Jahan rose from the low chair where he had seated himself to hear Dara's story and began slowly to pace his bedchamber, arms wrapped around himself, head bowed. At first Dara's words had so disconcerted him that for a while he'd just sat silent and still. He had even wondered whether they were a product of his imagination conjured by the *hakims*' potions. Often, particularly during the early days of his illness, he'd felt caught midway between wakefulness and sleep, uncertain what was real and what emanated from his tired and troubled brain. Strange images had floated through his mind, often of the departed – his grandfather Akbar, his father Jahangir and above all Mumtaz smiling as she whispered '*Mubarak manzil*', the traditional greeting from an empress to a returning emperor.

Now, though, he realised he was back in the real world, confronting harsh realities – rebellion, and rebellion led not by traitorous subjects but by members of his immediate family. What madness could have possessed his younger sons? None of them was what he would have wished, but he had never suspected them of such naked treachery. It was as if the old days were returning – the days when the Moghuls' greatest enemies had been each other. He himself had been pushed into rebellion against his own father and to fighting with his half-brothers for the throne. But that was different ... Urged on by Mehrunissa, Jahangir had driven him to it. He had only acted to protect his family. His own sons had no such excuse and he would not allow the old wheel of family ambition, feuding and bloodshed to begin turning again. He would – he must – end this rebellion before it destroyed his family and everything the Moghuls had achieved.

He ceased his pacing and turned to Dara. 'Send out scouts to their provinces. Find out how big their armies are, how far they have advanced and who has declared for them. I need as much hard information as possible. And in the morning I will summon my council. They must hear everything that you've told me. One thing is already clear – we must act quickly and decisively before the rebels gain further momentum.'

'Jahanara suggested you should appear to your people on the *jharoka* balcony as soon as you can to quell any rumours that you are dead.'

'Jahanara? You've seen her?'

'Yes. I went to her immediately I reached the fort.' Shah Jahan gave Dara a penetrating look but said nothing as he continued, 'You have done her a great injustice. These stories about her and Nicholas Ballantyne are as malicious and baseless as the stories of your demise. She only asked Nicholas to come to her because she was worried about Aurangzeb. She wanted Nicholas to tell her what had happened during the northern campaign. She swears on the memory of our mother that she's innocent of any liaison with him ... Father, forgive me for speaking so bluntly, but from what I hear you condemned Jahanara unjustly. At least see her now ... let my sister herself show you how wrong you have been.' Dara waited. His father needed those members of his family like Jahanara still loyal to him. He tried again. 'Father ... you must believe me. I ...'

This time Shah Jahan did respond. 'Enough, Dara. I have heard what you've said.'

'You will see Jahanara?'

'Perhaps.'

Three hours later, with an apricot glow lightening the eastern horizon, Shah Jahan sipped the water his *qorchi* had just handed him. It was still cold from the well and he drank thirstily, holding the jade cup with hands that were still not quite steady. Was it the result of his illness – the strange weakness that had suddenly inflicted him and for which the *hakims* could find no explanation? Or agitation at Dara's news of rebellion? Or was it because soon Jahanara would be before him and he must ask her forgiveness once more?

He was still pondering when he heard a series of shrill trumpet blasts – the signal he had ordered to be given to rouse the people of Agra from their sleep and summon them to the banks of the Jumna to witness the reappearance of their emperor on his *jharoka* balcony. '*Qorchi*, bring me my robes, please.' Normally the emperor made his brief appearance on the balcony in a simple cotton tunic, but his people hadn't seen him for nearly three months. He would wear green brocade and sparkle with jewels when he stepped from his bedchamber on to the carved sandstone balcony as the rising sun warmed the earth. He would raise his arms to bless them and the day to come, remaining there longer than usual so that none could doubt that it was indeed their emperor, returned to health, before them.

Half an hour later, the task was done. Shah Jahan turned away from the cheering crowds gathered below and went back into his apartments. Jahanara would be waiting for him on his private terrace as he had asked. For a moment he hesitated, then made his way there, shading his eyes against the now brilliant light as he came outside again. Jahanara was standing there but did not come forward. For a moment they stood looking at one another, then Shah Jahan strode towards her.

He could find no words. Dara had been so eloquent on her behalf, so convincing in his explanations, so insistent that she was innocent, and in his heart Shah Jahan had known his son was right. How could he have reacted with such unthinking anger? Once again he had failed her. 'Forgive me,' he managed at last. 'I judged you in haste and in anger. I make no excuses . . .'

'It is past, Father. Perhaps we shouldn't speak of it again.' Jahanara's tone was measured, devoid of the conflicting emotions swirling within her.

'But tell me you forgive me or I will not be able to rest.'

'I forgive you.' As she spoke those words, as she knew she must for the sake of the dynasty, Jahanara saw her father visibly relax. But were they really true, she wondered. Could she forgive him again? Eventually, perhaps, though it would take time to forget his immediate, unthinking belief in her guilt and his unreasoning anger. But looking at her father with fresh eyes after so many weeks of separation, she realised with a shock how old he looked. His broad shoulders were bowed and his once muscular body – a warrior's body – looked thin and fragile. His still handsome face was riven with deep lines.

Had his illness really taken such a toll or was it that she was only now seeing him as he really was?

Pity welled within her and she managed a smile, but it faded as another thought struck her. 'I'm not the only one who has suffered an injustice. You wronged Nicholas Ballantyne too. He was blameless for what happened. I turned to him because I was worried about my brothers – Aurangzeb especially. I was too impulsive, I know. I should have reflected how my actions might appear to others. But Nicholas's only crime was to try to help me despite his reluctance. He is taking ship for England. Let me write to him. My letter may not reach him in time but I would like him to know that all is well . . . that our family are conscious of what they owe him.'

'Of course. Tell him I regret what happened and remember his past service with gratitude. Should he ever return to my court he will be welcome.' Shah Jahan put his hand on Jahanara's arm. He felt a deep relief that one breach at least was mended, but a deadly weariness followed. He sighed and for a moment closed his eyes.

'Father . . . are you all right? Should I summon your *hakims*?'

'No. I've been an invalid too long and must become an emperor once more.' Shah Jahan straightened his back. 'How much has Dara told you of your brothers' rebellion?'

'That they have used your illness as an excuse to raise troops and intend to challenge for the throne . . .'

Shah Jahan frowned. 'That is the gist of it. I keep thinking what your mother would have thought and how badly I have let her memory down. I should have paid more attention to what your brothers were doing and

266

controlled them better, making regular imperial progresses through their provinces. Instead I gave them and their ambitious counsellors time and opportunity to plot against me.'

Jahanara did not respond for a moment. Her father was right. Grief at Mumtaz's death had forced him into an emotional seclusion from which he had never fully emerged, blunting his empathy with all of his children, herself included, as his willingness to believe the worst of her had shown. But how could she say any of that to him? 'Father, the past is gone. Nothing you have done or failed to do can justify my brothers' rebellion. Concentrate on bringing them to heel.'

• ◆ •

Shah Jahan looked round the familiar circle of his counsellors, their faces proof that the news of his sons' insurrection which he had just broken was as great a surprise to them as it had been to him a few hours earlier. Unless, of course, some of them were good dissemblers. At least one had money worries – his lands had been badly affected by drought. What if Aurangzeb had offered him a handsome sum for his support, Shah Jahan wondered, looking hard into the man's face. And another over there near the door was known to have coveted a rich *jagir* that not long before his illness he'd granted to another. He too might have been bought. Who could say? Most men had their price. But at least his Rajput allies, Raja Jai Singh of Amber and Raja Jaswant Singh of Marwar were utterly loyal, he was sure, bound to the Moghuls since Akbar's time by family ties as well as those of honour. Raising his hands, he spoke again. 'I have told you only the main facts about the treachery of my three youngest sons. Now Prince Dara will give you as much detail about their movements and that of their forces as we've been able to gather.'

'Aurangzeb's army is already on the march from the Deccan,' Dara said. 'He is apparently claiming that this is not a rebellion – merely that there have been so many rumours that he wishes to come to Agra in person to satisfy himself that the emperor is indeed alive. Shah Shuja also has an army in the field, advancing west along the Ganges. It contains many war elephants bred in the jungles of Assam as well as a large number of horsemen and foot soldiers.'

'Aurangzeb of course already had standing forces ready to deploy against the rulers of the south, but how did Shah Shuja raise so many men so quickly?' asked Jai Singh.

Shah Jahan answered. 'Bengal's coffers are deep enough to buy him an army twice that size, and he also has the revenues of Bihar, which I was foolish enough to award him though others advised against it. Go on, Dara.'

'My brother Murad is as deeply implicated as the others. He's apparently also been mustering troops and buying equipment – or trying to, because unlike his brothers' his treasuries are nearly empty thanks to his extravagance and incompetence. He's attempting to raise loans among the wealthy merchants of Gujarat and that will delay him, but not for long, I fear . . .'

'You really think they all intend to bring their armies to Agra?' asked Jaswant Singh.

'It would seem so. I believe they have made a pact with one another, but whether it is to support one of them for the throne or to divide the empire between them isn't clear,' Dara replied.

'Then it will come to a battle unless I can prevent it,' said Shah Jahan. 'I have already sent messages by post riders to every one of my governors and senior officials in the provinces assuring them that I am returned to health – and that anyone who aids my rebellious sons will suffer a traitor's death. I have also written to my sons, demanding they cease their rebellion and reminding them of their duty to their father. But matters may well have advanced too far for that to have much effect on these ingrates. I have no choice but to command you to prepare the imperial troops immediately for war, summoning every warrior you can muster from your fiefs and ordering your vassals to do the same. Perhaps when the traitors realise the strength of the forces ranging against them they will see reason and pull back before Moghul sheds the blood of Moghul.'

Two hours later, after the last of the counsellors had left, Shah Jahan rose a little shakily from his silver chair. Dara hurried to support him but Shah Jahan waved him back. 'No. I must learn to be strong again ... and, Dara, there's something I must say to you. If I'd formally declared you my heir many years ago, this could never have happened. Now you will be forced to fight for what should have been yours by right. I regret it from the bottom of my heart, but more importantly I mean to try to make amends. Tomorrow, seated on my peacock throne and before all my court, I will formally declare you my successor and your brothers outlaws.'

Chapter 17

Nicholas Ballantyne turned restlessly on the straw mattress on which he had been trying to snatch a few hours' sleep and slapped at one of the many mosquitoes whining around him. In just three days the *Juno* would sail from Surat for Bristol, her hold packed with calicos, silks and indigo to add to the fat profits of the English East India Company. He would also be aboard. He'd negotiated a good price for his passage with the *Juno*'s burly red-faced captain but there was little pleasure in the prospect of the long and hazardous voyage round the Cape of Good Hope and a return to the country which, the more he'd thought about it, was scarcely any longer home.

Abandoning thoughts of sleep as pointless, Nicholas got up. Though dawn was barely an hour away heat still radiated from the mud-brick walls of the small, bare ground floor room of the inn and his near-naked body felt damp with perspiration. Going out into the courtyard he drew a bucket of water from the well and poured it over himself. Then, shaking himself like a dog, he went to sit beneath the spreading branches of a neem tree near a string charpoy on which an old man – supposedly the nightwatchman – was fast asleep. At least he need no longer worry about Princess Jahanara. The short letter that had caught up with him the day before had put his mind at rest, extinguishing any guilt he'd felt at fleeing Agra.

Jahanara was strong. She had learned to be, even in childhood when her family had fled from Jahangir. All the same, the thought of her standing accused of imaginary crimes had troubled him deeply, especially if the rumours circulating among the merchants in Surat were true. But could the emperor's younger sons really be in revolt? Jahanara's letter had said nothing explicitly, but she had mentioned her relief at being able again to be at her father's side with Dara, whatever fate held in store for them. Could this be an oblique reference designed not to alarm him on his voyage? Probably not. Far more likely Dara's brothers were just posturing. In this vast land, despite the imperial trunk roads and teams of post riders, news took time to travel. It often became distorted along the way and there were always credulous fools to be taken in.

Nicholas had risen to go inside when he heard a barrage of crashes and felt the ground shake. After a minute or two the noise began again, and this time didn't cease. It could only be cannon fire. Was Surat under attack? By the direction of the sound cannon were pounding the city from the landward side. From nearby streets came shouts of alarm. Nicholas hurried back into his room, hastily pulled on his shirt, breeches and boots and ran into the alley outside to find it already full of people – English merchants, some in their night clothes, some clutching their cash boxes; Indian clerks and shopkeepers. They must be making for the protection of the fort. The square, thick-walled tower lay about a quarter of a mile away on the tip of a promontory. The East India Company stored its treasure there in deep underground vaults and it was well fortified and guarded by a regiment of Company soldiers sent out from England. In case of serious trouble the Company also kept several ships well equipped with cannon riding at anchor beneath its walls.

And trouble, it seemed, had definitely arrived … Pressing himself into a doorway to allow the tide of humanity to sweep past, he looked back over their heads towards the city walls and sure enough in the pale light of dawn saw billowing columns of dust and smoke. Suddenly he caught sight of a young merchant he knew slightly, clutching a leather-bound ledger to his chest as he ran towards him. 'John, what's happening?' Nicholas yelled above the confusion. When the young man didn't appear to hear him Nicholas reached out a muscular arm and yanked him over as he passed. 'It's me, Nicholas. Do you know what's going on? Is it *dacoits*?' But even as he posed the question Nicholas knew it couldn't be. They might lurk outside the city to prey on caravan trains but where would they get large cannon?

'Someone said Prince Murad has hired Turkish mercenaries to attack Surat.'

'But he's the Governor of Gujarat! Why is he assaulting

its richest city – the one that pays him most in taxes?' The young merchant was trying to twist from his grip and Nicholas saw his pale eyes turn towards the stream of people who in their eagerness to get away from the danger and into the fort were now pushing and shoving each other as they ran.

'Because the prince asked the Company for a huge loan and the local board of directors refused him,' the young man gasped, feeling Nicholas's hold on him tighten.

'So now he's decided to help himself ...' Nicholas released his grip and the merchant dashed away to be swallowed up in the crowd. Nicholas stayed where he was. Should he too take sanctuary in the fort? He was no longer a Moghul commander with troops to deploy but a foreigner caught in the middle of someone else's problems on the eve of his return home. His first duty was to himself. Or was it? If Murad had indeed launched an attack on Surat this was anarchy. Shah Jahan would never have sanctioned such a thing, in which case the rumours must be true: the emperor's sons – or Murad at least – had indeed risen against their father.

Stepping out of the doorway, Nicholas barged his way through the jumbled mass of frightened people and back into the inn from which everyone else seemed to have fled. The string charpoy was empty and the only sign of life was a pale-furred dog that had taken refuge beneath the bed where it lay, head between its front paws, whimpering in fear as the bombardment continued. Running into his room Nicholas grabbed his two saddlebags from beneath the straw mattress. They were not heavy – so much for his many years' service in

Hindustan – but he still owed something to this land and he knew where he must go.

• ◆ •

There had been so little time to organise the imperial armies but delay was not an option, Shah Jahan reflected as he prepared to address his council once more. Like him, his counsellors were growing old. Barely a man under fifty. Not for the first time since the crisis had broken three weeks ago he regretted Dara's lack of military experience. He had wanted to keep his eldest son by his side, content, as in truth Dara had been also, for his younger brothers to go off on campaign, never for a moment thinking it was giving them the chance to develop skills they would one day turn against himself and Dara on the battlefield.

'My loyal counsellors, the latest reports I have through scouts and post riders are that Shah Shuja's forces are still advancing westward along the Ganges, making slow but steady progress,' he began. 'I have sent orders to those whose lands lie in his path to do all they can to obstruct him and deny him supplies, but I must meet force with force. Therefore I am despatching an army against Shah Shuja. My grandson, Dara's son Suleiman, will lead it, with you, Raja Jai Singh of Amber, as his adviser. Your force will consist of twenty thousand horsemen and five thousand foot soldiers. You and my grandson will be reinforced as you travel down the Ganges by my Afghan general Dilir Khan and his men.'

'Is Shah Shuja to be taken alive?' asked the raja.

'Yes. I want to avoid shedding my sons' blood. I wish him brought before me to answer for his crimes.'

'Is there any news of your other two sons, Majesty?' asked the Uzbek Khalilullah Khan, whose scarred face testified to his hard and loyal fighting at the side of Aurangzeb against his fellow countrymen in his northern campaign.

'The information on Murad is still patchy and vague. Some reports state that he has proclaimed himself emperor in Gujarat – that the *khutba* has been read in his name in the mosques and he has ordered coins to be struck to mark the start of his reign – others that he has murdered his revenue minister – Ali Naqi, a man who was always loyal to me – for protesting against his treasonous acts. They say Murad himself ran him through with a sword. There are also rumours that Murad plans to attack and loot Surat and then, when he has filled his war chest, to march from his capital at Ahmadabad to rendezvous with Aurangzeb as he moves up from the Deccan. Murad has apparently sent his women and children to safety in the fortress of Champanir, which means he anticipates a long campaign.'

'Surely if Prince Murad has already crowned himself emperor, he intends to fight Prince Aurangzeb, not join forces with him?' asked Raja Jaswant Singh of Marwar, running a finger along the hilt of the dagger hanging in its jewelled scabbard from a gold chain round his waist.

'I think not. Our scouts intercepted one of Aurangzeb's messengers riding north to Ahmadabad. He was carrying a letter bearing Aurangzeb's seal and addressed to Murad. Listen to what it says.' Shah Jahan motioned to an attendant to hand him the document. '*Our scheme for seizing the throne is now under way. Together we will trample the idolaters and infidels who bring shame upon the name of Islam and Moghul alike and enforce the word of the one God in this sinful country. You, my dear brother, have joined me in this great enterprise and I hereby reaffirm my promise to you that when we have prevailed – as we will, for our cause is just – your reward will be the provinces of Punjab, Afghanistan, Kashmir and Sind to govern without let or hindrance as your own, let God be my witness. When we meet, as we are pledged to do before reaching Agra, we will debate further about how we will bring these glorious things to pass and send our enemies to perdition.'* It may be a forgery, intended deliberately to fall into my hands and to mislead me. Aurangzeb is devious enough for that. But I think it's genuine. Aurangzeb is playing to Murad's conceit and vanity. He knows that Murad is much closer to Agra than he is and I suspect the reason he is insistent on their joining forces before reaching here is to avoid Murad's arriving before him and thus seizing some kind of advantage militarily or politically. What Aurangzeb's intentions are towards Shah Shuja I can only guess. But one thing I'm absolutely certain of – we must prevent either Aurangzeb or Murad from reaching Agra. I therefore intend to despatch another army south under you, Raja Jaswant Singh, to seek them out and confront them, either singly or together. God and right are on our side – not theirs.'

Shah Jahan sat down and for a moment closed his eyes. Dara knew that he was exhausted. Despite his continuing weakness he had sat up through much of the night with himself, Suleiman, Jai Singh, Jaswant Singh and his other commanders, studying maps and discussing logistics – how many troops were ready to move, how long it would take to muster further units, how many cannon he had, how many war elephants there were in the imperial stables and how many more could be provided by his Rajput allies. Only a few weeks ago Shah Jahan had been on his sickbed but now, even if it was draining any reserves of strength remaining in his frail body, his steely determination was inspiring confidence in others. Dara could see it in the counsellors' faces. He felt it in himself.

He rose to his feet and raised his arms. 'Long live my father, the emperor. *Zinderbad Padishah Shah Jahan!*' As the council's spirited response echoed around him, his own spirits rose further. As his father had said, their cause was just.

• ◆ •

'Father, Raja Jai Singh is here.' Dara's voice broke into Shah Jahan's slumber. Despite his recovery, he sometimes dozed after his midday meal – itself a much less sumptuous affair than when he had been in his prime. Just some chicken baked in the *tandoor* and a little saffron rice. Rubbing the sleep from his eyes, Shah Jahan sat up on the gold brocade couch on which he had been lying, his mind quickly focusing. In recent weeks he'd received few reports of the progress of Suleiman's army. 'What's Jai Singh's news? Why has he come in person?'

'I don't know yet. I've not seen him. I was in the *haram* resting with Nadira when an attendant told me of his arrival. I thought you and I should hear his report together. I've sent word that he should join us in your private audience chamber in a quarter of an hour.'

In fact it was only ten minutes before a *qorchi* announced the ruler of Amber to the imperial father and son. As the raja entered he looked as urbane and well groomed as ever, his luxuriant moustaches faultlessly curled and pomaded, his cream robe spotless. Despite the best efforts of attendants in an adjacent chamber pulling the strings of a great *punka* of peacock's feathers so that it swayed back and forth like a giant butterfly's wing above the emperor's head, the audience chamber was hot and airless, but Jai Singh wasn't even perspiring.

Anxious and unable to read from the raja's face what his news was, Dara in an unaccustomed breach of protocol spoke before his father. 'Is your news good or bad, Jai Singh?'

Slightly taken aback, the raja responded, 'A mixture, Highness.'

'Well then, Dara,' said Shah Jahan, 'Jai Singh must let me have his report of events in the order they happened so that I can judge them for myself.'

'I will, Majesty.' The raja bowed, recognising in Shah Jahan's words an implicit rebuke to his over-eager son. 'We made swift progress in our flotilla of barges down first the Jumna and then the Ganges, pausing only occasionally to exercise the horses and at Allahabad to take on more weapons and stores and to rendezvous with Dilir Khan. It took us less than a month to cover five hundred miles before – acting on information brought to us by a local vassal who had himself rowed from his riverside fort to intercept us – your grandson gave the order to disembark near Varanasi. In doing so, he followed the advice of myself and Dilir Khan, as he did in leaving some of the heavy equipment behind and setting out immediately to intercept Shah Shuja and his men, who the vassal had told us were moving west, parallel to the north bank of the river about twelve miles inland.

'During the late evening of the next day, some of our scouts returned to camp. They had been sweeping well ahead of our main body when they saw at a distance what looked like campfires burning. Dismounting and creeping closer they found Shah Shuja's camp quiet and scarcely a sentry posted. Hearing their report, we agreed in a war council to break camp just after midnight and attack Shah Shuja's army at dawn as they prepared for the day ahead. Mindful of your strictures not to shed the blood of your family, Prince Suleiman ordered us to avoid firing on what looked like command positions and to seek to capture rather than kill Shah Shuja.

'All went well until we were pushing through some scrubland less than a mile or so from Shah Shuja's camp. An agonised scream tore the air and our leading scout suddenly pitched from his saddle. His terrified mount galloped back towards us, reins dangling. For a moment we thought an unseen sentry had killed the scout but then, as the horse got closer, we saw great bleeding slashes on its rump as it pushed its way into and through our ranks, unsettling our own horses, followed by a great male tiger. He was the cause of the wounds and the scout's scream – not an enemy attack. On seeing our numbers the tiger veered away back into the night. However, the hubbub had roused the few sentries Shah Shuja had posted. They began to yell warnings.

'We immediately dug our heels into our horses' flanks and charged for the camp, levelling our lances and drawing our swords as we went. We were scarcely a hundred yards away from the nearest tents when a few ragged musket volleys crackled out and one of my *qorchis* tumbled from his horse. Then we were among the tents, slashing at the guy ropes with our swords to collapse them on to the occupants and thrusting into them with our lances. Soon the fabric of the tents was stained with blood and wounded men were struggling from beneath it to surrender. Within what could have been no more than a quarter of an hour, we had penetrated right into the centre of the camp. Then I saw a large phalanx of horsemen gallop away and disappear into a clump of woodland to the east. I shouted to Prince Suleiman that Shah Shuja must be among them but he replied to let them go . . . that we could deal with him later. For the moment it was better to concentrate on the rout of the remainder of Shah Shuja's forces and the seizure of the camp with all the valuable equipment it contained, including the magnificent war elephants he had never been able to deploy.'

'Was it my son who fled? If not, what happened to him?'

'I believe it was Shah Shuja, Majesty, but I can't be sure. The group escaped. We did not capture Shah Shuja anywhere else – nor was he among the dead or wounded,' Jai Singh added hastily, seeing the look on Shah Jahan's face.

'But surely this is all good news? Under your guidance Suleiman has defeated Shah Shuja.'

'Yes, Majesty, but what happened next is the bad news.'

'Do you mean Shah Shuja's forces regrouped and attacked you?'

'No, Majesty, it's not that – simply that your grandson

insisted that our forces follow the remnants of Shah Shuja's army, at least half of whom escaped one way or the other and were, we soon discovered, fleeing east towards Patna. Dilir Khan and I argued hard that Shah Shuja was already spent as a contender for your throne and that Aurangzeb and Murad who, as far as we knew, were undefeated, now posed a far greater threat. We wanted to lead our troops, whom we considered the very cream of your army, back west where they were most needed. Prince Suleiman just would not agree and as our commander we had to obey him. The most I could achieve was his permission to return to Agra with my personal retainers and bodyguard to report back to you while Dilir Khan stayed with him as his counsellor.'

'Have you heard any more from Suleiman's forces?'

'Yes, only yesterday. A hard-riding *cossid* reached me from Dilir Khan. He and Suleiman are a hundred and twenty miles east of Varanasi, pursuing their adversaries into the jungles and marshes of Bengal.'

Shah Jahan frowned. Jai Singh was right: the news was mixed. Shah Shuja had been routed but Suleiman was behaving as if he were on a hunt rather than engaged in a deadly contest. All would be well if Jaswant Singh succeeded in defeating Aurangzeb and Murad, but if not Suleiman's men would be needed. His reckless pursuit of Shah Shuja must stop. Shah Jahan would send orders at once recalling the prince to Agra.

• ◆ •

The spring sunshine – warm but not overly fierce – felt good on his face. Shah Jahan was glad to be on horseback again as he urged his bay stallion into a gallop. It wasn't long before the red sandstone gateway of Akbar's great tomb at Sikandra loomed before him. Needing time and solitude to absorb the latest news, he had felt a sudden impulse to visit the final resting place of the grandfather who had taught him so much about the duties of an emperor. What would Akbar have said about the crisis now confronting his favourite grandson? Akbar himself had never faced such peril, perhaps because he had been a better ruler, more assiduous and astute in reading the mood of his empire . . .

As green-turbaned guards snapped to attention, Shah Jahan dismounted stiffly. Either through age or the aftermath of his illness – probably both – the ride had tested and tired his muscles and bones more than he had anticipated. Throwing his reins to a *qorchi*, he signalled his escort to remain outside and walked alone through the gateway. As he emerged into the gardens beyond, a monkey, taken by surprise, scampered off screeching and a trio of deer grazing beneath a plane tree raised their heads and looked towards him. But Shah Jahan's eyes were on his grandfather's tomb directly ahead at the end of a long raised sandstone path shaded by trees. The tomb was too solid for beauty but its bulk seemed to embody Akbar's spirit. He had been a big and powerful man, physically and mentally, expanding his empire and placing it on foundations as firm and deep as those that supported his burial place. Slowly, Shah Jahan made his way down the path and reaching the end sat on one of two marble benches facing the tomb. He had come here to think but, exhausted by the ride and the shock of the day's events, almost immediately his eyes began to close.

Footsteps on the sandstone paving woke him with a

start. Standing, he turned to see someone walking quickly towards him but the shadows cast by the trees made it impossible to see who it was. Why had his bodyguards admitted anyone when he'd asked to be left alone? Instinctively his right hand went to the dagger at his belt. 'Who are you? Who permitted you to intrude on my privacy?' he called.

The newcomer paused. Shah Jahan saw golden hair – not as bright or as thick as it had once been but unmistakable all the same.

'Approach.' He waited as Nicholas Ballantyne came closer.

'Majesty, forgive me for interrupting you. The captain of your guard knows me. When I told him I had urgent information for you, he allowed me to enter.'

Shah Jahan let his hand drop back to his side. Now that the Englishman was closer he could see that his face was gaunt and there were deep circles beneath his eyes. 'My daughter wrote to you, I know, expressing my . . . regret at the . . . misunderstanding that caused you to leave Agra.'

'Majesty, that's not why I've ridden so hard to find you. I've something to tell you that cannot – must not – wait.' Nicholas's words tumbled out.

'Speak, then.'

'I was in Surat waiting to embark for England when the forces of your son Murad attacked the city. They smashed through the walls with their cannon and looted the East India Company's treasury . . . From what I learned from those I met on the road from Surat, one of Murad's generals led the assault. The prince himself was already riding south with an even larger force to rendezvous with

Prince Aurangzeb ... I knew I must bring you this news at once. I ...' Seeing Shah Jahan's faint, sad smile, Nicholas tailed off.

'I appreciate your coming, but I already knew about the attack on Surat. Even before the event I heard that Murad planned to seize the city and its treasuries but I had no troops to despatch who could arrive in time ...'

'I'm relieved you know, Majesty. My worry was that I'd be too late.'

'And what action do you think I've taken?'

'Sent an army to intercept Murad before he and his brother join forces?'

'Quite right. In fact, I did it before I heard the definitive news about Surat. You look surprised, Nicholas. You don't believe my rebellious sons' claims that I've become too enfeebled to rule, do you?'

Seeing Nicholas's hurt expression Shah Jahan softened his tone – after all, the Englishman had had no need to return to Agra rather than take ship for his homeland. 'Matters have moved more quickly than you realise. You've come back to Agra in one of my darkest hours since the death of my empress. You thought you had important news to tell me – for which I thank you. But now let me tell you something ... Only a few hours ago I learned that Aurangzeb and Murad had joined forces by the time Raja Jaswant Singh and the strong army I had sent to confront them caught up with them at Dharmat, not far from Ujjain. Jaswant Singh was misinformed – or perhaps deliberately misled – about the strength of his enemies' artillery and ordered a frontal attack. As his Rajput horsemen galloped into battle over open ground, the rebel cannon cut them down. When the rebels followed their cannonade with a cavalry charge of their own, our troops broke under the impact and scattered, many – Jaswant Singh included – into the Rajasthani desert.'

'Where are Aurangzeb and Murad now?'

'I don't know for certain. If I were them I'd be making for the Chambal river, the last obstacle between them and Agra. Naturally I've despatched scouts south to report to me the moment their forces appear.'

'What will you do then, Majesty?'

'The only thing I can – send my remaining troops to block their advance. Prince Dara must take the field for the honour and salvation of the empire – for everything my grandfather achieved and now hangs in the balance.'

Chapter 18

Nicholas sat relaxed on his chestnut horse atop a low hill rising from the plain about four miles southwest of Agra. Looking back in the soft early morning light he could still see the familiar outline of the Taj Mahal on the horizon. To him, the dome was a teardrop. The coarser minds among his mercenaries, of whom at his own request he had once more taken command, insisted it was nothing but a woman's breast and its gold finial a fine pert nipple. In the pre-dawn hours Dara had despatched Nicholas and his five hundred men – disease, wounds and desertions had much reduced their number since the beginning of the northern campaign – to check the early stages of his route before he himself led the main body of his army out towards the Chambal river.

As, flaming torches in their hands, they had made their way down the steep ramp, through the towering gateway and out across the plain they had come upon nothing to concern them militarily. Nicholas had relished what to him was the wonderful and unique scent of Hindustan – the mixture of the smells of earth, night-flowering plants such as the *champa*, dung cooking fires and spices, as the country dwellers began to awake and prepare for the new day. He had heard nothing beyond the jingling of the harnesses of his men's horses, the occasional wild screech of a peacock and the nocturnal howl of some wakeful village hound swiftly taken up by its newly roused fellows.

Now, though, the peace was being broken literally and metaphorically. Dara and his main army were beginning their march to face his brothers Aurangzeb and Murad in battle in person. Civil war was under way, with all its bitterness and divisions within families, high and low. He had seen enough of it during his early days in Hindustan as Shah Jahan fought for the throne to know its bloody perils and consequences. Later, letters from his older brother at home on the family estates in the west of England had told him of the civil war raging in his own country – of the execution of the king and the establishment of a people's parliament. Its puritanical leader insisted on the following of a fundamentalist faith as strict and austere as any prescribed by Aurangzeb and his mullahs, banning even harmless festivities such as dancing around the maypole and the theatre.

Almost instinctively Nicholas put his hand to one of the two pistols in his sash. They had arrived in a tightly bound parcel accompanying his brother's last letter. Such weapons were rarely seen in Hindustan. They should however prove useful in the fighting to come, even if he was unlikely to have the necessary time in the press of battle to reload them. He must make each of their single shots count, something his initial attempts had shown was difficult to achieve at much more than fifteen yards.

An ear-splitting blast jolted Nicholas from his reverie. It came from a long-stemmed trumpet held by an outrider of the vanguard as it approached.

The vanguard, all mounted on matching black horses and wearing tunics and turbans of Moghul green, were advancing thirty abreast. The front two ranks were made up of trumpeters interspersed with drummers who beat out a steady tattoo on the drums mounted on each side of the saddles of their horses who were so well trained as to appear oblivious of the noise. Behind the musicians the next ranks were of straight-backed cavalrymen. Except for those — one in every six, Nicholas guessed — who gripped the wooden staves of green banners blowing gently in the breeze, they held erect long lances with green pennants. Beyond them came further lines of horsemen, the pennants at their lance tips seeming to roll like the waves of a gentle sea swell or a ripple of wind through an autumn cornfield as their riders bobbed in their saddles.

After some minutes through the golden dust haze Nicholas saw a phalanx of war elephants approaching, each with a great howdah and a coat of overlapping steel plate armour. The individual plates were small to allow the elephants to move freely. Nicholas couldn't help remembering how he had once tried to count the number in each coat, getting to over three thousand before giving up. As well as their war coats, every elephant had an outsize cutlass securely tied to each tusk. The tusks themselves were painted blood red and some filed to a sharp point to inflict the maximum damage at close quarters. From about a third of the howdahs poked the barrels of *gajnals*, the small cannon so effective in a war of movement because the elephants could transport them relatively quickly into the thick of the action.

In the middle of the elephant phalanx was a formation of the largest beasts, their tusks painted not red but gold, keeping pace with each other as they walked forward to maintain the shape of a square. From the howdah at each corner of the square flew vast green banners much bigger than those carried by the horsemen, six feet high and perhaps twenty feet long and embroidered in gold with the names of the emperor and Dara Shukoh. At the centre of the square plodded the largest elephant of them all, the jewels in its tower-like howdah glittering and glinting in the rising sun. As the elephant slowly drew closer Nicholas made out ever more clearly the figure of Dara sitting in the centre of the howdah clad in a gold breastplate like his revered great-grandfather the emperor Akbar, two dark-bearded bodyguards with drawn swords squatting behind him. As the column passed Nicholas Dara raised a hand in his direction but Nicholas couldn't be sure whether he recognised him or was simply doing as a good general should – acknowledging any body of his troops he met along the way.

Half an hour later the army's cannon were passing Nicholas, who had been ordered to join the rearguard with his men. The air was becoming hot as the morning drew on and the ever-increasing dust was clogging his nose and mouth. However, taking a quick swig from his leather water bottle before drawing his blue face cloth tighter, he couldn't help being impressed by the magnificence of the artillery as he watched the largest of the cannon rumble past. How long their brass barrels, engraved with serpents and mystical birds, were – some nearly twenty feet. How many oxen were required to pull the great eight-wheeled limbers? He counted thirty straining to pull one of the weapons, urged on by white-loinclothed drivers running barefoot on skinny legs from one animal to another, cracking their long whips and tugging at the rope halters of recalcitrant beasts whose outraged bellowing he could sometimes hear over the general hubbub of the march.

Even more than the war elephants, the cannon – nearly a hundred and fifty years after their introduction into Hindustan by Dara's ancestor Babur – were at the heart of any modern army, being as well suited to disrupting a charge of horsemen or war elephants as to blasting and battering down the walls and gates of a resisting city. The makers of gunpowder – often Turkish mercenaries – were producing better powder mixtures all the time to give the weapons longer range and greater reliability. If only, thought Nicholas, the forge masters could make these great weapons lighter and thus more manoeuvrable and swifter to deploy.

After the cannon came wooden ox carts, some with tightly roped-down oiled covers – the powder wagons – and some with the cannon balls of stone or iron stacked in them. Behind them, mostly mounted but some on foot, were the musketeers, long weapons and ram rods either tied to their saddles or slung across their backs, together with their powder horns and pouches containing the balls for the muskets. Their weapons were mostly matchlocks, more reliable in Hindustani conditions than the newer flintlocks which were prone to failure to fire through dust or damp. Marching with the musketeers were armourers whose task it was to fashion new musket balls when required by pouring liquid lead into the moulds they carried.

Nicholas was growing ever more hot and tired and anxious to be on the move as the archers marched past. Although fewer in number than on previous campaigns their double bows and quiverfuls of feathered arrows still had the advantage of speed of fire over muskets, even if they were less deadly. Last before the rearguard came the infantry. Hardly any had footwear. Most wore only a loincloth and a simple turban to protect against the sun. A few carried swords. Many had simple spears. But some carried as weapons only the tools such as scythes and hoes which they had used to work the fields from which they had recently and hastily been plucked by their landlords to replace the more experienced men who had gone with Suleiman to confront Shah Shuja.

Nicholas had never found such raw infantry of great use in battle. They were either quick to panic and flee or easy for the enemy to cut down if they did resist. Perhaps their greatest function was by their very number to overawe civilian populations or other inexperienced armies. It took nearly another half-hour for their stumbling, already disorganised mass to pass. Then, with a great sigh of relief, he saw the mounted rearguard appear – a mixture of

Rajputs in pale yellow or orange robes mounted on prick-eared Mewari horses and heavily bearded and more bulky-bodied Punjabis on larger beasts, slower but of greater endurance.

With a joyful wave of his hand Nicholas gestured to his men, now all sweating like himself in the hot June sun, perspiration running in rivulets down their faces and coursing down their spines beneath their hot heavy backplates, to join their comrades. As he did so, he gave grateful thanks that he did not have to await the baggage train with its mixture of heavily loaded spitting camels, braying mules and protruding-ribbed donkeys to lumber past, still less the great body of camp followers who as far as he could see through the choking dust were straggling almost back to the gates of Agra. Still, the army needed the entertainment and pleasures the cooks, acrobats, nautch girls and snake charmers provided to while away the empty hours that were such a feature of campaign life, as well as to soothe worries and anxieties as battle approached. May this campaign be a short one and Dara triumphant, he thought, as he kicked his horse forward and the willing chestnut, as glad as Nicholas to be on the move once more, cantered down the small hill to join Dara's vast army.

• ◆ •

Two Sarus cranes rose slowly from the banks of the Chambal and flew along the river searching for fish, their large red heads and grey and white plumage reflected in the Chambal's glistening pewter waters. As Nicholas watched, seated on the stump of a decayed tree and grateful that the afternoon heat was slowly dying, the long, slim snout of a ghariyal snapped out of the water, also intent on an evening meal. The ghariyal was a crocodile unlike any other Nicholas had seen. Local people had assured him that it was harmless and ate only fish, while warning him that more familiar flesh-hungry crocodiles also lurked in the shallows and that on no account, however hot or tempted, should he swim in the river.

Hearing a noise behind him, Nicholas glanced round. It wasn't a crocodile – fish-eating or otherwise – but two or three of his fellow officers heading for Dara's command tent and a meeting to which he had also been summoned. Reminded of the time, Nicholas stood up, brushed down his clothes and also began to walk towards the tent. As he did so he wondered what the council was to be about. The army had arrived at the Chambal that morning after five days' hot, slow and dusty journey. He presumed the discussion would concern the crossing of the river to confront Aurangzeb and Murad – whether the Chambal was slow and shallow enough to ford safely or whether they needed to consume time in building a bridge of boats.

Five minutes into the meeting, standing in the second row of the sixty commanders clustering around the low divan on which Dara was seated beneath his tent's awning, Nicholas found out that he was wrong. Gesturing to a travel-grimed figure standing beside the divan, Dara said, 'Ravi Kumar here has just returned from a two-day scouting mission southwards along the Chambal. Ravi, tell me again what you saw there for the benefit of my officers.'

Ravi Kumar nodded. 'Last evening I encountered Aurangzeb and Murad's army fording the river twenty or so miles downstream. Much of the vanguard was already across, but the rest of the army were lighting cooking fires, seemingly prepared to spend the night on the far side.'

As the scout had spoken his first words a gasp of surprise had run round the assembled officers. Now one, a tall, clipped-bearded man Nicholas recognised as Raja Ram Singh Rathor, the ruler of a small state near Gwalior with a high reputation for both bravery and military sagacity, spoke. 'They've moved far faster than we'd thought, Highness. Do they have all their equipment with them?'

Dara motioned to Ravi Kumar to answer.

'I couldn't stay too long or get too close but I think they had the leading elements of their baggage train with them. Further wagons seemed to be arriving all the time and a dust cloud on the horizon suggested many more men and much equipment were yet to come. My guess is that it will take all of tomorrow for them to complete the crossing and re-form on the near bank.'

'Thank you, Ravi Kumar,' said Dara. He turned to his commanders. 'Can we break camp and reach them before they have finished crossing?'

After a brief pause Raja Ram Singh Rathor spoke once more, 'No, Highness. Not if we wish to have our heavy guns and war elephants with us as I think we must. Until now we've only made eight or so miles a day. Even if we pushed our animals harder I can't see the full strength of the army being able to reach the crossing in less than two days. By then Aurangzeb and Murad will be on the march to Agra and we'll be hard pressed to catch them.'

'I feared as much,' said Dara. 'In the short time since

Ravi and the other scouts returned I've been looking at maps and talking to some junior officers whose homes are along the Chambal. Even though our enemies have crossed the river, we are considerably to the north of them and much nearer to Agra than they are. However quickly they move, it seems to me if we break camp before dawn and head due west from here we should be able to cut them off and position ourselves across their path on advantageous ground. What do you think?'

'What sort of country do we have to traverse?' asked another voice. Nicholas couldn't see the speaker.

'I'm told it's mostly flat with few obstructions, although in places there is some deepish sand which may slow the heavy equipment a little. Still, we should have plenty of time for our march.'

The voice spoke again, 'Thank you, Highness. In that case there should be no problems. The men and animals are not so exhausted that they will not find sufficient refreshment in a truncated night's rest.' His words were convoluted but their meaning clear and they were greeted by general shouts of agreement and nodding of turbaned heads from some other officers.

'We're decided then,' said Dara. 'I leave it to you, my trusted commanders, to make the necessary preparations. Make sure the men get an extra ration of food. It will hearten them. Tell them that I will reward them well, as I will you, when victory is ours.' With that, Dara rose and walked slowly back into the interior of his tent.

As he too turned away to make his way in the evening sunlight back to his own quarters, Nicholas couldn't help wondering whether, generous as were Dara's words about food and rewards for the troops and welcome as was his confidence in his officers, the prince shouldn't himself be taking a more central role. Not least, it would give him a chance to get to know some of his commanders better, particularly some of the vassal rulers who had only arrived at Agra at his father's summons just before the army left the city and had had little chance to meet Dara. To have full loyalty to a leader – particularly a prospective emperor fighting a civil war – a subordinate needed to know him and his virtues in addition to obtaining a general warm feeling about his own future prospects. From his own experience of the two northern campaigns Nicholas knew that neither Aurangzeb nor even Murad would have been so casual, but then they lacked Dara's obvious charisma and their campaigns had ended in ignominious defeat. God willing they would suffer that fate again.

• ◆ •

The Frenchman collapsed slowly from his saddle to hit the sandy ground with a gentle thud. Quickly Nicholas jumped from his own horse and ran over to him. Yet another casualty from the heat, he was sure. Reaching the man's crumpled form he heaved him over on to his back and with the help of some other of his comrades quickly unbuckled the man's heavy steel breastplate and lifted it from his chest. It was hot to the touch from the blistering sun. The Frenchman's hands were twitching. His face was reddish-purple and his pale green eyes were rolling in his head as Nicholas unhooked his own water bottle from his belt, unstoppered it and tried to tip some of the warm liquid into the man's mouth. A little went between his cracked lips and half-clenched teeth. Most trickled down his stubbly chin and neck.

The man began to cough and Nicholas poured a little more water. 'Get a *dhooli* – a litter – to carry him back to the camp, but before you do put some damp cloths on his forehead,' he ordered. The man might still survive. He hoped he would. The Frenchman was a stern fighter who had come to Hindustan from Bordeaux with a French trading party which he had quit for reasons he had never quite made clear but others said were connected to a missing ruby the size of a duck egg. If he did live, he would be luckier than many others, thought Nicholas, taking a swig himself from his water bottle. Three others of his men had collapsed – two dying on the spot – and he had seen several lifeless bodies carried away from the neighbouring regiment of infantry, arms dangling over the edges of simple stretchers fashioned from dead branches and palm leaves.

Just as they had planned, after three days' gruelling march Dara's forces had succeeded in blocking Aurangzeb and Murad's army's route to Agra, siting their camp on some low-lying hills – hillocks, really – which straddled the great trunk road to Agra about ten miles from the city at a place Nicholas had been told was called Samugarh. When they had realised that their initial plan to march north had been thwarted Aurangzeb and Murad had turned west amid great clouds of dust, attempting to outflank Dara's vast army. In response he had countermarched his forces, shadowing his brothers and occasionally sending out small raiding parties to snatch prisoners or probe the strength of pickets. He and his officers had learned little in the process other than that his enemies seemed determined, prone neither to panic nor to surrender.

After two days of such manoeuvring back and forth on the plains around Samugarh, this morning, 7 June, the two armies had deployed in full battle formation, Dara retaining his slight initial advantage of the somewhat higher ground. As the airless morning had drawn on and the heat increased, none of the three brothers had appeared to wish to push for a decisive engagement. Nicholas had even wondered whether there might be a chance for negotiations, though this seemed unlikely. All that had happened for the past five hours was that both sides had stood still or sat on horseback in the broiling sun, which was now at its midday zenith. Both men and horses were falling victim to the heat. Flocks of bald-headed scrawny vultures were already perching on the bodies of some of the dead animals, pecking at eyes and bellies now spilling out skeins of bluish intestines, unwanted portents to the men of their own potential fate in battle when it was finally joined.

Glancing round, Nicholas saw that there was still little movement in the ranks of either army other than young water-bearers running with their gourds and bottles to attempt to slake the thirst of the soldiers although there were not enough of them – nor enough water – to prevent more men collapsing from the heat. In the next two hours Nicholas lost two further men, including one – a ginger-haired Scot named Alex Graham – who had soldiered with him since his first northern campaign with Murad and had begged him to take the five silver coins in the pouch at his waist and get them back to his family in the Scottish highlands. Nicholas had assured him he would, while realising how difficult it would be even if he himself survived, with civil unrest in Britain as well as Hindustan.

As he pondered this question he saw sudden movement in the ranks of the army opposite. Were they going to attack at last? Nicholas shouted to his men to prepare for action, glad that the waiting might be over — nothing could be worse than standing in this awful heat. A few minutes later he realised that there would be no battle that day. The enemy appeared to be retreating back to their camp, which was about a mile behind their current position. Soon the order came from Dara through one of his *qorchis* to return to their own camp on the hillocks. At least he would live another day, thought Nicholas as he turned his horse and gestured to his men to follow.

Chapter 19

The next morning Nicholas was up before dawn. In truth he had slept little that night. The war council he had attended the previous evening had agreed unanimously that rather than spend another day waiting for their opponents to make a move they should take advantage of their numerical superiority – eighty thousand men compared to their opponents' fifty thousand – and seize the initiative, attacking with some of their elite cavalry early in the morning. As for Nicholas and his mercenaries, Dara had ordered them to form a reserve just behind his command tent, ready to reinforce any weak points or exploit any breakthroughs. In doing so they were to utilise their military experience and steadiness under fire to the full, bolstering the nervous and restraining the rash.

Nicholas made a quick round of his men, shaking awake any so nerveless as still to be asleep, giving a word of encouragement here, checking the sharpness of a blade there, but above all exhorting everyone to carry as much water as they could. Afterwards he climbed with his morning meal to the top of the hillock around which his men were encamped to survey the opposing battle lines, each stretching more than a mile and a half as they faced each other across the dry plains. While he sipped his clay cup of lassi – a mixture of yogurt and water – ate several round chapattis, delicious when hot from the skillet as these were, and gnawed on a bony hunk of chicken thigh, he looked beyond Dara's scarlet command tent and his army's front lines to those of the enemy. He saw that Aurangzeb and Murad's men were also up and busy. Even at a distance his keen eyesight could make out howdahs being hoisted on to elephants and troops of horsemen preparing to mount in front of the orderly ranks of tents. Suddenly – it could not have been more than an hour after dawn – he heard the crash of artillery and white smoke billowed from the batteries of heavy bronze cannon opposite, drawn up in the centre of the enemy position near a large pavilion which he imagined must be the headquarters of Aurangzeb and Murad. So Dara's brothers were as unwilling as he was to put off the decisive encounter any longer.

Immediately Dara's own cannon boomed out their response. Many of their balls fell short as had many of the enemy's, sending up showers of grit and dust as they bit harmlessly into the dry ground. However, through the ever-increasing smoke Nicholas saw that one of the enemy cannon had been knocked from its limber. Then a loud explosion deafened him for a moment. It came from behind him and to the left where he remembered some of Dara's powder wagons had been positioned, as the war council had thought, out of enemy cannon range. Either a lucky and record-breaking shot from one of Aurangzeb's biggest cannon or more likely some carelessness by one of Dara's own gunners had resulted in the powder in an ammunition wagon's being detonated. Pray God the damage was not too great.

As if in response to this setback, Nicholas saw one of Dara's regiments of cavalry begin to deploy from the centre of his lines, passing through regiments of musketeers and foot soldiers and out beyond the advanced pickets into the open ground between the two armies. They were the same Rajputs and Punjabis who had formed the rearguard the day the army had left Agra. Now they would be the first into battle. Soon the regiment were moving into the gallop and charging straight for Aurangzeb and Murad's cannon. Their green banners were fluttering, their lances were levelled and they were resisting the temptation to bunch close together and thus make themselves more vulnerable to enemy fire. Even at that distance Nicholas could hear the Rajputs shouting their war cry of 'Ram! Ram! Ram!' as they rode. When they were around half a mile from them, Aurangzeb and Murad's cannon fired again. The galloping bay horse of the leading banner-bearer collapsed instantly, catapulting its rider over its head to lie motionless while his banner, its staff trapped beneath his sprawled, lifeless body, still fluttered feebly. More horses and riders fell while other horses swerved away, either injured themselves or because their riders were wounded and losing control of them.

Still the remaining horsemen pressed on, pace unslackened and helmeted heads bent low to their horses' necks.

Musketeers stationed in between Aurangzeb and Murad's cannon levelled their long-barrelled weapons on tripods to steady their aim and then added the weight of their fire to the cannonade. Their first disciplined volley emptied many more saddles and many more horses tumbled to the dust, rolling over, legs and hooves flailing. But then Dara's horsemen were up to the cannon, thrusting with their lances, slashing and cutting at the gunners and musketeers with their swords. Soon some of the enemy musketeers were fleeing, abandoning their weapons. To Nicholas's delight, the imperial troops seemed to be winning. Dara clearly thought so too. Nicholas could see him standing in the howdah of his great war elephant beside his scarlet tent, hands clenched over his head in triumph.

However, only a minute or two later, looking back towards the action around the enemy cannon, Nicholas saw a large body of Aurangzeb and Murad's horsemen gallop from their position on the left flank of their army to join the battle, and smash into Dara's cavalry. For some minutes the fighting washed around them like waves round ocean rocks sometimes receding, sometimes engulfing the cannon. Gradually, though, the enemy cavalry were gaining the upper hand as they were joined by more and more reinforcements.

After about twenty minutes Nicholas saw Dara's banners beginning to turn. Soon it was beyond doubt. Dara's horsemen, much depleted in numbers, were in retreat, riding hard for their own lines. Even though

Murad and Aurangzeb's cavalrymen did not pursue them, riders continued to fall, pitching from their saddles as they were hit by musket balls. One orange-clad Rajput's foot caught in his stirrup as he fell and he was dragged along until the leather broke and he rolled over several times before lying still. Elsewhere, a rider bravely turned his grey horse to ride back towards the enemy, zigzagging as he did so to put the opposing musketeers off their aim, before bending to scoop a fallen comrade up behind him. Other unhorsed riders were running or limping back towards their own lines, some throwing off their breastplates and helmets so that they could make better progress.

A riderless and panic-stricken horse – one of many – knocked to the ground a dismounted rider who tried to grab its dangling reins as it galloped past. The man struggled back to his feet and staggered on, now dragging his right leg behind him. Soon nearly all those who were still on horseback regained the comparative safety of their own lines. Among the last to arrive was a banner-bearer whose wounded mount got him to within a hundred yards of safety before collapsing slowly. Sliding from his saddle, its rider, a burly Punjabi, ran the remaining distance still holding on to his heavy banner. Elsewhere *syces*, grooms, were helping wounded men from their horses, gently placing the most severely injured on makeshift stretchers to be carried to the lines of *hakims'* tents.

Earlier that day Nicholas had glanced into one and seen the red-aproned doctors calmly laying out their saws, knives and other instruments while their assistants prepared the cauterising fires. He had quickly looked away, not wishing to dwell on his fate if wounded. Why hadn't Aurangzeb and Murad followed up the advantage they had gained in repulsing the cavalry charge, he mused, only to be interrupted by a *qorchi* summoning him to a war council in Dara's command tent.

Since he was stationed so close to it, Nicholas was among the first to arrive. As he ducked beneath the awning he saw Dara, now clad in his gold breastplate, standing staring towards his brothers' camp, where labourers were struggling in the growing heat to right some of the cannon overturned in the first attack. Others were unloading more cannon balls and stocks of powder from wagons which teams of oxen were pulling up to the artillery positions. Another small group of soldiers were going among the dead and wounded men and horses sprawled around the guns. Nicholas saw them carry away some of the wounded, presumably those of their own side. Another band were thrusting lances into the hearts of injured horses. Appearing to have completed the grisly task of putting the animals out of their misery, they turned to the remaining bodies, bending over them, perhaps to search for valuables, and then thrusting their lances into their chests. A wounded man, seeing what was happening, suddenly staggered to his feet and began to stumble back towards Dara's lines. One of the killers sprinted after him, caught him easily, pushed him to the ground then very deliberately spitted him with his lance.

Dara, who had clearly also been watching, cried, 'How can they be so brutal?'

'Highness, it is war and war is brutal, particularly civil war. But I have seen men suffer much worse deaths in enemy hands in our northern campaigns,' Nicholas replied.

'You have far greater experience of war than I. In truth I have little and want little more. The sooner this battle and this war are over the better.'

By now Dara's other commanders were assembled around him and he addressed them without any of the normal preliminaries or flowery courtesies of the court. 'I have seen our enemies kill those of our brave men who were left wounded as our horsemen retreated. I do not intend to give them that opportunity again. We will not retreat again. Our next attack will be in overwhelming force with every soldier we have at our disposal.'

'That is brave, Highness, but is it wise,' asked Raja Jai Singh, 'to commit all our forces to a single attack? Shouldn't we keep some regiments in reserve to guard against the unforeseen, or any setback?'

'Holding men back will only make setbacks more likely. I am determined to strike decisively now and end this rebellion today. How long will it take to ready our men?'

'An hour, perhaps, Highness,' said the raja, 'and in that time I recommend that to give the attack the greatest chance of success you begin a cannonade of enemy lines to disrupt their forces and knock out some of their remaining guns.'

'Give the necessary orders.'

'Don't forget, Highness, while we make our own preparations,' said a voice from the back, 'we should keep watch for any massing or movement of troops by our enemy or for signs of attempts to outflank us.'

Another wise comment, thought Nicholas. In war as in

chess it was not enough to plan your own moves well, you had to watch out for your enemy's and be flexible in responding to them.

'Yes, of course. We should advance more pickets and send out scouts to warn us of any manoeuvres on our enemy's part or of any reinforcements riding to join them. However, it seems to me that, being outnumbered, my brothers are prepared to sit on the defensive. I am not. Let us lose no more time. Make the necessary arrangements for the attack, Jai Singh. I am indebted to you all, my loyal and wise counsellors, and so too will be my father, our rightful emperor. Good luck and may God bless us with victory. The council is dismissed.'

Again Nicholas wondered whether, although Dara had been gracious in his final remarks, he might not have done better to allow a little more time for his officers to ask questions and make suggestions about his simple strategy, as well as to enthuse them more thoroughly with the reasons why victory was important for the empire and of course for them. Having known Dara for over thirty years he was well aware of his warmth, charm and abilities, so clearly displayed in his family and personal life and his relationship with close allies. He just wished he would be less distant and aloof in public discussion with the wider circle of his supporters. Still, with the superior forces at Dara's disposal, his battle plan should succeed and, God willing, by evening he and his men should be riding victorious for Agra.

An hour and a half later Nicholas, mounted on his chestnut horse, was again on the top of the hillock behind Dara's command tent. He was now fully dressed for war, sweating beneath steel back- and breastplates, his long sword at his right side and his two bulbous-handled pistols primed and stuck into his blue sash. He watched as drums began to beat and Dara's troops started to advance along the whole one and a half miles of their front line from Raja Ram Singh Rathor's Rajputs on the right to Khalilullah Khan's Uzbeks on the left, moving into the white smoke drifting across the plain between the two armies from the previous exchanges of cannon fire. Despite the amount of powder and shot expended by both sides in the previous eighty minutes, neither seemed to have suffered great damage – the most obvious casualties were three of Aurangzeb and Murad's elephants, hit as they strained to haul some of their cannon into a more advanced position and now slumped within a few feet of each other like great grey rocks.

More and more of Dara's men began to move forward. Soon Dara's own massive war elephant started to advance and as it did so he waved from its jewel-encrusted tower-like howdah to the surrounding troops. The size of his elephant and the construction of the howdah allowed him to see and be seen by many more of his troops than he could have been in any other way.

In obedience to his own orders, which were still to stay where he was with his men till he saw how the battle developed, Nicholas sat tight on the hillock as Dara's army pushed forward. Sometimes drifting smoke obscured his view, making it difficult for him to judge the progress of the fighting. On the right flank, Raja Ram Singh Rathor's orange and saffron-clad horsemen were outdistancing the rest of the army, swerving as they did so to attack the enemy's centre. Through another gap in the smoke Nicholas was able to guess why. Two great elephants with howdahs were moving along the enemy lines, surrounded by a squadron of banner-bearing horsemen. Aurangzeb and Murad were encouraging their own troops to stand firm and Raja Ram Singh Rathor must have determined to win glory for himself and his Rajputs while avenging the defeat of his cousin Jaswant Singh at Dharmat by killing or capturing the two rebellious brothers. His men were clearly suffering casualties as the price for their daring with many falling, brought down by musket balls or fire from the cannon batteries at the centre of the enemy lines.

Raja Ram Singh Rathor, distinguishable by his pure white stallion and the two standard-bearers riding beside him, both still also miraculously unscathed, was the first to smash into the horsemen surrounding the rebellious brothers' elephants, his much diminished force close behind him.

It was difficult at the distance for Nicholas to make out the details of the action but he saw a Rajput horseman attack one of the two elephants, urging his mount, specially trained and equipped with a face plate as some cavalry horses were, to rear on its hind legs to allow him to strike at the elephants' *mahouts*. A bodyguard in the howdah stood and thrust twice with his long lance. Both horse and rider dropped from view.

One of Raja Ram Singh Rathor's banner-bearers had fallen but the other remained close by his leader's side as he battered his way towards the other imperial elephant, opponents swerving away from him or faltering beneath his attack. Suddenly, the remaining Rajput banner-bearer pitched forward out of his saddle and became entangled in his orange banner as he hit the ground. Next, the raja's own white horse reared up. Was he too preparing to attack the elephant's *mahouts*? But in a moment the horse toppled backwards, clearly wounded, and the raja, still identifiable by his lemon turban and flowing orange and white robes, slipped from the saddle and ran, drawn sword in hand and almost bent double, towards the elephant. Bravely he tried to duck beneath its belly, perhaps attempting to cut the girths holding the howdah in place. Whatever was his aim he did not succeed in it but fell wounded, and as he tried to rise he was trampled beneath the elephant's feet.

Undaunted, his men fought on. Through the increasing smoke Nicholas saw they were being joined by the leading horsemen from Dara's centre, battle-hardened warriors from Oudh, Kashmir and elsewhere. Aurangzeb's and Murad's elephants had already turned and with their cavalry escort were heading back through their own lines seeking greater protection. Dara's cavalry were trying to follow them, slashing and cutting. Although they were making some progress the fighting was clearly hard and hand to hand. Nicholas could see Dara's towering howdah getting closer to the action. Even though Dara had only begun his main advance less than half an hour ago, to Nicholas the climax of the battle was fast approaching. He and his men must join the conflict, but where? As he scanned the battlefield again, he noticed that on the left Khalilullah Khan and his Uzbeks seemed to be lagging behind and as a consequence a gap was opening between them and the regiment advancing next to them.

Nicholas couldn't understand why this was happening. Khalilullah Khan had never hung back in the battles in the north. As Nicholas continued to watch the gap began to grow. To his horror Khalilullah Khan and his men were turning away from the battlefield, deserting Dara's cause. This must have been pre-planned. Khalilullah Khan had been close to Aurangzeb during the campaign against Samarkand and Nicholas had been a little surprised to find him among Dara's forces. When they had talked briefly Khalilullah Khan had said simply that he owed his loyalty to the crowned emperor whatever his past regard for Aurangzeb's abilities. He had clearly been dissimulating, biding his time until his defection could be most lethal.

As if to underline that Khalilullah Khan's desertion was prearranged, Nicholas saw a division of rebel horsemen charge immediately for the gap in Dara's advance, sweeping along the flank of Khalilullah Khan's departing forces, clearly aware that they need take no precautions against them. Dara must have seen Khalilullah Khan's defection because his elephant was turning in that direction, followed by his bodyguard. Nicholas gestured to his men to mount and to move out. He knew now what their duty was – to rally to Dara and help him to plug the breach in his lines.

Within two or three minutes Nicholas was galloping through the thick smoke drifting across the battlefield and stinging his eyes and nostrils. Through the breaks he could see that Dara's elephant had halted three or four hundred yards ahead. As he drew closer, urging on his horse with hands and heels, he saw why. Dara was climbing down from the howdah. As soon as he was close enough to be heard above the crashes and screams of battle, he shouted to a captain of Dara's bodyguard, 'What's the matter? Why is the prince dismounting? Is the elephant wounded?'

'No, the elephant is fine. His Highness wishes to change to a horse so he can move more quickly about the field to meet the unexpected threat from Khalilullah Khan's treachery.'

Within a minute or two, Dara was mounted on a black stallion with a distinctive white blaze on its forehead and galloping towards the crisis on the left flank, followed by his bodyguard and Nicholas and his men and leaving the *mahouts* to turn the imperial elephant with its empty howdah back towards Dara's camp.

Soon Dara, Nicholas and their followers were charging a large phalanx of well-equipped rebel riders who were arrowing their way into Dara's ranks, hacking and thrusting as they rode. Nicholas drew his long double-edged sword and slashed hard at a rebel fighter as their horses passed. The man knocked Nicholas's blow aside and in the same movement aimed a swing with his scimitar at Nicholas, who in turn swayed back in his saddle to avoid the blade as it carved the air in front of his nose. Almost immediately, the rebel had turned his nimble horse – which was little larger than a pony – and was once more attacking Nicholas, who remained slightly off balance from his first assault.

Seeing this, and eager to finish his opponent, the rider carefully drew his arm back behind his head to deliver a decisive blow with his scimitar using all the power he possessed. His deliberation gave Nicholas just the short pause he needed to recover and to exploit the reach his height and the exceptional length of his sword gave him by thrusting the weapon into the rebel's unprotected armpit. The man screamed and swerved away, dropping his scimitar. A second rebel thrust at Nicholas with his lance but its tip splintered against Nicholas's strong steel breastplate and Nicholas succeeded in slashing into the man's upper arm with a hurried sword stroke. This rebel too sheered off, throwing down his now useless lance as blood from his wound coursed down his arm.

Looking round, Nicholas saw that Dara's bodyguard and his own mercenaries were steadily pushing back Aurangzeb and Murad's troops, several of whom lay sprawled dead or wounded, but there had also been casualties among his own men. A Burgundian who had served with him for many years was lying face down in a pool of blood with his brains spilling into his ginger hair from a great gash in his skull. Nicholas was preparing to re-join the fight, determined to avenge the waste of his comrade's life on those who by rebelling had caused it, when he heard above the general din of battle a drumming of many fast approaching hooves behind him. Turning, he saw a group of horsemen with a green banner galloping wildly for the rear, all clearly Dara's men. He shouted to the leading riders, 'Why are you retreating?' The first few who passed him were too intent on securing their safety even to respond, but one horseman, who appeared little more than a youth, reined in for a moment. 'Prince Dara is fleeing, so we must too. So should you if you value your life.'

'But the prince has not fled,' Nicholas shouted back.

'You're wrong. We've seen the imperial elephant head for the rear.'

'But didn't you see the howdah was empty?'

'No. But in that case the prince must be dead.' With that and before Nicholas could utter another word the young man dug his heels into the flanks of his blowing horse and urged it after his quickly disappearing comrades. Nicholas looked round to see where Dara was but he had been carried away from him by the press of the fighting. Even as his eyes searched the heaving, sweating battle line in front of him, he heard more horses galloping behind him. Turning once more he saw the oncoming riders were also from his own side and fleeing headlong.

'Prince Dara is safe! We are winning the fight!' he yelled at them as they passed, knowing that even if he could be heard he would be unlikely to be heeded. He was right. The group passed quickly without even a glance in his direction, all except for one green-clad horseman whose mount stumbled over the body of a dead rebel and fell, throwing the man from the saddle to land in a crumpled heap. As he struggled to rise he was knocked down and trampled by the riders following, who in their fear did not even seem to attempt to avoid him.

Dara needed to show himself and soon or it would be too late. The battle would be irretrievably lost and the road to Agra open for Aurangzeb and Murad. As Nicholas scanned the fighting he suddenly saw the black stallion with the white blaze emerge from a melee about two hundred yards away. It was limping and had a great bleeding gash in its rump but no one in its saddle. Dara must have been knocked or fallen from the animal. Nicholas urged his horse towards the place where he had first seen the stallion. Getting closer he saw three of Dara's green and gold-clad bodyguards, still mounted, trying to protect a recumbent figure in a gold breastplate lying motionless on the ground.

Almost immediately one of the guards dropped from his saddle, hit by a stroke from a black-clad rebel rider. Only a few moments later a second fell forward on to his horse's neck, clearly wounded. The third fought on against four attackers. Yelling as loudly as he could for all his men to rally to him, Nicholas kicked towards the action, fearing he would be too late. Suddenly he remembered his brace of pistols. Throwing off his heavy gauntlet, he pulled one from his sash. His sweaty hand slipped on the rounded handle but he quickly restored his grip, levelled the weapon and fired. One of the rebels flung up his arms and fell from his horse, hit by what Nicholas knew was a lucky shot at a distance. As he grabbed for his other pistol, the bodyguard knocked another rebel from the saddle with a sword stroke.

Levelling the second pistol, Nicholas fired at one of the two remaining enemy fighters but as he did so his horse skittered and he missed the rider and instead hit his horse in the rump. The rebel lost control as his frightened and wounded animal twisted and reared, running from the battle, but it only covered a short distance before collapsing, trapping the rider beneath it. That only left one man, but as Nicholas closed on him he knocked the remaining bodyguard from his horse with a stroke of his sword. By then Nicholas was up with him. The man thrust hard at Nicholas. Nicholas still had one of his pistols gripped in his hand, and he reversed the weapon and smashed its bulbous handle into the rebel's mouth. Frothing blood and broken pieces of tooth mingled with the man's black beard, and before he could recover Nicholas threw aside the pistol, drew his sword and with a reverse stroke slashed into the nape of his adversary's neck just beneath his helmet, crunching into bone and sinew. The man fell.

As more of Nicholas's own troops as well as of Dara's bodyguard arrived Nicholas jumped from his horse and ran across to Dara's motionless form. Turning the prince on to his back, Nicholas quickly examined his body. There were no obvious wounds beyond a large and swollen bruise on his forehead. Pray God he was merely knocked out. Pulling his water bottle from his belt, Nicholas unstoppered it and tipped some of its contents over the face of Dara who seemed to stir, then carefully poured a little of the liquid into the prince's mouth. Dara began to cough.

'He's alive,' Nicholas shouted to the men now surrounding him. 'Whoever's got the best horse, dismount and we'll use it for the prince. That rider, double up with someone else. See if any of the three bodyguards have any life left in them. If so, get them on horseback too, even if you have to tie them across your saddles.'

Grabbing the pistol he had discarded, he slipped it back into his sash with the other one and looked round. Everywhere as far as he could see through the drifts of smoke Dara's men were retreating. That was the polite way of putting it. Most were fleeing for their lives. Nicholas knew that there was no chance to rally them with Dara at best semi-conscious. The prince's only hope was to reach Agra and the *hakims* and survive to fight another day.

'Mount up,' Nicholas yelled, 'and head for Agra as quickly as we can.'

Chapter 20

Alone on the sandstone battlements of the Agra fort Shah Jahan scanned the sun-scorched countryside. The dust cloud rising for the past hours on the horizon confirmed the reports brought by messengers that the two armies had engaged. If only he could be there himself, with the bitter smell of cannon smoke in his nostrils and the energy of battle in his veins. Instead his years and his health had decreed his fate was to wait for news, impotently hoping that it was good. As if his thoughts had conjured them, he began to make out riders approaching on the far side of the Jumna. As they came nearer he saw that some had other soldiers mounted behind them or what looked like badly wounded men slung across their saddles. As they forded the river and approached the fort, their dress told him they were Dara's troops. The trickle of horsemen quickly became a steady flow. What did it mean? Had they left the battle because they needed the attention of the *hakims* or were Dara's men fleeing the field?

A coldness gripped his stomach as he made out the glittering steel breastplates of some of the imperial bodyguard. A group of about two dozen of them was slowly approaching in close formation. Among them he noticed Nicholas Ballantyne but then forgot everything else on seeing Dara at their centre, slumped forward over his saddle pommel, the reins of his horse held by a *qorchi* riding close beside him. Shah Jahan could wait no longer. Turning away, he hurried along the dusty battlements to a dimly lit seldom-used staircase spiralling straight down to the main courtyard. He had to brush cobwebs from his face as he descended the narrow, sharp-edged steps. He reached the courtyard just as Dara and his escort were emerging from the tall carved gateway. Seeing his father, Dara straightened himself and tried to speak, but then shook his head as if words were too much. His dazed-looking face was heavily bruised and there was congealed blood on his right temple.

The prince dismounted slowly, and as his feet touched the ground he swayed a little. Hurrying forward, Shah Jahan put out an arm to support him. Attendants ran up to assist too but Shah Jahan waved them away. He could help his own son. Conscious of the many eyes upon them in the courtyard and anxious not to reveal his terrible anxiety about both his son and the outcome of the battle, Shah Jahan called to a *qorchi* to summon his *hakim*. Then, an arm round Dara's shoulders, he walked slowly with him across the courtyard towards the broad main staircase leading to the imperial apartments.

As father and son entered, Jahanara, who had been waiting there for news, ran forward. Together she and Shah Jahan lowered Dara on to a stool. Moments later the *hakim* arrived. He stooped over Dara and stared hard into his eyes, examining his pupils. Then, rinsing a piece of cloth in a basin of warm water, he washed away the dried blood so he could examine his temple. At last he straightened up. 'The wound is superficial, Majesty. The prince has suffered no lasting injury, though he seems disorientated. What happened to him?'

Nicholas, who had followed them into the room, answered. 'He was knocked from his horse and fell hard.'

Dara himself nodded and tried to get to his feet but Shah Jahan placed a restraining hand on his shoulder. 'Father . . . we were betrayed . . . Khalilullah Khan deserted us at the height of the battle. Our troops began to panic. I dismounted from my war elephant because I wanted to ride among them on horseback and encourage them to fight on but it was a mistake . . . My men didn't understand what I was doing. When they saw I was no longer in my howdah they thought I'd been wounded or killed . . . even that I had fled the fighting. I could hear the panic-stricken cries all around. I tried to show I was still with them but it was too late . . . they were already fleeing . . . and then I was felled from my horse. Father, I've failed you . . . Aurangzeb and Murad can't be far behind. It's all over.' Dara put his head in his hands and seemed about to weep.

'Please leave us,' Shah Jahan ordered the *hakim*. 'You as well,' he said, turning to the attendants. As soon as the doors closed, Shah Jahan knelt by his son's side and shook him gently by the shoulders. 'You haven't failed me . . . you could never do that.' For a moment he enfolded Dara in his arms but then rose and addressed Nicholas, who was standing near the door, unsure whether to go or stay.

'What is the situation? Is the battle indeed lost as my son believes?'

'Yes, Majesty, I fear so. It happened as the prince said. When we took him from the field, groups of our fighters were continuing to resist but becoming isolated and, as they were surrounded, being killed by the enemy. Many others were already dead or, I am sad to say, throwing down their weapons and fleeing for their lives. It was becoming a rout . . . I wish I could give you better news, but you must know the truth.' Nicholas looked at the floor.

Shah Jahan was silent. For the sake of them all and of the empire he realised he must think calmly and above all appear calm. 'It's clear we have little time,' he said after a few moments. 'Aurangzeb and Murad won't delay their advance on Agra for long. The most important thing, Dara, is for you and your family to get away from here . . . On no account must you be taken prisoner.'

'No!' Dara said. 'Surely enough of our men will have managed to get back to Agra to defend the fort against my brothers. We can hold out until Suleiman and his army arrive from the east . . .'

'We've still had no news of Suleiman's whereabouts and I won't take the risk. If your brothers capture you, their position becomes almost unassailable. I won't let you be a hostage for the second time in your life . . .'

'But I can't leave you, Father . . .'

'I don't fear Aurangzeb and Murad – my own sons. Anyway, I'm not giving you a choice. As your emperor and your father I'm commanding you to go.' Shah Jahan turned to Jahanara, standing silent and very still by her brother's side. 'Go to Nadira Begum. She is with Roshanara and Gauharara. Tell her what's happened and to prepare herself to leave Agra immediately. Have Sipihr told to ready himself too.' As Jahanara hurried from the room, Shah Jahan turned back to his son. 'Listen to my instructions. Gather as many of your men as you can and ride immediately for Delhi. With Suleiman still absent, the scattering of Jaswant Singh's army at Ujjain and the defeat you have just suffered we have too few men to defend the Agra region. Our remaining strength – and it is substantial – lies in the north and the northwest. Mobilise them effectively and we will still be victorious. I will give you a letter for the Governor of Delhi ordering him to turn the imperial forces under his command over to you so you can organise the city's defences against your brothers, who I'm certain won't be long in following you. I will also instruct him to open the imperial treasuries to you so you can recruit more men to rebuild your army.'

Alarmed by the doubt in his still dazed son's eyes, Shah Jahan took Dara's head between his hands and looked into his eyes. 'Listen to me, Dara. You must leave Agra not only because I say so but because it is your duty to yourself and your family. You were defeated at Samugarh but that was only one battle in this war. You must not lose heart. I suffered setbacks on the battlefield but I never let them crush me. In fact, they only made me more determined that next time I would be the victor. Remember the advantages you still have over your brothers. I have proclaimed you heir to the Moghul throne. That gives you a power and an authority they don't possess. Use it and you can still prevail.' He was placing a mighty burden of leadership on his son, Shah Jahan thought, one from which he had shielded him so far, but now there was no choice.

'Majesty, I will accompany the prince to Delhi if he will permit me,' said Nicholas.

Dara managed a faint smile. 'I would be glad of it. You have already saved my life today. Perhaps the time will come when I can repay you ... Now I should go to Nadira and help her prepare ... she will be very anxious.'

'I will come with you to the *haram*.' Shah Jahan helped Dara to his feet again, then led the way from the apartments. Nicholas heard the customary cries of 'the emperor approaches' preceding them and then slowly fade as they went through the series of doors into the *haram*. But for how much longer would Shah Jahan be emperor, he wondered as he mopped his brow. It seemed unthinkable that such a mighty ruler could be toppled from his throne by a single battle and yet who would ever have thought that Aurangzeb and Murad's rebellion would get this far?

He was about to leave the imperial apartments as well, to gather the few possessions he would take with him on the ride to Delhi, when to his surprise Jahanara returned. For a few moments they looked at one another in silence. Then Jahanara burst out, 'Dara tells me that you have offered to go with him ... Why are you so generous to us after everything that happened?'

'It's not generosity. I belong in Hindustan. I hadn't realised that until I was about to leave. Your family has done me much kindness despite the event to which you refer . . .' Nicholas's voice trailed off for a moment, but then he continued, 'It will be an honour to fight for Dara as I once fought for your father.'

'Then on behalf of my father and Dara I thank you. But I must also ask your forgiveness. My thoughtlessness put you in terrible danger . . . I'm so sorry . . . I was only thinking of my own worries, never imagining . . .'

'You have nothing to be sorry for,' he interrupted her gently. 'You were acting from the best of motives.'

Above her filmy purple veil, Jahanara's eyes filled with tears. 'I have no truer friend than you and I know you will help Dara in any way you can. He is the true heir of everything our great-grandfather Akbar strove for – justice for all, regardless of their faith. Aurangzeb would only divide our people, setting Hindus against Muslims. If he ever became emperor, his intolerance would scar this land just as fire once scarred this face of mine.' With her right hand she slowly lowered her veil to reveal her blemished cheek. For a moment Nicholas stared at the mark, then reached out very gently to touch it, his blue eyes looking deep into hers. But then from outside came a series of shrill trumpet blasts, doubtless rallying Dara's men ready for departure.

Nicholas's hand dropped to his side. 'I must go . . . but I will do all that I can, I promise you.' Then without a backward glance he was gone.

Half an hour later, Jahanara watched through a *jali* screen as a small body of men began issuing from the fort.

Somewhere among the riders would be her brother and Nicholas. As the column vanished into the gathering twilight she realised that she and Dara had never said goodbye.

• ◆ •

Three days later, Dara, with Nicholas riding at his side, urged his sweat-scummed black horse up a low ridge. As they reached the crest they saw the city of Delhi laid out before them, sun glinting on the white marble domes of mosques visible above the crenellated walls, most of which were shrouded in purple shadow.

'Delhi at last,' said Dara. 'And no sign of any rebel troops blocking our approach.'

'We have been fortunate again, Highness, as we were when skirting Mathura.'

'Besides, it would take a strong force to oppose us now on open ground given the numbers of men who have joined us.'

Nicholas nodded. Spread out behind them were nearly ten thousand men who had rallied to Dara's flag over the past seventy-two hours. Some were elements of the imperial army defeated at Samugarh, others the garrisons of small forts along the road and yet others new recruits under local rulers responding to the urgent summons to arms issued by Shah Jahan.

'Should we wait to take closer order before making our final approach to the city?' Nicholas asked.

'There is no need with no sign of opposition. Let's hurry. Soon we'll be relaxing with the governor in his apartments and planning how our joint forces will defeat my brothers,' said Dara, and with a wave to his bodyguard to follow he kicked his black horse into a canter down the ridge towards the city about five miles away.

How much Dara's mood had improved, thought Nicholas, as he followed him. The dazed and disconsolate prince had quickly recovered his spirits as forces had joined him, seeming to grow physically as well as mentally, so much straighter was he sitting on his horse.

A quarter of an hour later, shading his eyes against the setting sun, Nicholas peered towards Delhi's great southern gateway a mile away. The gates themselves were closed, weren't they . . . ? 'Highness, the gates are shut.'

'A wise precaution in these troubled times,' Dara responded. 'The scouts I sent to alert the governor to our arrival should return soon. They've already been gone longer than I expected.'

Dara was right. Almost at once the gates opened just far enough to allow a small group of horsemen to emerge. A few minutes later the riders – as expected, Dara's scouts – galloped up, leaving clouds of golden dust hanging in the still evening air behind them.

'Is the governor preparing apartments to receive me?' Dara asked, a broad smile on his face.

There was no answering grin from the tall bearded Punjabi who was the leader of the scouts. 'They will not admit Your Highness,' he said simply.

'What do you mean? You must have handed over my father's letter to the governor . . .'

'We did, Highness. The captain of the guard took it to the governor. We were surprised that he did not return for half an hour. When he did, the governor was with him. He told us the letter was a forgery, that you were a renegade and that we were lucky he did not have us executed. Then he handed us this letter.' The Punjabi produced a folded parchment from his green tunic.

Dara, a look of incredulity on his face, snatched it from the man's grasp. As he broke the seal and read it, his expression changed to anger. 'How low will my brothers stoop? Have they no respect either for truth or my father? Read this, Nicholas.'

Prince Dara,

The letter you have sent me is a forgery. I have been forewarned by your brothers that you are attempting to usurp the throne of your father whose mind is declining to such an extent that he is scarcely capable of either ruling or understanding the depths of your treachery against him. They have informed me that as loyal sons – unlike yourself – they are protecting him and have already defeated you once on the field of battle. They warned me that you are capable of any snake-like intrigue to further your impious and unnatural ambitions and to be on my guard against them. I have told them that being a loyal subject I will follow their orders. Therefore be gone. If you approach any nearer the city be in no doubt that my men will fire upon you.

'How dare my brothers produce such perverted lies – an exact reversal of the truth – and how can the governor be such a fool as to believe them?'

'Or perhaps pretend to,' said Nicholas. 'He is clearly aware of your defeat at Samugarh. Messengers from Aurangzeb or Murad must have alerted him to your likely arrival and I suspect brought him extravagant promises of reward if he adheres to them and forestalls your attempt to revive your fortunes.'

'I will not be thwarted. The governor will regret his insolence when he grovels before me in the courtyard of his captured citadel. I must call a war council at once to plan our attack.' Dara spoke with vehemence, jerking so much in his saddle that his black horse began to skitter sideways.

'Highness, before you summon the council think what is possible or practical. You must give your commanders realistic prospects of success or else those who have recently joined us may equally quickly disappear again. And – if I may speak frankly – it is not realistic for us at present to attempt to besiege Delhi, let alone to contemplate a full frontal attack. We have insufficient men and, because we have had to move so fast, no cannon. Besides, we know Aurangzeb and Murad's men cannot be far behind us. We've been lucky to outstrip them so far. They could easily attack us in the rear while we were assaulting the city, crushing us against these imposing walls.'

The light of hope seemed to die in Dara's eyes just as the light of day was leaving Delhi, and it was some time before he spoke. 'You may be right, Nicholas ... I may only have one further chance to turn the tide of my fortunes. I cannot afford to be rash, particularly since I have Nadira and Sipihr with me. It is probably better that for the moment I turn away to the northwest where I can reflect with you and my other officers on our next move at more length and in greater security.'

· ◆ ·

Nicholas reined in his horse beneath the shade of a group of densely leaved mango trees and patted its sweating neck. Dara rode up beside him and they dismounted. In the dappled light filtering through the branches the prince's face looked drawn. Dara had said little during their ride from Delhi after the war council had, just as Nicholas anticipated, decided to move northwest towards Lahore where they might expect to find some support. However, what had there been to say? Who could have anticipated that the Governor of Delhi in defiance of orders from Shah Jahan himself would have barred the gates of the city? It was a sign of how quickly the balance of power had shifted since Dara's defeat at Samugarh.

Now what fate awaited Dara? Secure within Delhi's great Red Fort, Dara would have been in a strong position. He could have used the contents of the treasure vaults to buy further men and support. Instead, what was he – little more than a fugitive? Not for the first time Nicholas thought back to those days when he had accompanied Shah Jahan himself in flight with Mumtaz and their children from Jahangir. But Dara's circumstances were even more desperate. Shah Jahan had still had some allies. Dara, it seemed, had very few after his defeat in battle and repulse from Delhi. Though he'd sent messengers to nobles whose loyalty he'd thought he could rely on, he'd not received a single firm promise of support – only unctuous excuses and in some cases not even that. Every day the number of his troops lessened as officers and men drifted away on the flimsiest of pretexts – some presumably to offer their services to his brothers, others to return to their estates or villages to wait out the storm that was surely breaking over Hindustan.

'My wife's still feeling unwell. You must have heard her coughing in her palanquin. I've ordered a tent to be erected for her in the shade. To help her recover we'll rest here until the heat drops – perhaps even make camp until tomorrow. We should be safe enough concealed among these trees and scrubland.' Dara opened his water bottle and took a long swallow. 'Aurangzeb and Murad must know that we headed northwest from Delhi. I don't understand why our scouts patrolling to our rear have seen no signs of pursuit. Do my brothers think I'm such a spent force they needn't bother?'

'Perhaps they've decided to consolidate their hold on Delhi and Agra first . . . There would be logic in it.'

'I hope so. I need time. Last night, as Nadira tossed and coughed beside me, I lay awake wondering about Suleiman and his army – whether he ever received my father's orders to return or whether he's still chasing Shah Shuja. His troops were the pick of the imperial forces and with them I'd have a chance . . . I also worry what is happening to my father and my sisters in Agra.'

'The emperor was in no mood to capitulate. He'll hold out in the fort as long as he can, I'm certain.'

Dara squatted on the ground and picking up a stick traced patterns in the red earth. 'I wish I had some way of communicating with him – of finding out what he would wish me to do. I can't wander aimlessly.'

'Highness, in my country we have a saying: "If wishes were horses, beggars would ride." We would all want things to be different but we have to accept them as they

330

are. Don't forget that when his family rebelled against him Babur lived in caves in Ferghana with far fewer men than you have here. You must believe in yourself.'

'Forgive my weakness. The change in my fortune has been so sudden. As a first step in planning our revival, how many men did we have left at the last count?'

'Fifteen hundred or thereabouts.'

'That's no army ... Why are so few willing to follow me? I'm my father's chosen heir.'

'In uncertain times like these, many prefer not to take sides if they can avoid it. Giving allegiance is risky until the outcome is certain.'

'But they have a duty to me. Their honour demands it.'

'Men often overlook matters of honour when their lives and property are at stake.' Nicholas saw Dara frown. He hoped he'd reflect on his words. For all his cleverness and scholarship the prince sometimes seemed naïve about men's motives and the real world outside the court ... but then how much contact had he actually had with it?

However, Dara's thoughts were clearly elsewhere. Then suddenly his face brightened and with an exclamation he tossed the twig aside and got to his feet. 'I've been a fool not to think of it earlier. There is someone whose help I can ask and who I know won't refuse me.'

'Who?'

'A Baluchi leader called Malik Jiwan. A few years ago he ordered the execution of a Moghul tax collector. The governor of the province sent him in chains to Delhi where my father sentenced him to die beneath the elephant's foot. But Malik Jiwan appealed to me, claiming the tax gatherer had killed a farmer on his estates who

331

had refused his demand for a bribe and had threatened to petition the emperor. Malik Jiwan said the tax gatherer had deserved to die. I believed him and asked my father to stay his execution while I looked into his case. The officials I sent to investigate found his claim was undoubtedly true so I urged my father to pardon him, which he did. He also granted Malik Jiwan in recompense a rich *jagir* perhaps fifty or sixty miles north of here with a fortress which he has made his home. He should be able to provide me with a sizeable force. We'll remain here while I send scouts to bring him to me.'

The scouts must have made good progress, Nicholas thought, watching the arrival, just before sunset two days later, of Malik Jiwan with a small escort of blue-turbaned retainers. He was a tall, well-built man in his late forties and his expression as he dismounted from his cream-coated mare and saw Dara was jovial and warm.

'You are very welcome, Malik Jiwan.'

'I came as soon as I received you message. You once did me a great service and I'm glad a time has come when I can repay you.'

'It has. But first I have something to confer on you in recognition of my gratitude.' Dara clapped his hands and at the signal the unveiled figure of his wife appeared from behind the screen of oiled cloth that separated the two *haram* tents from the rest of the camp. Nadira, clearly unwell, was carrying a small silver cup and leaning heavily on the arm of an attendant while another attendant followed holding a silver bowl half filled with liquid. Intrigued, Nicholas came a little closer. Even in a rough camp like this, the women stayed hidden away in the

332

haram quarters. In all his years in Hindustan he had never seen a woman of Nadira's elevated social status – an imperial princess and mother of imperial princes – appear in the open before a complete stranger. Neither had Dara mentioned anything about what seemed like some kind of ceremony to greet the new arrival.

'My wife, Her Highness Nadira Begam,' Dara said to the chief, who looked a little taken aback but then bowed low before her.

Standing very erect Nadira spoke, her voice so hoarse that Nicholas strained to catch her words. 'You are an honoured visitor to our camp. As a Baluchi you may not know the ancient customs of my people. Please let me explain. In this bowl is water in which I have washed my breasts. I offer you a cup to drink in token of my husband's esteem for you. By drinking this – the symbol of my milk – you become a proxy member of the imperial Moghul family and my husband's own brother.' Slowly and gracefully, Nadira dipped the cup into the bowl her servant was holding and offered it to Malik Jiwan. After a moment's hesitation he took it, sipped from it and with a courteous inclination of his head handed it back. Then he turned to Dara. 'It is a great honour, Highness. I do not know what to say . . .'

'There is no need for you to say anything. You have responded to my call at a time of great need and I have conferred on you the greatest gift I can offer any man – one that creates a lifelong bond. When, with your help, my cause prospers, my father the emperor will heap gold and silver on you, my new brother. Now let us relax together.' As Nadira returned slowly to her tent, her progress interrupted by a bout of coughing, Dara put his arm round Malik Jiwan and led him to where carpets and cushions had been spread. They were soon deep in conversation.

The next morning, Nicholas woke to the sound of neighing horses and jingling bridles. In a moment he was on his feet, sword in hand, peering through the pale dawn light. He had spent a restless night dreaming the camp was being overrun. Still half asleep, for a moment he'd thought that that was indeed happening. Then in the light of the already smoking cooking fires he saw that Dara's bodyguard were stowing possessions in their saddlebags and that the grooms were readying their mounts. As he looked round, puzzled, Dara – fully dressed with his riding cloak over his arm – came striding towards him, his face exuding a once more recovered confidence.

'What's happening, Highness? Are we striking camp?'

'No. I am taking Sipihr and my bodyguard and accompanying Malik Jiwan to his fort, where he tells me he has already begun mustering troops. I wish to see with my own eyes what calibre of soldiers they are and how well equipped. He has also suggested that if I and my son appear before them it will encourage others to answer his call. I am leaving you in command of the camp.'

'But you've only got about fifty bodyguards mounted and ready to go with you. Wouldn't it be better to take your entire force?' Nicholas looked round, then lowered his voice. 'What if Malik Jiwan is trying to trick you? Are you so certain he's to be trusted?'

'You saw what happened yesterday. I know you've lived in Hindustan for many years but perhaps you still don't understand our ways. The honour you witnessed Nadira

334

confer on Malik Jiwan is a rare one. He is now bound to me by ties that can never be broken.' Suddenly Dara reached forward and placed his hand on Nicholas's arm. 'I don't mean to give offence. In fact, I have a great service to ask of you. My wife is feeling no better. In fact she is worse, alternately sweating and shivering. I want her to stay here and rest. May I entrust her to your care? Make her safety your first priority. Promise me that you will guard her and her honour well.'

'I promise.'

Fifteen minutes later, flanked by Sipihr and Malik Jiwan, and followed by his bodyguards and the Baluchi's escort, Dara trotted out of the camp and was soon lost to view among the deeper shadows of the trees.

• ◆ •

'It's Her Highness ... she has an even higher fever.' Nicholas, who was squatting on the ground cleaning the barrel of his musket, looked up to find one of Nadira's attendants – an elderly woman called Selima who had been nursemaid to Sipihr – standing before him. Above her white cotton veil, her old eyes looked anxious.

'How bad is she?'

'During the night her cough grew worse and she began thrashing and crying out. Her clothes and even her bedding were wet with sweat. I tried to calm her but it was useless, and in a few more hours she became delirious. She no longer knows me or where she is. She thinks she's back in the *haram* in Agra. She keeps asking for things I can't bring her. I don't know what to do ...'

Nicholas got to his feet. In truth, neither did he. When he'd promised Dara to keep Nadira safe he'd meant protecting her in the event of an attack ... not from illness. They had no *hakim* with them. If she'd been a man he could at least have taken a look at her himself – he'd seen plenty of cases of fever among his soldiers on campaign – but if Nadira's condition was really so serious, he'd have to try to get help from one of the settlements they'd passed. That would take time and it would also be risky, but he had no choice. In the meantime he must think what else might help. The leaves of the wormwood tree were said to be good for fever – on campaign he'd watched doctors pound the leaves and then pour boiling water over them to make tea. He'd also watched *hakims* make a paste of neem leaves to smear on the sufferer's tongue.

'Go back to your mistress. Give her plenty of water to drink and keep fanning her. I will send men to fetch assistance from one of the villages, also look for herbs that may help.' Should he send a rider to find Dara, Nicholas wondered as Selima hurried off. But the prince had already been gone for three days and would surely soon be returning. Also, Dara's description of the location of Malik Jiwan's fort had been vague. He would be foolish to weaken the camp's defences by sending out men on what might be a pointless quest. No, it was better to focus his attention on finding a doctor. Putting down his musket he went to look for two scouts – Amul and Raziq – he knew he could trust.

Fours hours later, with the sun beginning to dip in the sky, Nicholas made his way back towards the camp with the long, pointed wormwood leaves he'd finally managed to find piled in the crown of his broad-brimmed hat, which he was carrying carefully in both hands. He'd no idea if wormwood tea really worked but it was worth a try. In his long experience of Hindustan it had often seemed to him that the best hope of fever sufferers was their own constitution. Nadira was still quite young, he reflected hopefully. Her own strength should carry her through. All the same, his spirits rose when, as he passed through the cordon of pickets stationed around the camp's perimeter, he saw that one of the two scouts, the tall Punjabi, Amul, had returned and was waiting for him outside his tent.

'So, Amul, you must have had good luck?' called Nicholas. But as he came closer he saw the Punjabi's grim expression. 'What is it? How is Her Highness? Not worse . . . ?'

Amul shook his head. 'I don't know anything about that. But I have something to tell you in private.'

Pulling up the flap of his tent, Nicholas ducked inside and gestured to Amul to follow. With the light fast fading outside, Nicholas lit an oil lamp that sent inky shadows dancing over the tent's hide walls and ceiling. Then he pulled the flap closed.

'What is it, Amul?'

'To avoid being seen, we were keeping among the trees flanking a road that we hoped would lead eventually to a settlement. We'd not been gone from here more than a couple of hours when we spotted a long caravan of horses, mules and camels making its way slowly westward. Knowing that such caravans often have *hakims* with them, we approached. We'd invented a story that we were on a hunting expedition and that one of our number had fallen ill. But

337

before we could recount it, the elderly *cafila bashee*, the caravan leader, had a story of his own to tell us. He said that on the previous day his caravan had been passed by a group of soldiers taking two prisoners to Delhi. The soldiers stopped to buy camel meat and milk from the caravan and one of them boasted to the *cafila bashee* that the prisoners they were escorting were no ordinary men but the son and grandson of the emperor, being sent as a gift by the chieftain Malik Jiwan to Princes Aurangzeb and Murad. The *cafila bashee* said he saw the two princes with his own eyes, tied to their saddles with their hands bound behind their backs.'

'Where is Raziq?'

'Riding on, hoping to catch up with the soldiers and confirm what the *cafila bashee* said, while I returned to report to you. If we strike camp at once we might be able to overtake the soldiers and free the princes. The *cafila bashee* said there were only about a hundred of them.'

'We can't. I promised the prince I'd take care of his wife. Unless she is any better we must stay here. I cannot divide our small force. Wait here . . .' Nicholas ducked out of the tent again. He'd tried to warn Dara . . . he should have been more forceful. 'Bring Selima to me,' he ordered a *qorchi* and waited impatiently for the old woman to appear. When she did her face was haggard.

'How is your mistress?'

'Very bad.' Selima was unveiled and tears were running down her lined face. 'She still doesn't know me, her coughing racks her body, her skin feels as if it was on fire and her pulses are faint and racing.'

Nicholas remembered the wormwood leaves and bending down scooped a fistful from his hat, which he'd

338

left on the ground outside his tent. 'Make her some tea from these. It might help,' he said gently But even as he spoke, Selima's face sagged with disappointment.

'You have found no *hakims*?'

'No, I'm afraid not. If her condition worsens, tell me.'

Selima gave him a look that said as clearly as words, 'Why should I? What can you do to help?' and walked stiffly away on ancient legs, the already shrivelling wormwood leaves in her cupped hands. Whatever happened to Nadira, recovery or death, let it be quick, Nicholas found himself praying. Otherwise what choice did he have but for the time being to abandon Dara?

• ◆ •

Beneath a cloudless sky of a hard metallic blue Nicholas galloped along the great trunk road leading to Delhi, avoiding the wandering cows, the children playing barefoot in the dust and the peasants trudging to their fields with their tools on their shoulders, as well as the occasional train of ox carts or camels belonging to some merchant. It was the rural India he loved but he had little time to enjoy its eternal charms. The last earth had barely been piled on Nadira's simple grave and the last prayers recited before he had mounted up six days previously. Though a third scout he'd sent out had managed to locate a *hakim*, the man had been able to do nothing for Nadira, whose delirium had increased hour after hour and whose lung-bursting coughing and agonised shrieks for Dara had tormented Nicholas as he'd paced helplessly about by the screens surrounding the *haram* tents. Now she was at peace, and he was free to discover what had happened to Dara and Sipihr. Why had Malik Jiwan betrayed them despite the apparently great honour of the gift of the breast water, however strange that appeared to a European? Had Malik Jiwan seen the gift as disproportionate and desperate, indicating that he should join the winning side? Perhaps seeing the small number of Dara's followers had played a part too. Or had he already been committed to Aurangzeb and Murad?

Although the collapse of Shah Jahan's power and with it Dara's hopes had seemed swift, it was becoming clear that it had been long in the fermenting. By remaining in Agra and keeping Dara at his side, Shah Jahan had gradually lost touch with his provincial commanders and officials, leaving his other sons free to sow sedition, making promises and winning allies as they travelled across their provinces and to and from Agra. Unlike Dara, basking in his father's favour and taking his succession for granted, his brothers had known that to realise their ambitions they needed to act. Whatever the case, there might be little he could do to help Dara now . . . As the news of his capture had spread through the camp, even those who had remained loyal to him till now had begun to leave, slipping away quietly in ones and twos at first and then more openly in larger groups. In the end so few had remained that Nicholas had chosen to make his journey to Delhi alone. At least that way he would attract less notice.

As the sandstone walls of the city finally took substance on the horizon, Nicholas reined in, contemplating what might be happening there. Would Aurangzeb and Murad really harm their brother? Before he could discover the truth, he needed to disguise himself further. He'd already exchanged his usual breeches and leather jerkin for loose-fitting dun-coloured cotton pantaloons and a long tunic with a broad purple sash into which he'd tucked his pistols and a dagger. Now he tugged on a round felt cap that Amul had given him, tucking his hair inside, and pulled his dusty cotton neckcloth higher to cover the lower part of his face.

Two hours later, having left his tired horse at a caravanserai just outside the city, Nicholas joined what seemed an unusually large crowd of people passing through the main gate. Both the gatehouse and the adjacent walls were hung with flags of Moghul green silk – in normal times a sign that the emperor was in residence, but who were they honouring today? The emperor's usurping sons? Several hundred yards beyond the gate Nicholas turned into the broad thoroughfare leading north to Delhi's new Red Fort. This seemed the direction in which nearly everyone was heading, jostling one another in their haste to get ahead, as if anxious not to miss something. Perhaps today was a festival. Nicholas allowed himself to be carried along with the throng until it finally disgorged into a great paved square in front of the fort, whose massive sandstone walls rose up about two hundred yards away on the opposite side. Peering over a mass of heads, Nicholas saw that a large raised platform of roughly hewn wood had been erected immediately beneath an ornate carved balcony jutting from the wall of the fort – the place where Shah Jahan stood to address his people when he was in the city. Soldiers surrounded the platform.

Nicholas pushed his way forward, trying to get a better view. Above the noise of the crowd he thought he could hear solemn steady drum beats. Others heard them too and he caught fragments of conversation. 'They're coming . . .' an old man said, craning his skinny neck, 'it won't be long now.' Who was coming? And why? Aurangzeb and Murad, perhaps, making a triumphal tour of the city their troops had occupied? That would explain the flags on the gatehouse. The drumbeats were growing louder and then he saw a column of foot soldiers, long staves in their hands, enter the square from a street to the left of the fort. Wielding their staves, they began forcing a way through the crowds to clear a passage across the square to the platform. They acted so roughly that a few scuffles broke out, but soon they had made a path five or six yards wide and then stationed themselves, arms linked, on either side of it.

People were now looking expectantly towards the entrance to the street from which the soldiers had just emerged, and a great hubbub rose as a squadron of mounted troops riding two abreast entered the square. The two leading riders had drums tied to either side of their saddles and were striking them in turn: first one, then the other, and then both together. The anticipation of whatever was about to happen seemed too much for the crowds. Nicholas found himself being pushed forward again. He heard a scream as someone fell, and was trampled on by those behind as the great wave of people continued to press onwards, unstoppable as the tide.

Then, as suddenly as the rush had started, it ceased. A hush descended, to be followed by a strange sound like a great, collective sigh. Then Nicholas saw the cause . . . A single elephant was making its way into the square – no gorgeously caparisoned beast from the imperial *hati mahal* with jewelled headplate and gilded tusks but a broken-down, scarred old animal with a ripped ear led by a shaggy-headed man wearing a simple *dhoti*. But like everyone else, Nicholas was looking not at the elephant but at the two wretched figures riding in a rough wooden howdah on its back – Dara and Sipihr, dressed in rags, with garlands of what looked like rotting flowers round their necks. Dara was sitting very straight, looking to neither right nor left, but his son was slumped forward. Nicholas gazed in horror and instinctively tried to push forward towards the captives, but people were thirty deep at least ahead of him and a tall, red-turbaned man directly in front turned round and swore into his face. Nicholas ignored the stream of spittle-flecked abuse. All he could think of was that Aurangzeb and Murad were parading their brother and nephew through the streets of Delhi as if they were common criminals. But then Nicholas realised something else. If the traitors had hoped the populace would welcome such a spectacle they had misjudged. Cries of disgust were rising from all around him and some people were picking up stones and lumps of animal dung and hurling them at the soldiers, who stood their ground as the elephant continued its slow progress towards the wooden platform where it finally halted.

At that moment, the drumming ceased and a tall, broad-shouldered figure appeared on the balcony above. Nicholas saw at once that it was Aurangzeb. The shouting ceased as suddenly everyone turned their attention to him. What was he about to do? Make a speech? Denounce

343

Dara? But it seemed that Aurangzeb had no such intention. As he raised a hand, trumpets on the battlements above him sounded three shrill blasts. At the sign, two of the soldiers who had been standing around the platform stepped forward and pulled Dara roughly down from the elephant's howdah. The crowd gasped as Dara fell to the ground. Nicholas lost sight of him for a moment then saw him as he struggled, hands bound, to his feet. The two soldiers took hold of him again, this time pushing him up the three steps of a wooden ladder on to the platform.

Dara turned to face the crowds as they pressed against the barrier of the soldiers' staves. At this distance he appeared haggard and his unkempt hair straggled in rat's tails over his shoulders. Yet there was still pride and defiance in his posture, in the carriage of his head. His brothers had stripped away every external trapping of an imperial prince but they hadn't managed to rob him of his dignity, thought Nicholas. Slowly Dara turned and looked directly up at Aurangzeb, standing motionless on the balcony above. Nicholas heard Dara call out something but couldn't catch the words. Aurangzeb, though, clearly had. Immediately he signalled to the two soldiers standing next to Dara, who seized hold of him and, turning him back to face the crowd, pushed him to his knees.

Then a gate in the fort wall to the platform's right opened and a heavily built man appeared. He was wearing a leather apron that reached almost to the ground and in his hand gleamed a broad-bladed scimitar. Nicholas heard himself shout 'No! ... No!' As the man mounted the platform, Dara began frantically struggling. Breaking free, he jumped from the platform and ran to the side of the elephant on which Sipihr was still sitting. He tried to reach up to his son but Aurangzeb's soldiers seized him and threw him back on to the platform where the other two soldiers grabbed hold of him again. They pulled Dara on to his knees, then each took one of his arms and stretched it behind him so that his head was pushed forward. The executioner looked up at Aurangzeb, who gave him a nod. A terrible sound between a gasp and a groan rose from the crowd as the man swung his scimitar high in the air and brought it down in a single sweeping slash. Dara's body slumped bloodily forward, but his head rolled across the platform and fell to the ground where a soldier quickly retrieved it.

As people shoved and pushed for a better view, Nicholas looked up at the balcony. Aurangzeb had gone. Sipihr was now bent almost double and seemed to be weeping as his elephant was led onward into the fort, carrying him to whatever future his murderous uncles had in store for him.

Chapter 21

'Has there been any serious damage yet Father?' As Jahanara was still speaking there was a distant boom. The daily bombardment of the fort usually ceased about now as night began to fall and the first cooking fires to glow in the rebel encampment just visible through the trees half a mile away across the Jumna. As had become his habit since the siege began, Shah Jahan spent much of the late afternoon on the battlements watching the exchange of cannon fire as the rebel gunners attacked the fort's outer defences and his own artillery responded. Guessing she would find him here, Jahanara had just come from the *haram* to join him.

Shah Jahan shook his head. 'No. They're still only using small cannon and targeting points along our defences at random. Only a concerted and prolonged attack by their biggest guns centred on a single point would breach these double walls. I remember my grandfather showing me the plans when he was rebuilding the fort – how proud he was of the walls' solid construction and their height. I don't suppose he ever imagined that one day a member of his own family would be assaulting them, any more than I ever thought to be under attack from my own sons . . .'

'Why doesn't Murad bring up his heavy guns? This siege has already lasted a month and what progress has he made? None!'

'I agree. If Murad were serious he'd deploy all his firepower. But perhaps he isn't. Maybe he's no real intention of trying to batter his way into the fort.'

'In that case why bombard us at all?'

'My guess is that he wants to remind us of his presence and warn us against sallying from the fort. He knows that if he keeps us isolated we cannot contact supporters with the truth about the rebels' actions, nor direct our remaining loyal forces. The only version of events that will reach the provinces will be their perverted one and I can scarcely blame the officials there if they believe it, or at least take no action to question it while the outcome of our struggle is uncertain.'

'Perhaps he also hopes to demoralise the garrison and so precipitate our surrender.'

'Maybe, but whatever his intentions I mean to stand up to him. We have enough food and water as well as troops, powder and shot to hold out for a long time and even to inflict serious casualties on our enemy. I've promised our gunners five hundred rupees for every rebel cannon they silence.'

'Perhaps Murad's motives aren't what you think.

Perhaps he's regretting that things have come to such a pass and is anxious not to do anything to harm you . . . or his sisters. Maybe he is even thinking of reconciliation . . .'

'Murad must know he's gone too far to think he could ever win my forgiveness. He and Aurangzeb have killed my soldiers on the battlefield and put my appointed heir – their own brother – to flight.' At the mention of Dara Shah Jahan saw Jahanara's expression falter. 'I know how hard this is for you,' he went on more softly. 'These past weeks have been difficult for both of us. Every day, like you, I hope for word of Dara.'

'Not knowing is the hardest. Shut up in this fort we've no way of finding out what's happening in the world outside. And the only news we have had has been bad . . .'

Shah Jahan knew exactly what she meant – the letter from the Governor of Delhi brought by a messenger that Murad had allowed through his lines three weeks ago, which had reported the governor's decision to refuse to admit Dara into the city. His justification had been that Aurangzeb had assured him that the emperor was far too ill to have issued any order to hand over the city and its treasure to Dara . . .

Prince Aurangzeb tells me that Prince Dara is acting on his own account in a bid to seize the throne and that the instruction he claims to be from your Imperial Majesty is his forgery. By denying him I believe I am acting in the best interests of both my emperor and the empire. Instead I have given Delhi into the stewardship of Prince Aurangzeb who, I am convinced, is your loving and obedient son, seeking only to safeguard your Imperial Majesty's position. May God in his great goodness grant you a swift return to health.

'I hope one day Dara and I will be in a position to punish the governor for his duplicity and hypocrisy. I'd like to see him executed. That I cannot even send a reply condemning his action only brings home the harder how powerless I've become to impose my will on my empire.'

'Do you think Aurangzeb is still pursuing Dara?'

'Yes. Dara is the greatest threat to him. I doubt Aurangzeb'll rest until he's satisfied he's driven Dara far away from Agra and Delhi. But he'll want to get back here as soon as he can. He daren't risk leaving Murad in sole command for too long. Aurangzeb must secretly fear that Murad means to seize the whole empire if he can – as doubtless he does himself. My hope is that the two of them will soon quarrel. If they do, it may give Dara a chance, especially if Suleiman brings back his army from the east. This war isn't over yet . . .'

For a while he and Jahanara stood in silence. That was how it often was these days, she reflected. Cut off as they were from the outside world, what was there to talk about? Speculation was painful, raising fresh anxieties that each doubtless wished to spare the other. With every day she sensed her father retreating more and more into himself and she was doing the same. Sometimes her thoughts turned to Nicholas. The world around her – once so full of certainties – had become such a fragile place. Nicholas was one of the very few she knew she could still trust. She hadn't forgotten his gentle touch on her scarred face. What had she felt at that moment? Not suprise, or shock, but . . . and it had taken her a little time to realise this . . . gratitude for such a human gesture at such a bleak time. If Roshanara had witnessed it, she would doubtless have interpreted it very differently.

The thought of Roshanara reminded Jahanara that she should return to the *haram* for the evening meal, which since the start of the siege she had taken to eating with her sisters. Her relationship with Roshanara was still strained and they said little to one another, but she knew that the boom of the cannon frightened Gauharara. Though she was no child but a grown woman, her youngest sister was eating little and sleeping badly. Every evening Jahanara tried to reassure her and turn her mind to happier things.

'Father, with your permission I will return to the *haram*.' He nodded but said nothing. Just as in the days of peace the evening torches were lit on either side of the gates leading into the main courtyard of the *haram* as Jahanara approached.

As the Turkish female guards swung the gates open to admit her, she heard laughter. Three young women were sitting together on the marble edge of a splashing fountain in the centre of the courtyard. For a moment, listening to them, she could pretend that nothing was amiss with the world. Soon she would order the evening meal for herself and her sisters, but first she would go and tell Roshanara what their father had said about defending the fort.

But when she entered Roshanara's apartments on the far side of the courtyard she saw that her sister wasn't there. Neither were her attendants. Perhaps she had gone to the bath house? She was turning to leave when she noticed a piece of folded paper lying on top of her sister's gilded jewellery box. Curious, she picked it up and saw that it was a letter addressed to their father in Roshanara's neat hand and sealed with her sister's emblem of a displaying peacock. How odd that Roshanara should write to their father when she could see him whenever she wished . . . Jahanara was about to put the letter back when she noticed something else – the box's silver clasps were unfastened despite the fact that Roshanara kept her finest rubies and carved emeralds, including a necklace that had belonged to their great-great-grandmother Hamida, in it. How could her attendants have been so careless? She raised the lid and looked inside. The box was empty except for a few silver bangles.

Letting the heavy lid drop back, Jahanara scanned the room. It was not as tidy as usual. A Kashmir shawl was hanging out of a chest and a gold-tasselled silk skirt was crumpled on the floor. Could there have been a robbery? Surely not in the well-guarded *haram*. But then a thought struck her . . . She was being ridiculous and yet . . . Almost before she knew what she was doing she broke the seal of the letter she was still holding and as fragments of green wax showered the carpet, read what her sister had written.

My dear father,
  By the time you read this I will have left the fort to go to my brothers. Please forgive me but I owe my loyalty to those you have wronged and who have the best interests of the empire at heart. I must obey my conscience. May we meet again in happier times.

For a moment Jahanara stood there, scarcely able to take in the meaning of those few lines. Then, refolding the letter, she went to the door and called to an attendant.

'Ask the *khawajasara* to come at once. Tell her it's urgent.'

Barely two minutes later the *haram* superintendent appeared, carved ivory staff of office in hand, and anxiety on her normally calm and dignified face. 'Highness?'

'When I came to visit my sister she wasn't here. Instead I found this letter saying she's left the fort.'

'But that's impossible . . . quite, quite impossible.'

'I think you're wrong. When did you last see her?'

The *khawajasara* hesitated. 'Probably when I spoke to her early this morning . . . about an incident in the *haram* . . .'

'What incident?'

'I didn't think I needed to trouble you with it, Highness. Yesterday evening one of the *haram* servants, an elderly latrine cleaner, died. She was a Hindu from the town and her last wish was that her body be taken from the fort and returned to her people for cremation. The poor creature was very agitated at the last and I promised to do my best, though to be honest I doubted it would be possible. Somehow Princess Roshanara learned of the death and summoned me. I was surprised. It was unlike her to take such an interest in a humble member of my staff. She questioned me closely, then said that it was our duty to do our very best to fulfil the woman's dying request. At first light this morning she sent a note to the garrison commander asking him to send a messenger to Prince Murad's camp under flag of truce before the day's

352

bombardment began, carrying a letter she'd already written and sealed appealing for permission for the corpse to be carried from the fort ... at least that's what she claimed was in the letter ...' The *khawajasara's* voice tailed off. 'Madam, I ...'

'Go on.'

'Our messenger brought back word that at dusk we would be permitted to send the woman's body from the fort in safety. We had everything in readiness and shortly after you had gone to join His Majesty on the battlements four white-clad *haram* attendants carried the corpse from the fort ...' The *khawajasara* clapped a hand to her mouth. 'That must be how she managed it. One of the women must have been your sister in disguise. They were all heavily veiled and it never occurred to me to check their identities ...'

'Which gate did they use?'

'The same side gate as our messenger had earlier – a small one facing the town.'

So that was why she and her father, looking out across the Jumna, had seen nothing, Jahanara thought. When they had been standing talking Roshanara had slipped away ... How could she have done such a thing? And how dare she write about conscience when she plainly didn't have one? But then a fresh worry struck Jahanara.

'What about Princess Gauharara? When did you last see her?'

'She has been in her apartments all day with a bad headache. At least, that's what her attendants said and I'd no reason to disbelieve them ... I promise you I've always taken my responsibilities very seriously.'

But Jahanara wasn't listening. With the *khawajasara* close behind, Jahanara rushed to her youngest sister's rooms across the courtyard. Gauharara hadn't deserted their father as well, had she? The ivory-clad doors were closed, just as they'd been to Roshanara's quarters. Jahanara's heart was thumping as she pushed them open. The blinds were lowered over the casements and only a few lamps were burning. Some herbal smell – camomile perhaps – filled the air. Squinting into the gloom Jahanara made out a form lying on a divan, then heard a querulous voice. 'Who is it? My head is splitting.'

The voice sounded like Gauharara's but she must be certain this wasn't yet another trick. Taking an oil lamp from a niche Jahanara went closer. By its flickering light she saw her sister's thin face . . . thank goodness.

'Oh, it's you, Jahanara. I thought it might be Satti al-Nisa. I've been asking for her all day. She's the only one who knows how to get rid of these headaches of mine but she hasn't been near me.'

'Madam, I haven't seen Satti al-Nisa since this morning,' said the *khawajasara*, who had followed Jahanara into the room.

Looking over her shoulder Jahanara signalled to the woman to say nothing further. There was no point in telling Gauharara about Roshanara's flight yet. She turned back to her sister. 'I'm sorry you're not well. I'll see if I can find Satti al-Nisa for you.' Still accompanied by the *khawajasara*, Jahanara turned into the thickly carpeted, silk-hung corridor at the far end of which was the room Satti al-Nisa had occupied for nearly three decades – ever since she had become Mumtaz's confidante. Satti al-Nisa was the one person she could rely on to tell her what was happening, yet she didn't seem to have detected anything of Roshanara's plans. Had her sister simply taken an opportunity when it appeared or had she been planning this for a long time?

As soon as Jahanara pushed aside the curtains and entered her friend's room she saw that something was wrong. Satti al-Nisa was slumped on a silk bolster on the floor, her long silvery-grey hair loose around her. Had she had a seizure? She was still so vigorous it was easy to forget how old she was. Kneeling beside her, Jahanara took Satti al-Nisa's hand in hers. It felt chill, and as she chafed it there was no response ... neither was there any sign of the rise and fall of her breast. No, it couldn't be ... Jahanara's eyes filled with tears as she put her face closer to Satti al-Nisa's. Then she felt – or thought she did – a faint exhalation of breath against her own skin. Gently releasing Satti al-Nisa's hand, she rose to her feet. 'She's very ill but I think she's still alive ... Fetch help quickly,' she shouted to the *khawajasara* standing in the doorway.

The woman returned a few minutes later with a purple-robed companion whose forehead was curiously tattooed. 'This is Yasmin. She is from Arabia, where she learned some of the skills of the *hakim* from her doctor father.'

As Jahanara moved aside to give her room, Yasmin leant over Satti al-Nisa, felt for her pulse and then raised one of her eyelids to reveal a dark, dilated pupil.

'What's wrong with her? Has she had a fit?' Jahanara asked.

'No, Highness. I think she has swallowed opium and is in a very deep drugged sleep.'

'Opium? Are you certain? I have never known her take it.'

Turning, Yasmin picked up a silver cup standing on a low white marble table, dipped in her right forefinger and then licked it. 'The bitter taste of the poppy is un-mistakeable, even when mixed, as it has been here, with rose-flavoured sherbet.'

'Someone must have deliberately drugged her. That's the only explanation.' Jahanara could guess who. Roshanara had left as little as possible to chance and given opium to an old woman who had looked after her nearly all her life. 'You're absolutely certain she's in no danger?'

'There should be no lasting harm. She'll be herself again in a few hours, though her head will ache and she will feel weak and sick.'

'Stay with her and let me know at once when she wakes.' With that, Jahanara turned and left the room. How would she break the news of all this to her father? Yet tell him she must and as quickly as possible . . . Just a few minutes later, slightly out of breath, she re-joined him.

'What is it? Why have you returned so soon?'

She hesitated, but there was no way to disguise the truth – that yet again her father had been betrayed by his own flesh and blood. 'It's Roshanara. She's left the fort and gone to Murad. She wrote you this . . . Forgive me. In my haste to find out what had happened I opened it.'

Shah Jahan took Roshanara's note from her and scanned the short message. Then he crumpled the paper and let it fall to the ground.

'It seems she disguised herself as one of a party of

mourners carrying the body of a dead Hindu woman out of the fort. She . . .'

Shah Jahan held up a hand. 'How she did it is of no consequence,' he said quietly. 'What about Gauharara?'

'She is still here, Father.'

'I am glad.' Shah Jahan said no more but turned away from her so that she couldn't see his face. She had expected him to be very angry but she sensed only a deep sadness in him. She understood it very well, because she felt exactly the same. How had their family become so divided? Could scars like this within any family – let alone an imperial one – ever truly heal? Probably not.

• ◆ •

'Welcome to my camp. It's time you and I celebrated properly now that I've returned to Agra.' Aurangzeb clapped Murad on the back. 'I've arranged for food to be served separately to your escort but we two will eat in my tent.'

'I came as soon as I received your invitation. Roshanara sends greetings. Wasn't it good she found a way of escaping from the fort and joining me?'

'I only wish Jahanara would see sense, but you know what she's like. She sets loyalty to our father above the good of the dynasty . . .' Aurangzeb led the way to his command tent, where silk cushions had been spread on the rug-covered floor and a cloth already laid on a low table for the meal to come.

As Murad lay back on some of the cushions, an attendant poured water into a brass bowl for him to wash his hands. Then another offered wine. 'I thought you'd renounced alcohol, Aurangzeb?'

Aurangzeb smiled. 'I have, in accord with what I believe

are the tenets of our religion, but I know you haven't. And as I said, this is a moment to savour and be generous, not to be too strict . . . I will not drink, but you should take as much as you wish in celebration.'

'You really believe we've won?'

'Yes. Think about it for a moment. Dara's dead. Who else is there to challenge us? That's certainly what most of the important nobles and vassals seem to think . . . even those who fought for Dara are rushing to abase themselves and declare allegiance to us. I've been receiving such messages almost daily and you must have been as well.'

Murad nodded and then said, 'But what about Father and the forces in the fort? He's showing no sign of giving in.'

'He's not the man he was. It can't be long before even he sees reason – especially when he hears that I've returned to Agra with my army to reinforce you. And if he doesn't, we'll find a way to compel him to capitulate.'

Murad took a long swallow of wine from the cup and leaned back, beaming. 'You were right all along . . . You always said we'd win even when I had doubts – even after Samugarh. After all, Dara had our father and most of the imperial armies behind him . . .'

'Yes, but he squandered his advantages, especially by being over-confident. He didn't bother to woo powerful supporters like Khalilullah Khan – in his conceit he just assumed they'd follow him. But I knew Khalilullah Khan from our time campaigning in the north and I knew he could be, let's say, "encouraged" to join us . . .'

'These past days I've thought about Dara a lot . . . whether his death was necessary. He was our brother.

358

There must have been other ways . . . exile, or a pilgrimage to Mecca?'

'You were always kind-hearted as a child. It was him or us. If we'd let Dara live he'd only have plotted against us. The whole conflict might have reignited and more lives been lost.'

'I suppose you're right.'

'I know I am. Anyway, it's done. Put it out of your mind. I took the decision alone and will answer for it.'

'It's ironic, isn't it? Father criticised both of us for our handling of the campaign in the north yet we're the ones who've ultimately triumphed. Perhaps he'll now regret being so unfair.' Murad took another swig before adding, 'It's a pity Shah Shuja isn't with us. This is his victory as well and he'd have enjoyed our celebration. I've heard nothing from him. Have you?'

'Not for a long time. But I've sent messengers east to find him and tell him the good news. Perhaps it will give him the backbone to deal with Suleiman.'

'Backbone?'

'Yes. By letting Suleiman defeat him and then fleeing he damaged our credibility.'

'But in a way it worked to our advantage. Shah Shuja kept Suleiman in the east instead of returning to Agra. If Suleiman had joined forces with his father at Samugarh, the outcome might have been different.'

'Perhaps . . . thought not ultimately. Suleiman has some of his father's failings as well as some of his own . . . he's impulsive as well as over-confident, and doesn't think.'

'So he's not a threat?'

'Not a serious one. Once news of Dara's death reaches

Suleiman's camp, I expect some of his troops to desert and others to lose heart. It would be preferable if Shah Shuja can exploit that situation and defeat him. But if he doesn't think he has the manpower, I've suggested that he bring his forces straight back to Agra. It's time the three of us were together again so we can decide how to divide the provinces of the empire between us. But that's enough serious talk for the moment . . . let's eat.'

Murad held out his cup for an attendant to refill as others brought in dishes of roasted lamb, quails stuffed with raisins, pheasant breasts flavoured with saffron and pulaos sprinkled with dried cherries and apricots. For a while the two brothers ate, Murad hungrily and in quantity, Aurangzeb more sparingly. The sky, visible through the tent's half-open flap, was filling with stars and a crescent moon was rising when Murad lay back with a grunt of satisfaction, took another drink from his wine cup and said, 'You remembered my favourite dishes. I'm flattered . . .'

'Of course, my pleasure-loving little brother. And I've arranged something else you like.' At a clap of Aurangzeb's hands a cloaked and veiled woman, face entirely concealed, entered the tent and touched her hand to her breast. 'I'll leave you alone to enjoy my gift – I understand she has skills you'll appreciate. If you do, you can take her into your service? It's getting late. Why don't you spend the night with her here so that we can talk again in the morning?'

As Aurangzeb withdrew and the tent flap closed behind him, Murad beckoned the woman nearer. 'Let me see your face.' As she unfastened her veil, Murad saw brown

eyes steadily regarding him. Without waiting for further
instructions she pushed back her hood, revealing thick
hair hanging loose.

Murad's smile broadened. He loved voluptuous women,
as his brother well knew . . . Aurangzeb really was showing
his appreciation.

'What's your name?'

'Zainab.'

'Well, Zainab, let's see whether you can fulfil my
brother's promises . . .'

Swaying slightly with the effects of the wine, Murad
rose to his feet and reaching out released the single clasp
of her cloak, which slid to the floor revealing her naked
body, skin gleaming like marble and the nipples of her full
high breasts painted golden. Stepping closer, Murad ran
his hands down her body, exploring the curves of her
slender waist, the soft swell of her buttocks, and buried his
face in that glorious hair, which smelled of jasmine. She
was perfect . . . With one hand still gripping her right
buttock, with his other he reached between her legs.

'Wait, my prince – let me massage you first. It will
heighten the pleasure, I promise you. Your brother told
you I have special skills . . . he wants me to use them to
please you . . . don't disappoint him.'

Intrigued, Murad released Zainab and nodded.

'Good. You won't be sorry. First, let me undress you.'
Swiftly she removed his clothes and when he too was
naked looked at him appraisingly for a moment, then
smiled. 'Any woman would be glad to spend the night
with you . . . Come, lie face down on those cushions.'

As Murad did so, he felt Zainab straddle him. Then she

began gently to caress his shoulders with her breasts, brushing her nipples back and forth against his skin. At the same time he felt her begin to move her hips, rubbing his lower back with the most intimate part of her body and making him groan aloud. 'See, didn't I tell you how good it would be? Soon it will be your turn to pleasure me, my prince, but not too soon . . .' As she leaned forward, her thick hair fell over him like a scented curtain. From somewhere outside in the camp rose the trumpeting of an elephant, but Murad was oblivious of everything now except the feel of Zainab's warm, voluptuous body moving against his, and closing his eyes he gave himself up to her.

Drowsy with wine and pleasure, it took him some moments to realise that Zainab had climbed off him and he stretched languorously. What now? Did she have some other way of heightening his anticipation or had the time for the climax arrived? Turning over, he looked up, but the eyes regarding him steadily weren't wide and female but narrow, black and male. 'What . . . ?'

Before he could say anything further, a voice from the direction of the tent entrance called out, 'Seize him!' Alert too late to the danger, Murad tried to rise, but as he did so the black-eyed man who had been looking down at him put the tip of his dagger to his throat while two other men came out of the shadows to pinion his arms. He opened his mouth to call for his escort, hoping that at least some might be in earshot, but the man pushed his dagger point into his skin, drawing blood, and bent lower over him.

'Don't resist!'

'How dare you! How did you get in here? Where's my brother?'

'He doesn't want to see you. We're his men. He left to take control of your camp. And you're going on a journey as well – a longer one.' Then, glancing quickly round at his two companions holding Murad down, the man said, 'Get him on his feet, quickly.'

As the men hoisted the dazed and unresisting Murad up and began bundling him into clothes that he realised dimly weren't his own but like the guards' own uniform, the man with the dagger strode over to the tent flap and, opening it far enough to reveal a black triangle of night sky, peered briefly outside.

'Good.' He nodded, then said to the two guards, 'Take him outside. The elephants are waiting. You know what to do.'

• ◆ •

'Fetch my sword Alamgir!' Shah Jahan ordered a startled *qorchi*, who immediately hurried from his private apartments. Though previously he had considered giving the Moghuls' ancestral sword – the weapon first brought to Hindustan by his ancestor Babur – to Dara, a feeling that it would be a bad omen to part with it while he still reigned on the peacock throne had stopped him.

A few minutes later, as he once more held the sword in his hands, feeling its ornately fashioned eagle hilt – strong as well as beautiful – and admiring the red glitter of the bird's ruby eyes, he was glad. Tomorrow, with Alamgir in its jewelled scabbard at his waist and Timur's heavy gold ring on his finger, he would ride into battle perhaps for the last time. Whatever happened to him – even death – it would be good to feel a man and a warrior once more and to wield that perfectly balanced weapon again. As he had done so many times before on the eve of conflict he ran a finger along one edge of the steel blade. If it cut his skin he would know it was sharp enough. He pressed his right forefinger gently on to it but no bead of blood appeared. 'Send this to my armourer for sharpening,' he ordered the *qorchi*.

The youth had not been long gone when the doors opened again to admit Jahanara. He could guess her reaction when he told her what he planned to do, but he would not be dissuaded. He might be old but he was an emperor and a warrior and he would show his rebellious children – daughters as well as sons – exactly what that meant.

'Is it true that Aurangzeb has written to you at last? I came here from the *haram* as soon as I heard the story.'

Shah Jahan nodded. Aurangzeb had returned to Agra a week ago – he had witnessed his son's boastful return, banners flying, drums beating, from the battlements himself – but it had taken Aurangzeb till now to send any communication.

'What does he say? Was it him who gave the order to stop the cannonade?'

'Yes. He writes that Murad should never have begun the bombardment of a fort housing a man so old and frail as myself. However, this is not because he intends us any good. He claims it is his duty both to me – who am no longer fit to rule or even to command the fort garrison – and to the empire to force my surrender as soon as possible so that he can restore order. What's more, he also claims that he has found a means of doing so.'

'How?'

'By cutting off the fort's water supply. A rebel detachment has seized the fort's water gate opening on to the Jumna so we can no longer take in fresh water. All we have are a few stagnant long disused wells . . . He hopes in this summer heat to break the spirit of our troops.'

'I don't understand him . . . I'd hoped that even having come this far he and Murad might yet draw back . . .'

'They have no sense of shame or guilt.'

'Does Aurangzeb say anything about Dara?'

'Nothing. My hope is that Aurangzeb has returned to Agra because Dara has evaded him.'

'I will write to my brothers . . . I will make Aurangzeb and Murad see reason.'

'They will not listen and I won't let you demean yourself by pleading with traitors.'

'I wouldn't plead . . . I am their equal . . .'

'Even so, I forbid it. I am still emperor. I'm not going to remain here in the fort waiting impotently for my sons' next outrages against me. They have told the world that I am too old and ill to rule but I will show them and my subjects otherwise.'

'What do you mean to do?'

'Ride out to face them at the head of my men. The garrison are still loyal and will follow me, I am certain.' As he spoke, Shah Jahan drew himself up. 'I've been inactive too long. I should have taken to the field myself instead of sending Dara against his brothers. It gave credence to their claims that I was losing my powers but it still isn't too late. Even if I am killed, I will have regained my pride, and in time Dara and Suleiman may return to avenge me.'

'Father, you can't do this . . . Please . . .'

'It is the only way. I have left a letter with my steward to be given to Aurangzeb and Murad if I die, telling them it is my last my wish that they treat you with all honour and respect. Despite everything that has happened and their malice towards me, I still trust them to do so. You mustn't be afraid.'

'I'm not – at least not for myself, but I fear for you . . . Aurangzeb knows your nature. He has provoked you to this. Forgive me, Father, but you are acting rashly and in haste.'

'Perhaps, but at least I am acting. I may no longer have the body of a warrior, but I have the warrior spirit.'

For a moment he saw his wife's lovely face before him. Many, many times she had watched him ride off to battle and he had always returned to her. Never had he thought that she would be the one to die and leave him . . . but that was long ago and perhaps he would soon be with her in Paradise. Hearing a knock on the door, he rose as Jahanara drew her veil. Was it the *qorchi* returning with his sword? If so, the youth had been quick. But as the doors opened he saw that it was his garrison commander.

'Majesty, a further messenger has arrived under flag of truce from your sons. He insists on seeing you in person. He says he has something for you from Prince Aurangzeb.'

'What? Another letter?'

'No, Majesty. It looks like some kind of parcel. When I ordered my men to inspect it, the messenger resisted, saying he had been instructed to hand it only to you and he would not yield it up. If you wish it, Majesty, I will order my men to take it from him.'

'No, search him for weapons then bring him to me under close guard.'

Shah Jahan and Jahanara exchanged glances but neither said anything as they waited. A few minutes later the commander returned, followed by eight of his guards surrounding a tall, bearded man with the neat black turban and plain flowing robes of an official. He was carrying a large brocade bag secured with a piece of silken cord.

'I understand you have something for me. What is it?' Shah Jahan asked.

'My master did not tell me – only that I must hand it to you and no one else.'

'Very well. Place it on the carpet in front of you then step well back. Guards, keep an eye on him.' Shah Jahan waited until the man had retreated and his guards were stationed round him. Then he approached the brocade bag and carefully lifted it. Despite its bulk it wasn't very heavy. Placing it back on the carpet, he leaned over and unfastened the silk cord. Inside was another bag, this time of a coarser material, fastened round the top with a piece of thin rope. Shah Jahan lifted it out carefully. Tucked beneath the rope was a sliver of folded paper. Pulling it out, Shah Jahan opened it: *The only punishment for heresy is death. God's will has been done and those in the gardens of Paradise rejoice.*

Shah Jahan flung the note aside and ripped open the bag. As he did so, a sickly sweet stench – the once encountered never forgotten stench of death – filled his nostrils and his gorge rose. Yet another parcel was inside the bag, this time cocooned in a swathe of black silk. He unravelled the silk with frantic hands and at last something rolled out across the carpet: Dara's head, no longer handsome, with creamy white maggots crawling around his dead eyes and in and out of his gaping mouth and blood-encrusted nostrils.

With Jahanara's anguished cries coming as if from far away, Shah Jahan's eyes remained fixed on the rotting object before him for some moments. Then he said dully, 'I can bear no more. Let it be over. Open the gates . . .'

Chapter 22

Shah Jahan had been wondering when the officer Aurangzeb had placed in control of the Agra fort would present himself. He had already been told that he was an Uzbek – one of Khalilullah Khan's men who with his commander had deserted Dara at Samugarh. Now Makhdumi Khan stood before him and he could see him for himself. He was tall, with a close-cropped grey beard and a pink shiny scar that looked recent across his right eyebrow. He made no attempt at obeisance but nor did he meet Shah Jahan's gaze, keeping his eyes averted.

'Why have you ignored the messages I sent you? Answer me now! Where are my daughters?' Shah Jahan demanded.

'Princess Gauharara has left the fort at her own request to join Princess Roshanara in the palace she now occupies along the Jumna. Your other daughter remains confined here in the imperial *haram*.'

'I wish to see Princess Jahanara as soon as possible. I must be sure you are treating her with the respect due to her rank.'

'I can assure you your daughter is in good health and being well treated. It isn't for me to say when you will be permitted to see one another. Please listen to what your son Aurangzeb has commanded me to tell you. He has ordered you to be confined here in your apartments. He has also instructed me to post guards outside day and night to ensure your safety.'

'I have always had guards at my door to protect me. I assume these are to prevent me from leaving?'

Makhdumi Khan said nothing.

'And why have my attendants and *qorchis* been replaced? I do not wish to be served by strangers I neither know nor trust.'

'It was on His Majesty's orders . . .'

'What do you mean, "His Majesty"? Who are you talking about?'

'The Emperor Aurangzeb.'

'There is no such person. I, Shah Jahan, am Emperor of Hindustan and no other.'

'I am only the bearer of His Majesty the Emperor Aurangzeb's messages. I cannot debate with you,' Makhdumi Khan said awkwardly.

With an immense effort of will, Shah Jahan had been speaking slowly and calmly, masking emotions still in turmoil even though it was nearly three weeks since he had been confronted by Dara's rotten head and the awful reality of his murder. After he had ordered the fort's surrender he had retreated to his rooms. There he had contemplated ending his life and only the thought of Jahanara, whose distress he knew would be as great as his own and whom he could not desert, had stayed his hand. As the days had passed, a determination to defy – and ultimately to defeat – his traitorous sons had begun to strengthen him. He had waited with growing impatience for the moment when he could confront Aurangzeb and Murad face to face, rehearsing again and again the words he would use to them. But neither had come to him. Instead, cowards as well as traitors, they had simply sent soldiers to occupy and garrison the fort.

Suddenly something else about the commander's words struck Shah Jahan. 'At least tell me this. Why do you only mention Aurangzeb? What about his ally in rebellion, my son Murad?'

Makhdumi Khan looked surprised. 'Don't you know?'

'How can I know anything when I'm kept in seclusion like this?'

'I thought an attendant would have told you . . . Not long after Aurangzeb returned to Agra he ordered Prince Murad to be arrested.'

'On what grounds?'

'That while he was your governor in Gujarat he murdered his finance minister, Ali Naqi. Aurangzeb said that it was a crime before man and before God and his conscience could not allow it to go unpunished even though it was committed by his own brother.' Shah Jahan almost smiled. He had wondered how Aurangzeb would get rid of his rival. The hypocrisy was breathtaking – Aurangzeb himself had ordered Dara's murder yet he could pretend to be shocked by his brother's killing of an official. 'Didn't Murad resist?'

'He didn't understand what was happening until too late. Aurangzeb invited him to his tent in his camp a mile or so away from his own to celebrate their victory alone together. While refusing it himself on account of his strict religious beliefs he ordered his brother to be plied with wine, then called for a concubine to massage the prince and lie with him. While the prince was naked and off guard in his brother's tent, Aurangzeb's guards came for him.'

Aurangzeb had foolishly feared to be alone with Dara in his underground room. Why had Murad not had the sense to beware being alone in Aurangzeb's tent, knowing he had killed his older brother, thought Shah Jahan. 'Surely Murad's own soldiers fought to defend him when they learned what was happening?'

'That is where His Majesty was so clever.' Despite himself the Uzbek's face cracked into a smile that showed deep admiration for Aurangzeb's cunning. 'The prince knew his brother would not be missed until the morning and had previously ordered four near-identical elephants to be readied with their howdahs closely curtained. While most of the camp slept he had Prince Murad, still bemused from the effects of the wine, placed in one of the howdahs. Then, to confuse those of his brother's followers whom he had not already secretly won over with promises of money and advancement and hinder them from rescuing him, while it was still dark he despatched each elephant to a separate point of the compass with a strong escort. In fact, the elephant bearing Murad headed south, making for the fort at Gwalior. By the time his few loyal commanders had discovered what had happened pursuit was impossible and they were easily persuaded to accept the inevitable.'

Gwalior ... The huge cliff-top fortress with its many-turreted and brightly painted walls was a formidable prison. Many of the Moghuls' enemies had disappeared into its deep dungeons, seldom to see daylight again.

'I heard that he is in a cell near your grandson Prince Sipihr,' the governor went on.

'Sipihr?' So Dara's younger son was still alive ... Shah Jahan gave private thanks to God.

'Yes. Aurangzeb has not yet decided his fate.'

'What about Murad? What is to happen to him?'

'His Majesty says that he does not wish to spill the blood of a brother who fought beside him against the heretic Dara. Therefore he has not had him executed. Instead every day he is to be fed *pousta*.'

Shah Jahan stared at the Uzbek. They both knew perfectly well what that meant. *Pousta* was a concoction made from the milky juice of the opium poppy, so potent that any man dosed on it turned first into a mumbling idiot before eventually – and it could take years – dying. It was a terrible and protracted end – better by far to perish on the battlefield. For a moment, Shah Jahan thought of Murad as he had been in his childhood – so good-looking and full of energy and daring. A son any man could be proud of. Yet this was what he had come to – first treachery against his own father, then cold condemnation by his brother to a slow death that would rot both body and mind. The burst of compassion he was experiencing at Murad's plight and his own inability to help him was hard to reconcile with his anger at his previous behaviour. Perhaps it was proof that a father's feelings for a son, especially the instinct to protect, never entirely dissipated whatever the circumstances . . . however badly the child behaved. Perhaps in his heart his own father Jahangir had felt the same towards him.

'I have further orders from the emperor.' Makhdumi Khan broke into his thoughts. 'Your steward has already given me the keys to the imperial treasury, but you are to hand over to me your personal jewels since living a life of retirement you will no longer need them. In particular, you have a gold ring that once belonged to Timur the Great. I am instructed to be sure that the ring is included among the jewels you are to relinquish.'

'No! I will hand over nothing – not the smallest diamond or pearl. And if my son covets Timur's ring he must come to me and cut it from my finger himself!' Shah Jahan's eyes blazed defiance as he locked his left hand over the middle finger of his right hand on which he was wearing the heavy ring engraved with its snarling tiger. 'Tell my son he is no more than a common thief stealing from his lawful emperor and that as the good Muslim he claims to be he should know there will be a reckoning in the next life if not in this.'

'I will tell your son that you refuse, and ask for his further instructions.'

Shah Jahan saw that the Uzbek's expression was more respectful than at the start of their interview and drew himself up, conscious that though a prisoner he still retained the aura of imperial authority his grandfather Akbar had so strongly urged him to cultivate. The governor hesitated, then said softly, 'You maintain that you are still emperor, but if you watch from your terrace this evening towards sunset you will see that age and events overtake everyone.'

'What do you mean?'

But Makhdumi Khan clearly felt he had said enough. He gave an almost imperceptible bow of his head before turning to stride from the room.

All that afternoon there was frenetic activity on the riverbank across from Shah Jahan's apartments. At first, he paid no attention. All his thoughts were focused on the son who was dead and the son and grandson who were still alive but incarcerated in Gwalior. Would Aurangzeb order *pousta* to be fed to Sipihr too? He wished Jahanara were here with him ... he needed her good sense and compassion more than ever as darkness enveloped his family – a miasma conjured by Aurangzeb for reasons that he still struggled to comprehend. Ambition was one thing – it had driven the Moghuls to great as well as terrible deeds – but spite and vindictiveness were something else.

Sending Dara's decomposing head had been an act of deliberate malice. Why did Aurangzeb hate him so much, and when had those feelings begun? Had they already been festering that day when Aurangzeb had defied his order to inspect the underground chamber of Dara's mansion? At the time he had been too angry to consider what really lay behind his son's strange behaviour ... whether he had genuinely thought Dara intended to kill him and that his father would collude in his murder. Surely not. But Aurangzeb's suspicions and insecurities ran deeper and further back than he had ever suspected. His humiliation and killing of Dara was calculated, cold-hearted revenge against his father as well as a brother he had envied and despised. It signalled a determination to rid himself of anyone who posed a threat. First Dara, then Murad. Who would be next? Probably Shah Shuja – wherever he might be – and his grandson Suleiman? Ever since Dara's flight from Agra after the battle of Samugarh a good portion of Shah Jahan's hopes had focused on Suleiman. He had longed to hear that his army was marching on Agra, but no more. Having slaughtered Dara, Aurangzeb wouldn't hesitate to kill his eldest son, now his most serious rival for the throne. He wouldn't care whether it was a clean death in battle or by the blade of a paid assassin creeping into Suleiman's camp. One way or another Aurangzeb would have his way . . .

Shah Jahan remained deep in contemplation – all of it bleak and dark – until finally the raucous clamour outside grew too loud to be ignored any longer. He had no intention of going out on to his terrace where he might be observed, but looking through a carved *jali* screen he could see well enough what was happening. About two hundred feet away on the opposite side of the Jumna soldiers had almost finished erecting a large green silk pavilion edged with gold and supported by tall, slender poles striped green and gold. At each corner, the fabric was tied back on either side with golden cords on to which, from the bright sparkle, gems had been sewn. Beneath the canopy the troops had spread the earth with rich carpets while on the strip of ground between the pavilion and the river itself they were arranging more carpets in rows like prayer rugs in the mosque. Two jewelled incense burners shaped like crouching tigers and almost as large had been positioned on either side of the pavilion and thin trails of white smoke were already issuing from the tigers' open jaws, inside which perfumed crystals must have been lit.

Curious crowds had already assembled. Straining to see what was going on, they were being held back by soldiers who had formed a cordon from one side of the canopy round its back to the other. Excited cries and shouts filled the air. He had long realised – even before the crowd roared their approval of Ismail Khan's execution at the beginning of his reign – how fickle the people were and how short were their memories and loyalties. So many times he'd ridden at the head of his troops into the Agra fort while his attendants flung ornaments of beaten gold to his cheering subjects as they roared their enthusiasm for their ruler. Did a single person waiting so expectantly on the riverbank have a sympathetic thought to spare for their true emperor standing betrayed just across the river? Probably not. Like children craving entertainment and trinkets, not caring from whom they came, all their thoughts would be focused on the coming spectacle and Aurangzeb's potential largesse.

What was Aurangzeb planning? It wasn't too long before he had his answer. A large, flat-bottomed barge of a design Shah Jahan had not seen before came slowly into view from downstream, rowed by a dozen men whom Shah Jahan did recognise as imperial boatmen who crewed the vessels usually kept moored beneath the fort walls for the emperor's use. Bare backs glistening with sweat in the late afternoon sun, they were straining at the oars not only because they were battling the current but because of the weight of a tall object covered with a piece of oiled cloth positioned in the middle of the boat. It was so heavy that the vessel seemed to ride low in the water. As the boatmen nudged the bow in at an angle against the far bank, soldiers ran forward to grab ropes the oarsmen flung to them and heaved the boat a little farther up on to the flat, muddy bank.

Soon soldiers climbed into the boat. One drew his dagger and began to saw at the thick ropes holding the object's covering in place. It took some minutes before the ropes fell away and other men were finally able to pull off the oiled cloth. Shah Jahan gasped as he saw what it had been concealing. Facing towards him was his golden peacock throne. The twelve emerald-studded pillars supporting its domed roof blazed green in the sunlight. The gem-studded peacocks and trees set with rubies, diamonds, emeralds and pearls atop the pillars were dazzling.

For a moment a kind of pride pushed aside Shah Jahan's troubles. He and he alone had created this fabulous thing, personally selecting the best jewels from the treasure of his empire. No ruler since the days of King Solomon had possessed such a throne . . . When the idea had first come to him at the start of his reign he had still been young and full of hope. For just a few moments he was that man again, with his glory days still ahead of him and his family around him, but then the feeling faded. His family had imploded. This was no longer his throne. A usurping son had stolen it from him. As he watched, two of the oarsmen lowered the front of the barge, which must have been specially constructed for this purpose. A group of soldiers edged behind the throne and began to push. Slowly and painfully they inched it forward. When at last it started to emerge from the boat on to the bank Shah Jahan could see that it had been placed on a wooden platform with rollers at either end. After twenty more minutes' pushing, the throne was finally in place beneath the canopy, its gleaming, glittering front facing directly towards the fort.

Towards sunset, Makhdumi Khan had said . . . Glancing towards the horizon, Shah Jahan saw it wasn't far off. As if on cue, moments later a series of strident trumpet blasts sounded, apparently from somewhere along the fort's battlements. Then the great, silver-oared imperial barge – *his* barge – appeared from the same direction as the boat that had carried the throne. It had been re-gilded and banners of Moghul green fluttered from prow and stern, and its decks were deep with rose petals that drifted in the breeze like pink snowflakes. In the centre of the vessel shielded from the sun beneath a giant green umbrella stood Aurangzeb, dressed in cream-coloured robes with long ropes of pearls round his neck. On his head was the imperial turban with its white egret feathers and his fingers gleamed with gems. Everything about the way he was holding himself, from his straight back to his raised chin, suggested pride and authority.

Two more boats were following. Shah Jahan recognised nearly every one of the thirty bright-robed courtiers aboard. Some were Aurangzeb's commanders and nobles but among them were men he had thought loyal to him, even a few who had helped defend the fort during the siege. Aurangzeb had bought them . . . or had they too simply bowed to the inevitable?

Saddened by the sight, Shah Jahan left the *jali* screen and walked the room, feeling a little like one of his hunting leopards restlessly prowling its cage – except that the leopards sometimes had the chance to run free. He might never know freedom again . . . But eventually, even though he knew that whatever he was about to witness could only bring him pain, further fanfares of trumpets followed by the booming of kettledrums drew him back to the *jali* screen.

Aurangzeb had disembarked and, flanked on each side by twelve bodyguards in silver breastplates, was making his way towards the peacock throne followed at a respectful distance by the courtiers. Reaching the throne, Aurangzeb paused for a moment, looked up at the dazzling canopy, then mounted its golden steps, turned and sat down. His courtiers ranged themselves before him. Then at a single shrill trumpet blast they fell to the ground, prostrating themselves in the age-old obeisance of the *korunush*, arms spread wide and faces pressed against the earth. At the further sounding of a trumpet they rose again. Next, a bearded man whom Shah Jahan hadn't noticed before stepped forward. Dressed in a white robe and black turban he looked like a mullah. At a sign from Aurangzeb, he turned to face the courtiers and began a loud chant that Shah Jahan recognised at once as the prayer inaugurating the reign of a new Moghul emperor:

'*By the grace of God, and in succession to the glorious reigns of the mighty Genghis Khan and Timur, of Babur the Great and Humayun, of Akbar and Jahangir, of Shah Jahan . . .*'

As Shah Jahan heard his own name, for a moment he clenched his eyes tight shut.

'. . . I now proclaim that Aurangzeb is the new Emperor of Hindustan. May his glorious reign bring light to his people so that they and their descendants will bless his name for centuries without end and his memory will be as a shaft of sunlight driving away the darkness of the world. Long life to the Ruler of the Age!'

As the mullah ceased his sonorous chanting, Aurangzeb raised his right hand. From behind the throne emerged a line of *qorchis*, each carrying a heaped tray. From the glint Shah Jahan guessed what they were carrying – gold rupees, the traditional gift of a new emperor to his people. At a nod from Aurangzeb, the *qorchis* divided, half making their way to the right, the other half to the left, where the spectators were waiting. As they reached the cordon of soldiers they threw the contents of the trays into the air, showering the crowds with golden coins. There was a wild scrambling as people rushed for a share of the new emperor's largesse. Meanwhile, more *qorchis* brought silken robes of honour and small bags doubtless containing money and jewels which Aurangzeb began handing to his nobles as each in turn approached the throne and knelt before him. Shah Jahan's eyes narrowed as the tall figure of Khalilullah Khan advanced and Aurangzeb presented him with a sword whose jewelled scabbard flashed in the dying rays of the sun. The reward of treachery.

By the time Aurangzeb had finished, the light was fading and attendants were thrusting burning torches into the ground at intervals along the riverbank. From the battlements of the fort came the crack and whizz of fireworks and bursts of gold and green stars patterned the sky above Aurangzeb. Unseen drums and trumpets were sounding and attendants carrying lanterns waited to escort the emperor and his courtiers back to the boats. So many lamps had been lit on the imperial barge that the dark waters of the Jumna shimmered gold around it.

What had this ritual really been about, Shah Jahan wondered. Why had Aurangzeb chosen the riverbank as the place to proclaim himself emperor instead of the Hall of Public Audience within the fort? There was only one answer . . . Aurangzeb had chosen a spot directly opposite his father's apartments in the fort because he had wanted, just as Makhdumi Khan had hinted, to show his father who was emperor now. Taking one last look through the *jali*, Shah Jahan saw his son still seated on his throne erect and motionless and looking directly towards him, as if he knew his father was watching and that after all these years he had his full attention at last.

Chapter 23

'He refuses to come to Agra to see me. Look what he writes ... that I have forfeited the rights of a father ...' Shah Jahan held out Aurangzeb's letter to Jahanara, whom Makhdumi Khan was now allowing to visit him each day.

Over the past six months of their incarceration she herself had written several times to her brother begging him to come to Shah Jahan. She had advanced every argument she could think of – Shah Jahan's age and frailty, the duty owed by a son to his father, even the love Aurangzeb had once had for her. She had reminded him of how he had rushed to her bedside after she had nearly burned to death. His replies had been polite but cold, their implication that by choosing to give her loyalty to their father she had forfeited any rights to his affection or attention, but as she read Aurangzeb's brutal words to Shah Jahan she gasped.

You ask me to come to you. Why should I? What good would it do either of us?

You demand to know how I can treat you, my father, in this way. The answer is simple. You were never a father to me and so can have no claims on me.

You never loved me. You slighted and neglected me in favour of your other children – the more so after the death of my mother. You scorned me when I advised you to follow more closely the teachings of our religion in your own life and that of the empire.

You upbraid me for my treatment of the heretic Dara and of the murderer Murad as if the fact that they are my brothers should make me excuse their crimes. They deserved their fates and I acted within the law in punishing them. Indeed I would have been culpable if I had not. What's more, your protests are the purest hypocrisy. You appear to forget you had my uncles Khusrau and Shahriyar killed for no better reason than that they stood between you and the fulfilment of your ambition, yet under the customs of our people their claims to the throne were no less than yours. You, not I, are the murderer – the truly guilty man.

Father and daughter were silent for a minute or two. Then Shah Jahan said, 'There is some truth in what he writes. I was responsible for the deaths of my half-brothers, but they had to die for the safety of all of you – my children – and of the dynasty. They died so that my sons, full brothers, would never have to face the dangers I had to. I was never easy in my mind about their deaths. Now it seems it was all for nothing . . . the old cycle of blood, of father against son, of brother against brother, has begun again. I blame myself.

I was complacent when I should have been vigilant. I believed the rivalries that have cursed the Moghuls for generations could never happen in my family.'

'You couldn't have foreseen Aurangzeb's behaviour.'

'You did – you tried to warn me about him!'

'No. I was worried that you and he were drawing apart but I never dreamed his discontent would lead him to rebel against you or to kill Dara . . .' Jahanara's voice shook. Fighting to retain her composure, she turned back to the rest of Aurangzeb's letter.

But now I must raise practical matters. I have wished to be merciful and give you time to adjust to your new circumstances. I have tolerated your abusive and accusing letters as the outpourings of an old man whose mental and physical powers are fading and who cannot accept that the times have moved on and he is no longer emperor. I have also borne your continued refusal over these past months to give up your imperial jewels, but my patience is becoming exhausted. You will either send me what I ask – including Timur's ring – or I will have them taken from you. I hope you will act with dignity, but the choice is yours.

Hearing a movement, Jahanara looked up. Her father was on his knees before the leather-bound chest in which he kept his most precious possessions. Taking a key on a slender gold chain from round his neck, he opened the chest and then reaching inside began flinging out the contents – enamelled chains, necklaces of rubies, emeralds and diamonds and heavy gold bracelets. Out they all came to lie gleaming on the carpet.

'Father, what are you doing?'

'He has stolen my throne but some things will never be his . . . like Timur's ring, which will go with me to my grave – or this!' So saying he took out what he must have been searching for – a roll of dark green velvet. Clearing a space, he laid it down on the carpet and unrolled it to reveal a long, triple-stranded necklace of creamy, perfectly matched lustrous pearls. 'My father gave me this when I won my first battle. It once belonged to my grandfather Akbar.'

Getting to his feet with some difficulty, with the pearls trailing from his right hand, Shah Jahan walked to the corner of the room and knelt down again, this time next to a large inlaid marble carpet weight. Spreading the pearls out in front of him, he picked up the weight with both hands and began pounding the pearls, crushing some to a powder while others, freed from the silk cord on which they'd been strung, went rolling across the floor.

'Father . . . Father, please don't!' But Shah Jahan paid no attention to Jahanara. There was something frightening about his cold, concentrated expression as he continued to crush the pearls, sending up clouds of filmy white dust. When he had finished, he looked up at her, chest heaving with effort and tears in his eyes.

• ◆ •

Roshanara stared into Jahanara's face. 'Timur's ring must be found.'

An hour earlier Jahanara had been surprised to hear a fanfare of trumpets, and hurrying outside had been in time to watch the painted elephant carrying her sister in a closed silver howdah that had once been her own make

386

its slow way into the *haram* courtyard. Roshanara was magnificently dressed in stiff gold-embroidered maroon silk. Gems glittered on her fingers and round her neck while a filet of twisted gold set with rubies was wound through her hennaed hair, which beneath the dye would be as grey as Jahanara's own. Now she knew what had brought Roshanara back to the Agra fort after all these months.

'I've already told you that I don't know what Father has done with it. He's surrendered the rest of his jewels . . . isn't that enough?'

'No. Timur's ring is our greatest family heirloom. Aurangzeb says that Father must be brought to his senses.'

'Is that why he has dismissed Makhdumi Khan and sent his head eunuch to be the new governor?'

'Yes. He thinks that Makhdumi Khan was over-indulgent towards our father, encouraging his arrogance and his obstinacy. Itibar Khan understands his duty better.'

'By refusing to allow our father to leave his apartments to walk in the gardens? By further reducing the number of his attendants? By restricting the length of my visits to him?'

'Yes. It is all on Aurangzeb's orders.'

'It is vindictiveness and spite towards an old man – his own father.'

'Aurangzeb won't relent until he has the ring. You know how stubborn he can be.'

'Father is stubborn as well, and he has cause to be. Can't you and Aurangzeb understand how much the ring means to him? Aurangzeb has taken everything else – the peacock throne on which he now sits in the Red

Fort in Delhi, the imperial treasuries, all the Moghul palaces and estates. Can't he show enough greatness of spirit to be content? He pretends to be an emperor but he behaves like a *dacoit* preying on the weak and vulnerable.'

'I have no voice in the matter. I came to the fort to see you because Aurangzeb asked me to. He believes you could make Father see reason if you wanted to. If you help him in this matter he will make your life more comfortable. Of course, if you refuse . . .'

'Tell Aurangzeb I will try to persuade Father to give up the ring but not because of his promises or his threats. I will do it for Father's sake. Every time Aurangzeb demands the ring Father becomes so agitated that I fear for him. I want him to live the remainder of his years quietly and peacefully with no further harassment – just as you should!'

Roshanara said nothing.

'All these months I've waited for some word from you,' Jahanara continued, her emotions rising. 'Even if you didn't wish to visit us, would it have hurt you to write a few words to me or to Father? You must have known how he would react to Dara's death. Did you know Aurangzeb was planning to send Dara's head to him? Imagine how he felt when he lifted it out of the bag and saw what it was . . . Couldn't you have stopped Aurangzeb doing such a cruel thing, or didn't you care?'

'I didn't know what Aurangzeb meant to do,' Roshanara said slowly. 'Believe me, if I had I would have tried to dissuade him. But don't ask me to feel too sorry for Dara. Aurangzeb did what he had to for the sake of the empire.'

'Aurangzeb did what was good for him as he's always done – just as you've always done what was best for you. Why have you really come in your silks and jewels? To make me jealous? Do you think I envy your position as First Lady of the Empire, doing the bidding of a brother with blood on his hands? I just wonder at the woman you've become – no conscience, no charity, no compassion – as hard as those diamonds on your fingers.'

'I have nothing to be ashamed of. If my presence is distasteful to you I will leave, though I have some news for you.'

'What news?'

'Our nephew Suleiman has been captured.'

Jahanara's thoughts flew instantly to Shah Jahan. He would be grief-stricken. 'How? What happened?'

'After Dara's arrest, Suleiman's army deserted him. He himself tried to flee north but he was betrayed and handed over to one of Aurangzeb's generals. He was brought to Delhi in chains and appeared before our brother in the Hall of Private Audience. I observed everything from the women's gallery.'

'What sentence did Aurangzeb pronounce?' Jahanara's voice was a whisper.

'He was merciful. He has ordered Suleiman to be sent to the Gwalior fort.'

'To be fed *pousta* like Murad?'

Roshanara didn't answer. Then she said quietly. 'There is something else you should know. Murad is dead.'

'From the opium?'

'No. The brother of Ali Naqi, the official murdered by Murad, petitioned Aurangzeb claiming he and his family

389

had the right to compensation in blood or in money for his death. Aurangzeb acknowledged the justice of his case. He offered him gold but the man refused, insisting on a life for a life.'

'And Aurangzeb agreed, of course,' said Jahanara. How convenient to be able to get rid of a rival all in the name of the law. Perhaps he had even encouraged Ali Naqi's brother to come forward . . .

'Aurangzeb had no choice. He asked the man to forgive him for allowing brotherly sentiment to override duty and had Murad publicly beheaded. Afterwards, he rewarded the man for his determination to see his brother avenged and his refusal to be bought off. As Aurangzeb said, many would have been tempted by the gold.'

Jahanara's mind was numb. As if from far away she heard Roshanara say, 'But now I must leave. Send word to me about the ring.' Then with a rustle of silk her sister was gone.

So Murad was dead . . . At least he had been spared the torments of *pousta*. But what about the captive Suleiman, perhaps even at this moment already on the long path to destruction by poppy . . . Her thoughts cleared. Nothing could be done for Murad, but she could still help her nephew. Timur's ring must be traded for Aurangzeb's promise not to harm him. Knowing her father as she did, she was certain he wouldn't hesitate.

Chapter 24

Agra Fort, January 1666

'Aurangzeb has refused me. I thought he would. He writes that his campaigns in the south are costly and he can't afford expensive building projects. He dismisses the idea as an old man's fantasy and tells me not to raise the question again ...'

Jahanara sighed. Though in her heart she'd known it was unlikely, she'd still hoped that Aurangzeb might be swayed. It had long been her father's dream to construct a black marble counterpart of the Taj across the Jumna as his own tomb.

'You mustn't be sad, Father – not on your birthday.' Jahanara had dressed carefully in her best silks and jewels and sent special instructions to the kitchens for the preparation of her father's favourite dishes, even though she knew he'd not eat much. His appetite was growing smaller and smaller. Shah Jahan, though, would not be distracted.

'Aurangzeb's right, of course. I am old. No other Moghul emperor survived to this great age of mine. Akbar, the oldest, was over ten years younger than me when he died.'

'Seventy-four is not so old, Father . . .' But even as she spoke Jahanara thought how weary he looked – and how frail. As he neared his birthday Shah Jahan's strong constitution had begun to weaken and the slow but irreversible decline into deep old age to set in. In the last few weeks he had scarcely ventured from his comfortable apartments overlooking the right-hand bend in the Jumna beneath the fort and beyond that the Taj Mahal.

How handsome and strong her father had once been as he rode out at the head of his army, but now his once muscular warrior's frame was wasting away. Time had been unkind to him, as it was to most men, but in his case perhaps not as cruel as his own flesh and blood. In the seven years of Shah Jahan's imprisonment Aurangzeb had not visited him once nor written a single spontaneous letter. Any important news had continued to come from Roshanara . . . It was from her sister that she and her father had finally learned of Shah Shuja's disappearance on the eastern fringes of the empire. In his eagerness to escape Suleiman's approaching army the prince had ventured into the swamplands ruled by wild Arakan pirates and never been seen again. Of the four brothers who had once been so close, only one had survived . . . Aurangzeb.

'I was born under the sign of Libra . . .' Shah Jahan was continuing. Jahanara guessed what was coming next. She had heard him say it many times before. 'The conjunction of the planets at the moment of my birth was the same as at the birth of Timur. My grandfather named me Khurram, "joyous". He said I was "a riband in the cap of royalty and more resplendent than the sun."' Shah Jahan looked up at her from the divan where he was resting and such a smile lit his face that for a moment the years rolled back to reveal the man he had once been. She was glad that he could take such pleasure in the past. The present sometimes seemed so bleak, even though Aurangzeb had honoured his promise to make their confinement more comfortable. Their apartments were well furnished and they had enough servants. But what could compensate for their loss of liberty? Often she found her father looking across the Jumna towards the Taj Mahal. It was his dearest wish to be allowed to visit Mumtaz's tomb and walk in the gardens he himself had planted, but Aurangzeb had repeatedly refused to allow him to leave the fort.

'Father, tell me that story again – the one about how my great-grandfather led you through the streets of Agra on the back of a baby elephant to the imperial mosque school to begin your education. I always enjoy hearing it . . .'

It wasn't a lie. She enjoyed the stories of his boyhood only a little less than he did telling them. Now, as she listened to his soft, low voice, she saw before her a young boy – exactly four years, four months and four days old as tradition demanded – with Akbar by the side of his gorgeously caparisoned elephant, looking excitedly around him as the crowds cheered and flung rose petals . . . She pictured the beturbaned scholars, Hindus as well as Muslims, grouped at the entrance to the school, waiting to take the child inside so he could begin his education as an imperial prince.

But when Shah Jahan was still only about halfway through his tale, Jahanara saw his eyes closing and his head beginning to nod forward. He slept so much these days. Rising quietly from her stool so as not to disturb him, she walked to the casement. At first her legs felt a little stiff, but then she herself was getting older – in April she would be fifty-two. Her hair, though still thick, was growing white as the snows of Kashmir she hadn't seen for so many years. Yet what did it matter how she looked? There were few to see her now ...

From the casement she watched a young boy leading a camel down to the Jumna to drink and other children running along the riverbank and shouting. The sight gave her pleasure, yet their high spirits and simple joy in each other's company cost her a pang. How narrow and constrained her own existence seemed in comparison. Yet her youth had been full of life and of people – her mother and six brothers and sisters, the endless bustle and activity of the court, their journeyings, the attendants who had become friends, like Satti al-Nisa, now at rest in her tomb in the grounds of the Taj Mahal ... and of course there was Nicholas Ballantyne.

Some months before her death Satti al-Nisa had smuggled a letter from him into the fort. It had come all the way from England – a journey that, from the date, had taken over a year. It had said simply that he had reached home and was living quietly on his brother's estates but that he missed the heat and colour of Hindustan and of course his friends at court. When she had read the letter her eyes had filled with tears. She'd been relieved that Nicholas had at last returned to his cold, rain-washed island but she'd often wondered whether he could ever find contentment there. The sadnesses of disappointment and unfulfilled hope were part of life, whether that of an imperial princess or an adventurer like Nicholas, just as they were of the most humble peasant.

• ◆ •

Jahanara woke with a start. The pale light of a late winter dawn was filtering into her apartment, throwing into relief the intricate sandstone carving around the casement. Getting up, she walked across to the window and looked out through the mists that so often shrouded the Jumna at this time of year. Suddenly a shiver ran through her, not of cold, even though the morning was a chill one, but of apprehension. She must go to her father, whose frailty had seemed to increase daily since his birthday two weeks before. Without pausing to question her intuition she called for her attendants and quickly began to dress.

In less than a quarter of an hour, warmly clothed and with a soft Kashmiri shawl drawn across her face in place of a veil, Jahanara was hurrying to her father's apartments. Two of the *haram* eunuchs led the way and two of her own female attendants followed. Reaching the ivory-clad doors to her father's rooms the eunuchs knocked with the ebony staves of office they carried, and then as the doors were opened from inside stood back for Jahanara to enter. 'Has my father awoken yet?' she asked his chief servant, an elderly silver-haired Pathan.

'Yes, Highness,' he began, and relief flooded into Jahanara as he continued, 'He was awake about an hour ago when we looked in on him as we now regularly do. He told us he did not wish to rise but asked for a bed to be prepared beneath the domed pavilion just outside his room where he could rest longer.'

'Is he in the pavilion now?'

'Yes, Highness. It didn't take us long to ready the bed. He was dozing when I passed by ten minutes ago.'

'I will go to him.' Still feeling an unaccountable unease, Jahanara crossed the richly carpeted room and went through the exterior doors out to the pavilion. Her father was lying on a divan propped against brocade cushions and bolsters and swathed in soft wool blankets and shawls against the early morning cool. A gentle breeze caught a lock of the silver hair protruding from beneath the chintz-patterned shawl framing his head. Jahanara bent and tucked the strand of hair back beneath the shawl. At first Shah Jahan, whose eyes were half closed, did not seem to notice either her touch or her presence. But slowly his eyes opened a little further and focused.

'Jahanara, is that you?'

'Yes, Father.' Jahanara took his hand. How soft his skin felt. How little flesh there was on his palms and his long fingers.

'Good. I am so glad.'

For a moment or two neither said anything more. Watching Shah Jahan's shallow, rapid breathing Jahanara realised her forebodings had not been misplaced. His condition had deteriorated even in the few hours since she had last seen him. Then her father put her fears into words. 'I feel my life ebbing from me.' Seeing tears well in Jahanara's eyes he went on, 'Do not weep. Every man has his time to die and sometimes I feel I have gone beyond my own. I have no pain, just a sense of the life force draining from me.' Then his voice strengthened. 'Before I go, lift me higher against the bolsters so I can see your mother's tomb.'

Struggling to contain her tears, Jahanara hoisted her father's frail body up the bolsters and tucked more cushions behind his back.

'Thank you. Now give me your hand again. I have things I must say.'

Taking his hand once more in her own, Jahanara realised the futility of trying to convince him that he was mistaken about his condition and so just nodded. 'Go on. I am listening.'

'It may not matter to him, but tell Aurangzeb that I forgive him ... Above all beg him to do all he can to avoid conflict with and between his sons. Such animosities have plagued our dynasty since we first entered Hindustan. I wanted to end them ... but to my lasting regret I failed.'

'I will, Father,' Jahanara said softly.

'I hope I have not sinned too greatly. I know that I have done things that are wrong and done so more frequently than many men. But I believe that was because my ambition and my subsequent position gave me greater freedom than others and not because I was more wicked at heart. I have done what I have done out of love for my wife and my children and my dynasty.'

'None of us can doubt your love, Father. God will forgive you for your sins. Here on earth the tomb you have built for our mother will prove an incomparable monument to your great love which will long outlast other memories of you.' Jahanara heard her father's breathing become irregular and he gasped for air as she clasped his hand more tightly. 'Soon you will be in the gardens of Paradise with Mother.'

'I see her,' said Shah Jahan, fixing his eyes on the Taj Mahal standing proud above the Jumna mist. Slowly his pulses faded and his eyes glazed. The fifth Moghul emperor was dead and, as she realised this, his eldest daughter collapsed over his body, weeping warm tears for him, his wife and for all his children alive and dead, herself included.

After a minute or two, however, she lowered her father's body back on the divan and stood up, composed herself and straightened her back. She must remember she was a Moghul. She had a duty to give her father the burial he deserved. If he could not have a black marble tomb of his own he would join his wife in the luminous white one he had raised as a monument to her and to their love.

Historical Note

Unlike his father Jahangir, Shah Jahan did not write his own memoirs, but his life is well documented. Jahangir himself gives us a picture of the young Shah Jahan – or Prince Khurram as he then was – in his youthful days while he was still his father's favourite. When Jahangir became too infirm to keep a journal, he handed the task to Mutamid Khan who described Shah Jahan's revolt against his father. On becoming emperor, Shah Jahan asked Abdul Hamid Lahori to document his reign. Increasing infirmity prevented Lahori from covering more than the first twenty years of Shah Jahan's rule in his *Padshah-nama*. However, he described in detail the building of the Taj Mahal. Also, the scholar Inayat Khan, responsible for the imperial library, wrote a detailed history of Shah Jahan's reign, the *Shah-Jahan-nama*. In addition we have the writings of several court poets.

Foreigners of course wrote of what they saw at the

Moghul court and were amazed by its opulence. Englishman Peter Mundy, in India from 1628 to 1633, witnessed the early construction of the Taj Mahal, writing: 'the building ... goes on with excessive labour and cost, prosecuted with extraordinary diligence, gold and silver esteemed but common metal and marble but as ordinary stone.' The Venetian adventurer Niccolao Manucci was eyewitness to the rivalry and disintegration of Shah Jahan's family. His *Storia do Mogor* describes how he fought for Dara Shukoh and graphically captures the tragedy of the final battle of Samugarh.

As always, though, the sources need handling with care. Official chroniclers were constrained in what they could write and eulogy and propaganda play their part in their accounts. Foreign visitors to the Moghul court were far freer to write what they wanted but were often attracted by the sensational as well as being hampered by ignorance of local customs and languages from understanding what was really going on. Nevertheless, certain themes emerge consistently through the sources, whoever the author and whatever their purpose, especially the unshakeable bond between Shah Jahan and Mumtaz and his collapse after her death, and the emerging rivalries between the surviving children of Mumtaz and Shah Jahan, undetected until too late by Shah Jahan himself.

As in the earlier books in the series, nearly all the main characters existed in real life – the imperial Moghul family themselves, the Rajput rulers, the Moghuls' close confidants like Satti al-Nissa. A few, though, are composite characters, like Nicholas Ballantyne who first made his appearance in *The Tainted Throne* and is based in part on

Niccolao Manucci and the Rajput prince Ashok Singh. The main events and battles all happened though I've sometimes altered timescales to maintain the narrative pace. I've also omitted some events to focus on those which best capture this tipping point in the story of one of the world's greatest dynasties.

Research took me to many places that still speak of the love between Shah Jahan and Mumtaz and the tragedy that overtook the dynasty in the next generation. I travelled south, following the route taken by Shah Jahan and Mumtaz on their final journey together to the ill-omened fortress-palace of Burhanpur on the Tapti river. Here staff of the Archaeological Survey of India showed me the chamber where most believe Mumtaz died. Across the river, surrounded by fields, I found the Zainabad garden – an old Moghul hunting ground – where the Baradari pavilion beneath which Mumtaz's body was temporarily laid to rest still stands.

The Agra fort where Mumtaz spent her brief time as empress still conjures the imperial family's luxurious life, bathing in marble *hammams* flowing with rosewater and eating from jade dishes. Standing in the many-pillared Chamber of Public Audience, I thought of Shah Jahan, ablaze with gems, dispensing justice to his subjects while an equally glittering Mumtaz watched from behind a carved *purdah* screen. In the fort's marble pavilions – built by Shah Jahan overlooking the Jumna river and destined to become his prison – the colours of the flowers inlaid into the white marble remain as vivid as when the craftsmen first sliced the leaves and petals from semi-precious stones and the marble floors and pillars feel cool to the touch. Loveliest of all is the bronze-canopied octagonal tower where a fluidly carved marble pool fills the centre of the floor and sculpted friezes of swaying irises and yet more jewelled flowers overlay walls and pillars. I could picture Shah Jahan in his imprisonment looking from the tower towards the Taj Mahal, floating mirage-like beyond the ox-bow bend in the Jumna, and like Shakespeare's Troilus sighing his soul as he thought of the long-dead Mumtaz.

I roamed Shah Jahan's *mahtab bagh*, his moonlight garden, from where, before his overthrow, he often contemplated the melancholy beauty of the Taj Mahal. And of course I returned to the Taj itself. Though I've seen it many times I always find it enduringly lovely, whether at sunrise when it emerges ethereal through the early morning mists, at sunset when purple shadows wrap around the dome, or by the light of the silvering moon. People argue about what makes it so perfect. Artistry, symmetry, setting all play their part, yet the heart of its magic is surely the knowledge that it is above all a monument to love and loss.

Additional Notes

Chapter 1

Shah Jahan came to the throne at the beginning of January 1628 and faced several assassination attempts during his reign. He was born on 5 January 1592. His wife Mumtaz was a year younger. They married in May 1612.

Khusrau's wife Jani did take her life by swallowing a hot coal.

Shah Jahan's court poets wrote many verses in praise of Mumtaz including those quoted here, which are from Kalim's *Padshah Nama*.

The Deccan crisis which drew Shah Jahan south erupted towards the end of 1629.

Chapter 2

The Archaeological Survey of India are currently restoring the fortress palace of Burhanpur.

Chapter 3

The famine around Burhanpur was extremely severe. Shah Jahan's historian recorded how 'During the past year no rain had fallen ... and the drought had been especially severe ... dog's flesh was sold for goat's flesh, and the pounded bones of the dead [people] were mixed with flour and sold [to make bread] ... Destitution at length reached such a pitch that men began to devour each other, and the flesh of a son was preferred to his love'. To aid his stricken subjects, Shah Jahan remitted taxes and ordered his officials to open feeding stations in Burhanpur and other cities, where bread and broth were doled out to the hungry. He also ordered 5,000 rupees to be distributed amongst the poor every Monday.

Chapter 4

Delicate frescoes still cover the ceiling of the marble *hammam* in the fortress palace of Burhanpur where Mumtaz bathed in warm scented water.

Mumtaz spent some of her pregnancy planning the marriage between Dara Shukoh and Nadira, daughter of Shah Jahan's half-brother Parvez. It was a dynastically sensible alliance and perhaps Mumtaz also hoped to heal rifts within the imperial family. Whatever the case, her husband and son welcomed the suggestion and Shah Jahan despatched messengers to Agra with instructions to his officials to prepare for a magnificent ceremony.

Mumtaz died on 7 June 1631. Gauharara was the fourteenth child born to her, of whom only the seven who are characters in this volume survived to adulthood.

Some archaeologists believe they have identified the chamber overlooking the Tapti river where Mumtaz died.

Chapter 5

The chronicles agree on the immense emotional and physical effect on Shah Jahan of Mumtaz's unexpected death, and capture his despair at the fleeting nature of human happiness, even for emperors: 'Alas! This transitory world is unstable, and the rose of its comfort is embedded in a field of thorns. In the dustbin of the world, no breeze blows which does not raise the dust of anguish; and in the assembly of the world, no one happily occupies a seat who does not vacate it full of sorrow.' They record how Shah Jahan went into deep mourning, exchanging his 'night-illuminating gems and costly clothes' for 'white garb, like dawn' – the most celebrated poet of his reign wrote: *running tears turned his garments white In Hind, white is the colour of mourning.*

Similarly they record his hair went white overnight and even that he contemplated abdication. In an age when marriage was not seen as a partnership, as now, Shah Jahan, who approved daily the content of his court chronicle, sanctioned the inclusion of the following:

The friendship and concord between them had reached such an extent the like of which has never been known between a husband and wife from among the classes of sovereigns, or the rest of the people and this was not merely out of carnal desire but high virtues and pleasing habits, outward and

*inward goodness, and physical and spiritual compatibility
on both sides had been the cause of great love and affection
and abundant affinity and familiarity.*

Shah Jahan is said to have lamented: '*Even though the
Incomparable Giver had conferred on us such great bounty . . .
yet the person with whom we wanted to enjoy it has gone.*'

Shah Jahan did ask Dara and Jahanara to accompany
Mumtaz's body back to Agra and a court poet wrote of
'the indigo of grief' covering the land.

Chapter 6

Various claims have been made for the architect of the Taj
Mahal but the most credible candidate is probably
Ustad Ahmad Lahori. During the 1930s a researcher
discovered an early eighteenth-century manuscript of a
poem written by one of Lahori's sons, claiming he was
architect of both the Taj Mahal and the Red Fort at
Delhi. Whatever the case, Shah Jahan's chroniclers show
that he himself took a very close personal interest in
the design. He had a fine appreciation of architecture
– something for which, even in his youth, his father
Jahangir commended him.

The English word 'paradise' is a simple transliteration of
the old Persian word *pairideza*, meaning a walled garden.
The association of gardens with an eternal idyll is
common to both Christianity and Islam with their
shared roots in the Old Testament and the arid Middle
East. The Book of Genesis states that '. . . a river went
out of Eden to water the garden and from thence it was
parted and became into four heads'.

The site chosen by Shah Jahan for the Taj Mahal was about one and a half miles from the Agra fort, downstream from a sharp approximately right-angled bend in the river at the Agra fort which formed a watershed, thus reducing the thrust of the Jumna. The land in question was owned by the Raja of Amber who willingly offered it to the emperor. However, Islamic tradition considers that women like Mumtaz Mahal, who die in childbirth, are martyrs and thus that their burial sites should become places of pilgrimage. Tradition also requires that there should be no perceived element of coercion – whether real or not – in the acquisition of such holy sites. Therefore Shah Jahan gave the Raja not one but four separate properties in exchange. The Raja of Amber also supplied Shah Jahan with marble from his quarries at Makrana.

Chapter 7

In June 1632, Shah Jahan returned to Agra where he could personally oversee the building of the Taj Mahal. Englishman Peter Mundy witnessed the return of the imperial court minus its empress, writing that it made 'a most gallant show'.

According to Lahori, work on the Taj Mahal site began in January 1632 while Shah Jahan was still in the Deccan.

The jewelled inlay decorating the Taj Mahal astonished contemporaries. A court poet wrote: *They set the stone flowers in the marble That by their colour, if not their perfume Surpass real flowers.*

Gem experts estimate that over forty different types of gems were used. Many were personally selected by

Shah Jahan himself. French jeweller Jean–Baptiste Tavernier was impressed by the emperor's knowledge of gems, writing that 'in the whole empire of the Great Moghul no one was more proficient in the knowledge of stones'.

Masons working on the Taj complex did carve their marks into the stone. The Archaeological Survey of India have found over 250 marks – stars, squares, arrows and even a lotus flower.

For a full historical account of Shah Jahan's building of the Taj Mahal and the heaven on earth he was seeking to create, as well as of the events of his reign, see the non-fiction work *A Teardrop on the Cheek of Time* by Diana and Michael Preston.

The description of Dara Shukoh's wedding is in part based on a surviving illustration from Lahori's *Padshah-nama* – one of forty-four illustrations covering the first decade of Shah Jahan's reign preserved in the royal library of Windsor Castle.

The elephant fight during which Aurangzeb displayed his cool courage is a true incident.

Chapter 8

Amanat Khan was the only artist allowed by Shah Jahan to inscribe his name on the Taj. His signature is visible in two places – above the south arch on the interior of the mausoleum and towards the bottom of the same arch.

European visitors to the Moghul court describe Shah Jahan's frenetic sexual adventures as he sought physical compensation for his emotional loss. The Venetian

Manucci described the opportunities afforded to Shah Jahan by the Meena Bazaar: 'In those eight days, the king visited the stalls twice every day, seated on a small throne carried by several Tartar women, surrounded by several matrons, who walked with their sticks of enamelled gold in their hands, and many eunuchs, all brokers for the subsequent bargaining; there were also a set of women musicians. Shah Jahan moves past with his attention fixed, and seeing any seller that attracts his fancy, he goes up to the stall, and making a polite speech, selects some of the things and orders whatever she asks for them to be paid to her. Then the king gives an agreed-on signal and having passed on, the matrons, well versed in these matters, take care that they get her; and in due time, she is produced in the royal presence.'

Chapter 9

Shah Jahan indeed made Aurangzeb his viceroy in the Deccan and Shah Shuja his governor in Bengal and Orissa.

Jahanara was badly burned in an incident on 4 April 1644 described thus by Inayat Khan:

. . . the border of her chaste garment brushed against a lamp left burning on the floor in the middle of the hall. As the dresses worn by the ladies of the palace are made of the most delicate fabrics and perfumed with fragrant oils, her garment caught fire and was instantly enveloped in flames. Four of her private attendants were at hand, and they immediately tried to extinguish the fire; yet as it spread itself over their garments as well, their efforts proved

unavailing. As it all happened so quickly, before the alarm could be given and water procured, the back and hands and both sides of the body of that mine of excellence were dreadfully burned.

It is my suggestion that the accident was caused by Shah Jahan mistaking Jahanara for Mumtaz in his wine and opium-dazed state. Some foreign visitors to the Moghul court reported rumours of incest between Shah Jahan and Jahanara. Peter Mundy wrote that: 'The Great Moghul's daughters are never suffered to marry . . . This Shah Jahan, among the rest, hath one named Chiminy begum [Jahanara], a very beautiful creature by report, with whom (it was openly bruited and talked of in Agra) he committed incest, being very familiar with her many times.' However, Niccolao Manucci, who was much closer to the imperial family, dismissed the stories of incest as rubbish, attributing them to the fact that Jahanara served her father 'with the greatest love and diligence' and that 'It was from this cause that the common people hinted that she had intercourse with her father.' The official sources are of course silent on the relationship between Jahanara and her father.

Chapter 10
A French doctor indeed wrote that it was impossible to find his patient's pulse because of the ropes of gems coiled around her arms.

Chapter 11
A lakh is one hundred thousand. Many contemporaries

commented on the great cost of building the Taj Mahal. Shah Jahan's *mahtab bagh* garden lay forgotten, its pools and pavilions crumbling beneath layers of slit, until in the 1990s archaeologists uncovered evidence that it was designed as an integral part of the Taj Mahal complex. Today the gardens are being restored. Conservationists have planted 10,000 trees and shrubs, including the richly scented white *champa* – a member of the magnolia family that blooms at night – and the flowerbeds are again a vivid, jostling mass of nasturtiums, pansies, marigolds and stocks.

Aurangzeb's refusal to enter an underground chamber in Dara's new mansion for fear of being murdered was reported by a courtier. Clearly some sort of showdown occurred since the sources agree that in the aftermath of Jahanara's accident, Aurangzeb lost his father's favour and relations between them soured. Lahori wrote somewhat obliquely that Aurangzeb had fallen 'under the influence of ill-advised and short-sighted companions'. More specific clues are offered in a letter from Aurangzeb to Jahanara written some years later in which he stated that 'I knew my life was a target [for rivals]'. Plainly, the person he suspected of plotting against him was Dara, their father's favourite and in Aurangzeb's eyes a religious heretic. Accounts agree that Jahanara interceded on Aurangzeb's behalf with Shah Jahan.

Chapter 12

Shah Jahan did despatch Aurangzeb to Gujarat and give the Central Asian command to the younger, less experienced Murad.

Chapter 13

When Murad failed to advance on and capture Samarkand, Shah Jahan did turn to Aurangzeb who also failed in what was the first major setback of Shah Jahan's reign.

Chapter 14

Kandahar had been lost to the Persians in Jahangir's reign then regained by Shah Jahan in 1638. In February 1649, the city fell to the armies of Shah Abbas II and Shah Jahan's subsequent attempts to retake – one under the command of Dara Shukoh – all failed. Kandahar was never again in Moghul hands.

Chapter 15

At the height of battle Aurangzeb was indeed observed unfurling a mat to kneel down and pray.

Foreign travellers like François Bernier recorded rumours that Jahanara had lovers on whom Shah Jahan wrought a terrible revenge, for example ordering one to be boiled alive in a cauldron. There is, however, no evidence that Jahanara, denied the chance to marry, took lovers.

Chapter 16

Inayat Khan recorded that Shah Jahan fell seriously ill in December 1657. His three younger sons, in their distant provinces, indeed began plotting how to seize the throne. None allowed emerging proof that Shah Jahan was in fact recovering to destroy their momentum. Manucci – a supporter of Dara – later claimed that

Aurangzeb ordered any letters reaching the Deccan suggesting that Shah Jahan still lived to be burned and their bearers immediately beheaded.

Chapter 17

Murad indeed ordered his forces to plunder Surat so he could raise a large army to support his bid for the throne. He also murdered his finance minister, Ali Naqi – an act that would later prove his downfall.

Dara's son Suleiman and the Rajput general Jai Singh of Amber defeated Shah Shuja at Bahadur near Benares in February 1658, after which Shah Shuja retreated along the Ganges. Suleiman could not resist giving chase.

Aurangzeb and Murad routed the imperial Moghul forces commanded by Maharaja Jaswant Singh of Marwar at Dharmat on 15 April 1658.

Chapter 18

Dara tried to stop Aurangzeb and Murad from getting their armies across the Chambal river but they were too quick for him and crossed using a little-known and unguarded ford.

Chapter 19

The pivotal battle of Samugarh, east of Agra, took place on 29 May 1658. Dara indeed dismounted from his elephant at a critical moment when the battle was going in his favour. Manucci, who was fighting with Dara's forces, wrote: 'This was as if he had quitted victory.' The story of Khalilullah Khan's defection is true.

Chapter 20

A distraught Shah Jahan sent orders to the Governor of Delhi to throw the imperial treasury open to Dara. In fact Dara fled Agra just in time. The next day, riding out of Agra to join Dara, Manucci found Aurangzeb's troops blocking the road. They told Manucci that the government had already changed hands and 'Aurangzeb was the victor'.

Malik Jiwan did owe his life to Dara but betrayed him to Aurangzeb. The story of how Dara's wife Nadira offered a raja water to drink with which she had washed her breasts is true, though it was not Malik Jiwan but another ruler earlier in her and Dara's flight. Nadira died of exhaustion and dysentery.

After their capture, Aurangzeb paraded Dara and Sipihr in rags on a filthy elephant through the streets of Delhi. Frenchman Bernier witnessed the 'disgraceful procession'.

In reality, Dara was beheaded in his cell, not in public, in late August 1659. His tomb is on the platform surrounding Humayun's tomb in Delhi.

Chapter 21

There is clear evidence that Roshanara had early allied herself with Aurangzeb and was one of his chief sources of information about what was happening at court, especially in the period of Shah Jahan's illness.

Aurangzeb did cut off the water supply to the Agra fort.

Manucci recounts that a vengeful Aurangzeb sent Dara's head to Shah Jahan.

Chapter 22

Aurangzeb indeed captured Murad through subterfuge and dispatched him on one of four elephants sent to the four points of the compass to hinder Murad's supporters from following him. Murad was later executed on the charge of having murdered his finance minister, Ali Naqi.

Aurangzeb first declared himself emperor in a simple ceremony on 21 July 1658. Nearly a year later, on 5 June 1659 – a day deemed auspicious by his astrologers – he held a second and far more elaborate ceremony.

Chapter 23

The story that Shah Jahan ground up his pearls rather than surrender them to Aurangzeb is true. It is my suggestion that Shah Jahan tried to save Suleiman's life. Whatever the case, he didn't succeed. Aurangzeb ordered Suleiman Shukoh to be fed daily on *pousta* which first turned him into a zombie and eventually killed him. Aurangzeb kept Dara's other son Sipihr in prison for many years and then married him to one of his daughters.

Shah Shuja was last heard of in the lands of the pirate king of Arakan, east of Bengal, where most believe he perished.

Chapter 24

Jahanara was her father's companion throughout his imprisonment.

Shah Jahan never saw Aurangzeb during his imprisonment although during the first year of Shah Jahan's incarceration father and son exchanged letters, full of reproaches on Shah Jahan's side and pious self-justifications on

Aurangzeb's. In one letter Aurangzeb wrote, 'I was convinced that Your Majesty loved not me' – a clue to his long-standing sense of alienation.

The only evidence that Shah Jahan wished to build a black marble Taj Mahal as his own tomb comes from Frenchman Jean-Baptiste Tavernier who wrote that 'Shah Jahan began to build his own tomb on the other side of the river but the war with his sons interrupted his plan.' Shah Jahan had previously counterpointed white marble buildings with black ones. If he had wished to build his own Taj Mahal the place he would surely have chosen would have been his *mahtab bagh*, or moonlight garden. Archaeologists have found no foundations for such a building in the *mahtab bagh* yet the idea would not have been out of keeping with Shah Jahan, a man who saw art on a grand scale. Also, he loved to contrast white marble with black. This is exemplified by his building of a counterpointing black marble pavilion in the Shalimar Gardens in Srinagar in Kashmir in 1630, just before Mumtaz Mahal's death. The Taj Mahal also contains much black marble. For example the joints between each of the white marble blocks of the four minarets are inlaid with it, the low wall around the mausoleum plinth is inlaid with the same material and the mausoleum itself has black marble in its framing and calligraphy – what better transition to a black Taj over the water? However, we shall probably never know the truth. What is clear is that he did not intend to be buried in the Taj Mahal, which he designed for Mumtaz alone. Her sarcophagus lies on the central axis of the complex, his is squashed in to one side, the only asymmetrical element in the whole design. It encroaches on the black and white tiled border surrounding Mumtaz's tomb while lacking one of its own. Again, for more details see *A Teardrop on the Cheek of Time*.

Shah Jahan died in the Agra fort in the early hours of 22 January 1666. Aurangzeb did not sanction a grand state funeral but ordered his father to be laid quietly beside Mumtaz in the crypt of the Taj Mahal.

Main Characters

Shah Jahan's close family

Mumtaz Mahal (formerly Arjumand Banu), Shah Jahan's wife

Jahanara, eldest surviving daughter of Shah Jahan and Mumtaz

Dara Shukoh, eldest surviving son of Shah Jahan and Mumtaz

Shah Shuja, second surviving son of Shah Jahan and Mumtaz

Roshanara, second surviving daughter of Shah Jahan and Mumtaz

Aurangzeb, third surviving son of Shah Jahan and Mumtaz

Murad, youngest surviving son of Shah Jahan and Mumtaz

Gauharara, youngest surviving daughter of Shah Jahan and Mumtaz

Nadira, Dara Shukoh's wife

Suleiman, Dara Shukoh's elder son

Sipihr, Dara Shukoh's younger son

Jahangir, Shah Jahan's father

Akbar, Shah Jahan's grandfather

Humayun, Shah Jahan's great-grandfather

Khusrau, Shah Jahan's half-brother and Jahangir's eldest son

Parvez, Shah Jahan's half-brother and Jahangir's second son

Shahriyar, Shah Jahan's half-brother and Jahangir's youngest son

Mehrunissa (known also as Nur Jahan and Nur Mahal), Jahangir's last wife and aunt of Mumtaz Mahal

Asaf Khan, father of Mumtaz Mahal and brother of Mehrunissa

Jani, Khusrau's widow

Ismail Khan, Jani's nephew

Imperial household and members of the court

Satti al-Nisa, Mumtaz's confidante and later Jahanara's friend

Aslan Beg, Shah Jahan's elderly steward

Tuhin Roy, Moghul ambassador to Shah Abbas of Persia

Ustad Ahmad, architect of the Taj Mahal

Nasreen, Jahanara's attendant formerly in Roshanara's employ

Ali Naqi, revenue minister of Gujarat

Shah Jahan's chief commanders and officers

Ashok Singh, Rajput prince and friend of Shah Jahan

Nicholas Ballantyne, Englishman and former squire to
    the English ambassador to the Moghul court
Kamran Iqbal, commander of the Agra garrison
Ahmed Aziz, commander in the Deccan
Abdul Aziz, son of Ahmed Aziz
Zafir Abas, Ahmed Aziz's second-in-command
Mahabat Khan, Shah Jahan's commander-in-chief early
    in his reign
Malik Ali, Shah Jahan's master of horse
Sadiq Beg, Baluchi veteran.
Rai Singh, a Rajput and one of Shah Jahan's chief scouts
Suleiman Khan, an officer
Raja Jaswant Singh of Marwar
Khalilullah Khan, an Uzbek veteran
Raja Jai Singh of Amber
Dilir Khan, an Afghan general
Raja Ram Singh Rathor, a Rajput ruler

Others
Malik Jiwan, betrayer of Dara Shukoh and his son Sipihr
Makhdumi Khan, governor of the Agra fort and Shah
    Jahan's jailor
Itibar Khan, Aurangzeb's chief eunuch and later Shah
    Jahan's jailor

ALEX RUTHERFORD

Empire of the Moghul: Raiders from the North

The first book in the gripping and brilliant *Empire of the Moghul* series, chronicling the rise and fall of the Moghul Emperors of Central Asia, one of the most powerful dynasties in history.

It is 1494, and the new ruler of Ferghana, twelve-year-old Babur, faces a seemingly impossible challenge. Babur is determined to equal his great ancestor, Tamburlaine, whose conquests stretched from Delhi to the Mediterranean, from wealthy Persia to the wild Volga. But he is dangerously young to inherit a crown and treasonous plots, tribal rivalries, rampaging armies and ruthlessly ambitious enemies will threaten his destiny, his kingdom, even his survival.

'Alex Rutherford's glorious, broad-sweeping adventure in the wild lands of the Moghul sees the start of a wonderful series . . . Babur [is] a real-life hero, with all the flaws, mistakes and misadventures that spark true heroism . . . a vast, colourful cast, savage, glorious battles and a powerful narrative' Manda Scott, author of *Boudica*

'Alex Rutherford has set the bar high for his sequels' *Daily Mail*

978 0 7553 4753 7

headline
review

ALEX RUTHERFORD

Empire of the Moghul: Brothers at War

The second book in the gripping and brilliant Empire of the Moghul series – chronicling the rise and fall of the Moghul rulers of India – follows the troubled reign of Humayun: son to the founder of one of the most powerful dynasties in history.

1530. Emperor Humayun's father, Babur, has bequeathed him wealth, glory and an extensive empire. He must now build on this legacy to match the greatness of their forebear, Tamburlaine. But Humayun's half-brothers are already plotting against him, doubting he has the strength, the will and the brutality to succeed. The emperor faces a terrible battle: not only for his crown, not only for his life, but for the very existence of the empire itself.

Praise for Alex Rutherford:

'A totally absorbing narrative filled with authentic historical characters and sweeping action set in an age of horrifying but magnificent savagery. The writing is as compelling as the events described and kept me eagerly leaping from one page to the next' Wilbur Smith

'Glorious . . . Will march straight up to join the ranks of Conn Iggulden and Simon Scarrow. Breathtaking stuff' Manda Scott, author of *Boudica*

'Alex Rutherford has set the bar high for his sequels' *Daily Mail*

978 0 7553 4756 8

headline
review